Cocktails *for* Three

Cocktails for Three

Madeleine Wickham

THOMAS DUNNE BOOKS
St. Martin's Griffin
New York

THOMAS DUNNE BOOKS.
An imprint of St. Martin's Press.

COCKTAILS FOR THREE. Copyright ©2000 by Madeleine Wickham. All rights reserved. Printed in the United States of America. No part of this book may be used or reproduced in any manner whatsoever without written permission except in the case of brief quotations embodied in critical articles or reviews. For information, address St. Martin's Press, 175 Fifth Avenue, New York, N.Y. 10010.

ISBN 0-7394-6510-4

First St. Martin's Griffin Edition: March 2006

Printed in the U.S.A.

Many thanks to my agent Araminta Whitley, to Linda Evans and Sally Gaminara and all at Transworld, for their constant enthusiasm and encouragement during the writing of this book. To my parents and sisters for their continual, cheerful support and to my friends Ana-Maria and George Mosley, for always being there with a cocktail shaker at the ready.

And finally to my husband Henry, without whom this book would have been impossible, and to whom it is dedicated.

Chapter One

Candice Brewin pushed open the heavy glass door of the Manhattan Bar and felt the familiar swell of warmth, noise, light and clatter rush over her. It was six o'clock on a Wednesday night and the bar was already almost full. Waiters in dark green bow ties were gliding over the pale polished floor, carrying cocktails to tables. Girls in slippy dresses were standing at the bar, glancing around with bright, hopeful eyes. In the corner, a pianist was thumping out Gershwin numbers, almost drowned by the hum of metropolitan chatter.

It was getting to be too busy here, thought Candice, slipping off her coat. When she, Roxanne and Maggie had first discovered the Manhattan Bar, it had been a small, quiet, almost secretive place to meet. They had stumbled on it almost by chance, desperate for somewhere to drink after a particularly fraught press day. It had then been a dark and old-fashioned-looking place, with tatty bar stools and a peeling mural of the New York skyline on one wall. The patrons had been few and silent – mostly tending towards elderly gentlemen with much younger female companions. Candice, Roxanne and Maggie had boldly ordered a round of cocktails and then several more – and by the end of the evening had decided, amid fits of giggles, that the place had a certain terrible charm and must be re-visited. And so the monthly cocktail club had been born.

But now, newly extended, relaunched and written up in every glossy magazine, the bar was a different place. These days a young, attractive after-work crowd came flocking in every evening. Celebrities had been spotted at the bar. Even the waiters all looked like models. Really, thought Candice, handing her coat to the coat-check woman and receiving an art deco silver button in return, they should find somewhere else. Somewhere less busy, less obvious.

At the same time, she knew they never would. They had been coming here too long; had shared too many secrets over those distinctive frosted martini glasses. Anywhere else would feel wrong. On the first of every month, it had to be the Manhattan Bar.

There was a mirror opposite, and she glanced at her reflection, checking that her short cropped hair was tidy and her make-up – what little there was of it – hadn't smudged. She was wearing a plain black trouser suit over a pale green T-shirt – not exactly the height of glamour, but good enough.

Quickly she scanned the faces at the tables, but couldn't see Roxanne or Maggie. Although they all worked at the same place – the editorial office of the *Londoner* – it was rare they made the walk to the bar together. For a start, Roxanne was a freelance, and at times only seemed to use the office to make long-distance calls, arranging the next of her foreign jaunts. And Maggie, as editor of the magazine, often had to stay for meetings later than the others.

Not today, though, thought Candice, glancing at her watch. Today, Maggie had every excuse to slip off as early as she liked.

She brushed down her suit, walked towards the tables and, spotting a couple getting up, walked quickly forward. The young man had barely made it out of his chair before she was sliding into it and smiling gratefully up at him. You couldn't hang about if you wanted a table at the Manhattan Bar. And the three of them always had a table. It was part of the tradition.

Maggie Phillips paused outside the doors of the Manhattan Bar, put down her bulky carrier bag full of bright, stuffed toys, and pulled unceremoniously at the maternity tights wrinkling around her legs. Three more weeks, she thought, giving a final tug. Three more weeks of these bloody things. She took a deep breath, reached for her carrier bag again and pushed at the glass door.

As soon as she got inside, the noise and warmth of the place made her feel faint. She grasped for the wall, and stood quite still, trying not to lose her balance as she blinked away the dots in front of her eyes.

'Are you all right, my love?' enquired a voice to her left. Maggie swivelled her head and, as her vision cleared, made out the kindly face of the coat-check lady.

'I'm fine,' she said, flashing a tight smile.

'Are you sure? Would you like a nice drink of water?'

'No, really, I'm fine.' As if to emphasize the point she began to struggle out of her coat, self-consciously aware of the coat-check lady's appraising gaze on her figure. For pregnancy wear, her black Lycra trousers and tunic were about as flattering as you could get. But still there it was, right in front her, wherever she moved. A bump the size of a helium balloon. Maggie handed over her coat and met the coat lady's gaze head on.

If she asks me when it's due, she thought, I swear I'll smother her with Tinky Winky.

'When's it due?'

'The 25th of April,' said Maggie brightly. 'Three weeks to go.'

'Got your bag packed?' The woman twinkled at her. 'Don't want to leave it too late, do you?' Maggie's skin began to prickle. What bloody business was it of anyone's whether she'd packed her bag or not? Why did everyone keep *talking* to her about it? A complete stranger had come up to her in the pub at lunchtime, pointed to her wine glass and said, 'Naughty!' She'd nearly thrown it at him.

'Your first, is it,' the lady added, with no hint of interrogation in her voice.

So it's that obvious, thought Maggie. It's that clear to the rest of the world that I, Maggie Phillips – or Mrs Drakeford as I'm known at the clinic – have barely ever touched a baby. Let alone given birth to one.

'Yes, it's my first,' she said, and extended her palm, willing the lady to hand over her silver coat-check button and release her. But the woman was still gazing fondly at Maggie's protruding belly.

'I had four myself,' she said. 'Three girls and a boy. And each time, those first few weeks were the most magical time of all. You want to cherish those moments, love. Don't wish it all away.'

'I know,' Maggie heard herself saying, her mouth in a false beam.

I don't know! she yelled silently. I don't know anything about it. I know about page layout and editorial ratios and commissioning budgets. Oh God. What am I doing?

'Maggie!' A voice interrupted her and she wheeled round. Candice's round, cheerful face smiled back at her. 'I thought I saw you! I've nabbed a table.'

'Well done!' Maggie followed Candice through the throng, aware of the path her unwieldy bulk created; the curious glances following her. No-one else in the bar was pregnant. No-one was even fat. Everywhere

10

she looked she could see girls with flat stomachs and stick legs and pert little breasts.

'OK?' Candice had reached the table and was carefully pulling out a chair for her. Biting back a retort that she wasn't ill, Maggie sat down.

'Shall we order?' said Candice. 'Or wait for Roxanne?'

'Oh, I dunno.' Maggie gave a grumpy shrug. 'Better wait, I suppose.'

'Are you OK?' asked Candice curiously. Maggie sighed.

'I'm fine. I'm just sick of being pregnant. Being prodded and patted and treated like a freak.'

'A freak?' said Candice in disbelief. 'Maggie, you look fantastic!'

'Fantastic for a fat woman.'

'Fantastic full stop,' said Candice firmly. 'Listen, Maggie – there's a girl across the road from me who's pregnant at the moment. I tell you, if she saw the way you look, she'd throw up in jealousy.'

Maggie laughed. 'Candice, I adore you. You always say the right things.'

'It's true!' Candice reached for the cocktail menu – tall green leather with a silver tassle. 'Come on, let's have a look, anyway. Roxanne won't be long.'

Roxanne Miller stood in the ladies' room of the Manhattan Bar, leaned forward and carefully outlined her lips in cinnamon-coloured pencil. She pressed them together, then stood back and studied her reflection critically, starting – as she always did – with her best features. Good cheekbones. Nothing could take away your cheekbones. Blue eyes a little bloodshot, skin tanned from three weeks in the Caribbean. Nose still long, still crooked. Bronzy-blond hair tumbling down from a beaded comb in her hair. Tumbling a little too wildly, perhaps. Roxanne reached into her bag for a hairbrush and began to smooth it down. She was dressed, as she so often was, in a white T-shirt. In her opinion, nothing in the world showed off a tan better than a plain white T-shirt. She put her hairbrush away and smiled, impressed by her own reflection in spite of herself.

Then, behind her, a lavatory flushed and a cubicle door opened. A girl of about nineteen wandered out and stood next to Roxanne to wash her hands. She had pale, smooth skin and dark sleepy eyes, and her hair fell straight to her shoulders like the fringe on a lampshade. A mouth like a plum. No make-up whatsoever. The girl met Roxanne's eyes and smiled, then moved away.

When the swing doors had shut behind her, Roxanne still stayed, staring at herself. She suddenly felt like a blowsy tart. A thirty-three-year-old woman, trying too hard. In an instant, all the animation disappeared from her face. Her mouth drooped downwards and the gleam vanished from her eyes. Dispassionately, her gaze sought out the tiny red veins marking the skin on her cheeks. Sun damage, they called it. Damaged goods.

Then there was a sound from the door and her head jerked round.

'Roxanne!' Maggie was coming towards her, a wide smile on her face, her nut-brown bob shining under the spotlights.

'Darling!' Roxanne beamed, and gaily thrust her make-up bag into a larger Prada tote. 'I was just beautifying.'

'You don't need it!' said Maggie. 'Look at that tan!'

'That's Caribbean sun for you,' said Roxanne cheerfully.

'Don't tell me,' said Maggie, putting her hands over her ears. 'I don't want to know. It's not even approaching fair. Why did I never do a single travel feature while I was editor? I must have been mad!' She jerked her head towards the door. 'Go and keep Candice company. I'll be out in a moment.'

As she entered the bar, Roxanne saw Candice sitting alone, reading the cocktail menu, and an involuntary smile came to her lips. Candice always looked the same, wherever she was, whatever she was wearing. Her skin always looked well scrubbed and glowing, her hair was always cut in the same neat crop, she always dimpled in the same place when she smiled. And she always looked up with the same wide, trusting eyes. No wonder she was such a good interviewer, thought Roxanne fondly. People must just tumble into that friendly gaze.

'Candice!' she called, and waited for the pause, the lift of the head, the spark of recognition and wide smile.

It was a strange thing, thought Roxanne. She could walk past scores of adorable babies in pushchairs and never feel a tug on her maternal instinct. But sometimes, while looking at Candice, she would, with no warning, feel a pang in her heart. An obscure need to protect this girl, with her round face and innocent, childlike brow. But from what? From the world? From dark, malevolent strangers? It was ridiculous, really. After all, what was the difference between them in years? Four or five at most. Most of the time it seemed like nothing – yet sometimes Roxanne felt a generation older.

She strode up to the table and kissed Candice twice.

'Have you ordered?'

'I'm just looking,' said Candice, gesturing to the menu. 'I can't decide between a Summer Sunset or an Urban Myth.'

'Have the Urban Myth,' said Roxanne. 'A Summer Sunset is bright pink and comes with an umbrella.'

'Does it?' Candice wrinkled her brow. 'Does that matter? What are you having?'

'Margarita,' said Roxanne. 'Same as usual. I lived on Margaritas in Antigua.' She reached for a cigarette, then remembered Maggie and stopped. 'Margaritas and sunshine. That's all you need.'

'So – how was it?' said Candice. She leaned forward, eyes sparkling. 'Any toyboys this time?'

'Enough to keep me happy,' said Roxanne, grinning wickedly at her. 'One return visit in particular.'

'You're terrible!' said Candice.

'On the contrary,' said Roxanne, 'I'm very good. That's why they like me. That's why they come back for more.'

'What about your—' Candice broke off awkwardly.

'What about Mr Married with Kids?' said Roxanne lightly.

'Yes,' said Candice, colouring a little. 'Doesn't he mind when you . . . ?'

'Mr Married with Kids is not allowed to mind,' said Roxanne. 'Mr Married with Kids has got his wife, after all. Fair's fair, don't you think?' Her eyes glinted at Candice as though to forbid any more questions, and Candice bit her lip. Roxanne always discouraged talk of her married man. She had been with him for all the time that Candice had known her – but she had resolutely refused to divulge his identity, or even any details about him. Candice and Maggie had jokingly speculated between themselves that he must be somebody famous – a politician, perhaps – and certainly rich, powerful and sexy. Roxanne would never throw herself away on someone mediocre. Whether she was really in love with him, they were less sure. She was always so flippant, almost callous-sounding about the affair – it was as though she were using him, rather than the other way around.

'Look, I'm sorry,' said Roxanne, reaching again for

14

her cigarettes. 'Foetus or no foetus, I'm going to have to have a cigarette.'

'Oh, smoke away,' said Maggie, coming up behind her. 'I'm sure it can't be worse than pollution.' As she sat down, she beckoned to a cocktail waitress. 'Hi. Yes, we're ready to order.'

As the fair-haired girl in the green waistcoat came walking smartly over, Candice stared curiously at her. Something about her was familiar. Candice's eyes ran over the girl's wavy hair; her snub nose; her grey eyes, shadowed with tiredness. Even the way she shook her hair back off her shoulders seemed familiar. Where on earth had she seen her before?

'Is something wrong?' said the girl, politely, and Candice flushed.

'No. Of course not. Ahm . . .' She opened the cocktail menu again and ran her eyes down the lists without taking them in. The Manhattan Bar served over a hundred cocktails; sometimes she found the choice almost too great. 'A Mexican Swing, please.'

'A Margarita for me,' said Roxanne.

'Oh God, I don't know what to have,' said Maggie. 'I had wine at lunchtime . . .'

'A Virgin Mary?' suggested Candice.

'Definitely not.' Maggie pulled a face. 'Oh, sod it. A Shooting Star.'

'Good choice,' said Roxanne. 'Get the kid used to a bit of alcohol inside its system. And now . . .' She reached inside her bag. 'It's present time!'

'For who?' said Maggie, looking up in surprise. 'Not for me. I've had *heaps* of presents today. Far too many. Plus about five thousand Mothercare vouchers . . .'

'A Mothercare voucher?' said Roxanne disdainfully. 'That's not a present!' She produced a tiny blue box and put it on the table. 'This is a proper present.'

'Tiffany?' said Maggie incredulously. 'Really? Tiffany?' She opened the box with clumsy, swollen fingers and carefully took something silver from its tiny bag. 'I don't believe it! It's a rattle!' She shook it, and they all smiled with childish delight.

'Let me have a go!' said Candice.

'You'll have the most stylish baby on the block,' said Roxanne, a pleased expression on her face. 'If it's a boy, I'll get him cufflinks to match.'

'It's wonderful,' said Candice, staring admiringly at it. 'It makes my present seem really . . . Well, anyway.' She put the rattle down and started to rummage in her bag. 'It's here somewhere . . .'

'Candice Brewin!' said Roxanne accusingly, peering over her shoulder. 'What's that in your bag?'

'What?' said Candice, looking up guiltily.

'More tea towels! And a sponge.' Roxanne hauled the offending items out of Candice's bag and held them aloft. There were two blue tea towels and a yellow sponge, each wrapped in cellophane and marked 'Young People's Cooperative'. 'How much did you pay for these?' demanded Roxanne.

'Not much,' said Candice, at once. 'Hardly anything. About . . . five pounds.'

'Which means ten,' said Maggie, rolling her eyes at Roxanne. 'What are we going to do with her? Candice, you must have bought their whole bloody supply, by now!'

'Well, they're always useful, aren't they, tea towels?' said Candice, flushing. 'And I feel so bad, saying no.'

'Exactly,' said Maggie. 'You're not doing it because you think it's a good thing. You're doing it because if you don't, you'll feel bad.'

'Well, isn't that the same thing?' retorted Candice.

'No,' said Maggie. 'One's positive, and the other's negative. Or . . . something.' She screwed up her face. 'Oh God, I'm confused now. I need a cocktail.'

'Who cares?' said Roxanne. 'The point is, no more tea towels.'

'OK, OK,' said Candice, hurriedly stuffing the packets back in her bag. 'No more tea towels. And here's my present.' She produced an envelope and handed it to Maggie. 'You can take it any time.'

There was silence around the table as Maggie opened it and took out a pale pink card.

'An aromatherapy massage,' she read out disbelievingly. 'You've bought me a massage.'

'I just thought you might like it,' said Candice. 'Before you have the baby, or after . . . They come to your house, you don't have to go anywhere—' Maggie looked up, her eyes glistening slightly.

'You know, that's the only present anyone's bought for me. For *me*, as opposed to the baby.' She leaned across the table and gave Candice a hug. 'Thank you, my darling.'

'We'll really miss you,' said Candice. 'Don't stay away too long.'

'Well, you'll have to come and see me!' said Maggie. 'And the baby.'

'In your country manor,' said Roxanne sardonically. 'Mrs Drakeford At Home.' She grinned at Candice, who tried not to giggle.

When Maggie had announced, a year previously, that she and her husband Giles were moving to a cottage in the country, Candice had believed her. She had pictured a quaint little dwelling, with tiny crooked windows and a walled garden, somewhere in the middle of a village.

The truth had turned out to be rather different. Maggie's new house, The Pines, had turned out to be situated at the end of a long, tree-lined drive. It had turned out to have eight bedrooms and a billiards room and a swimming pool. Maggie, it had turned out, was secretly married to a millionaire.

'You never told us!' Candice had said accusingly as they'd sat in the vast kitchen, drinking tea made on the equally vast Aga. 'You never told us you were rolling in it!'

'We're not rolling in it!' Maggie had retorted defensively, cradling her Emma Bridgwater mug. 'It just . . . looks bigger because it's in the country.' This remark she had never been allowed to forget.

'It just looks bigger . . .' Roxanne began now, snorting with laughter. 'It just *looks* bigger . . .'

'Oh, shut up, y'all,' said Maggie good-naturedly. 'Look, here come the cocktails.'

The blond-haired girl was coming towards them, holding a silver tray on the flat of her hand. Three glasses were balanced on it. One a Margarita glass, frosted round the rim, one a highball decorated with a single fanned slice of lime, and one a champagne flute adorned with a strawberry.

'Very classy,' murmured Roxanne. 'Not a cherry in sight.'

The girl set the glasses down expertly on their paper coasters, added a silver dish of salted almonds, and discreetly placed the bill – hidden inside a green leather folder – to one side of the table. As she stood up, Candice looked again at her face, trying to jog her memory. She knew this girl from somewhere. She was sure of it. But from where?

'Thanks very much,' said Maggie.

'No problem,' said the girl, and smiled – and as she did so, Candice knew, in a flash, who she was.

'Heather Trelawney,' she said aloud, before she could stop herself. And then, as the girl's eyes slowly turned towards her, she wished with all her soul that she hadn't.

Chapter Two

'I'm sorry,' began the girl puzzledly. 'Do I—' She stopped, took a step nearer and peered at Candice. Then suddenly her face lit up. 'Of course!' she said. 'It's Candice, isn't it? Candice . . .' She wrinkled her brow. 'Sorry, I've forgotten your last name.'

'Brewin,' said Candice in a frozen voice, barely able to utter the syllables. Her name seemed to rest in the air like a physical presence; a target, inviting attack. *Brewin*. As she saw Heather frowning thoughtfully, Candice flinched, waiting for the jolt of recognition, the anger and recriminations. Why had she not just kept her stupid mouth shut? What hideous scene was going to ensue?

But as Heather's face cleared, it was obvious that she recognized Candice as nothing but an old school acquaintance. Didn't she know? thought Candice incredulously. *Didn't she know?*

'Candice Brewin!' said Heather. 'That's right! I should have recognized you straight away.'

'How funny!' said Maggie. 'How do you two know each other?'

'We were at school together,' said Heather brightly. 'It must be *years* since we've seen each other.' She looked again at Candice. 'You know, I thought there was something about you, when I took your order. But

'. . . I don't know. You look different, somehow. I suppose we've all changed since then.'

'I suppose so,' said Candice. She picked up her glass and took a sip, trying to calm her beating heart.

'And I know this is going to sound bad,' said Heather, lowering her voice, 'but after you've been waitressing for a while, you stop looking at the customers' faces. Is that awful?'

'I don't blame you,' said Maggie. 'I wouldn't want to look at our faces either.'

'Speak for yourself,' retorted Roxanne at once, and grinned at Maggie.

'You know, I once took an order from Simon Le Bon,' said Heather. 'Not here, at my old place. I took the order, and I didn't even notice who he was. When I got back to the kitchen, everyone was going "what's he like?" and I didn't know what they were talking about.'

'Good for you,' said Roxanne. 'It does these people good not to be recognized.'

Maggie glanced at Candice. She was staring at Heather as though transfixed. What the hell was wrong with her?

'So, Heather,' she said quickly, 'have you been working here long?'

'Only a couple of weeks,' said Heather. 'It's a nice place, isn't it? But they keep us busy.' She glanced towards the bar. 'Speaking of which, I'd better get on. Good to see you, Candice.'

She began to move off, and Candice felt a jolt of alarm.

'Wait!' she said. 'We haven't caught up properly.' She swallowed. 'Why don't you . . . sit down for a minute?'

'Well, OK,' said Heather after a pause. She glanced again at the bar. 'But I can't be long. We'll have to pretend I'm advising you on cocktails or something.'

20

'We don't need any advising,' said Roxanne. 'We *are* the cocktail queens.' Heather giggled.

'I'll just see if I can find a chair,' she said. 'Back in a tick.'

As soon as she had walked away, Maggie turned to Candice.

'What's wrong?' she hissed. 'Who is this girl? You're staring at her as though you've seen a bloody ghost!'

'Is it that obvious?' said Candice in dismay.

'Darling, you look as if you're practising to play Hamlet,' said Roxanne drily.

'Oh God,' said Candice. 'And I thought I was doing quite well.' She picked up her cocktail with a shaking hand and took a gulp. 'Cheers, everybody.'

'Never mind bloody cheers!' said Maggie. 'Who is she?'

'She's—' Candice rubbed her brow. 'I knew her years ago. We were at school together. She – she was a couple of years below me.'

'We know all that!' said Maggie impatiently. 'What else?'

'Hi!' Heather's bright voice interrupted them, and they all looked up guiltily. 'I found a chair at last.' She set it at the table and sat down. 'Are the cocktails good?'

'Wonderful!' said Maggie, taking a gulp of her Shooting Star. 'Just what the midwife ordered.'

'So – what are you up to now?' said Heather to Candice.

'I'm a journalist,' said Candice.

'Really?' Heather looked at her wistfully. 'I'd love to do something like that. Do you write for a newspaper?'

'A magazine. The *Londoner.*'

'I know the *Londoner!*' said Heather. 'I've probably even read articles you've written.' She looked around the table. 'Are you all journalists?'

'Yes,' said Maggie. 'We all work together.'

21

'God, that must be fun.'

'It has its moments,' said Maggie, grinning at Roxanne. 'Some better than others.'

There was brief silence, then Candice said, with a slight tremor in her voice, 'And what about you, Heather? What have you done since school?' She took another deep gulp of her cocktail.

'Oh well . . .' Heather gave a quick little smile. 'It was all a bit grim, actually. I don't know if you know – but the reason I left Oxdowne was my father lost all his money.'

'How awful!' said Maggie. 'What – overnight?'

'Pretty much,' said Heather. Her grey eyes darkened slightly. 'Some investment went wrong. The stock markets or something – my dad never said exactly what. And that was it. They couldn't afford school fees any more. Or the house. It was all a bit horrendous. My dad got really depressed over it, and my mum blamed him . . .' She broke off awkwardly. 'Well, anyway.' She picked up a paper coaster and began to fiddle with it. 'They split up in the end.'

Maggie glanced at Candice for a reaction, but her face was averted. She had a cocktail stirrer in her hand and was stirring her drink, round and round.

'And what about you?' said Maggie cautiously to Heather.

'I kind of lost it, too, for a bit.' Heather gave another quick little smile. 'You know, one minute I was at a nice fee-paying school with all my friends. The next, we'd moved to a town where I didn't know anyone, and my parents were arguing all the time, and I went to a school where they all gave me a hard time for talking posh.' She sighed, and let the coaster drop from her fingers. 'I mean, looking back, it was quite a good comprehensive. I should have just stuck it out and gone on to college . . . but I didn't. I left as soon as I was sixteen.' She pushed back her thick, wavy hair. 'My dad was living in London by then so I moved in with him and got a job in a wine bar. And that was it, really. I never did a degree, or anything.'

'What a shame,' said Maggie. 'What would you have done, if you'd stayed on?'

'Oh, I don't know,' said Heather. She gave an embarrassed little laugh. 'Done something like you're doing, maybe. Become a journalist, or something. I started a creative writing course once, at Goldsmiths', but I had to give it up.' She looked around the bar and shrugged. 'I mean, I do like working here. But it's not really . . . Anyway.' She stood up and tugged at her green waistcoat. 'I'd better get going, or André will kill me. See you later!'

As she walked away, the three of them sat in silence, watching her. Then Maggie turned to Candice, and said carefully,

'She seems nice.'

Candice didn't reply. Maggie looked questioningly at Roxanne, who raised her eyebrows.

'Candice, what's wrong?' said Maggie. 'Is there some history between you and Heather?'

'Darling, speak to us,' said Roxanne.

Candice said nothing, but continued stirring her cocktail, faster and faster and faster, until the liquid threatened to spill over the sides of the glass. Then she looked up at her friends.

'It wasn't the stock markets,' she said in a flat voice. 'It wasn't the stock markets that ruined Frank Trelawney. It was my father.'

Heather Trelawney stood at the corner of the bar, by the entrance to the kitchen, watching Candice Brewin's face through the crush of people. She couldn't take her eyes off the sight. Gordon Brewin's daughter, large as life, sitting at the table with her friends. With her nice haircut, and her good job, and money for cocktails

23

every night. Oblivious of what suffering her father had caused. Unaware of anything except herself.

Because she'd come out all right, hadn't she? Of course she had. Good-Time Gordon had been very clever like that. He'd never used his own money. He'd never put his own life on the line. Only other people's. Other poor saps, too greedy to say no. Like her poor reckless, stupid dad. At the thought, Heather's chin tightened, and her hands gripped her silver tray harder.

'Heather!' It was André, the head waiter, calling from the bar. 'What are you doing? Customers waiting!'

'Coming!' called back Heather. She put down her silver tray, shook out her hair and tied it back tightly with a rubber band. Then she picked up her tray and walked smartly to the bar, never once taking her eyes off Candice Brewin.

'They called him Good-Time Gordon,' said Candice in a trembling voice. 'He was there at every single party. Life and soul.' She took a gulp of her cocktail. 'And every school function. Every concert, every gym display. I used to think it was because – you know, he was proud of me. But all the time, he just wanted to pick up new contacts to do business with. Frank Trelawney wasn't the only one. He got to all our friends, all our neighbours . . .' Her hand tightened around her glass. 'They all started popping up after the funeral. Some had invested money with him, some had lent him money and he'd never paid it back . . .' She took a swig of her cocktail. 'It was horrendous. These people were our friends. And we'd had no idea.'

Roxanne and Maggie glanced at each other.

'So how do you know Heather's father was involved?' said Maggie.

'I found out when we went through the paperwork,' said Candice blankly. 'My mother and I had to go into

24

his study and sort out the mess. It was . . . just awful.'

'How did your mum take it?' asked Maggie curiously.

'Terribly,' said Candice. 'Well, you can imagine. He'd actually told some people he needed to borrow money from them because she was an alcoholic and he wanted to put her through rehab.'

Roxanne snorted with laughter, then said,

'Sorry.'

'I still can't talk to her about it,' said Candice. 'In fact, I think she's pretty much persuaded herself it never happened. If I even mention it, she gets all hysterical . . .' She lifted a hand and began to massage her forehead.

'I had no idea about this,' said Maggie. 'You've never even mentioned any of this before.'

'Yes, well,' said Candice shortly. 'I'm not exactly proud of it. My father did a lot of damage.'

She closed her eyes as unwanted memories of that dreadful time after his death came flooding back into her mind. It had been at the funeral that she'd first noticed something wrong. Friends and relatives, clumped in little groups, had stopped talking as soon as she came near. Voices had been hushed and urgent; everyone had seemed to be in on one big secret. As she'd passed one group, she'd heard the words, '*How much?*'

Then the visitors had started arriving, ostensibly to pay their condolences. But sooner or later the conversation had always turned to money. To the five or ten thousand pounds that Gordon had borrowed. To the investments that had been made. No hurry, of course – they quite understood things were difficult . . . Even Mrs Stephens, their cleaning lady, had awkwardly brought up the subject of a hundred pounds, loaned some months ago and never repaid.

At the memory of the woman's embarrassed face,

Candice felt her stomach contract again with humiliation; with a hot, teenage guilt. She still felt as though she were somehow to blame. Even though she'd known nothing about it; even though there was nothing she could have done.

'And what about Frank Trelawney?' said Maggie. Candice opened her eyes dazedly, and picked up the cocktail stirrer again.

'He was on a list of names in the study,' she said. 'He'd invested two hundred thousand pounds in some venture capital project which folded after a few months.' She began to run the silver stirrer around the rim of her glass. 'At first I didn't know who Frank Trelawney was. It was just another name. But it seemed familiar . . . And then I suddenly remembered Heather Trelawney leaving school with no warning. It all made sense.' She bit her lip. 'I think that was the worst moment of all. Knowing that Heather had lost her place at school because of my father.'

'You can't just blame your father,' said Maggie gently. 'This Mr Trelawney must have known what he was doing. He must have known there was a certain risk.'

'I always used to wonder what happened to Heather,' said Candice, as though she hadn't heard. 'And now I know. Another life ruined.'

'Candice, don't beat yourself up about this,' said Maggie. 'It's not your fault. You didn't do anything!'

'I know,' said Candice. 'Logically, you're right. But it's not that easy.'

'Have another drink,' advised Roxanne. 'That'll cheer you up.'

'Good idea,' said Maggie, and drained her glass. She lifted her hand and, on the other side of the room, Heather nodded.

Candice stared at Heather as she bent down to pick up some empty glasses from a table and wipe it over, unaware she was being watched. As she stood up again, Heather gave a sudden yawn and rubbed her face with tiredness, and Candice felt her heart contract with emotion. She had to do something for this girl, she thought suddenly. She had to absolve her guilt for at least one of her father's crimes.

'Listen,' she said quickly, as Heather began to approach the table. 'They haven't got a new editorial assistant for the *Londoner* yet, have they?'

'Not as far as I know,' said Maggie in surprise. 'Why?'

'Well, what about Heather?' said Candice. 'She'd be ideal. Wouldn't she?'

'Would she?' Maggie wrinkled her brow.

'She wants to be a journalist, she's done creative writing . . . she'd be perfect! Oh, go on, Maggie!' Candice looked up, to see Heather approaching. 'Heather, listen!'

'Do you want some more drinks?' said Heather.

'Yes,' said Candice. 'But . . . but not just that.' She looked at Maggie entreatingly. Maggie gave her a mock-glare, then grinned.

'We were wondering, Heather,' she said, 'if you'd be interested in a job on the *Londoner*. Editorial assistant. It's pretty low-ranking, and the money's not great, but it's a start in journalism.'

'Are you serious?' said Heather, looking from one to the other. 'I'd love it!'

'Good,' said Maggie, and took out a card from her bag. 'This is the address, but it won't be me processing the applications. The person you need to write to is Justin Vellis.' She wrote the name on the card and handed it to Heather. 'Just write a letter about yourself, and pop in a CV. OK?'

Candice stared at her in dismay.

'Great!' said Heather. 'And . . . thanks.'

'And now I suppose we'd better choose some more

cocktails,' said Maggie cheerfully. 'It's a tough old life.'

When Heather had departed with their order, Maggie grinned at Candice and leaned back in her chair.

'There you are,' she said. 'Feel better now?' She frowned at Candice's expression. 'Candice, are you OK?'

'To be honest, no!' said Candice, trying to stay calm. 'I'm not! Is that all you're going to do? Give her the address?'

'What do you mean?' said Maggie in surprise. 'Candice, what's wrong?'

'I thought you were going to give her the job!'

'What, on the spot?' said Maggie, beginning to laugh. 'Candice, you must be joking.'

'Or an interview . . . or a personal recommendation, at least,' said Candice, flushing in distress. 'If she just sends in her CV like everyone else, there's no *way* Justin will give her the job! He'll appoint some awful Oxford graduate or something.'

'Like himself,' put in Roxanne with a grin. 'Some nice smarmy intellectual.'

'Exactly! Maggie, you know Heather hasn't got a chance unless you recommend her. Especially if he knows she's anything to do with me!' Candice flushed slightly as she said the words. It was only a few weeks since she had broken up with Justin, the features editor who was taking over from Maggie as acting editor. She still felt a little awkward, talking about him.

'But Candice, I can't recommend her,' said Maggie simply. 'I don't know anything about her. And neither, let's face it, do you. I mean, you haven't seen her for years, have you? She could be a criminal for all you know.'

Candice stared into her drink miserably, and Maggie sighed.

'Candice, I can understand how you feel, truly I can,'

she said. 'But you can't just leap in and procure a job for some woman you hardly know, just because you feel sorry for her.'

'I agree,' said Roxanne firmly. 'You'll be giving the tea towel girl a personal recommendation next.'

'And what would be wrong with that?' said Candice with a sudden fierceness. 'What's wrong with giving people a boost every so often if they deserve it? You know, we three have had it very easy, compared to the rest of the world.' She gestured round the table. 'We've got good jobs, and happy lives, and we haven't the first idea what it's like to have nothing.'

'Heather doesn't have nothing,' said Maggie calmly. 'She has good looks, she has a brain, she has a job, and she has every opportunity to go back to college if she wants to. It's not your job to sort her life out for her. OK?'

'OK,' said Candice after a pause.

'Good,' said Maggie. 'Lecture over.'

An hour later, Maggie's husband Giles arrived at the Manhattan Bar. He stood at the side of the room, peering through the throng – then spotted Maggie's face. She was clutching a cocktail, her cheeks were flushed pink and her head was thrown back in laughter. Giles smiled fondly at the sight, and headed towards the table.

'Man alert,' he said cheerfully as he approached. 'Kindly cease all jokes about male genitals.'

'Giles!' said Maggie, looking up in slight dismay. 'Is it time to go already?'

'We don't have to,' said Giles. 'I could stay for a drink or two.'

'No,' said Maggie after a pause. 'It's OK, let's go.'

It never quite worked when Giles joined the group. Not because the other two didn't like him – and not because he didn't make an effort. He was always genial

29

and polite, and conversation always flowed nicely. But it just wasn't the same. He wasn't one of them. Well – how could he be? thought Maggie. He wasn't a woman.

'I've got to go soon, anyway,' said Roxanne, draining her glass and putting her cigarettes away. 'I have someone to see.'

'Would that be Someone?' said Maggie with a deliberate emphasis.

'Possibly.' Roxanne smiled at her.

'I can't believe this is it!' said Candice, looking at Maggie. 'We won't see you again till you've had the baby!'

'Don't remind me!' said Maggie, flashing an overcheerful smile.

She pushed back her chair and gratefully took the hand Giles offered. They all slowly made their way through the crowds to the coat-check, and surrendered their silver buttons.

'And don't think you're allowed to give up on the cocktail club,' said Roxanne to Maggie. 'We'll be round your bed in a month's time, toasting the babe.'

'It's a date,' said Maggie, and suddenly felt her eyes fill with easy tears. 'Oh God, I'm going to miss you guys.'

'We'll see you soon,' said Roxanne, and gave her a hug. 'Good luck, darling.'

'OK,' said Maggie, trying to smile. She suddenly felt as though she were saying goodbye to her friends for ever; as though she were entering a new world into which they wouldn't be able to follow.

'Maggie doesn't need luck!' said Candice. 'She'll have that baby licked into shape in no time!'

'Hey, baby,' said Roxanne, addressing Maggie's stomach humorously. 'You are aware that your mother is the most organized woman in Western civilization?' She pretended to listen to the bump. 'It says it wants to have someone else. Tough luck, kid.'

'And listen, Candice,' said Maggie, turning to her kindly. 'Don't let Justin lord it over you just because he's in charge for a few months. I know it's a difficult situation for you . . .'

'Don't worry,' said Candice at once. 'I can handle him.'

'Justin the bloody wunderkind,' said Roxanne, dismissively. 'You know, I'm glad we can all be rude about him now.'

'You always were rude about him,' pointed out Candice. 'Even when I was going out with him.'

'Well, he deserves it,' said Roxanne, unabashed. 'Anyone who comes to a cocktail bar and orders a bottle of claret is obviously a complete waste of space.'

'Candice, they can't seem to find your coat,' said Giles, appearing at Maggie's shoulder. 'But here's yours, Roxanne, and yours, darling. I think we should get going, otherwise it'll be midnight before we get back.'

'Right, well,' said Maggie in a shaky voice. 'This is it.'

She and Candice looked at each other, half grinning, half blinking back tears.

'We'll see each other soon,' said Candice. 'I'll come and visit.'

'And I'll come up to London.'

'You can bring the baby up for day trips,' said Candice. 'They're supposed to be the latest accessory.'

'I know,' said Maggie, giving a little laugh. She leaned forward and hugged Candice. 'You take care.'

'And you,' said Candice. 'Good luck with . . . everything. Bye, Giles,' she added. 'Nice to see you.'

Giles opened the glass door of the bar, and after one final backwards glance, Maggie walked out into the cold night air. Roxanne and Candice watched silently through the glass as Giles took Maggie's arm and they disappeared down the dark street.

31

'Just think,' said Candice. 'In a few weeks, they won't be a couple any more. They'll be a family.'

'So they will,' said Roxanne in indeterminate tones. 'A happy little family, all together in their huge, fuck-off happy house.' Candice glanced at her.

'Are you OK?'

'Of course I'm OK!' said Roxanne. 'Just glad it isn't me! The very thought of stretchmarks . . .' She gave a mock-shudder then smiled. 'I've got to shoot off, I'm afraid. Do you mind?'

'Of course not,' said Candice. 'Have a good time.'

'I always have a good time,' said Roxanne, 'even if I'm having a terrible time. See you when I get back from Cyprus.' She kissed Candice briskly on each cheek and disappeared out of the door. Candice watched her hailing a taxi and jumping in; after a few seconds, the taxi zoomed off down the street.

Candice waited until it had disappeared, counted to five – then, feeling like a naughty child, swivelled round to face the crowded bar again. Her stomach felt taut with expectation; her heart was thumping quickly.

'I've found your coat!' came the voice of the coat-check lady. 'It had fallen off its hanger.'

'Thanks,' said Candice. 'But I've just got to . . .' She swallowed. 'I'll be back in a moment.'

She hurried through the press of people, feeling light and determined. She had never felt so sure of herself in her life. Maggie and Roxanne meant well, but they were wrong. This time, they were wrong. They didn't understand – why should they? They couldn't see that this was the opportunity she'd unconsciously been waiting for ever since her father's death. This was her chance to make things right. It was like . . . a gift.

At first she couldn't see Heather, and she thought with a sinking heart that she was too late. But then, scanning the room again, she spotted her. She was behind the bar, polishing a glass and laughing with one

32

of the waiters. Fighting her way through the crowds, Candice made her way to the bar and waited patiently, not wanting to interrupt.

Eventually Heather looked up and saw her – and to Candice's surprise, a flash of hostility seemed to pass over her features. But it disappeared almost at once, and her face broke into a welcoming smile.

'What can I get you?' she said. 'Another cocktail?'

'No, I just wanted a word,' said Candice, feeling herself having to shout over the background hubbub. 'About this job.'

'Oh yes?'

'If you like, I can introduce you to the publisher, Ralph Allsopp,' said Candice. 'No guarantees – but it might help your chances. Come to the office tomorrow at about ten.'

'Really?' Heather's face lit up. 'That would be wonderful!' She put down the glass she was polishing, leaned forward and took Candice's hands. 'Candice, this is really good of you. I don't know how to thank you.'

'Well, you know,' said Candice awkwardly. 'Old school friends and all that . . .'

'Yes,' said Heather, and smiled sweetly at Candice. 'Old school friends.'

Chapter Three

As they reached the motorway, it began to rain. Giles reached down and turned on Radio Three, and a glorious soprano's voice filled the car. After a few notes, Maggie recognized the piece as 'Dove Sono' from *The Marriage of Figaro* – in her opinion, the most beautiful, poignant aria ever written. As the music soared over her, Maggie stared out of the rain-spattered windscreen and felt foolish tears coming to her eyes, in sympathy with the fictitious Countess. A good and beautiful wife, unloved by her philandering husband, sadly recalling moments of tenderness between them. *I remember . . .*

Maggie blinked a few times and took a deep breath. This was ridiculous. Everything was reducing her to tears at the moment. The other day, she'd wept at an advertisement on television in which a boy cooked supper for his two small sisters. She'd sat on the living-room floor, tears streaming down her face – and when Giles had come into the room, had had to turn away and pretend to be engrossed in a magazine.

'Did you have a good send-off?' asked Giles, changing lanes.

'Yes, lovely,' said Maggie. 'Heaps of presents. People are so generous.'

'And how did you leave it with Ralph?'

'I told him I'd call him after a few months. That's what I've told everybody.'

'I still think you should have been honest with them,' said Giles. 'I mean, you know you've no intention of going back to work.'

Maggie was silent. She and Giles had discussed at length whether she should return to work after the baby was born. On the one hand, she adored her job and her staff, was well paid, and felt that there were still things she wanted to achieve in her career. On the other hand, the image of leaving her baby behind and commuting to London every day seemed appalling. And after all, what was the point of living in a large house in the country and never seeing it?

The fact that she had never actually wanted to move to the country was something which Maggie had almost successfully managed to forget. Even before she'd become pregnant, Giles had been desperate for his future children to have the rough-and-tumble, fresh-air upbringing which he had enjoyed. 'London isn't healthy for children,' he had pronounced. And although Maggie had pointed out again and again that the London streets were full of perfectly healthy children; that parks were safer places to ride bicycles than country lanes; that nature existed even in cities, Giles had still not been persuaded.

Then, when he'd started applying for the details of country houses – glorious old rectories, complete with panelled dining rooms, acres of land and tennis courts – she'd found herself weakening. Wondering if it was indeed selfish to stay in London. On a wonderfully sunny day in June, they'd gone to look at The Pines. The drive had crackled under the wheels of their car; the swimming pool had glinted in the sun, the lawns had been mowed in light and dark green stripes. After showing them round the house, the owners had poured them glasses of Pimm's and invited them to sit under the weeping willow, then tactfully moved away. And Giles had looked at Maggie and said, 'This could be ours, darling. This life could be ours.'

And now that life was theirs. Except it wasn't so much a life yet as a large house which Maggie still didn't feel she knew very well. On working days, she barely saw the place. At the weekends, they often went away, or up to London to see friends. She had done none of the redecorations she had planned; in some strange way she felt as though the house wasn't really hers yet.

But things would be different when the baby arrived, she told herself. The house would really become a home. Maggie put her hands on her bump and felt the squirming, intriguing movements beneath her skin. A smooth lump rippled across her belly and disappeared as though back into the ocean. Then, with no warning, something hard jabbed into her ribs. A heel, perhaps, or a knee. It jabbed again and again, as though desperate to break out. Maggie closed her eyes. It could be any time now, her pregnancy handbook had advised her. The baby was fully matured; she could go into labour at any moment.

At the thought, her heart began to thump with a familiar panic, and she began quickly to think reassuring thoughts. Of course, she was prepared for the baby. She had a nursery full of nappies and cotton wool; tiny vests and blankets. The Moses basket was ready on its stand; the cot had been ordered from a department store. Everything was waiting.

But somehow – despite all that – she secretly still didn't feel quite ready to be a mother. She almost didn't feel *old* enough to be a mother. Which was ridiculous, she told herself firmly, bearing in mind she was thirty-two years old and had had an entire nine months to get used to the idea.

'You know, I can't believe it's really happening,' she

36

said. 'Three weeks away. That's nothing! And I haven't been to any classes, or anything . . .'

'You don't need classes!' said Giles. 'You'll be great! The best mother a baby could have.'

'Really?' Maggie bit her lip. 'I don't know. I just feel a bit . . . unprepared.'

'What's to prepare?'

'Well, you know. Labour, and everything.'

'One word,' said Giles firmly. 'Drugs.'

Maggie giggled. 'And afterwards. You know. Looking after it. I've never even *held* a baby.'

'You'll be fantastic!' said Giles at once. 'Maggie, if anyone can look after a baby, you can. Come on.' He turned and flashed a smile at her. 'Who was voted Editor of the Year?'

'I was,' she said, grinning proudly in spite of herself.

'Well then. And you'll be Mother of the Year, too.' He reached out and squeezed her hand, and Maggie squeezed gratefully back. Giles's optimism never failed to cheer her.

'Mum said she'd pop round tomorrow,' said Giles. 'Keep you company.'

'Oh good,' said Maggie. She thought of Giles's mother, Paddy – a thin, dark-haired woman who had, unaccountably, produced three huge, cheerful sons with thick, fair hair. Giles and his two brothers adored their mother – and it had been no coincidence that The Pines was in the next-door village to Giles's old family home. At first, Maggie had been slightly discomfited at the proximity of their new house to her in-laws. But, after all, her own parents were miles away, in Derbyshire and, as Giles had pointed out, it would be useful to have at least one set of grandparents around.

'She was saying, you'll have to get to know all the other young mums in the village,' said Giles.

'Are there many?'

'I think so. Sounds like one long round of coffee mornings.'

'Oh good!' said Maggie teasingly. 'So while you slave away in the City I can sip cappuccinos with all my chums.'

'Something like that.'

'Sounds better than commuting,' said Maggie, and leaned back comfortably. 'I should have done this years ago.' She closed her eyes and imagined herself in her kitchen, making coffee for a series of new, vibrant friends with cute babies dressed in designer clothes. In the summers they would hold picnics on the lawn. Roxanne and Candice would come down from London and they would all drink Pimm's while the baby gurgled happily on a rug. They would look like something from a lifestyle magazine. In fact, maybe the *Londoner* would run a piece on them. *Former editor Maggie Phillips and her new take on rural bliss.* It was going to be a whole new life, she thought happily. A whole wonderful new life.

The brightly lit train bounced and rattled along the track, then came to an abrupt halt in a tunnel. The lights flickered, went off, then went on again. A group of party-goers several seats down from Candice began to sing 'Why are we waiting', and the woman across from Candice tried to catch her eye and tut. But Candice didn't see. She was staring blindly at her shadowy reflection in the window opposite, as memories of her father which she had buried for years rose painfully through her mind.

Good-Time Gordon, tall and handsome, always dressed in an immaculate navy blazer with gilt buttons. Always buying a round, always everyone's friend. He'd been a charming man, with vivid blue eyes and a firm handshake. Everyone who met him had admired him. Her friends had thought her lucky to have such a fun-loving father – a dad who let her go to the pub; who bought her stylish clothes; who threw holiday brochures down on the table and said 'You choose' and meant it. Life had been endless entertainment. Parties, holidays, weekends away, with her father always at the centre of the fun.

And then he'd died, and the horror had begun. Now Candice could not think of him without feeling sick, humiliated; hot with shame. He'd fooled everybody. Taken them all for a ride. Every word he'd ever uttered now seemed double-edged. Had he really loved her? Had he really loved her mother? The whole of his life had been a charade – so why not his feelings, too?

Hot tears began to well up in her eyes, and she took a deep breath. She didn't usually allow herself to think about her father. As far as she was concerned he was dead, gone, excised from her life. In the midst of those dreadful days full of pain and confusion, she'd walked into a hairdresser's and asked to have all her long hair cropped off. As the lengths of hair had fallen onto the floor, she'd felt as though her connections with her father were, in some way, being severed.

But of course, it wasn't as easy as that. She was still her father's daughter; she still bore his name. And she was still the beneficiary of all his shady dealings. Other people's money had paid for her clothes and her skiing trips and the little car she'd been given for her seventeenth birthday. The expensive year off before university – history of art lessons in Florence followed by trekking in Nepal. Other people's hard-earned money had been squandered on her pleasure. The thought of it still made her feel sick with anger; with self-reproach. But how could she have known? She'd only been a child. And her father had managed to fool everybody. Until his car crash, halfway through her first year at university. His sudden, horrific, unexpected death.

Candice felt her face grow hot all over again, and tightly gripped the plastic armrests of her seat as, with a jolt, the train started up again. Despite everything, she still felt grief for her father. A searing, angry grief – not only for him, but for her innocence; her childhood. She grieved for the time when the world had seemed to make sense; when all she'd felt for her father was love and pride. The time when she'd happily held her head high and been proud of her name and family. Before everything had suddenly darkened and become coated in dishonesty.

After his death, there hadn't been nearly enough money left to pay everyone back. Most people had given up asking; a few had taken her mother to court. It had been several years before everyone was finally settled and silenced. But the pain had never been alleviated; the damage had never been properly repaired. The consequences to people's lives could not be settled so quickly.

Candice's mother Diana had moved away to Devon, where no-one had heard of Gordon Brewin. Now she lived in a state of rigid denial. As far as she was concerned, she had been married to a loving, honourable man, maligned after his death by evil rumours – and that was the end of it. She allowed herself no true memories of the past, felt no guilt; experienced no pain.

If Candice ever tried to bring up the subject of her father, Diana would refuse to listen, refuse to talk about it; refuse to admit – even between the two of them – that anything had happened. Several years after moving to Devon she had begun a relationship with a mild-mannered, elderly man named Kenneth – and he now acted as a protective buffer. He was always present when Candice visited, ensuring that conversation never ventured beyond the polite and inconsequential. And so Candice had given up trying to get her mother to confront the past. There was no point, she had decided – and at least Diana had salvaged some happiness in her life. But she rarely visited her mother any more. The duplicity and weakness of the whole situation – the fact that Diana wouldn't admit the truth, even to her own daughter – slightly sickened Candice.

As a result, she had found herself shouldering the entire burden of memories herself. She would not allow herself the easy option, like her mother; she would not allow herself to forget or deny. And so she had learned to live with a constant guilt; a constant, angry shame. It had mellowed a little since those first nightmare years; she had learned to put it to the back of her mind and get on with her life. But the guilt had never quite left her.

Tonight, however, she felt as though she'd turned a corner. Perhaps she couldn't undo what her father had done. Perhaps she couldn't repay everyone. But she could repay Heather Trelawney – if not in money, then in help and friendship. Helping Heather as much as she possibly could would be her own private atonement.

As she got off the tube at Highbury and Islington, she felt light and hopeful. She briskly walked the few streets to the Victorian house where she had lived for the last two years, let herself in at the front door and bounded up the flight of stairs to her first-floor flat.

'Hey, Candice.' A voice interrupted her as she reached for her Yale key, and she turned round. It was Ed Armitage, who lived in the flat opposite. He was standing in the doorway of his flat, wearing ancient jeans and eating a Big Mac. 'I've got that Sellotape, if you want it back.'

'Oh,' said Candice. 'Thanks.'

'Give me a sec.' He disappeared into his flat, and

Candice leaned against her own front door, waiting. She didn't want to open her door and find him inviting himself in for a drink. Tonight, to be honest, she wasn't in the mood for Ed.

Ed had lived opposite Candice for as long as she'd lived there. He was a corporate lawyer at a huge City law firm, earned unfeasibly large amounts of money, and worked unfeasibly long hours. Taxis were frequently to be heard chugging outside the house for him at six in the morning, and didn't deliver him back home until after midnight. Sometimes he didn't come home at all, but caught a few hours' sleep on a bed at the office, then started again. The very thought of it made Candice feel sick. It was pure greed that drove him so hard, she thought. Nothing but greed.

'Here you are,' said Ed, reappearing. He handed her the roll of tape and took a bite of his Big Mac. 'Want some?'

'No thanks,' said Candice politely.

'Not healthy enough?' said Ed, leaning against the banisters. His dark eyes glinted at her as though he were enjoying his own private joke. 'What do you eat, then? Quiche?' He took another bite of hamburger. 'You eat quiche, Candice?'

'Yes,' said Candice impatiently. 'I suppose I eat quiche.' Why couldn't Ed just make polite small talk like everyone else? she thought. Why did he always have to look at her with those glinting eyes, waiting for an answer – as though she were about to reveal something fascinating? It was impossible to relax while talking to him. No idle comment could go unchallenged.

'Quiche is fucking cholesterol city. You're better off with one of these.' He gestured to his hamburger, and a piece of slimy lettuce fell onto the floor. To Candice's horror, he bent down, picked it up, and popped it in his mouth.

42

'See?' he said as he stood up. 'Salad.'

Candice rolled her eyes. Really, she felt quite sorry for Ed. He had no life outside the office. No friends, no girlfriend, no furniture even. She had once popped across to his flat for a drink in order to be neighbourly – and discovered that Ed possessed only one ancient leather chair, a wide-screen TV and a pile of empty pizza boxes.

'So, have you been sacked or something?' she said sarcastically. 'I mean, it's only ten p.m. Shouldn't you be hammering out some deal somewhere?'

'Since you ask, I'll be on gardening leave as from next week,' said Ed.

'What?' Candice looked at him uncomprehendingly.

'New job,' said Ed. 'So I get to spend three months doing sod-all. It's in my contract.'

'Three months?' Candice wrinkled her brow. 'But why?'

'Why do you think?' Ed grinned complacently and cracked open a can of Coke. 'Because I'm bloody important, that's why. I know too many little secrets.'

'Are you serious?' Candice stared at him. 'So you don't get paid for three months?' Ed's face creased in a laugh.

'Of course I get paid! These guys love me! They're paying me more to do nothing than I used to get working my arse off.'

'But that's . . . that's immoral!' said Candice. 'Think of all the people in the world desperate for a job. And you're getting paid to sit around.'

'That's the world,' said Ed. 'Like it or slit your wrists.'

'Or try to change it,' said Candice.

'So you say,' said Ed, taking a slurp of Coke. 'But then, we can't all be as saintly as you, Candice, can we?'

Candice stared furiously at him. How did Ed always manage to wind her up so successfully?

43

'I've got to go,' she said abruptly.

'By the way, your man's in there,' said Ed. 'Ex-man. Whatever.'

'Justin?' Candice stared at him, her cheeks suddenly flaming. 'Justin's in the flat?'

'I saw him letting himself in earlier,' said Ed, and raised his eyebrows. 'Are you two back together again?'

'No!' said Candice.

'Now, that's a shame,' said Ed. 'He was a really fun guy.' Candice gave him a sharp look. On the few occasions that Ed and Justin had met, it had been clear that the two had absolutely nothing in common.

'Well, anyway,' she said abruptly, 'I'll see you around.'

'Sure,' said Ed, shrugging, and disappeared back into his flat.

Candice took a deep breath, then opened her front door, her head whirling. What was Justin doing there? It was a good month since they'd split up. And more to the point, what the hell was he still doing with a key to her flat?

'Hi?' she called. 'Justin?'

'Candice.' Justin appeared at the end of the corridor. He was dressed, as ever, in a smart suit which verged on trendy, and holding a drink. His dark curly hair was neatly glossed back and his dark eyes glowed in the lamplight; he looked to Candice like an actor playing the role of a moody intellectual. 'A young Daniel Barenboim,' someone had once admiringly described Justin – after which, for several evenings, she had noticed him sitting casually in front of the piano, and sometimes even fingering the keys, despite the fact he couldn't play a note.

'I apologize for dropping in unannounced,' he said now.

'Glad to see you've made yourself at home,' said Candice.

'I expected you back earlier,' said Justin, in a slightly resentful tone. 'I won't be long – I just thought we should have a little chat.'

'What about?'

Justin said nothing, but solemnly ushered her down the corridor into the sitting room. Candice felt herself prickling with annoyance. Justin had a unique ability to make it seem as though he was always in the right and everyone else was in the wrong. At the beginning of their relationship, he had been so convincing that she too had believed he was always right. It had taken six months and a series of increasingly frustrating arguments for her to realize that he was just a self-opinionated pompous show-off.

When they'd first met, of course, he had dazzled her. He had arrived at the *Londoner* fresh from a year's experience on the *New York Times*, with the reputation of a huge intellect and a barrage of impressive connections. When he had asked her out for a drink she had felt flattered. She had drunk copious quantities of wine, and gazed into his dark eyes, and had listened admiringly to his views – half persuaded by everything he said, even when she would normally have disagreed. After a few weeks he had begun to stay the night at her flat every so often, and they had tentatively planned a holiday together. Then his flat-share in Pimlico had fallen apart, and he had moved in with her.

It was really then that things had gone wrong, thought Candice. Her hazy admiration had melted away as she saw him in close proximity – taking three times longer than herself to get ready in the mornings; claiming proudly that he couldn't cook and didn't intend to learn; expecting the bathroom to be clean but never once cleaning it himself. She had come to realize the full extent of his vanity; the strength of his arrogance and eventually – with a slight shock – that he considered her no intellectual match for himself. If she tried to argue intelligently with him he patronized her until she made a winning point, at which he grew sullen and angry. Never once would he admit defeat – his self-image simply would not allow it. For in his own mind, Justin was destined for great things. His ambition was almost frightening in its strength; it drove him like a steamroller, flattening everything else in his life.

Even now, Candice couldn't be sure which had been hurt most when she had ended the relationship – his feelings or his pride? He had almost seemed more sorrowful for her than anything else, as though she'd made a foolish mistake which he knew she would soon regret.

However, so far – a month on – she hadn't regretted her decision for an instant.

'So,' she said as they sat down. 'What do you want?'

Justin gave her a tiny smile.

'I wanted to come and see you,' he said, 'to make sure you're absolutely OK about tomorrow.'

'Tomorrow?' said Candice blankly. Justin smiled at her again.

'Tomorrow, as you know, is the day I take over as acting editor of the *Londoner*. Effectively, I'll be your boss.' He shook out his sleeves, examined his cuffs, then looked up. 'I wouldn't want any . . . problems to arise between us.' Candice stared at him.

'Problems?'

'I realize it may be a rather difficult time for you,' said Justin smoothly. 'My promotion coinciding with the break-up of our relationship. I wouldn't want you feeling at all vulnerable.'

'Vulnerable?' said Candice in astonishment. 'Justin, it was me who ended our relationship! I'm fine about it.'

'If that's the way you want to see it,' said Justin

kindly. 'Just as long as there are no bad feelings.'

'I can't guarantee that,' muttered Candice.

She watched as Justin swirled his glass of whisky, so that the ice-cubes in it clinked together. He looked as though he were practising for a television ad, she thought. Or a *Panorama* profile: 'Justin Vellis: the genius at home'. A giggle rose through her, and she clamped her lips together.

'Well, I mustn't keep you,' said Justin at last, and stood up. 'See you tomorrow.'

'Can't wait,' said Candice, pulling a face behind his back. As they reached the door she paused, her hand on the latch. 'By the way,' she said casually, 'do you know if they've appointed a new editorial assistant yet?'

'No they haven't,' said Justin, frowning. 'In fact, to tell you the truth, I'm a bit pissed off about that. Maggie's done absolutely nothing about it. Just disappears off into domestic bliss and leaves me with two hundred bloody CVs to read.'

'Oh dear, poor you,' said Candice innocently. 'Still, never mind. I'm sure someone'll turn up.'

Roxanne took another sip of her drink and calmly turned the page of her paperback. He had said nine-thirty. It was now ten past ten. She had been sitting in this hotel bar for forty minutes, ordering Bloody Marys and sipping them slowly and feeling her heart jump every time anyone entered the bar. Around her, couples and groups were murmuring over their drinks; in the corner, an elderly man in a white tuxedo was singing 'Someone to watch over me'. It could have been any bar in any hotel in any country of the world. There were women like her all over the globe, thought Roxanne. Women sitting in bars, trying to look lively, waiting for men who weren't going to show.

A waiter came discreetly towards her table, removed

her ashtray and replaced it with a fresh one. As he moved off, she sensed a flicker in his expression – sympathy, perhaps. Or disdain. She was used to both. Just as years of exposure to the sun had hardened her skin, so years of waiting, of disappointment and humiliation, had toughened her internal shell.

How many hours of her life had she spent like this? How many hours, waiting for a man who was often late and half the time didn't show up at all? There was always an excuse, of course. Another crisis at work, perhaps. An unforeseen encounter with a member of his family. Once, she'd been sitting in a London restaurant, waiting for their third anniversary lunch – only to see him entering with his wife. He'd glanced over at her with an appalled, helpless expression, and she'd been forced to watch as he and his wife were ushered to a table. To watch, with pain eating like acid at her heart, as his wife sat frowning at him, obviously bored by his company.

He'd later told her that Cynthia had bumped into him on the street and insisted on joining him for lunch. He'd told her how he'd sat in misery, unable to eat; unable to make conversation. The next weekend, to make up, he'd cancelled everything else and taken Roxanne to Venice.

Roxanne closed her eyes. That weekend had been an intoxication of happiness. She'd known a pure single-minded joy which she'd never since experienced; a joy she still desperately sought, like an addict seeking that first high. They had walked hand in hand through dusty ancient squares; along canals glinting in the sunshine; over crumbling bridges. They'd drunk Prosecco in Piazza San Marco, listening to Strauss waltzes. They'd made love in the old-fashioned wooden bed at their hotel, then sat on their balcony watching the gondolas ride past; listening to the sounds of the city travelling over the water.

They hadn't mentioned his wife or family once. For that weekend, four human beings simply hadn't existed. Gone, in a puff of smoke.

Roxanne opened her eyes. She no longer allowed herself to think about his family. She no longer indulged in wicked fantasies about car crashes and avalanches. Down that road lay pain; self-reproach; indecision. Down that road lay the knowledge that she would never have him to herself. That there would be no car crash. That she was wasting the best years of her life on a man who belonged to another woman; a tall and noble woman whom he had vowed to love and cherish for all his life. The mother of his children.

The mother of his fucking children.

A familiar pain seared Roxanne's heart and she drained her Bloody Mary, placed a twenty in the leather folder containing her bill and stood up in an unhurried motion, her face nonchalant.

As she made her way to the door of the bar, she almost bumped into a girl in a black Lurex dress, with thick make-up, over-dyed red hair and shiny gilt jewellery. Roxanne recognized her calling at once. There were women like this all over London. Hired as escorts for the evening from a fancy-named firm; paid to laugh and flirt and – for a fee – much more. Several steps up from the hookers at Euston; several steps down from the trophy wives in the dining room.

Once upon a time she would have despised such a person. Now, as she met the girl's eyes, she felt something like empathy pass between them. They'd both fallen out of the loop. Both ended up in situations which, if predicted, would have made them laugh with disbelief. For who on earth planned to end up an escort girl? Who on earth planned to end up the other woman for six long years?

A bubble, half sob, half laughter rose up in Roxanne's throat, and she quickly strode on past the escort girl, out of the bar and through the hotel foyer.

'Taxi, madam?' said the hotel doorman as she emerged into the cold night air.

'Thanks,' said Roxanne, and forced herself to smile brightly, hold her head high. So she'd been stood up, she told herself firmly. So what was new? It had happened before and it would happen again. That was the deal when the love of your life was a married man.

Chapter Four

Candice sat in the office of Ralph Allsopp, publisher of the *Londoner*, biting her nails and wondering where he was. She had hesitantly knocked on his door that morning, praying that he was in; praying that he wouldn't be too busy to see her. When he'd opened the door, holding a phone to his ear, and gestured her in, she'd felt a spurt of relief. First hurdle over. Now all she had to do was persuade him to see Heather.

But before she'd been able to launch into her little speech, he'd put the phone down, said, 'Stay there', and disappeared out of the room. That was about ten minutes ago. Now Candice was wondering whether she should have got up and followed him. Or perhaps said boldly, 'Where are you going – can I come too?' That was the sort of gumption Ralph Allsopp liked in his staff. He was famous for hiring people with initiative rather than qualifications; for admiring people not afraid to admit ignorance; for prizing and nurturing talent. He admired dynamic, energetic people, prepared to work hard and take risks. The worst crime a member of his staff could possibly commit was to be feeble.

'Feeble!' would come his roaring voice from the top floor. 'Bloody feeble!' And all over the building, people would pull their chairs in, stop chatting about the weekend, and begin typing.

But those who made the grade, Ralph treated with the utmost respect. As a result, staff tended to join Allsopp Publications and stay for years. Even those who left to become freelance or pursue other careers would keep in touch; pop in for a drink or do some photocopying and float their latest ideas past Ralph's enthusiastic ear. It was a sociable, relaxed company. Candice had been there five years and had never considered leaving.

She leaned back in her chair now and looked idly around Ralph's desk – legendary for its untidiness. Two wooden in-trays overflowed with letters and memos; copies of the company's publications competed for space with galley proofs covered in red ink; a telephone was perched on a pile of books. As she looked at it, the phone began to ring. She hesitated for a second, wondering if she ought to answer someone else's phone – then imagined Ralph's reaction if he came in to see her just sitting there, letting it ring. 'What's wrong, girl?' he'd roar. 'Afraid it'll bite you?'

Hastily she picked up the receiver.

'Hello,' she said in a businesslike voice. 'Ralph Allsopp's office.'

'Is Mr Allsopp there?' enquired a female voice.

'I'm afraid not,' said Candice. 'May I take a message?'

'Is this his personal assistant?' Candice glanced out of the office window at the desk of Janet, Ralph's secretary. It was empty.

'I'm . . . standing in for her,' said Candice. There was a pause, then the voice said, 'This is Mr Davies's assistant Mary calling from the Charing Cross Hospital. Please could you tell Mr Allsopp that Mr Davies is unfortunately unable to make the two o'clock appointment, and wondered if three would be convenient instead.'

'Right,' said Candice, scribbling on a piece of paper. 'OK. I'll tell him.'

She put the phone down and looked curiously at the message.

'So! My dear girl.' Ralph's breezy voice interrupted her, and she gave a startled jump. 'What can I do for you? Here to complain about your new editor already? Or is it something else?'

Candice laughed.

'Something else.'

She watched as he made his way round to the other side of the desk, and thought again what an attractive man he must have been when he was younger. He was tall – at least six foot three – with dishevelled greying hair and intelligent, gleaming eyes. He must be in his fifties now, she guessed – but still exuded a relentless, almost frightening energy.

'You just got this message,' she said almost unwillingly, handing him the bit of paper.

'Ah,' said Ralph, scanning it expressionlessly. 'Thank you.' He folded the note up and put it in his trouser pocket.

Candice opened her mouth to ask if he was all right – then closed it again. It wasn't her place to start enquiring about her boss's health. She had intercepted a private call; it was nothing to do with her. Besides, it occurred to her, it might be something minor and embarrassing that she didn't want to hear about.

'I wanted to see you,' she said instead, 'about the editorial assistant's job on the *Londoner.*'

'Oh yes?' said Ralph, leaning back in his chair.

'Yes,' said Candice, garnering all her courage. 'The thing is, I know somebody who I think would fit the bill.'

'Really?' said Ralph. 'Well, then, invite him to apply.'

'It's a girl,' said Candice. 'And the thing is, I don't think her CV is that spectacular. But I know she's talented. I know she can write. And she's bright, and enthusiastic . . .'

'I'm glad to hear it,' said Ralph mildly. 'But you know, Justin's the one you should be talking to.'

'I know,' said Candice. 'I know he is. But—' She broke off, and Ralph's eyes narrowed.

'Now, look,' he said, leaning forward. 'Tell me plainly – is there going to be trouble between you two? I'm quite aware of the situation between you, and if it's going to cause problems . . .'

'It's not that!' said Candice at once. 'It's just that . . . Justin's very busy. It's his first day, and I don't want to bother him. He's got enough on his plate. In fact . . .' She felt her fingers mesh tightly together in her lap. 'In fact, he was complaining yesterday about having to read through all the applications. And after all, he is only *acting* editor . . . So I thought perhaps—'

'What?'

'I thought perhaps you could interview this girl yourself?' Candice looked entreatingly at Ralph. 'She's downstairs in reception.'

'She's *where*?'

'In reception,' said Candice falteringly. 'She's just waiting – in case you say yes.'

Ralph stared at her, an incredulous look on his face, and for a dreadful moment Candice thought he was going to bellow at her. But suddenly his face broke into a laugh. 'Send her up,' he said. 'Since you've dragged her all this way, let's give the poor girl a chance.'

'Thanks,' said Candice. 'Honestly, I'm sure she'll be—' Ralph raised a hand to stop her.

'Send her up,' he said. 'And we'll see.'

Maggie Phillips sat alone in her magnificent Smallbone kitchen, sipping coffee and staring at the table and wondering what to do next. She had woken that morning at the usual early hour and had watched as Giles got dressed, ready for his commute into the City.

'Now, you just take it easy,' he'd said, briskly

knotting his tie. 'I'll try and be home by seven.'

'OK,' Maggie had said, grinning up at him. 'Give the pollution my love, won't you.'

'That's right, rub it in,' he'd retorted humorously. 'You bloody ladies of leisure.'

As she'd heard the front door slam, she'd felt a delicious feeling of freedom spread through her body. No work, she'd thought to herself. No work! She could do what she liked. At first, she'd tried to go back to sleep, closing her eyes and deliberately snuggling back under the duvet. But lying down was, perversely, uncomfortable. She was too huge and heavy to find a comfortable position. So after a few tussles with the pillows, she'd given up.

She'd come downstairs and made herself some breakfast and eaten it, reading the paper and admiring the garden out of the window. That had taken her until eight-thirty. Then she'd gone back upstairs, run a bath and lain in it for what seemed like at least an hour. When she emerged, she discovered she'd been in there for twenty minutes.

Now it was nine-thirty. The day hadn't even begun yet, but she felt as though she'd been sitting at her kitchen table for an eternity. How was it that time – such a precious, slipping-away commodity in London – seemed here to pass so slowly? Like honey dripping through an hourglass.

Maggie closed her eyes, took another sip of coffee and tried to think of what she was usually doing at this hour. Any number of things. Strap-hanging on the tube, reading the paper. Striding into the office. Buying a cappuccino from the coffee shop on the corner. Answering a thousand e-mails. Sitting in an early meeting. Laughing, talking, surrounded by people.

And stressed out, she reminded herself firmly, before the images became too positive. Buffeted by the crowds, choked by taxi fumes; deafened by the noise;

pressured by deadlines. Whereas here, the only sound was that of a bird outside the window, and the air was as clean and fresh as spring water. And she had no pressures, no meetings, no deadlines.

Except the big one of course – and that was utterly outside her own control. It almost amused her, the thought that she, who was so used to being boss, who was so used to running the show, was in this case utterly powerless. Idly, she reached for her pregnancy handbook and allowed it to fall open. 'At this point the pains will become stronger,' she found herself reading. 'Try not to panic. Your partner will be able to offer support and encouragement.' Hastily she closed the book and took another gulp of coffee. Out of sight, out of fright.

Somewhere at the back of her mind, Maggie knew she should have taken the midwives' advice and attended classes on childbirth. Each of her friendly, well-meaning midwives had pressed on her a series of leaflets and numbers, and exhorted her to follow them up. But didn't these women realize how busy she was? Didn't they appreciate that taking time off work for hospital appointments was disruptive enough – and that the last thing she and Giles felt like doing at the end of a busy day was trekking off to some stranger's house in order to sit on bean bags and talk about, frankly, quite private matters? She had bought a book and half watched a video – fast-forwarding through the gruesome bits – and that would have to be enough.

Firmly she pushed the book behind the breadbin, where she couldn't see it – and poured herself another cup of coffee. At that moment, the doorbell rang. Frowning slightly in surprise, Maggie heaved herself out of her chair and walked through the hall to the front door. There on the front step was her mother-in-law, dressed in a Puffa jacket, a stripy shirt and a blue corduroy skirt, straight to the knee.

'Hello, Maggie!' she said. 'Not too early, am I?'

'No!' said Maggie, half laughing. 'Not at all. Giles said you might pop round.' She leaned forward and awkwardly kissed Paddy, stumbling slightly on the step.

Although she had been married to Giles for four years, she still did not feel she had got to know Paddy very well. They had never once sat down for a good chat – principally because Paddy never seemed to sit down at all. She was a thin, energetic woman, always on the move. Always cooking, gardening, running someone to the station or organizing a collection. She had run the village Brownies for twenty-five years, sang in the church choir, and had made all Maggie's bridesmaids' dresses herself. Now she smiled, and handed Maggie a cake tin.

'A few scones,' she said. 'Some raisin, some cheese.'

'Oh, Paddy!' said Maggie, feeling touched. 'You shouldn't have.'

'It's no trouble,' said Paddy. 'I'll give you the recipe, if you like. They're terribly easy to rustle up. Giles always used to love them.'

'Right,' said Maggie after a pause, remembering her one disastrous attempt to make a cake for Giles's birthday. 'That would be great!'

'And I've brought someone to see you,' said Paddy. 'Thought you'd like to meet another young mum from the village.'

'Oh,' said Maggie in surprise. 'How nice!'

Paddy beckoned forward a girl in jeans and a pink jersey, holding a baby and clutching a toddler by the hand.

'Here you are!' she said proudly. 'Maggie, meet Wendy.'

As Candice tripped down the stairs to reception she felt elated with her success. Powerful, almost. It just showed what could be achieved with a little bit of initiative, a little effort. She arrived at the foyer and walked quickly to the chairs where Heather was sitting, dressed in a neat black suit.

'He said yes!' she said, unable to conceal her triumph. 'He's going to see you!'

'Really?' Heather's eyes lit up. 'What, now?'

'Right now! I told you, he's always willing to give people chances.' Candice grinned with excitement. 'All you've got to do is remember everything I told you. Lots of enthusiasm. Lots of drive. If you can't think of an answer to the question, tell a joke instead.'

'OK.' Heather tugged nervously at her skirt. 'Do I look all right?'

'You look brilliant,' said Candice. 'And one more thing. Ralph is sure to ask if you've brought an example of your writing.'

'What?' said Heather in alarm. 'But I—'

'Give him this,' said Candice, suppressing a grin, and handed a piece of paper to Heather.

'What?' Heather gazed at it incredulously. 'What is it?'

'It's a short piece I wrote a few months ago,' said Candice. 'On how ghastly London transport is in summer. It was never used in the magazine, and the only other person who read it was Maggie.' A couple of visitors entered the foyer, and she lowered her voice. 'And now it's yours. Look – I've put your byline at the top.'

'"London's Burning",' read Heather slowly. '"By Heather Trelawney."' She looked up, eyes dancing. 'I don't believe it! This is wonderful!'

'You'd better read it over quickly before you go in,' said Candice. 'He might ask you about it.'

'Candice . . . this is so good of you,' said Heather. 'I don't know how I can repay you.'

'Don't be silly,' said Candice at once. 'It's a pleasure.'

'But you're being so kind to me. Why are you being

so kind to me?' Heather' s grey eyes met Candice's with a sudden intensity, and Candice felt her stomach give a secret guilty flip. She stared back at Heather, cheeks growing hot and, for a heightened instant, considered telling Heather everything. Confessing her family background; her constant feeling of debt; her need to make amends.

Then, almost as she was opening her mouth, she realized what a mistake it would be. What an embarrassing situation she would put Heather – and herself – in by saying anything. It might make her feel better, it might act as a kind of catharsis – but to unburden herself would be selfish. Heather must never find out that her motives were anything but genuine friendship.

'It's nothing,' she said quickly. 'You'd better go up. Ralph's waiting.'

Paddy had insisted on making the coffee, leaving Maggie alone with Wendy. Feeling suddenly a little nervous, she ushered Wendy into the sitting room, and gestured to the sofa. This was the first fellow mother she'd met. And a neighbour, too. Perhaps this girl would become her bosom pal, she thought. Perhaps their children would grow up lifelong friends.

'Do sit down,' she said. 'Have you . . . lived in the village long?'

'A couple of years,' said Wendy, dumping her huge holdall on the floor and sitting down on Maggie's cream sofa.

'And . . . do you like living here?'

'S'all right, I suppose. Jake, leave that alone!'

Maggie looked up and, with a spasm of horror, saw Wendy's toddler reaching up towards the blue Venetian glass bowl Roxanne had given them as a wedding present.

'Oh gosh,' she said, getting to her feet as quickly as her bulk would allow. 'I'll just . . . move that, shall I?'

She reached the glass bowl just as Jake's sticky fingers closed around it. 'Thanks,' she said politely to the toddler. 'Ahm . . . would you mind . . .' His fingers remained tight around it. 'It's just that . . .'

'Jake!' yelled Wendy, and Maggie jumped in fright. 'Leave it!' Jake's face crumpled, but his grip obediently loosened. Quickly, Maggie withdrew the bowl from his grasp and placed it on top of the tallboy.

'They're monsters at this age,' said Wendy. Her eyes ran over Maggie's bump. 'When are you due?'

'Three weeks,' said Maggie, sitting back down. 'Not long now!'

'You might be late,' said Wendy.

'Yes,' said Maggie after a pause. 'I suppose I might.' Wendy gestured to the baby on her lap.

'I was two weeks late with this one. They had to induce me in the end.'

'Oh,' said Maggie. 'Still—'

'Then he got stuck,' said Wendy. 'His heartbeat started to fall and they had to pull him out with forceps.' She looked up and met Maggie's eye. 'Twenty-nine stitches.'

'Dear God,' said Maggie. 'You're joking.' Suddenly she thought she might faint. She took a deep breath, gripping the edge of her chair, and forced herself to smile at Wendy. Get off the subject of childbirth, she thought. Anything else at all. 'So – do you . . . work at all?'

'No,' said Wendy, staring at her blankly. 'Jake! Get off that!' Maggie turned, to see Jake balancing precariously on the piano stool. He gave his mother a murderous stare and began to bang on the piano keys.

'Here we are!' Paddy came into the room, carrying a tray. 'I opened these rather nice almond biscuits, Maggie. Is that all right?'

'Absolutely,' said Maggie.

'Only I know what it's like when you've planned all

your meals in advance, and then someone else comes and disrupts your store cupboard.' She gave a short little laugh, and Maggie smiled feebly back. She suspected that Paddy's idea of a store cupboard and her own were somewhat different.

'I've got some squash for Jake somewhere,' said Wendy. Her voice suddenly rose. 'Jake, pack it in or you won't get a drink!' She deposited the baby on the floor and reached for her holdall.

'What a pet!' said Paddy, looking at the baby wriggling on the floor. 'Maggie, why don't you hold him for a bit?' Maggie stiffened in horror.

'I don't think—'

'Here you are!' said Paddy, picking the baby up and putting him in Maggie's awkward arms. 'Isn't he a poppet?'

Maggie stared down at the baby in her arms, aware that the other two were watching her, and felt a prickling self-consciousness. What was wrong with her? She felt nothing towards this baby except distaste. It was ugly, it smelt of stale milk and it was dressed in a hideous pastel Babygro. The baby opened his blue eyes and looked at her, and she gazed down, trying to warm to him; trying to act like a mother. He began to squirm and chirrup, and she looked up in alarm.

'He might need to burp,' said Wendy. 'Hold him upright.'

'OK,' said Maggie. With tense, awkward hands, she shifted the baby round and lifted him up. He screwed up his face and for an awful moment she thought he was going to scream. Then his mouth opened, and a cascade of warm regurgitated milk streamed onto her jersey.

'Oh my God!' said Maggie in horror. 'He's thrown up on me!'

'Oh,' said Wendy dispassionately. 'Sorry about that. Here, give him to me.'

'Never mind,' said Paddy briskly, handing Maggie a muslin cloth. 'You'll have to get used to this kind of thing, Maggie! Won't she, Wendy!'

'Oh yeah,' said Wendy. 'You just wait!'

Maggie looked up from wiping her jersey to see Paddy and Wendy both looking complacently at her, as though in triumph. *We've got you*, their eyes seemed to say. Inside, she began to shiver.

'Wanta do a poo,' Jake announced, wandering over to Wendy's side.

'Good boy,' she said, putting down her cup. 'Just let me get the potty out.'

'Dear God, no!' cried Maggie, getting to her feet. 'I mean – I'll make some more coffee, shall I?'

In the kitchen she flicked on the kettle and sank into a chair, shaking, her jersey still damp with milk. She didn't know whether to laugh or cry. Was this really what motherhood was all about? And if so, what the hell had she done? She closed her eyes and thought, with a pang, of her office at the *Londoner*. Her organized, civilized office, full of grown-ups; full of wit and sophistication and not a baby in sight.

She hesitated, glancing at the door – then picked up the phone and quickly dialled a number.

'Hello?' As she heard Candice's voice, Maggie exhaled with relief. Just hearing those friendly, familiar tones made her relax.

'Hi, Candice! It's Maggie.'

'Maggie!' exclaimed Candice in surprise. 'How's it going? Are you all right?'

'Oh, I'm fine,' said Maggie. 'You know, lady of leisure . . .'

'I suppose you're still in bed, you lucky cow.'

'Actually,' said Maggie gaily, 'I'm hosting a coffee morning. I have a real-live Stepford mum in my living room.' Candice laughed, and Maggie felt a warm glow of pleasure steal over her. Thank God for friends, she thought. Suddenly the situation seemed funny; an entertaining anecdote. 'You won't *believe* what happened just now,' she added, lowering her voice. 'I'm sitting on the sofa, holding this pig-ugly baby, and he starts to wriggle. And the next minute—'

'Actually, Maggie,' interrupted Candice, 'I'm really sorry, but I can't really chat. Justin's holding some stupid meeting and we've all got to go.'

'Oh,' said Maggie, feeling a stab of disappointment. 'Well . . . OK.'

'But we'll talk later, I promise.'

'Fine!' said Maggie brightly. 'It doesn't matter at all. I was just calling on the off-chance. Have a good meeting.'

'I doubt that. Oh, but listen. Before I go, there's something I must tell you!' Candice's voice grew quieter. 'You remember that girl, Heather, we saw last night? The cocktail waitress?'

'Yes,' said Maggie, casting her mind back to the evening before. 'Of course I do.' Was it really only last night that they were all sitting in the Manhattan Bar? It seemed like a lifetime ago.

'Well, I know you told me not to – but I introduced her to Ralph,' said Candice. 'And he was so impressed, he offered her the job on the spot. She's starting as editorial assistant next week!'

'Really?' said Maggie in astonishment. 'How extraordinary!'

'Yes,' said Candice, and cleared her throat. 'Well, it turns out she's . . . she's very good at writing. Ralph was really impressed with her work. So he's decided to give her a chance.'

'Typical Ralph,' said Maggie. 'Well, that's great.'

'Isn't it fantastic?' Candice lowered her voice even further. 'Mags, I can't tell you what this means to me. It's as though I'm finally making amends for what my father did. I'm finally . . . doing something positive.'

'Then I'm really glad for you,' said Maggie more warmly. 'I hope it all works out well.'

'Oh, it will,' said Candice. 'Heather's a really nice girl. In fact, we're having lunch today, to celebrate.'

'Right,' said Maggie wistfully. 'Well, have fun.'

'We'll toast you. Look, Mags, I've got to run. Talk soon.' And the phone went dead.

Maggie stared at the receiver for a moment, then slowly replaced it, trying not to feel left out. Already, within twenty-four hours, office life had moved on without her. But of course it had. What did she expect? She gave a sigh, and looked up, to see Paddy standing in the doorway, watching her with a curious expression.

'Oh,' said Maggie guiltily. 'I was just talking to an old colleague about a . . . a work matter. Is Wendy all right?'

'She's upstairs, changing the baby's nappy,' said Paddy. 'So I thought I'd give you a hand with the coffee.'

Paddy went to the sink, turned on the hot tap, then turned round and smiled pleasantly.

'You know, you mustn't cling onto your old life, Maggie.'

'What?' said Maggie in disbelief. 'I'm not!'

'You'll soon find you put down roots here. You'll get to know some other young families. But it does require a bit of effort.' Paddy squirted washing-up liquid into the bowl. 'It's a different way of life down here.'

'Not that different, surely,' said Maggie lightly. 'People still have fun, don't they?' Paddy gave her a tight little smile.

'After a while, you may find you have less in common with some of your London friends.'

And more in common with Wendy? thought Maggie. I don't think so.

'Possibly,' she said, smiling back at Paddy. 'But I'll

make every effort to keep in touch with my old friends. There's a threesome of us who always meet up for cocktails. I'll certainly carry on seeing them.'

'Cocktails,' said Paddy, giving a short laugh. 'How very glamorous.'

Maggie stared back at her and felt a sudden stab of resentment. What business was it of hers who her friends were? What business of hers was it what kind of life she led?

'Yes, cocktails,' she said, and smiled sweetly at Paddy. 'My own personal favourite is Sex on the Beach. Remind me to give you the recipe some time.'

Chapter Five

The doorbell rang and Candice jumped, despite the fact that she'd been sitting still on the sofa, waiting for Heather's arrival, for a good twenty minutes. She glanced once more round the sitting room, making sure it was neat and tidy, then nervously headed towards the front door. As she opened it, she gasped in surprise, then laughed. All she could see was a huge bouquet of flowers. Yellow roses, carnations and freesias nestling in dark greenery, wrapped in gold-embossed cellophane and crowned with a large bow.

'These are for you,' came Heather's voice from behind the bouquet. 'Sorry about the hideous bow. They put it on before I could stop them.'

'This is so kind of you!' said Candice, taking the rustling bouquet from Heather and giving her a hug. 'You really shouldn't have.'

'Yes I should!' said Heather. 'And more.' Her eyes met Candice's earnestly. 'Candice, look at everything you're doing for me. A job, a place to stay . . .'

'Well, you know,' said Candice awkwardly, 'I do have two bedrooms. And if your other place was grim . . .'

It had been purely by chance that, during their lunch together, Heather had happened to start talking about the flat where she lived. As she had talked, making light of its awfulness, Candice had suddenly hit on the idea of asking Heather to move in with her – and to her delight, Heather had agreed on the spot. Everything was falling wonderfully into place.

'It was like a hovel,' said Heather. 'Six to a room. Utterly sordid. But this place . . .' She put down her suitcases and walked slowly into the flat, looking around incredulously. 'Is this all yours?'

'Yes,' said Candice. 'At least, I had a flatmate when I first moved in, but she moved out, and I never got round to—'

'It's a palace!' interrupted Heather, looking around. 'Candice, it's beautiful!'

'Thanks,' said Candice, flushing in pleasure. 'I . . . well, I like it.'

She was secretly rather proud of her attempts at home decoration. She'd spent a long time the previous summer stripping down the brown swirly wallpaper left by the previous occupant of the flat and covering the walls in a chalky yellow paint. The whole thing had taken rather longer than she'd imagined, and her arms had ached by the end of it, but it had been worth it.

'Look – the flowers I brought go perfectly with your walls,' said Heather, and her eyes danced a little. 'We obviously think alike, you and me. That's a good omen, don't you think?'

'Absolutely!' said Candice. 'Well, let's get your luggage in and you can . . .' She swallowed. 'You can see your room.'

She picked up one of Heather's cases and hefted it down the hall, then, with a slight tremor, opened the first bedroom door.

'Wow,' breathed Heather behind her. It was a large room, decorated simply, with lavender walls and thick cream-coloured curtains. In the corner was a huge, empty oak armoire; on the night-stand beside the double bed was a pile of glossy magazines.

'This is fantastic!' said Heather. 'I can't believe this place.' She looked round. 'What's your room like? Is it this door?'

'It's . . . fine,' said Candice. 'Honestly . . .'

But Heather was too quick for her. She had already opened the door, to reveal a much smaller room, furnished with a single bed and a cheap pine wardrobe.

'Is this yours?' she said in puzzlement – then looked slowly back at the lavender-painted room. 'That one's yours, isn't it?' she said in surprise. 'You've given me your room!'

She seemed astonished – almost amused – and Candice felt herself flush with embarrassment. She had felt so proud of her little gesture; had hummed merrily the night before as she'd transferred all her clothes out of her own bedroom to make way for Heather. Now, looking at Heather's face, she realized it had been a mistake. Heather would, of course, insist on swapping back. The whole incident would bring an awkwardness to their arrangement.

'I just thought you'd want your own space,' she said, feeling foolish. 'I know what it's like, moving into someone else's home – sometimes you need to get away. So I thought I'd give you the bigger room.'

'I see,' said Heather, and looked again at the lavender room. 'Well – if you're quite sure.' She beamed at Candice and kicked one of her suitcases into the room. 'It's very good of you. I'll love being in here.'

'Oh,' said Candice, half relieved, half secretly discomfited. 'Right. Well . . . good. I'll leave you to unpack, then.'

'Don't be silly!' said Heather. 'I'll unpack later. Let's have a drink first.' She reached into her holdall. 'I brought some champagne.'

'Flowers *and* champagne!' Candice laughed. 'Heather, this is too much.'

'I always drink champagne on special occasions,' said Heather, and her eyes sparkled at Candice. 'And this occasion is very special indeed. Don't you agree?'

As Candice popped the champagne in the kitchen, she could hear the wooden floorboards of the sitting room creaking slightly as Heather moved about. She filled two champagne flutes – free gifts from a reception she'd once attended sponsored by Bollinger – then took them, together with the bottle, into the sitting room. Heather was standing by the mantelpiece, her blond hair haloed in the lamplight, gazing up at a framed photograph. As she saw her, Candice's heart began to thump. Why hadn't she put that photograph away? How could she have been so stupid?

'Here,' she said, handing Heather a glass of champagne and trying to draw her away from the mantelpiece. 'Here's to us.'

'To us,' echoed Heather, and took a sip. Then she turned back to the mantelpiece, picked up the photograph and looked at it. Candice took another gulp of champagne, trying not to panic. If she just acted naturally, she told herself, Heather would suspect nothing.

'This is you, isn't it?' said Heather, looking up. 'Don't you look sweet! How old were you there?'

'About eleven,' said Candice, forcing a smile.

'And are these your parents?'

'Yes,' said Candice, trying to keep her voice casual. 'That's my mother, and – ' she swallowed ' – and that's my father. He . . . he died a while back.'

'Oh, I'm sorry,' said Heather. 'He was a handsome man, wasn't he?' She stared at the picture again, then raised her head and smiled. 'I bet he spoiled you rotten when you were a kid.'

'Yes,' said Candice, and attempted a laugh. 'Well – you know what fathers are like . . .'

'Absolutely,' said Heather. She gave the photograph

69

one last look, then replaced it on the mantelpiece. 'Oh, this is going to be fun,' she said suddenly. 'Don't you think?' She came towards Candice and put her arm affectionately round her waist. 'The two of us, living together. It's going to be such fun!'

At midnight that night, after a four-course dinner and more than her fair share of a bottle of divine Chablis, Roxanne arrived back at her suite at the Aphrodite Bay Hotel, to find her bed turned down, the lights dimmed, and a message light blinking on her telephone. Kicking off her shoes, she sat down on the bed, pressed the message button and began to unwrap the chocolate mint which had been placed on her pillow.

'Hi, Roxanne? It's Maggie. Hope you're having a good time, you lucky cow – and give me a call some time.' Roxanne stiffened in excitement, and was about to pick up the phone, when the machine beeped again, indicating a second message.

'No, you dope, I haven't had the baby,' came Maggie's voice again. 'This is something else. Ciao.' Roxanne grinned, and stuffed the chocolate mint into her mouth.

'End of messages,' said a tinny voice. Roxanne swallowed the mint, reached for the phone and pressed three digits.

'Hello, Nico?' she said as the phone was answered. 'I'll be down in a minute. I just have to make a quick call.' She pointed her toes, admiring her tan against her pink-polished toenails. 'Yes, order me a Brandy Alexander. See you in a moment.' She replaced the receiver, then picked it up again and dialled Maggie's number from memory.

'Hello?' said a sleepy voice.

'Giles!' said Roxanne, and guiltily looked at her watch. 'Oh God, it's late, isn't it? Sorry! I didn't think. It's Roxanne. Were you asleep?'

'Roxanne,' said Giles blearily. 'Hi. Where are you?'

'Give it to me!' Roxanne could hear Maggie saying in the background, then, in a more muted voice, 'Yes, I know it's late! I want to talk to her!' There was a scuffling noise, and Roxanne grinned, imagining Maggie wrenching the phone determinedly from her husband's grasp. Then Maggie's voice came down the receiver. 'Roxanne! How are you?'

'Hi, Mags,' said Roxanne. 'Sorry I woke Giles up.'

'Oh, he's OK,' said Maggie. 'He's already fallen asleep again. So, how's life in Cyprus?'

'Bearable,' drawled Roxanne. 'A Mediterranean paradise of blazing sun, blue waters and five-star luxury. Nothing to speak of.'

'I don't know how you stand it,' said Maggie. 'I'd complain to the management if I were you.' Then her voice grew more serious. 'Listen, Roxanne, the reason I called – have you spoken to Candice recently?'

'Not since I came out here. Why?'

'Well, I rang her this evening,' said Maggie, 'just for a chat – and that girl was there.'

'Which girl?' said Roxanne, leaning back against the padded headrest of her bed. Through her uncurtained french windows, she could see fireworks from some distant revelry or other exploding into the night sky like coloured shooting stars.

'Heather Trelawney. The cocktail waitress in the Manhattan Bar, remember?'

'Oh yes,' said Roxanne, yawning slightly. 'The one Candice's father ripped off.'

'Yes,' said Maggie. 'Well, you know Candice got her the editorial assistant job on the *Londoner*?'

'Really?' said Roxanne in surprise. 'That was quick work.'

'Apparently she went to see Ralph the next morning, and made some special plea. God knows what she said.'

'Oh well,' said Roxanne easily. 'She obviously feels very strongly about it.'

'She must do,' said Maggie. 'Because now this girl's moved in with her.'

Roxanne sat up, frowning. 'Moved in with her? But, I mean, she hardly knows her!'

'I know,' said Maggie. 'Exactly. Don't you think it seems a bit . . .'

'Mmm,' said Roxanne. 'Sudden.'

There was silence down the line, punctuated by crackles and Giles coughing in the background.

'I just have a bad vibe about it,' said Maggie eventually. 'You know what Candice is like. She'll let anyone take advantage of her.'

'Yes,' said Roxanne slowly. 'You're right.'

'So I was thinking – maybe you could try and keep tabs on this girl? There's not much I can do . . .'

'Don't worry,' said Roxanne. 'As soon as I get back, I'll suss it out.'

'Good,' said Maggie, and exhaled gustily. 'I'm sure I'm just a bored pregnant woman worrying about nothing. It'll probably all turn out fine. But . . .' She paused. 'You know.'

'I do,' said Roxanne. 'And don't fret. I'm on the case.'

The next morning Candice woke to a sweet, mouth-watering smell wafting through the air. She rolled puzzledly over in bed, opened her eyes and found herself staring at an unfamiliar white wall. What was going on? she wondered blearily. What was she doing . . .

Then her brain clicked into place. Of course. She was in the spare room. Heather was living here. And from the smell of it, she was already up and cooking something. Candice swung her legs out of bed and sat up, groaning slightly at the heaviness of her head.

Champagne always got her like that. She stood up, put on a robe, and tottered down the hall to the kitchen.

'Hi!' said Heather, looking up from the stove, with a beam. 'I'm making pancakes. Do you want one?'

'Pancakes?' said Candice. 'I haven't had pancakes since . . .'

'Coming right up!' said Heather, and opened the oven. Candice stared in amazement, to see a pile of light, golden-brown pancakes, warming gently in the oven's heat.

'This is amazing,' she said, starting to laugh. 'You can stay.'

'You don't get pancakes every day,' said Heather, gazing at her in mock severity. 'Only when you've been good.'

Candice giggled. 'I'll make some coffee.'

A few minutes later, they sat down at Candice's marble bistro table, each with a pile of pancakes, sugar and lemon juice, and a steaming mug of coffee.

'We should have maple syrup, really,' said Heather, taking a bite. 'I'll buy some.'

'This is delicious!' said Candice, her mouth full of pancake. 'Heather, you're an utter star.'

'It's a pleasure,' said Heather, smiling modestly down at her plate.

Candice took another bite of pancake and closed her eyes, savouring the pleasure. To think she'd actually had some last-minute qualms about inviting Heather to live with her. To think she'd wondered if she was making a mistake. It was obvious that Heather was going to make a wonderful flat-mate – and a wonderful new friend.

'Well, I guess I'd better go and get ready.' Candice looked up to see a sheepish grin flash across Heather's face. 'Actually, I'm a bit nervous about today.'

'Don't be,' said Candice at once. 'Everyone's very friendly. And remember I'll be there to help you.' She smiled at Heather, filled with a sudden affection for her. 'It'll all go fine, I promise.'

Half an hour later, as Candice brushed her teeth, Heather knocked on the bathroom door.

'Do I look OK?' she asked nervously, as Candice appeared. Candice gazed at her, feeling impressed and a little taken aback. Heather looked incredibly smart and polished. She was wearing a smart red suit over a white T-shirt and black high-heeled shoes.

'You look fantastic!' said Candice. 'Where's the suit from?'

'I can't remember,' said Heather vaguely. 'I bought it ages ago, when I had a windfall.'

'Well, it looks great!' said Candice. 'Just give me a sec, and we'll go.'

A few minutes later, she ushered Heather out of the flat and banged the door shut. Immediately Ed's front door swung open and he appeared on the landing, dressed in jeans and a T-shirt and clutching an empty milk bottle.

'Well, hello there!' he said, as though in surprise. 'Fancy bumping into you, Candice!'

'What a coincidence,' said Candice.

'Just putting the milk out,' said Ed unconvincingly, his eyes glued on Heather.

'Ed, we don't have a milkman,' said Candice, folding her arms.

'Not yet, we don't,' said Ed, and waved the milk bottle at Candice. 'But if I put this out as bait, maybe I can lure one this way. It works for hedgehogs. What do you think?'

He put the milk bottle down on the floor, looked at it consideringly for a moment, then moved it a little towards the stairs. Candice rolled her eyes.

'Ed, this is my new flat-mate, Heather. You may have heard her arrive last night.'

'Me?' said Ed innocently. 'No, I heard nothing.' He stepped forward, took Heather's hand and kissed it. 'Enchanted to meet you, Heather.'

'You too,' said Heather.

'And may I say how delightfully smart you look?' added Ed.

'You may,' said Heather, dimpling at him. She gave a satisfied glance at her own appearance and brushed a speck of dust off her immaculate red skirt.

'You know, you should take a few tips from Heather,' said Ed to Candice. 'Look – her shoes match her bag. Very chic.'

'Thanks, Ed,' said Candice. 'But the day I take sartorial tips from you is the day I give up wearing clothes altogether.'

'Really?' Ed's eyes gleamed. 'Is that a move you're planning in the near future?'

Heather giggled.

'What do you do, Ed?' she asked.

'He does nothing,' said Candice. 'And he gets paid for it. What is it today, Ed? Loafing around the park? Feeding the pigeons?'

'Actually, no,' said Ed. He leaned against the door frame of his flat and his eyes glinted in amusement. 'Since you ask, I'm going to go and look at my house.'

'What house?' said Candice suspiciously. 'Are you moving away? Thank God for that.'

'I've inherited a house,' said Ed. 'From my aunt.'

'Of course you have!' said Candice. 'Obviously. Some people inherit debts; Ed Armitage inherits a house.'

'Dunno what I'm going to do with it,' said Ed. 'It's down in Monkham. Bloody miles away.'

'Where's Monkham?' said Candice, wrinkling her brow.

'Wiltshire,' said Heather surprisingly. 'I know Monkham. It's very pretty.'

'I suppose I'll sell it,' said Ed. 'But then, I'm quite fond of it. I spent a lot of time there when I was a kid . . .'

'Sell it, keep it . . . who cares?' said Candice. 'What's an empty property here or there? It's not like there are people starving on the streets, or anything—'

'Or turn it into a soup kitchen,' said Ed. 'A home for orphans. Would that satisfy you, St Candice?' He grinned, and Candice scowled at him.

'Come on,' she said to Heather. 'We'll be late.'

The editorial office of the *Londoner* was a long, large room with windows at each end. It held seven desks – six for members of editorial staff and one for the editorial secretary, Kelly. At times it could be a loud and noisy place to work; on press day it was usually mayhem.

As Candice and Heather arrived, however, the room was full of the usual mid-month, Monday morning lethargy. Until the eleven o'clock meeting, no real work would be done. People would open their post, exchange stories about the weekend, make pots of coffee and nurse their hangovers. At eleven o'clock they would all cluster into the meeting room and report on the progress of the June issue; at twelve o'clock they would all emerge feeling motivated and energetic – and promptly go off for lunch. It was the same every Monday.

Candice stood at the door to the room, grinned encouragingly at Heather, and cleared her throat.

'Everybody,' she said, 'this is Heather Trelawney, our new editorial assistant.'

A murmur of hungover greetings went round the room, and Candice smiled at Heather.

'They're very friendly really,' she said. 'I'll introduce you properly in a moment. But first we should try to find Justin . . .'

'Candice,' came a voice behind her, and she jumped. She turned round to see Justin standing in the corridor. He was dressed in a dark purple suit, holding a cup of coffee and looking harassed.

'Hi!' she said. 'Justin, I'd like you to . . .'

'Candice, a word,' interrupted Justin tersely. 'In private. If I may.'

'Oh,' said Candice. 'Well . . . OK.'

She glanced apologetically at Heather, then followed Justin to the corner by the photocopying machine. Once upon a time, she thought, he would have been leading her off into the corner to whisper in her ear and make her giggle. But now, as he turned round, the expression on his face was distinctly unfriendly. Candice folded her arms and stared back at him defiantly.

'Yes?' she said, wondering if she'd made some horrendous gaffe in the magazine without realizing. 'Is something wrong?'

'Where were you on Friday?'

'I took the day off,' said Candice.

'In order to avoid me.'

'No!' said Candice, rolling her eyes. 'Of course not! Justin, what's wrong?'

'What's wrong?' echoed Justin, as though he could barely believe her effrontery. 'OK, tell me this, Candice. Did you or did you not go over my head to Ralph last week – *deliberately* undermining my credibility – simply in order to secure a job for your little friend?' He jerked his head towards Heather.

'Oh,' said Candice, taken aback. 'Well, not on purpose. It just . . . happened that way.'

'Oh yes?' A tense smile flickered across Justin's face. 'That's funny. Because the way I heard it was that after our discussion the other night, you went straight up to Ralph Allsopp, and told him I was too busy to process the applications for editorial assistant. Is that what you told him, Candice?'

'No!' said Candice, feeling herself colouring. 'At least . . . I didn't mean anything by it! It was just—'

She broke off, feeling slightly uncomfortable. Although – of course – she'd been acting primarily to help Heather, she couldn't deny that it had given her a slight *frisson* of pleasure to have outwitted Justin. But that hadn't been the *main* reason she'd done it, she thought indignantly. And if Justin were just a bit less arrogant and snobbish, maybe she wouldn't have had to.

'How do you think that makes me look?' hissed Justin furiously. 'How do you think Ralph rates my management skills now?'

'Look, it's no big deal!' protested Candice. 'I just happened to know someone who I thought would be good for the job, and you'd said you were busy—'

'And you happened to see a neat way to sabotage my position on day one,' said Justin, with a little sneer.

'No!' said Candice in horror. 'God, is that the way you think my mind works? I would never do anything like that!'

'Of course you wouldn't,' said Justin.

'I *wouldn't*!' said Candice, and glared at him. Then she sighed. 'Look, come and meet Heather – and then you'll see. She'll be an excellent editorial assistant. I promise.'

'She'd better be,' said Justin. 'We had two hundred applicants for that job, you know. Two *hundred*.'

'I know,' said Candice hurriedly. 'Look, Justin, Heather'll be great. And I didn't mean to undermine you, honestly.'

There was a tense silence, then Justin sighed.

'OK. Well, perhaps I over-reacted. But I'm having problems enough as it is today.' He took a sip of coffee and scowled. 'Your friend Roxanne hasn't helped.'

'Oh really?'

'She described some new hotel as a "vulgar

monstrosity" in the last issue. Now I've got the company on the phone, demanding not only a retraction, but a free full-page advertisement. And where's the woman herself? On some bloody beach somewhere.'

Candice laughed.

'If she said it's a monstrosity, it probably is.' She felt a movement at her arm and looked up in surprise. 'Oh, hello, Heather.'

'I thought I'd come and introduce myself,' said Heather brightly. 'You must be Justin.'

'Justin Vellis, Acting Editor,' said Justin, holding out his hand in a businesslike fashion.

'Heather Trelawney,' said Heather, shaking it firmly. 'I'm so delighted to be working for the *Londoner.* I've always read it, and I look forward to being part of the team.'

'Good,' said Justin shortly.

'I must just also add,' said Heather, 'that I love your tie. I've been admiring it from afar.' She beamed at Justin. 'Is it Valentino?'

'Oh,' said Justin, as though taken aback. 'Yes, it is.' His fingers reached up and smoothed the tie down. 'How . . . clever of you.'

'I love men in Valentino,' said Heather.

'Yes, well,' said Justin, flushing very slightly. 'Good to meet you, Heather. Ralph's told me about the high quality of your writing, and I'm sure you're going to be an asset to the team.'

He nodded at Heather, glanced at Candice, then strode away. The two girls looked at each other, then started to giggle.

'Heather, you're a genius!' said Candice. 'How did you know Justin had a thing about his ties?'

'I didn't,' said Heather, grinning. 'Just call it instinct.'

'Well, anyway, thanks for rescuing me,' said

79

Candice. 'You got me out of a tight corner there.' She shook her head. 'God, Justin can be a pain.'

'I saw you arguing,' said Heather casually. 'What was the problem?' She looked at Candice, and a curious expression came over her face. 'Candice, you weren't arguing about . . . me, were you?' Candice felt herself flush red.

'No!' she said hastily. 'No, of course we weren't! It was . . . something else completely. It really doesn't matter.'

'Well – if you're sure,' said Heather, and gazed at Candice with luminous eyes. 'Because I'd hate to cause any trouble.'

'You're not causing trouble!' said Candice, laughing. 'Come on, I'll show you your desk.'

Chapter Six

Maggie was in her large, cool bedroom, sitting by the rain-swept window and staring out at the muddy green fields disappearing into the distance. Fields and fields, as far as the eye could see. Proper, old-fashioned English countryside. And twenty acres of it belonged to her and Giles.

Twenty whole acres – vast by London standards. The thought had thrilled her beyond measure in those first exhilarating months after they'd decided to move. Giles – used to his parents' paddocks and fields full of sheep – had been pleased to acquire the land, rather than excited. But to Maggie, after her own suburban upbringing and the tiny patch of land they'd called a garden in London, twenty acres had seemed like a country estate. She'd imagined striding around her land like a gentleman farmer, getting to know every corner, planting trees; picnicking in her favourite shady spot.

That first October weekend after they'd moved in, she'd made a point of walking to the furthest point of the plot and looking back towards the house – greedily taking in the swathe of land that now belonged to her and Giles. The second weekend it had rained, and she'd huddled inside by the Aga. The third weekend, they'd stayed up in London for a friend's party.

Since then, the thrill of ownership had somewhat paled. Admittedly, Maggie still liked to drop her twenty acres into the conversation. She still liked to think of herself as a landowner and talk carelessly about buying a horse. But the thought of going and actually trudging through her own muddy fields exhausted her. It wasn't as if they were particularly beautiful or interesting. Just fields.

The phone rang and she looked at her watch. It would be Giles, wanting to know what she had been doing with herself. She had told herself – and him – that she would go up to the attic bedrooms today and plan their redecoration. In fact, she had done nothing more than go downstairs, eat some breakfast and come back upstairs again. She felt heavy and inert; slightly depressed by the weather; unable to galvanize herself into action.

'Hi, Giles?' she said into the receiver.

'How are you doing?' said Giles cheerily down the line. 'It's lashing it down here.'

'Fine,' said Maggie, shifting uncomfortably in her chair. 'It's raining here, too.'

'You sound a bit down, my sweet.'

'Oh, I'm OK,' said Maggie gloomily. 'My back hurts, it's pissing with rain and I haven't got anyone to talk to. Apart from that, I'm doing great.'

'Did the cot arrive?'

'Yes, it's here,' said Maggie. 'The man put it up in the nursery. It looks lovely.'

Suddenly she felt a tightening across the front of her stomach, and drew in breath sharply.

'Maggie?' said Giles in alarm.

'It's OK,' she said, after a few seconds. 'Just another practice contraction.'

'I would have thought you'd had enough practice by now,' said Giles, and laughed merrily. 'Well, I'd better shoot off. Take care of yourself.'

'Wait,' said Maggie, suddenly anxious for him not to disappear off the line. 'What time do you think you'll be home?'

'It's bloody frantic here,' said Giles, lowering his voice. 'I'll try and make it as early as I can – but who knows? I'll ring you a bit later and let you know.'

'OK,' said Maggie disconsolately. 'Bye.'

After he'd rung off she held the warm receiver to her ear for a few minutes more, then slowly put it down and looked around the empty room. It seemed to ring with silence. Maggie looked at the still telephone and felt suddenly bereft, like a child at boarding school. Ridiculously, she felt as though she wanted to go home.

But this was her home. Of course it was. She was Mrs Drakeford of The Pines.

She got to her feet and lumbered wearily into the bathroom, thinking that she would have a warm bath to ease her back. Then she must have some lunch. Not that she felt very hungry – but still. It would be something to do.

She stepped into the warm water and leaned back, just as her abdomen began to tighten again. Another bloody practice contraction. Hadn't she had enough already? And why did nature have to play such tricks, anyway? Wasn't the whole thing bad enough as it was? As she closed her eyes, she remembered the section in her pregnancy handbook on false labour. 'Many women,' the book had said patronizingly, 'will mistake false contractions for the real thing.'

Not her, thought Maggie grimly. She wasn't going to have the humiliation of summoning Giles from the office and rushing excitedly off to the hospital, only to be told kindly that she'd made a mistake. You think *that's* labour? the silent implication ran. Ha! You just wait for the real thing!

Well, she would. She'd wait for the real thing.

*   *   *

Roxanne reached for her orange juice, took a sip and leaned back comfortably in her chair. She was sitting at a blue and green mosaic table on the terrace of the Aphrodite Bay Hotel, overlooking the swimming pool and, in the distance, the beach. A final drink in the sunshine, a final glimpse of the Mediterranean, before her flight back to England. Beside her on the floor was her small, well-packed suitcase, which she would take onto the plane as hand luggage. Life was far too short, in her opinion, to spend waiting by airport carousels for suitcases of unused clothes.

She took another sip and closed her eyes, enjoying the sensation of the sun blazing down on her cheeks. It had been a good week's work, she thought. She had already written her two-thousand-word piece for the *Londoner* on holidaying in Cyprus. She had also visited enough new property developments to be able to write a comprehensive survey for the property pages of one of the national newspapers. And for one of their rivals, under a pseudonym, she would pen a light-hearted diary-type piece on living in Cyprus as an expatriate. The *Londoner* had funded half the cost of her trip – with these extra pieces of work she would more than pay for the rest of it. Nice work if you can get it, she thought idly, and began to hum softly to herself.

'You are enjoying the sun,' came a voice beside her and she looked up. Nico Georgiou was pulling a chair out and sitting down at the table. He was an elegant man in his middle years, always well dressed; always impeccably polite. The quieter, more reserved of the two Georgiou brothers.

She had met them both on her first trip to Cyprus, when she had been sent to cover the opening of their new hotel, the Aphrodite Bay. Since then, she had never stayed anywhere else in Cyprus, and over the years, had got to know Nico and his brother Andreas well. Between them, they owned three of the major hotels on the island, and a fourth was currently under construction.

'I adore the sun,' said Roxanne now, smiling. 'And I adore the Aphrodite Bay.' She looked around. 'I can't tell you how much I've enjoyed my stay here.'

'And we have, as always, enjoyed having you,' said Nico. He lifted a hand, and a waiter came rushing to attention.

'An espresso, please,' said Nico, and glanced at Roxanne. 'And for you?'

'Nothing else, thanks,' said Roxanne. 'I have to leave soon.'

'I know,' said Nico. 'I will drive you to the airport.'

'Nico! I've booked a taxi.'

'And I have unbooked it,' said Nico, smiling. 'I want to talk to you, Roxanne.'

'Really?' said Roxanne. 'What about?'

Nico's coffee arrived and he waited for the waiter to retreat before he spoke again.

'You have been to visit our new resort, the Aphrodite Falls.'

'I've seen the construction site,' said Roxanne. 'It looks very impressive. All those waterfalls.'

'It will be impressive,' said Nico. 'It will be unlike anything previously seen in Cyprus.'

'Good!' said Roxanne. 'I can't wait till it opens.' She grinned at him. 'If you don't invite me to the launch party you're in trouble.' Nico laughed, then picked up his coffee spoon and began to balance it on his cup.

'The Aphrodite Falls is a very high-profile project,' he said, and paused. 'We will be looking for a . . . a dynamic person to run the launch and marketing of the resort. A person with talent. With energy. With contacts in journalism . . .' There was silence, and Nico looked up. 'Someone, perhaps, who enjoys the

Mediterranean way of life,' he said slowly, meeting Roxanne's eyes. 'Someone, perhaps, from Britain?'

'Me?' said Roxanne disbelievingly. 'You can't be serious.'

'I am utterly serious,' said Nico. 'My brother and I would be honoured if you would join our company.'

'But I don't know anything about marketing! I don't have any qualifications, any training—'

'Roxanne, you have more intelligence and flair than any of these so-called qualified people,' said Nico, gesturing disparagingly. 'I have hired these people. The training seems to dull their wits. Young people go into college with ideas and enthusiasm, and come out with only flip-charts and ridiculous jargon.'

Roxanne laughed. 'You do have a point.'

'We would provide accommodation for you,' said Nico, leaning forward. 'The salary would be, I think, generous.'

'Nico—'

'And, of course, we would expect you to continue with a certain amount of travel, to other comparable resorts. For . . . research purposes.' Roxanne looked at him suspiciously.

'Has this job been tailor-made for me?'

A smile flickered over Nico's face. 'In a way . . . perhaps yes.'

'I see.' Roxanne stared into her glass of orange juice. 'But . . . why?'

There was silence for a while – then Nico said in a deadpan voice, 'You know why.'

A strange pang went through Roxanne and she closed her eyes, trying to rationalize her thoughts. The sun was hot on her face; in the distance she could hear children shrieking excitedly on the beach. 'Mama!' one of them was calling, 'Mama!' She could live here all year round, she thought. Wake up to sunshine every day. Join the Georgiou family for long, lazy celebration meals – as she once had for Andreas's birthday.

And Nico himself. Courteous, self-deprecating Nico, who never hid his feelings for her – but never forced them on her either. Kind, loyal Nico; she would die rather than hurt him.

'I can't,' she said, and opened her eyes to see Nico gazing straight at her. The expression in his dark eyes made her want to cry. 'I can't leave London.' She exhaled sharply. 'You know why. I just can't—'

'You can't leave him,' said Nico, and, in one movement, drained his espresso.

Something was ringing in Maggie's mind. A fire alarm. An alarm clock. The doorbell. Her mind jerked awake and she opened her eyes. Dazedly, she glanced at her watch on the side of the bath and saw to her astonishment that it was one o'clock. She'd been in her bath for almost an hour, half dozing in the warmth. As quickly as she could, she stood up, reached for a towel, and began to dry her face and neck before getting out.

Halfway out of the bath another practice contraction seized her and in slight terror she clung onto the side of the bath, willing herself not to slip over. As the painful tightness subsided, the doorbell rang again downstairs, loud and insistent.

'Bloody hell, give me a minute!' she yelled. She wrenched angrily at a towelling robe on the back of the door, wrapped it around herself and padded out of the room. As she passed the mirror on the landing she glanced at herself and was slightly taken aback at her pale, strained reflection. Hardly a picture of blooming health. But then, in the mood she was in, she didn't care what she looked like.

She headed for the front door, already knowing from the thin shadowy figure on the other side of the frosted glass that her visitor was Paddy. Barely a day went by without Paddy popping in with some excuse or other

– a knitted blanket for the baby, a cutting from the garden, the famous recipe for scones, copied onto a flowery card. 'She's keeping bloody tabs on me!' Maggie had complained, half jokingly, to Giles the night before. 'Every day, like clockwork!' On the other hand, Paddy's company was better than nothing. And at least she hadn't brought Wendy back for a visit.

'Maggie!' exclaimed Paddy, as soon as Maggie opened the door. 'So glad to have caught you in. I've been making tomato soup, and, as usual, I've made far too much. Can you use some?'

'Oh,' said Maggie. 'Yes, I should think so. Come on in.' As she stood aside to let Paddy in, another contraction began – this one deeper and more painful than the others. She gripped the door, bowing her head and biting her lip, waiting for it to pass – then looked up at Paddy, a little out of breath.

'Maggie, are you all right?' said Paddy sharply.

'Fine,' said Maggie, breathing normally again. 'Just a practice contraction.'

'A what?' Paddy stared at her.

'They're called Braxton-Hicks contractions,' explained Maggie patiently. 'It's in the book. Perfectly normal in the last few weeks.' She smiled at Paddy. 'Can I make you a cup of coffee?'

'You sit down,' said Paddy, giving Maggie an odd look. 'I'll do it. Are you *sure* you feel all right?'

'Really, Paddy, I'm fine,' said Maggie, following Paddy into the kitchen. 'Just a bit tired. And my back aches a bit. I'll take some paracetamol in a minute.'

'Good idea,' said Paddy, frowning slightly. She filled the kettle, switched it on and took two mugs down from the dresser. Then she turned round.

'Maggie, you don't think this could be it?'

'What?' Maggie stared at Paddy and felt a little plunge of fear. 'Labour? Of course not. I'm not due for another two weeks.' She licked her dry lips. 'And I've been having practice contractions like this all week. It's . . . it's nothing.'

'If you say so.' Paddy reached inside a cupboard for the jar of coffee, then stopped.

'Shall I run you up to the hospital, just to make sure?'

'No!' said Maggie at once. 'They'll just tell me I'm a stupid woman and send me home again.'

'Isn't it worth being on the safe side?' said Paddy.

'Honestly, Paddy, there's nothing to worry about,' said Maggie, feeling the tightness begin again inside her. 'I'm just . . .' But she couldn't manage the rest of her sentence. She held her breath, waiting for the pain to pass. When she looked up, Paddy was standing up and holding her car keys.

'Maggie, I'm no expert,' she said cheerfully, 'but even I know that wasn't a practice contraction.' She smiled. 'My dear, this is it. The baby's coming.'

'It can't be,' Maggie heard herself say. She felt almost breathless with fright. 'It can't be. I'm not ready.'

It was raining, a soft slithery rain, when Roxanne emerged from London Underground at Barons Court. The skies were dark with clouds, the pavements were wet and slimy, and an old Mars Bar wrapper was floating in a puddle next to a pile of *Evening Standards*. It felt, to Roxanne, like the middle of winter. She picked up her case and began to walk briskly along the street, wincing as a passing lorry spattered her legs with dirty water. It seemed hardly believable that only a few hours ago she'd been sitting in the blazing heat of the sun.

Nico had driven her to the airport in his gleaming Mercedes. He had, despite her protestations, carried her suitcase into the airport terminal for her, and had ensured that everything was in order at the check-in desk. Not once had he mentioned the job at the

Aphrodite Bay. Instead he had talked generally, about politics and books, and his planned trip to New York – and Roxanne had listened gratefully, glad of his tact. Only as they'd been about to bid farewell to one another at the departure desk had he said, with a sudden vehemence, 'He is a fool, this man of yours.'

'You mean I'm a fool,' Roxanne had responded, trying to smile. Nico had shaken his head silently, then taken her hands.

'Come back to visit us soon, Roxanne,' he'd said in a low voice. 'And . . . think about it? At least think about it.'

'I will,' Roxanne had promised, knowing that her mind was already made up. Nico had scanned her face, then sighed and kissed her fingertips.

'There is no-one like Roxanne,' he'd said. 'Your man is very lucky.'

Roxanne had smiled back at him, and laughed a little, and waved cheerfully as she went through the departure gate. Now, with rain dripping down her neck and buses swooshing by every few seconds, she felt less cheerful. London seemed a grey unfriendly place, full of litter and strangers. What was she living here for, anyway?

She reached her house, ran up the steps to the front door and quickly felt inside her bag for her keys. Her tiny little flat was on the top floor, with what estate agents described as far-reaching views over London. By the time she reached the top of the stairs, she was out of breath. She unlocked the door to her flat, pushed it open, and stepped over a pile of post. The air was cold and unheated and she knew her hot water would be off. Quickly she went into the little kitchen and switched on the kettle, then wandered back into the hall. She picked up her mail and began to flip through it, dropping all the uninteresting bills and circulars back onto the floor. Suddenly, at a handwritten white envelope, she stopped. It was a letter from him.

With cold hands, still wet from the rain, she tore it open and sank her eyes into the few lines of writing.

My darling Rapunzel

As many apologies as I can muster for Wednesday night. Will explain all. Now as my deserved punishment – must wait jealously for your return. Hurry home from Cyprus. Hurry, hurry.

The letter ended, as ever, with no name but a row of kisses. Reading his words, she could suddenly hear his voice; feel his touch on her skin; hear his warm laughter. She sank to the floor and read the letter again, and again, devouring it greedily with her eyes. Then eventually she looked up, feeling in some strange way restored. The truth was, that there was no conceivable alternative. She couldn't stop loving him; she couldn't just move to a new country and pretend he didn't exist. She needed him in her life, just as she needed food and air and light. And the fact that he was rationed, the fact that she could not have him properly, simply made her crave him all the more.

The phone rang and, with a sudden lift of hope, she reached for the receiver. 'Yes?' she said lightly, thinking that if it was him, she would get in a taxi and go to him straight away.

'Roxanne, it's Giles Drakeford.'

'Oh,' said Roxanne in surprise. 'Is Maggie all—'

'It's a girl,' said Giles, sounding more emotional than she'd ever heard him. 'It's a girl. Born an hour ago. A perfect little girl. Six pounds eight. The most beautiful baby in the world.' He took a deep, shuddering breath. 'Maggie was . . . fantastic. She was so quick, I only just made it in time. God, it was just the most amazing experience. Everyone cried, even the midwives. We've decided we're going to call her Lucia. Lucia Sarah Helen. She's . . . she's perfect. A perfect little daughter.' There was silence. 'Roxanne?'

'A daughter,' said Roxanne, in a strange voice. 'Congratulations. That's . . . that's wonderful news.'

'I can't talk long,' said Giles. 'To be honest, I'm bloody shattered. But Maggie wanted you to know.'

'Well, thanks for calling,' said Roxanne. 'And congratulations again. And s-send all my love to Maggie.'

She put the phone down, and looked at it silently for a minute. Then, with no warning at all, she burst into tears.

Chapter Seven

The next day dawned bright and clear, with the smell
of summer and good spirits in the air. On the way to
the office, Roxanne stopped off at a florist and chose an
extravagantly large bunch of lilies for Maggie from
an illustrated brochure entitled 'A New Arrival'.

'Is it a boy or a girl?' enquired the florist, typing the
details into her computer.

'A girl,' said Roxanne, and beamed at the woman.
'Lucia Sarah Helen. Isn't that pretty?'

'LSH,' said the florist. 'Sounds like a drug. Or an
exam.' Roxanne gave the woman an annoyed glance,
and handed her a Visa card. 'They'll go out this afternoon,' added the woman, swiping the card. 'Is that all
right?'

'Fine,' said Roxanne, and imagined Maggie sitting
up like one of the women in the brochure, in a crisp
white bed, rosy-cheeked and serene. A tiny sleeping
baby in her arms, Giles looking on lovingly and
flowers all around. Deep inside her she felt something
tug at her heart, and quickly she looked up with a
bright smile.

'If you could just sign there,' said the florist, passing
a slip of paper to Roxanne, 'and write your message in
the box.' Roxanne picked up the biro and hesitated.

'Can't wait to mix Lucia her first cocktail,' she wrote

eventually. 'Much love and congratulations to you both from Roxanne.'

'I'm not sure that'll fit on the card,' said the florist doubtfully.

'Then use two cards,' snapped Roxanne, suddenly wanting to get away from the sickly scent of flowers; the brochure full of winsome photographs of babies. As she strode out of the shop, a petal fell from a garland onto her hair like confetti, and she brushed it irritably away.

She arrived at the editorial office a little after nine-thirty, to see Candice sitting cross-legged on the floor sketching something out on a piece of paper. Sitting next to her, head also bent over the piece of paper, was the blond-haired girl from the Manhattan Bar. For a few moments Roxanne gazed at them, remembering Maggie's phone call. Was this girl really trouble? Was she really using Candice? She looked outwardly innocuous, with her freckled snub nose and cheerful smile. But there was also, Roxanne noticed, a firmness to her jaw when she wasn't smiling, and a curious coolness to her grey eyes.

As she watched, the blond girl looked up and met Roxanne's gaze. Her eyes flickered briefly, then she smiled sweetly.

'Hello,' she said. 'You probably don't remember me.'

'Oh yes I do,' said Roxanne, smiling back. 'It's Heather, isn't it?'

'That's right.' Heather's smile became even sweeter. 'And you're Roxanne.'

'Roxanne!' said Candice, looking up, eyes shining. 'Isn't it wonderful news about the baby?'

'Fantastic,' said Roxanne. 'Did Giles call you last night?'

'Yes. He sounded absolutely overwhelmed, didn't you think?' Candice gestured to the piece of paper. 'Look, we're designing a card for the Art Department to make up. Then we'll get everyone to sign it. What do you think?'

'It's an excellent idea,' said Roxanne, looking fondly at her. 'Maggie'll love it.'

'I'll take it down to the studio,' said Candice, standing up. Then she looked a little hesitantly from Heather to Roxanne. 'You remember Heather, don't you, Roxanne?'

'Of course,' said Roxanne. 'Maggie told me all about Heather joining the team. That certainly was quick work.'

'Yes,' said Candice, colouring slightly. 'It's . . . it's all worked out really well, hasn't it?' She glanced again at Heather. 'Right, well – I'll just pop down with this card. I won't be long.'

When she'd gone, there was silence between them. Roxanne gave Heather an appraising look and Heather stared back innocently, twisting a lock of hair around her finger.

'So, Heather,' said Roxanne at last, in a friendly tone. 'How are you enjoying the *Londoner*?'

'It's wonderful,' said Heather, gazing at her earnestly. 'I feel so lucky to be working here.'

'And I gather you're living with Candice now.'

'Yes, I am,' said Heather. 'She's been so incredibly kind.'

'Has she?' said Roxanne pleasantly. 'Well, you know, that doesn't surprise me at all.' She paused thoughtfully. 'Candice is a very kind, generous person. She finds it very difficult to say no to people.'

'Really?' said Heather.

'Oh yes. I'm surprised you haven't picked that up.' Roxanne nonchalantly examined her nails for a moment. 'In fact, her friends – including myself – sometimes get quite worried about her. She's the sort of person it would be so easy to take advantage of.'

'Do you think so?' Heather smiled sweetly at

Roxanne. 'I would have thought Candice could take pretty good care of herself. How old is she now?'

Well, thought Roxanne, almost impressed. She certainly gives as good as she gets.

'So,' she said, abruptly changing the subject, 'I gather you've never worked on a magazine before.'

'No,' said Heather unconcernedly.

'But you're a very good writer, I hear,' said Roxanne. 'You obviously impressed Ralph Allsopp tremendously at your interview.'

To her surprise, a faint pink flush began to creep up Heather's neck. Roxanne stared at it with interest until it faded away again.

'Well, Heather,' she said. 'Lovely to meet you again. We'll be seeing lots of each other, I'm sure.'

She watched as Heather sauntered away, into Justin's office, noticing that Justin looked up with a smile as Heather entered. Typical male, she thought acidly. He'd clearly already been seduced by Heather's sweet smile.

Roxanne stared through the window at Heather's cute, snub-nosed profile, trying to work her out. She was young, she was pretty, and probably talented to some degree. She was charming – on the surface. At face value, a lovely girl. So why did she make Roxanne's hackles rise? The consideration passed through Roxanne's mind that she might simply be jealous of Heather – and immediately she dismissed it.

As she stood, staring, Candice came back into the office, holding a colour page proof.

'Hi!' said Roxanne, smiling warmly at her. 'Listen – fancy a quick drink after work?'

'I can't,' said Candice regretfully. 'I promised Heather I'd go shopping with her. I'm going to find a present for Maggie.'

'No problem,' said Roxanne lightly. 'Another time.'

She watched as Candice went into Justin's office, grinned at Heather and started talking. Justin immediately began to gesture, frowning, at the page proof – and Candice nodded earnestly and began to gesture herself. As they both stared, engrossed, at the proof, Heather slowly turned and met Roxanne's eyes coolly through the window. For a moment, they simply stared at each other – then Roxanne abruptly turned away.

'Roxanne!' Justin was looking up and calling. 'Can you come and have a look at this?'

'In a minute!' called Roxanne and strode out of the office. She didn't wait for the lift but hurried, with a sudden rush of adrenalin, up the stairs and straight along the corridor to Ralph Allsopp's office.

'Janet!' she said, stopping at his elderly secretary's desk. 'Can I see Ralph for a moment?'

'He's not in, I'm afraid,' said Janet, looking up from her knitting. 'Not in at all today.'

'Oh,' said Roxanne, subsiding slightly. 'Damn.'

'He does know about Maggie's baby, though,' said Janet. 'I told him when he rang in this morning. He was thrilled. Such a lovely name, too. Lucia.' She gestured to her knitting. 'I'm just running her up a little matinée jacket.'

'Really?' said Roxanne, looking at the bundle of lemon wool as though it were a curiosity from another land. 'That's very clever of you.'

'It takes no time, really,' said Janet, clicking briskly with her needles. 'And she doesn't want to be dressing the little thing in shop-bought cardigans.'

Doesn't she? thought Roxanne in puzzlement. Why on earth not? Then she shook her head impatiently. She wasn't here to talk about baby clothes.

'Listen, Janet,' she said. 'Can I ask you something?'

'You can ask,' said Janet, picking up her knitting again and beginning to click. 'Doesn't mean you'll get.'

Roxanne grinned, and lowered her voice slightly.

'Has Ralph said anything to you about this new editorial assistant, Heather?'

'Not really,' said Janet. 'Just that he was giving her the job.'

Roxanne frowned. 'But when he interviewed her. He must have said something.'

'He thought she was very witty,' said Janet. 'She'd written a very funny article about London Transport.'

'Really?' Roxanne looked at her in surprise. 'Was it really any good?'

'Oh yes,' said Janet. 'Ralph gave a copy of it to me to read.' She put down her knitting, leafed through a pile of papers on her desk and produced a piece of paper. 'Here. You'll like it.'

'I doubt that,' said Roxanne. She glanced at the piece of paper, then put it in her bag. 'Well, thanks.'

'And do give my love to Maggie when you speak to her,' added Janet fondly, shaking out the little yellow matinée jacket. 'I do hope motherhood isn't too much of a shock for her.'

'A shock?' said Roxanne in surprise. 'Oh no. Maggie'll be fine. She always is.'

A voice calling her name dragged Maggie from a vivid, frenzied dream in which she was running after something nameless and invisible. She opened her eyes in a flurry of panic and blinked a few times disorientatedly at the bright overhead light.

'Maggie?' Her eyes snapped into focus, and she saw Paddy, standing at the end of her hospital bed, holding an enormous bunch of lilies. 'Maggie, dear, I wasn't sure if you were asleep. How are you feeling?'

'Fine,' said Maggie in a scratchy voice. 'I'm fine.' She tried to sit up, wincing slightly at her aching body, and pushed her hair back off her dry face. 'What time is it?'

'Four o'clock,' said Paddy, looking at her watch,

'just gone. Giles will be along any moment.'

'Good,' whispered Maggie. Giles, along with all the other visitors, had been ejected from the ward at two o'clock so that the new mothers could catch up on some rest. Maggie had lain tensely awake for a while, waiting for Lucia to cry, then had obviously drifted off to sleep. But she didn't feel rested. She felt bleary and unfocused; unable to think straight.

'And how's my little granddaughter?' Paddy looked into the plastic cradle beside Maggie's bed. 'Asleep like a lamb. What a good little baby! She's been an angel, hasn't she?'

'She was awake quite a lot of the night,' said Maggie, pouring herself a glass of water with shaking hands.

'Was she?' Paddy smiled fondly. 'Hungry, I expect.'

'Yes.' Maggie looked through the glass of the crib at her daughter. A little bundle in a cellular blanket, her tiny, screwed-up face just visible. She didn't seem real. None of it seemed real. Nothing had prepared her for what this would be like, thought Maggie. Nothing.

The birth itself had been like entering another, alien world, in which her body responded to some force she had no control over. In which her dignity, her ideals, her self-control and self-image were obliterated; in which none of the rules of normal life applied. She had wanted to object; to call a halt to the whole proceedings. To produce some last-minute get-out clause. But it had been too late. There was no get-out clause; no escape route. No alternative but to grit her teeth and do it.

Already the hours of pain were fading from her memory. In her mind the whole event seemed to have kaleidoscoped around those last few minutes – the bright white lights and the arrival of the paediatrician and the actual delivery of the baby. And that, thought Maggie, had been the most surreal moment of all. The delivery of another, living, screaming human being

99

from inside her. Looking around the maternity ward at the faces of the other mothers, she could not believe how calmly they seemed to be taking this momentous, extraordinary event; how they seemed able to chat about brands of nappies and plots of soap operas, as though nothing of any importance had happened.

Or perhaps it was just that they'd all done it before. None of the other women on the ward was a first-time mother. They all dandled their little bundles with accustomed ease. They could simultaneously breast-feed and eat their breakfasts and talk to their husbands about redecorating the spare room. During the night, she had heard the girl in the bed next to hers joking with the midwife on duty about her baby.

'Greedy little bugger, isn't he?' she'd said, and laughed. 'Won't leave me alone.' And Maggie, on the other side of the floral curtain, had felt tears pouring down her face as, once again, she tried to persuade Lucia to feed. What was wrong with her? she had thought frantically, as, yet again, Lucia sucked for a few seconds, then opened her mouth in a protesting shout. As the baby's squawls had become louder and louder, a midwife had appeared, looked at Maggie and pursed her lips with disapproval.

'You've let her get too wound up,' she'd said. 'Try to calm her down first.'

Flushed with distress and humiliation, Maggie had tried to soothe a flailing, wailing Lucia. She had once read in an article that a newborn baby already knew its mother's smell; that a baby even a few hours old could be calmed by hearing its mother's voice. The article had concluded that the bond between mother and child was one that could not be paralleled. But as Maggie had rocked her own newborn baby, Lucia's screams had only become louder and louder. With a sigh of impatience, the midwife had eventually reached for her. She had laid the baby on the bed,

100

wrapped her up tightly in a blanket, and lifted her up again. And almost immediately, Lucia's cries had ceased. Maggie had stared at her own baby, peaceful and quiet in someone else's arms, and had felt cold with failure.

'There,' the midwife had said more kindly. 'Try again.' Stiff with misery, Maggie had taken the baby from her, fully expecting Lucia to protest. She had held Lucia to her breast and, almost magically, the baby had begun to feed contentedly.

'That's more like it,' the midwife had said. 'You just need a bit of practice.'

She had waited a few minutes, then had looked more closely at Maggie's red-rimmed eyes. 'Are you OK? Not feeling too down?'

'Fine,' Maggie had said automatically, and forced herself to smile brightly at the midwife. 'Honestly. I just need to get to grips with it.'

'Good,' the midwife had said. 'Well, don't worry. Everyone has trouble at first.'

She'd glanced at Lucia, then left the flowery cubicle. As soon as she'd gone, tears had begun to pour down Maggie's face again. She'd stared straight ahead at the end of her bed, feeling the hot wetness on her cheeks, but not daring to move or make a sound lest she disturbed Lucia – or even worse, was heard by one of the other mothers. They would think her a freak, to be crying over her baby. Everybody else in the ward was happy. She should be happy, too.

'These lilies arrived for you just as I was leaving,' Paddy was saying now. 'Shall we find another vase here, or shall I take them back to the house?'

'I don't know,' said Maggie, rubbing her face. 'Did . . . did my mother call?'

'Yes,' said Paddy, beaming. 'She's coming down tomorrow. Unfortunately she couldn't take today off. Some crucial meeting.'

101

'Oh,' said Maggie, trying not to let her disappointment show on her face. After all, she was a grown
woman. What did she need her mother for?

'And look, here's Giles!' said Paddy brightly. 'I'll go
and fetch us all a nice cup of tea, shall I?' She laid the
lilies carefully on the bed and walked off briskly.
Where she was going to find a nice cup of tea, Maggie
had no idea. But then, Paddy was that kind of woman.
Abandoned in the middle of the jungle with nothing
but a penknife, she would still, no doubt, be able to
rustle up a nice cup of tea – and probably a batch of
scones as well.

Maggie watched as mother and son greeted each
other. Then, as Giles approached her bed, she tried to
compose her features into light-hearted friendliness; a
suitable expression for a happy, loving wife. The truth
was, she felt dissociated from him, unable to com-
municate on anything but a surface level. In a matter of
twenty-four hours she had moved into a new world
without him.

She had not intended it to be that way. She had
wanted him there beside her; with her in every sense.
But by the time the message had got to him at work,
she had been well into the throes of labour. He had
arrived just in time for the last half-hour, by which
time she had barely been aware of his existence. Now,
although he could claim to have been present at his
daughter's birth, she felt that he had seen the denoue-
ment without experiencing any of the build-up; that he
would never fully understand what she had been
through.

As she had stared, shocked and silent at her new
daughter, he had cracked jokes with the nurses and
poured glasses of champagne. She had craved some
time alone together; a moment or two of quiet in which
to gather her thoughts. A chance for the two of them to
acknowledge the unbelievable nature of what had just

passed. A chance for her to talk honestly, without putting on an act. But after what seemed like only a few minutes, a midwife had come and gently told Giles it was time for all visitors to leave the maternity ward and that he could return in the morning. As he'd gathered his belongings, Maggie had felt her heart start to thud with panic. But instead of letting him see her fear, she'd smiled cheerfully as he'd kissed her good-bye, and even managed a crack about all the other women waiting for him at home. Now she smiled again.

'You took your time.'

'Did you have a nice sleep?' Giles sat down on the bed and stroked Maggie's hair. 'You look so serene. I've been telling everyone how wonderful you were. Everyone sends their love.'

'Everyone?'

'Everyone I could think of.' He looked at the crib. 'How is she?'

'Oh, fine,' said Maggie lightly. 'She hasn't done much since you left.'

'Nice flowers,' said Giles, looking at the lilies. 'Who are they from?'

'I haven't even looked!' said Maggie. She opened the little envelope and two embossed cards fell out. 'Roxanne,' she said, laughing. 'She says she's going to mix Lucia her first cocktail.'

'Typical Roxanne,' said Giles.

'Yes.' As Maggie stared down at the message, she could hear Roxanne's husky, drawling voice in her mind, and to her horror, felt the treacherous tears pricking her eyes again. Hurriedly she blinked, and put the cards down on the bedside table.

'Here we are!' came Paddy's voice. She was carrying a tray of cups and accompanied by a midwife Maggie didn't recognize. Paddy put the tray down and beamed at Maggie. 'I thought perhaps, after your tea, you could give Lucia her first bath.'

103

'Oh,' said Maggie, taken aback. 'Yes, of course.'

She took a sip of tea and tried to smile back at Paddy, but her face was red with embarrassment. It hadn't even occurred to her that Lucia would need a bath. It hadn't even occurred to her. What was wrong with her?

'Has she fed recently?' said the midwife.

'Not since lunchtime.'

'Right,' said the midwife cheerfully. 'Well, maybe you'd like to feed her now. Don't want to leave her too long. She's only a little thing.'

A renewed stab of guilt went through Maggie's chest and her face flushed even brighter.

'Of course,' she said. 'I'll . . . I'll do it now.'

Aware of everyone's eyes on her she reached into the crib, picked up Lucia and began to unwrap the tiny cellular blanket.

'Let me hold her for a moment,' said Giles suddenly. 'Let me just look at her.' He picked Lucia up, nestling her comfortably into the crook of his arm. As he did so, she gave an enormous yawn, then her tiny screwed-up eyes suddenly opened. She stared up at her father, her little pink mouth open like a flower.

'Isn't that the most beautiful sight?' said Paddy softly.

'Can I have a little look?' said the midwife.

'Of course,' said Giles. 'Isn't she perfect?'

'Such a healthy colour!' said Paddy.

'That's what I was wondering about,' said the midwife. She placed Lucia on the bed and briskly unbuttoned her sleepsuit. She stared at Lucia's chest, then looked up at Maggie. 'Has she always been this colour?'

'Yes,' said Maggie, taken aback. 'I . . . I think so.'

'She's got a tan,' said Giles, and laughed uncertainly.

'I don't think so,' said the midwife, and frowned. 'Someone should have picked this up. I think she's got jaundice.'

104

The unfamiliar word hung in the air like a threat. Maggie stared at the midwife and felt the colour drain from her cheeks; felt her heart begin to thump. They'd lied to her. They'd all lied. Her baby wasn't healthy at all.

'Is it very serious?' she managed.

'Oh no! It'll clear up in a few days.' The woman looked up at Maggie's face and burst into laughter. 'Don't worry, sweetheart. She'll live.'

Ralph Allsopp sat on a bench outside the Charing Cross Hospital, watching as a man with a broken leg painfully made his way past on crutches; as two nurses greeted each other and began to chatter animatedly. On his lap was a greetings card he had bought from the hospital shop, depicting a crib, a bunch of flowers and a winsome, grinning baby. 'My dear Maggie,' he had written shakily inside the card. Then he had stopped and put the pen down, unable to write any more.

He felt ill. Not from the disease itself: that had crept up quietly, unnoticed, like a friendly confidence trickster. It had slipped one silent toe inside him, and then another – and then had spread quickly about his body with the assurance of a welcome guest. Now it had squatter's rights. It could do as it pleased; could not be dislodged. It was stronger than him. And perhaps because of that fact – because it knew its own power – it had, until now, treated him with relative kindness. Or maybe that was all part of its strategy. It had tiptoed around him, setting up camp wherever it could find a foothold, letting him remain unaware of its presence until it was too late.

Now, of course, he was no longer unaware. Now he knew it all. He had had his disease explained to him carefully by three separate doctors. Each had apparently been concerned that he should understand every single detail completely, as though he were entering an exam on the subject. Each had looked him straight in the eye with a practised, compassionate expression; had mentioned counselling and hospices and Macmillan Nurses – then, after a pause, his wife. It had been taken for granted that his wife and family would be told; that his staff would be told; that the world would be told. It had been taken for granted that this dissemination of information was his task; his choice; his responsibility.

And it was this responsibility which made Ralph feel ill; which made him feel a coldness up and down his spine, a nausea in the pit of his stomach. The responsibility was too much. Whom to tell. What to tell. How many boats to rock at once. For the moment the words were out of his lips, everything would change. It seemed to him that he would immediately become public property. His life – his limited, diminishing life – would no longer be his own. It would belong to those he loved. And therein lay the problem; the heartache. To whom did those last months, weeks, days, belong?

By speaking now, he would grant the rest of his life to his wife, to his three children, to the closest of his friends. And so it should be. But to include was also to exclude; to reveal was also to attract scrutiny. By speaking now, it seemed to him, his last months would at once be placed under a giant magnifying glass, allowing no secrets; no intruders; no unexpected elements. He would be obliged to play out the remainder of his life in conventional, noble fashion.

For, after all, cancer patients were not adulterers, were they?

Ralph closed his eyes and massaged his brow wearily. Those doctors thought they owned the sum of the world's knowledge, with their graphs and scans and statistics. What they didn't know was that outside the consulting room, life was more complicated than that. That there were factors they knew nothing about. That the potential for hurt and misery was enormous.

He could, of course, have told them everything. Offered them his dilemma as he had offered his body; watched them whispering and conferring and consulting their textbooks. But what would have been the point? There was no solution, just as there was no cure to his illness. All ways forward would be painful; the most he could hope was to minimize the pain as much as possible.

Feeling a sudden shaft of determination, he picked up his pen again. 'A new little light in the world,' he wrote in the baby card. 'With many congratulations and love from Ralph.' He would buy a magnum of champagne, he suddenly decided, put the card in with that and send the whole lot by special delivery. Maggie deserved something special.

He sealed the envelope, stood up stiffly, and looked at his watch. Half an hour to go. Half an hour to rid his pockets of all leaflets, all pamphlets, all evidence; to rid his nostrils of that cloying hospital smell. To turn from a patient back into an ordinary person. A taxi was cruising slowly along the street and he hurried forward to hail it.

As it moved off through the thick evening traffic, he stared out of the window. People were bad-temperedly barging past one another as they crossed the road and he gazed at them, relishing the normality of their expressions after the guarded looks of the doctors. He would hold on to that normality for as long as possible, he thought fiercely. He would hold on to that easy, wonderful disregard for the miracle of human existence. People weren't designed to roam the earth constantly and gratefully aware of their healthy functioning bodies. They were designed to strive, to love, to fight and bicker; to drink too much and eat too much and lie too long in the sun.

He got out of the taxi at a corner and walked slowly along the street to the house in which she lived. As he looked up he could see all her windows lit up and uncurtained in a brilliant, defiant blaze. The sight seemed suddenly to have a strange poignancy. His unwitting Rapunzel in her tower, unaware of what the future held. A dart of pain went through his heart and for a moment, he desperately wanted to tell her. To tell her that very night; to hold her tight and weep with her into the small hours.

But he would not. He would be stronger than that. Taking a deep breath, he quickened his pace and arrived at her front door. He pressed the buzzer and after a few moments the front door was released. Slowly he climbed the stairs, arrived at the top and saw her waiting at her front door. She was wearing a white silk shirt and a short black skirt and the light from behind was burnishing her hair. For a few moments he just stared at her.

'Roxanne,' he said eventually. 'You look . . .'

'Good,' she said, and her mouth curved in a half-smile. 'Come on in.'

Chapter Eight

The gift shop was small and quiet and sweetly scented
– and, although the rest of the shopping mall seemed
to be crowded with people, practically empty. Candice
walked around, listening to her own footsteps on the
wooden floor and looking doubtfully at sampler
cushions and mugs saying 'It's a Girl!' She stopped by
a shelf of stuffed toys, picked up a teddy bear and
smiled at it. Then she turned it over to look at the price
and, as she saw the ticket, felt herself blanch.

'How much?' said Heather, coming up behind her.

'Fifty pounds,' said Candice in an undertone, and
hastily stuffed the bear back onto the shelf.

'Fifty quid?' Heather stared at the teddy incredulously, then began to laugh. 'That's outrageous! It
hasn't even got a nice face. Come on. We'll go somewhere else.'

As they walked out of the shop, Heather unself-
consciously took Candice's arm in hers, and Candice
felt herself blush slightly with pleasure. She could
hardly believe it was only a week since Heather had
moved in with her. Already they felt like old friends;
like soulmates. Every night, Heather insisted on cooking a proper supper and opening a bottle of wine; every
night she had another entertainment planned. One
evening she had given Candice a facial, another

evening she'd brought home videos and popcorn; the next, she'd brought home an electric juicer and announced she was setting up a juice bar in the kitchen. By the end of that evening their hands had been raw from peeling oranges and they'd produced approximately one glass of warm, unappealing juice – but they'd both been in fits of giggles. Even now, remembering it, Candice felt a giggle rising.

'What?' said Heather, turning towards her.

'The juicer.'

'Oh God,' said Heather. 'Don't remind me.' She paused by the entrance to a big department store. 'Here, what about in here? There must be a baby department.'

'Oh, that's a good idea,' said Candice.

'In fact, I'm just going to slip off,' said Heather. 'I've got something I need to buy. So I'll see you in the baby department.'

'OK,' said Candice, and headed for the elevator. It was seven o'clock at night, but the shop was as crowded and bustling as though it were the middle of the day. As she arrived at the baby department she felt a sudden slight selfconsciousness, but forced herself to walk forward, among all the pregnant women staring at prams. A row of little embroidered dresses took her eye and she began to leaf through the rack.

'Here you are!' Heather's voice interrupted her and she looked up.

'That was quick!'

'Oh, I knew what I wanted,' said Heather, and flushed slightly. 'It's . . . actually, it's for you.'

'What?' Puzzled, Candice took the paper bag Heather was holding out to her. 'What do you mean, it's for me?'

'A present,' said Heather, gazing earnestly at her. 'You've been so good to me, Candice. You've . . . transformed my life. If it weren't for you, I'd be . . . well. Something quite different.'

Candice stared back at her wide grey eyes and felt suddenly shamefaced. If Heather only knew. If she only knew the real reason for Candice's generosity; knew the trail of guilt and dishonesty that lay behind their friendship. Would she still be standing there, looking at Candice with such candid, friendly eyes?

Feeling suddenly sick at her own deceit, Candice ripped the bag open and drew out a slim silver pen.

'It's not much,' said Heather. 'I just thought you'd like it. For when you're writing up your interviews.'

'It's beautiful,' said Candice, feeling tears coming to her eyes. 'Heather, you really shouldn't have.'

'It's the least I can do,' said Heather. She took Candice's arm and squeezed it. 'I'm so glad I ran into you, that night. There's something really . . . special between us. Don't you think? I feel as if you're my closest friend.' Candice looked at her, then impetuously leaned forward and hugged her. 'I know your other friends don't like me,' came Heather's voice in her ear. 'But . . . you know, it doesn't matter.'

Candice withdrew her head and looked at Heather in surprise.

'What do you mean, my other friends don't like you?'

'Roxanne doesn't like me.' Heather gave a quick little smile. 'Don't worry about it. It doesn't matter.'

'But this is awful!' exclaimed Candice, frowning. 'Why don't you think she likes you?'

'I might have got it wrong,' said Heather at once. 'It was just a look she gave me . . . Honestly, Candice, don't hassle about it. I shouldn't have said anything.' She flashed a quick grin. 'Come on, choose one of these dresses, and then let's go and try on some proper clothes.'

'OK,' said Candice. But as she began to pick up the baby dresses again, her face was creased in a frown.

'Look, now I feel terrible!' said Heather. 'Please,

Candice, forget I said anything.' She lifted a thumb and ran it slowly down the crease in Candice's forehead. 'Forget about Roxanne, OK? I'm probably just sensitive. I probably got it all wrong.'

Roxanne lay happily on the sofa in a T-shirt, listening to low, jazzy music and, in the background, the sounds of Ralph cooking in the kitchen. He always cooked the supper – partly because he claimed to enjoy it, and partly because she was useless at it. She associated some of their happiest moments together with meals that he had cooked, after sex. Those were the times she cherished the most, she thought. The times when she could almost believe that they lived together; that they were a normal couple.

Of course, they weren't a normal couple. Perhaps they never would be. Automatically – and almost dispassionately – Roxanne's thoughts flicked to Ralph's youngest son Sebastian. Sweet little Sebastian, the afterthought. The blessing. The accident, let's face it. And still only a child; still only ten years old. Ten years, five months and a week.

Roxanne knew Sebastian Allsopp's age to the minute. His older brother and sister were in their twenties, safely off in their own lives. But Sebastian lived at home, went to school, brushed his teeth and still had a teddy bear. Sebastian was too young to bear the turmoil of a divorce. Not until he was eighteen, Ralph had said once after a few brandies. Eighteen. Another seven years, six months and three weeks. In seven years she would be forty.

For the sake of the children. It was a phrase which had once meant nothing to her. Now it seemed burnt into her soul with a branding iron. For the sake of Sebastian. He'd been four years old that night when she and Ralph had first danced together. A poppet in pyjamas, sleeping in his bed, while she looked into his

112

father's eyes and realized with a sudden urgency that she wanted more of them. That she wanted more of him. She'd been twenty-seven, then. Ralph had been forty-six. Anything in the world had seemed possible.

Roxanne closed her eyes, remembering. It had been at the first night of a star-laden visiting production of *Romeo and Juliet* at the Barbican. Ralph had been sent two complimentary tickets and, at the last minute, had wandered into the editorial office of the *Londoner,* looking for a second taker. When Roxanne had jumped at the chance, his face had registered slight surprise, which he had tactfully hidden. He had, he'd later confessed, always thought of her as a glossy, materialistic girl – bright and talented but with no real depth. When he turned to her at the end of the play to see her still staring forward, her face streaked unashamedly with tears, he'd felt a lurch of surprise, and an unexpected liking for her. Then, when she'd pushed her hair back off her brow, wiped her eyes and said, with her customary spirit, 'I'm bloody parched. How about a cocktail?' he'd thrown back his head and laughed. He'd produced two invitations for the post-performance party – which he hadn't been intending to use – had called his wife and told her that he would be a little later than he'd thought.

He and Roxanne had stood at the edge of a party full of strangers, drinking Buck's Fizz, talking about the play and inventing stories about all the other guests. Then a jazz band had struck up, and the floor had crowded with couples. And after hesitating a second, Ralph had asked her to dance. As soon as she'd felt his arms around her and looked up into his eyes, she'd known. She'd simply known.

A familiar spasm, half pain, half joy, went through Roxanne at the memory. She would always remember that night as one of the most magical in her life. Ralph had disappeared off to make a phone call which she hadn't allowed herself to think about. Then he had returned to the table at which she was sitting, trembling with excitement. He had sat down opposite her, had met her eyes and said slowly, 'I was thinking about going on somewhere from here. A hotel, perhaps. Would you . . . care to join me?' Roxanne had stared at him silently for a few seconds, then had put down her drink.

She had intended to play it cool; to maintain a sophisticated reserve for as long as possible. But the moment they had got into their taxi, Ralph had turned to her, and she had found herself gazing back with an almost desperate longing. As their lips met she had thought, with a brief flash of humour, Hey, I'm kissing the boss. And then his kiss had deepened and her eyes had closed and her mind had lost its capacity for coherent thought. A capacity which had only returned in the morning, as she woke up in a Park Lane hotel with an adulterous man nineteen years her senior.

'Glass of wine?' Ralph's voice interrupted her and she opened her eyes to see him gazing fondly down at her. 'I could open the bottle I brought.'

'Only if it's properly cold,' she said suspiciously. 'If it's warm, I'm sending it back.'

'This one is cold,' said Ralph, smiling. 'I put it in the fridge when I got here.'

'It'd better be,' said Roxanne. She sat up and hugged her knees as he went back out to the kitchen. A minute later Ralph returned with two glasses full of wine.

'Why weren't you in the office today, by the way?' said Roxanne. She lifted her glass. 'Cheers.'

'Cheers,' replied Ralph. He took a long sip, then looked up and said easily, 'I had a meeting with my accountant all morning and into lunch. It didn't seem worth coming in.'

'Oh, right,' said Roxanne, and took a sip of wine. 'Slacker.'

A half-smile flickered across Ralph's face and he lowered himself slowly into a chair. Roxanne stared at him and frowned slightly.

'Are you OK?' she said. 'You look knackered.'

'Bit of a late night last night,' said Ralph, and closed his eyes.

'Oh well,' said Roxanne cheerfully. 'In that case, you don't get any sympathy from me.'

Candice took another swig of wine and gazed around the packed restaurant.

'I can't believe how full it is!' she said. 'I had no idea late-night shopping was such a big thing.'

Heather laughed. 'Have you never been shopping in the evening before?'

'Of course. But I didn't realize what a . . . party atmosphere there was here.' She took another swig of wine and looked around again. 'You know, I might suggest to Justin that we do a piece on it. We could come down, interview some people, take some photographs . . .'

'Good idea,' said Heather, and sipped at her wine. In front of her was a paper menu and a pen which their waiter had left behind, and Heather idly picked it up. She began to doodle on the menu: spiky star-like creations with far-reaching glittering rays. Candice watched her, slightly mesmerized, slightly drunk. They had had to wait half an hour for a table, during which time they had consumed a gin and tonic each and half a bottle of wine. Somehow she seemed to be drinking more quickly than Heather, and on an empty stomach the alcohol seemed stronger than usual.

'It's funny, isn't it?' said Heather, looking up suddenly. 'We're so close, and yet we don't really know each other.'

'I suppose not,' said Candice, and grinned. 'Well, what do you want to know?'

115

'Tell me about Justin,' said Heather after a pause. 'Do you still like him?'

'No!' said Candice, then laughed. 'I suppose I can stand him as an editor. But I don't have any . . . feelings for him. I think that was all a huge mistake.'

'Really?' said Heather lightly.

'He impressed me when I first met him. I thought he was incredibly clever and articulate and wonderful. But he's not. Not when you actually listen to what he's saying.' She took another gulp of wine. 'He just likes the sound of his own voice.'

'And there's no-one else on the horizon?'

'Not at the moment,' said Candice cheerfully. 'And I can't say I mind.'

A waiter appeared at the table, lit the candle between them and began to lay out knives and forks. Heather waited until he'd gone, then looked up again, her face glowing in the candlelight.

'So . . . men aren't important to you.'

'I don't know,' said Candice, laughing a little. 'I suppose the right one would be.' She watched as Heather picked up the bottle of wine, replenished Candice's glass then looked up, her eyes shining with a sudden intensity.

'So what is?' she asked softly. 'What means most to you in the world? What do you . . . treasure?'

'What do I treasure?' Candice repeated the question thoughtfully, staring into her glass. 'I don't know. My family, I suppose. Although my mother and I aren't that close any more. And my friends.' She looked up with a sudden certainty. 'I treasure my friends. Roxanne and Maggie especially.'

'Your friends.' Heather nodded slowly. 'Friends are such important things.'

'And my job. I love my job.'

'But not for the money,' probed Heather.

'No! I don't care about money!' Candice flushed

slightly, and took a gulp of wine. 'I hate materialism. And greed. And . . . dishonesty.'

'You want to be a good person.'

'I want to try.' Candice gave an embarrassed little laugh and put her wine glass down. 'What about you? What do you treasure?'

There was a short silence, and a curious expression flitted across Heather' s face.

'I've learned not to treasure anything much,' she said eventually, and gave a quick smile. 'Because you can lose it all overnight, with no warning. One minute you have it, the next you don't.' She snapped her fingers. 'Just like that.'

Candice stared at her in guilty misery, suddenly wanting to talk more; perhaps even reveal the truth.

'Heather . . .' she said hesitantly. 'I've . . . I've never—'

'Look!' interrupted Heather brightly, gesturing behind Candice. 'Here comes our food.'

Roxanne took a last mouthful of pasta, put down her fork and sighed. She was sitting opposite Ralph at her tiny folding dining table, the lights were dim and Ella Fitzgerald was crooning softly in the background.

'That was bloody delicious.' Roxanne hugged her stomach. 'Aren't you eating yours?'

'Go ahead.' Ralph gestured to his half-full plate, and, wrinkling her brow slightly, Roxanne pulled it towards her.

'No appetite?' she said. 'Or is it still your hang-over?'

'Something like that,' said Ralph lightly.

'Well, I'm not going to let it go to waste,' said Roxanne, plunging her fork into the pasta. 'You know, I always miss your cooking when I go away.'

'Do you?' said Ralph. 'What about all those five-star chefs?'

Roxanne pulled a face. 'Not the same. They can't do pasta like you.' She tilted her dining chair back so that it rested against the sofa, took a sip of wine and comfortably closed her eyes. 'In fact, I think it's very selfish of you not to come and cook me pasta every night.' She took another sip of wine, then another.

Then, as the silence continued, she opened her eyes. Ralph was gazing speechlessly at her, a curious expression on his face.

'I am selfish,' he said at last. 'You're right. I've treated you appallingly selfishly.'

'No you haven't!' said Roxanne, giving a little laugh. 'I'm only joking.' She reached for the bottle of wine, replenished both their glasses, and took a gulp. 'Nice wine.'

'Nice wine,' echoed Ralph slowly, and took a sip.

For a while they were both silent. Then Ralph looked up and, almost casually, said, 'Suppose in a year's time you could be doing anything. Anything at all. What would it be?'

'In a year's time,' echoed Roxanne, feeling her heart start to beat a little more quickly. 'Why a year?'

'Or three years,' said Ralph, making a vague gesture with his wine glass. 'Five years. Where do you see yourself?'

'Is this a job interview?' said Roxanne lightly.

'I'm just interested, I suppose,' said Ralph, shrugging. 'Idle fantasies.'

'Well, I . . . I don't know,' said Roxanne, and took a sip of wine, trying to stay calm.

What was going on? She and Ralph, by tacit agreement, never discussed the future; never discussed any part of life that might cause hurt or resentment. They talked about work, about films, food and travel. They gossiped about colleagues and speculated about Roxanne's dubious-looking downstairs neighbour. They watched television soap operas together and, in fits of laughter, ridiculed the wooden-faced acting. But, even when they were staring at adultery on the screen, they never talked about their own situation.

In the early days, she had tearfully insisted on hearing about his wife, about his family; about every last detail. She had shaken with misery and humiliation each time he'd left; had thrown accusations and ultimatums at him to no avail. Now she behaved almost as though each evening, each night spent in his arms, were a one-off; a self-contained bubble. It was simple self-preservation. That way disappointment could creep up on her less easily. That way she could pretend – at least to herself – that she was conducting the relationship on her own terms; that this was what she'd wanted all along.

She looked up, to see Ralph still waiting for an answer and, as she saw his expression, felt her stomach give a little flip. He was staring straight at her, his eyes glistening slightly, as if her answer really mattered to him. She took a gulp of wine, playing for time, then pushed her hair back and forced herself to smile unconcernedly.

'In a year's time?' she said lightly. 'If I could be anywhere, I think I'd like to be lying on a white beach somewhere in the Caribbean – with you, naturally.'

'Glad to hear it,' said Ralph, his face crinkling into a smile.

'But not just you,' said Roxanne. 'A posse of attentive waiters in white jackets would see to our every need. They'd ply us with food and drink and witty stories. Then, as if by magic, they would discreetly disappear, and we'd be left on our own in the magical sunset.'

She broke off, and took a sip of wine, then, after a short silence, looked up. As she met Ralph's eyes, her heart was thumping. Does he realize, she thought, that what I have just described is a honeymoon?

119

Ralph was staring at her with an expression she'd never seen in his eyes before. Suddenly he took hold of her hands and drew them up to his lips.

'You deserve it,' he said roughly. 'You deserve it all, Roxanne.' She gazed at him, feeling a hotness growing at the back of her throat. 'I'm so sorry for everything,' he muttered. 'When I think what I've put you through . . .'

'Don't be sorry.' Roxanne blinked hard, feeling tears smarting at her eyes. She drew him close across the table and kissed his wet eyes, his cheeks, his lips. 'I love you,' she whispered, and felt a sudden swell of painful, possessive happiness inside her. 'I love you, and we're together. And that's all that counts.'

Chapter Nine

The hospital was a large, Victorian building, with well-tended gardens at the front and a fenced area for children to play in. As Roxanne and Candice got out of the car and began to walk along the path towards the main entrance, Roxanne started laughing.

'Typical Maggie,' she said, looking around the pleasant scene. 'Even the hospital's a bloody picture postcard. She couldn't have her baby in some grim London hell-hole, could she?'

'What do we want?' said Candice, squinting at a colour-coded signpost with arrows pointing in all directions. 'Gynaecology. Labour suite.' She looked up. 'We don't want that, do we?'

'You can visit the labour suite if you like,' said Roxanne, giving a little shudder. 'As far as I'm concerned, ignorance is bliss.'

'Neo-natal. Pre-natal. Maternity,' read Candice, and wrinkled her brow. 'I can't work this out at all.'

'Oh, come on,' said Roxanne impatiently. 'We'll find her.'

They strode into the spacious reception area and spoke to a friendly woman at a desk, who tapped Maggie's name into a computer.

'Blue Ward,' she said, looking up with a smile.

'Follow the corridor round as far as you can go, then take the lift to the fifth floor.'

As they walked along the corridors, Candice glanced around at the beige walls and pulled a face.

'I hate the smell of hospitals,' she said. 'Horrible places. I think if I ever had a baby, I'd have it at home.'

'Of course you would,' said Roxanne. 'With pan pipes playing in the background and aromatherapy candles scenting the air.'

'No!' said Candice, laughing. 'I'd just . . . I don't know. Prefer to be at home, I suppose.'

'Well, if I ever have a baby, I'll have it by Caesarean,' said Roxanne drily. 'Full anaesthesia. They can wake me up when it's three years old.'

They arrived at the lift and pressed the fifth-floor button. As they began to rise, Candice glanced at Roxanne. 'I feel nervous!' she said. 'Isn't that weird?'

'I feel a bit nervous, too,' said Roxanne, after a pause. 'I suppose it's just that one of us has finally grown up. Real life has begun. The question is – are we ready for it?' She raised her eyebrows, and Candice gazed at her critically.

'You look tired, actually,' she said. 'Are you feeling OK?'

'I'm great,' said Roxanne at once, and tossed her hair back. 'Never better.'

But as they rose up in the lift, she stared at her tinted reflection in the lift doors and knew that Candice was right. She did look tired. Since that night with Ralph she had found it difficult to sleep; impossible to wrench her mind away from their conversation and what it had meant. Impossible to stop hoping.

Of course, Ralph had said nothing definite. He had made no promises. After that one short conversation, he had not even referred to the future again. But

122

something was going on; something was different. Thinking back, she'd realized there had been something different about him from the moment he stepped in the door. Something different in the way he looked at her, and talked to her. As they'd said goodbye he'd stared at her for minutes without speaking. It was as though inside, behind his eyes, he was coming to the hardest decision of his life.

She knew it was a decision that couldn't be hurried; that couldn't be arrived at in a snap. But the stress of this constant uncertainty was unbearable. And they were both suffering because of it – Ralph looked more tired and strained these days than she'd ever seen him. She'd glimpsed him the other day at the office, and had realized with a shock that he was actually losing weight. What mental hell he must be going through. And yet if he would only make up his mind and take courage, the hell would be over for good.

Once again, a surge of painful hope rose through her, and she clasped her bag more tightly. She shouldn't allow herself to think like this. She should return to her former, disciplined state of mind. But it was too hard. After six frugal years of refusing to hope or even think about it, her mind was now gorging itself on fantasy. Ralph would leave his wife. They would both, finally, be able to relax; to enjoy each other. The long hard winter would be over; the sun would come out and shine. Life would begin again for both of them. They would set up house together. Perhaps they would even—

There she stopped herself. She could not let herself go that far; she had to keep some control on herself. After all, nothing had been said. Nothing was definite. But surely that conversation had meant something? Surely he was at least thinking about it?

And she deserved it, didn't she? She bloody well deserved it, after everything she'd been through. An unfamiliar resentment began to steal over her, and she forced herself to breathe slowly and calmly. Over the past few days, having let her mind break out into fantasy land, she had discovered that beneath the joyous hope there was a darker flip-side. An anger that she had suppressed for too many years. Six whole years of waiting and wondering and grabbing moments of happiness where she could. It had been too long. It had been a prison sentence.

The lift doors opened and Candice looked up at Roxanne.

'Well, here we are,' she said, and gave a little smile. 'At last.'

'Yes,' said Roxanne, and exhaled sharply. 'At last.'

They walked out of the lift and towards a swing door marked 'Blue Ward'. Candice glanced up at Roxanne, then hesitantly pushed the door open. The room was large, but divided into cubicles by unnamed floral curtains. Candice raised her eyebrows at Roxanne, who shrugged back. Then a woman in a dark blue uniform, holding a baby, approached them.

'Are you here to visit?' she said, smiling.

'Yes,' said Roxanne, staring down at the baby in spite of herself. 'Maggie Phillips.'

'No, it'll be Drakeford, won't it?' said Candice. 'Maggie Drakeford.'

'Oh yes,' said the woman pleasantly. 'In the corner.'

Roxanne and Candice glanced at each other, then advanced slowly down the ward. Slowly, Candice pushed back the curtain of the final cubicle, and there she was, Maggie, looking familiar but unfamiliar, sitting up in bed with a tiny baby in her arms. She looked up, and for a still moment none of them said anything. Then Maggie gave a wide smile, held up the baby to face them and said, 'Lucia, meet the cocktail queens.'

*   *   *

124

Maggie had had a good night. As she watched Roxanne and Candice advance hesitantly towards the bed, eyes glued on Lucia's tiny face, she allowed herself to feel a warm glow of contentment. A bit of sleep, that was all. A bit of sleep every night, and the world changed.

The first three nights had been hell. Utter misery. She had lain stiffly in the darkness, unable to relax; unable to sleep while there was even the smallest chance that Lucia might wake. Even when she had drifted off to sleep, every snuffle from the tiny crib would wake her. She would hear cries in her dreams and jerk awake in a panic, only to find Lucia peacefully asleep and some other baby wailing. Then she would fear that the other baby's cries would wake Lucia – and she would tense up with apprehension, unable to fall asleep again.

On the fourth night, at two in the morning, Lucia had refused to go back to sleep. She had cried when Maggie tried to place her in her cot, thrashed about when Maggie tried to feed her, and screamed protestingly when, in desperation, Maggie began to sing. After a few minutes, a face had appeared round Maggie's floral curtain. It was an elderly midwife on night duty whom Maggie had not met before, and at the sight of Lucia, she shook her head comically.

'Young lady, your mother needs her sleep!' she'd said, and Maggie's head had jerked up in shock. She had expected a lecture on demand feeding or mother-baby bonding. Instead, the midwife had advanced inside Maggie's cubicle, looked at her shadowed face and sighed. 'This is no good! You look exhausted!'

'I feel a bit tired,' Maggie had admitted in a wobbly voice.

'You need a break.' The midwife had paused, then said, 'Would you like me to take her to the nursery?'

'The nursery?' Maggie had stared at her blankly. Nobody had told her about any nursery.

'I can keep an eye on her, and you can have a sleep. Then, when she needs feeding, I can bring her back.'

Maggie had stared at the midwife, wanting to burst into tears with gratitude.

'Thank you. Thank you . . . Joan,' she had managed, reading the woman's name-badge in the dim light. 'I . . . will she be all right?'

'She'll be fine!' Joan had said reassuringly. 'Now, you get some rest.'

As soon as she had left the cubicle, wheeling Lucia's crib, Maggie had fallen into the first relaxed sleep she'd had since Lucia's birth. The deepest, sweetest sleep of her life. She had woken at six, feeling almost restored, to see Lucia back in the cubicle again, ready for feeding.

Since then, Joan had appeared at Maggie's bedside each night, offering the services of the nursery – and Maggie had found herself guiltily accepting every time.

'No need to feel guilty,' Joan had said one night. 'You need your sleep to produce milk. No good wearing yourself out. You know, we used to keep mothers in for two weeks. Now, they shoo you all off after two days. Two days!' She clucked disapprovingly. 'You'd be home already if it weren't for the baby's jaundice.'

But despite Joan's reassuring comments, Maggie did feel guilty. She felt she should be with Lucia twenty-four hours a day, as all the books recommended. Anything less was failure. And so she hadn't mentioned Joan to Giles or to Paddy – or, in fact, to anyone.

Now she smiled at Roxanne and Candice and said, 'Come on in! Sit down. It's so good to see you!'

'Mags, you look wonderful!' said Roxanne. She embraced Maggie in a cloud of scent, then sat down on the edge of the bed. She was looking thinner and more glamorous than ever, thought Maggie. Like an exotic bird of paradise in this room full of dopey-eyed mother

126

ducks. And for an instant, Maggie felt a twinge of jealousy. She'd imagined that straight after the birth she would regain her old figure; that she would slip back into her old clothes with no problem. But her stomach, hidden under the bedclothes, was still frighteningly flabby, and she had no energy to exercise it.

'So, Mags,' drawled Roxanne, looking around the ward. 'Is motherhood all it's cracked up to be?'

'Oh, you know.' Maggie grinned. 'Not too bad. Of course, I'm an old hand now.'

'Maggie, she's beautiful!' Candice looked up with shining eyes. 'And she doesn't look ill at all!'

'She's not, really,' said Maggie, looking at Lucia's closed-up, sleeping face. 'She had jaundice, and it's taken a while to clear up. It just meant we had to stay in hospital a bit longer.'

'Can I hold her?' Candice held out her arms and, after a pause, Maggie handed the baby over.

'She's so light!' breathed Candice.

'Very sweet,' said Roxanne. 'You'll be making me broody in a moment.'

Maggie laughed. 'Now, that *would* be a miracle.'

'Do you want to hold her?' Candice looked up at Roxanne, who rolled her eyes comically.

'If I must.'

She had held scores of babies before. Little bundles belonging to other people, that aroused in her no feeling other than tedium. Roxanne Miller did not coo over babies – she yawned over them. She was famous for it. Whether she was genuinely uninterested, or whether this was a defensive response deliberately cultivated over the years, she had never allowed herself to consider.

But as she looked into the sleeping face of Maggie's baby, Roxanne felt her defences begin to crumble;

127

found herself thinking thoughts she had never let herself think before. She wanted one of these, she found herself thinking. Oh God. She actually wanted one. The thought frightened her; exhilarated her. She closed her eyes and, without meaning to, imagined herself holding her own baby. Ralph's baby. Ralph looking fondly over her shoulder. The picture made her almost sick with hope – and with fear. She was treading on forbidden ground, allowing her mind to venture into dangerous places. And on what basis? On the basis of one conversation. It was ridiculous. It was foolhardy. But, having started, she couldn't seem to stop.

'So, what do you reckon, Roxanne?' said Maggie, looking at her amusedly. Roxanne stared at Lucia a few seconds longer, then forced herself to look up with a nonchalant expression.

'Very nice, as babies go. But I warn you, she'd better not pee on me.'

'I'll take her back,' said Maggie, smiling, and a ridiculous thud of disappointment went through Roxanne.

'Here you are then, Mummy,' she drawled, handing the bundle back.

'Oh, Maggie, I brought you these,' said Candice, rescuing the bouquet of flowers which she'd deposited on the floor. 'I know you'll have heaps already . . .'

'I did have,' said Maggie. 'But they're all dead. They don't last five minutes in here.'

'Oh good! I mean—'

'I know what you mean,' said Maggie, smiling. 'And they're lovely. Thank you.'

Candice looked around the cubicle. 'Have you got a vase?'

Maggie pulled a doubtful face.

'There might be one in the corridor. Or one of the other wards.'

'I'll find one.' Candice put the flowers down on the bed and headed out of the ward. When she'd gone, Maggie and Roxanne smiled at each other.

'So – how are you?' asked Maggie, stroking Lucia's cheek gently with the tip of her finger.

'Oh, fine,' said Roxanne. 'You know, life goes on . . .'

'How's Mr Married with Kids?' asked Maggie cautiously.

'Still got kids,' said Roxanne lightly. 'Still married.' They both laughed, and Lucia stirred slightly in her sleep. 'Although . . . you never know,' Roxanne couldn't resist adding. 'Changes may be afoot.'

'Really?' said Maggie in astonishment. 'You're not serious!'

'Who knows?' A smile spread over Roxanne's face. 'Watch this space.'

'You mean we might actually get to meet him?'

'Oh, I don't know about that.' Roxanne's eyes flashed in amusement. 'I've got used to him being my little secret.'

Maggie glanced at her, then looked around for her watch.

'What time is it? I should offer you a cup of tea. There's an urn in the day room . . .'

'Don't worry,' said Roxanne, suppressing a shudder at the idea. 'I've brought a little liquid refreshment. We can have it when Candice gets back.' She looked around the maternity ward, trying to find something polite to say about it. But it seemed, to her, an over-heated floral hell. And Maggie had been here for well over a week. How could she bear it? 'How much longer are you in here for?' she asked.

'I go home tomorrow. The paediatrician has to check Lucia over – and then we're out of here.'

'I bet you're relieved.'

'Yes,' said Maggie, after a pause. 'Yes, of course I am. But . . . but let's not talk about hospitals.' She smiled at

129

Roxanne. 'Tell me about the outside world. What have I been missing?'

'Oh God, I don't know,' said Roxanne lazily. 'I never know the gossip. I'm always away when things happen.'

'What about that girl of Candice's?' said Maggie, suddenly frowning. 'Heather Whatsername. Have you met her again?'

'Yes, I saw her at the office. Didn't exactly warm to her.' Roxanne pulled a face. 'Bit sickly sweet.'

'I don't know why I got so worked up about her,' said Maggie ruefully. 'Pregnancy paranoia. She's probably a lovely girl.'

'Well, I wouldn't go that far. But I tell you what – ' Roxanne sat up and reached for her bag. 'She can certainly write.'

'Really?'

'Look at this.' Roxanne pulled a sheet of paper from her bag. 'I got it from Janet. It's actually very funny.'

She watched as Maggie read the first two lines of the piece, frowned, then scanned further down to the end.

'I don't believe it!' she exclaimed as she looked up. 'Did she really get a job at the *Londoner* on the strength of this piece?'

'I don't know,' said Roxanne. 'But you've got to admit, it's on the nail.'

'Of course it is,' said Maggie drily. 'Everything Candice writes is on the nail.'

'What?' Roxanne stared at her.

'Candice wrote this for the *Londoner*,' said Maggie, hitting the piece of paper with her hand. 'I remember it. Word for word. It's her style and everything.'

'I don't believe it!'

'No wonder Ralph was impressed,' said Maggie, rolling her eyes. 'God, Candice can be an idiot sometimes.'

*   *   *

130

Candice had taken longer than she had expected to find a vase, and had struck up a conversation with one of the midwives on another ward. As she finally made her way, humming, back into the ward, she saw Roxanne and Maggie staring at her, ominous expressions on their faces.

'So,' said Roxanne as she neared the bed. 'What do you have to say for yourself?'

'What?' said Candice.

'This,' said Maggie, producing the piece of paper with a flourish. Candice stared at it in bewilderment – then, as her gaze focused on the text, realized what it was. A flush spread over her cheeks and she looked away.

'Oh, that,' she said. 'Well . . . Heather didn't have any examples of her writing. So I—' She broke off awkwardly.

'So you thought you'd supply her with an entire portfolio?'

'No!' said Candice. 'Just one little piece. Just . . . you know.' She shrugged defensively. 'Something to get her started. For God's sake, it's no big deal.'

Maggie shook her head.

'Candice, it's not fair. You *know* it's not fair. It's not fair on Ralph, it's not fair on all the other people who ₊plied for the job . . .'

'It's not fair on Heather, come to that,' put in Roxanne. 'What happens when Justin asks her to write another piece just like that one?'

'He won't! And she's fine. You know, she has got talent. She can do the job. She just needed a chance.' Candice looked from Roxanne to Maggie, feeling a sudden impatience with them both. Why couldn't they see that in some cases the ends more than justified the means? 'Come on, be honest,' she exclaimed. 'How many jobs are got through nepotism? How many people drop names and use contacts and pretend they're better than they are? This is just the same.'

There was silence – then Maggie said, 'And she's living with you.'

'Yes.' Candice looked from face to face, wondering if she'd missed something. 'What's wrong with that?'

'Is she paying you rent?'

'I . . .' Candice swallowed. 'That's our business, don't you think?'

She had not yet mentioned rent to Heather – nor had Heather ever brought the subject up. In her heart she had always assumed that Heather would offer to pay something, at least – but then even if she didn't, Candice thought with a sudden fierceness, what was the big deal? Some people paid rent to their friends, and some people didn't. And it wasn't as if she was desperate for the money.

'Of course it is,' said Roxanne mildly. 'As long as she isn't using you.'

'*Using* me?' Candice shook her head disbelievingly. 'After what my father did to her family?'

'Candice—'

'No, listen to me,' said Candice, her voice rising a little. 'I owe her one. OK? I owe her one. So maybe I got her this job under slightly false pretences, and maybe I'm being more generous to her than I normally would. But she deserves it. She deserves a break.' Candice felt her face growing hot. 'And I know you don't like her, Roxanne, but—'

'What?' said Roxanne in outrage. 'I've barely spoken to her!'

'Well, she has the impression you don't like her.'

'Maybe she doesn't like *me*. Had you thought of that?'

'Why wouldn't she like you?' retorted Candice indignantly.

'I don't know! Why wouldn't I like her, for that matter?'

'This is ridiculous!' cut in Maggie. 'Stop it, both of you!'

At her raised voice, Lucia gave a sudden wriggle and began to wail, plaintively at first, then more lustily.

'Now look what you've done!' said Maggie.

'Oh,' said Candice, and bit her lip. 'Sorry. I didn't mean to lose it like that.'

'No,' said Roxanne. 'Neither did I.' She put a hand out and squeezed Candice's. 'Don't get me wrong. I'm sure Heather's a great girl. We just . . . worry about you.'

'You're too blinking nice,' put in Maggie, then winced. The others turned and, in appalled fascination, watched her putting Lucia to her breast.

'Does it *hurt*?' said Candice, watching Maggie's face involuntarily screw up in pain.

'A bit,' said Maggie. 'Just at first.' The baby began to suck and gradually her face relaxed. 'There. That's better.'

'Bloody hell,' said Roxanne, staring blatantly at Maggie's breast. 'Rather you than me.' She pulled a face at Candice, who gave a sudden giggle.

'She likes a drink, anyway,' she said, watching Lucia greedily sucking.

'Like her mother,' said Roxanne. 'Speaking of which . . .' She reached into her bag and, after some rummaging, produced a large silver cocktail shaker.

'No!' exclaimed Maggie in disbelief. 'You haven't!'

'I told you we'd toast the baby with cocktails,' said Roxanne.

'But we can't!' said Maggie, giggling. 'If somebody sees us, I'll get thrown out of the Good Mother club.'

'I thought of that, too,' said Roxanne. With a completely straight face, she reached into the bag again and produced three little baby bottles.

'What—'

'Wait.'

133

She unscrewed each of the bottles, placed them in a row on the bedside table, picked up the cocktail shaker and gave it a good shake as the other two watched in amazement. Then she removed the lid of the cocktail shaker and solemnly poured a thick white liquid into each of the bottles.

'What is it?' said Candice, staring at it.

'Not milk, surely?' said Maggie.

'Pina Colada,' said Roxanne airily.

At once, Candice and Maggie exploded into giggles. Pina Colada was a standing joke between them – ever since that first uproarious night at the Manhattan Bar, when Roxanne had announced that if anyone ordered Pina Colada she was disowning them.

'I mustn't!' wailed Maggie, trying not to shake. 'I mustn't laugh. Poor Lucia.'

'Cheers,' said Roxanne, handing her a baby bottle.

'To Lucia,' said Candice.

'Lucia,' echoed Roxanne, holding her bottle up.

'And to you two,' said Maggie, smiling at Roxanne and Candice. She took a gulp and closed her eyes in delight. 'God, that's good. I haven't tasted proper alcohol for weeks.'

'The thing is,' said Candice, taking a slurp, 'that actually, Pina Colada is bloody delicious.'

'It's not bad, is it?' said Roxanne, sipping thoughtfully. 'If they could just call it something classier . . .'

'Talking of alcohol, Ralph Allsopp sent us a magnum of champagne,' said Maggie. 'Wasn't that nice of him? But we haven't opened it yet.'

'Great minds think alike,' said Roxanne lightly.

'Mrs Drakeford?' A man's voice came from outside the floral curtains and the three looked guiltily at each other. The next moment, a doctor's cheerful head popped round the side of the curtain and grinned at them all. 'Mrs Drakeford, I'm one of the paediatricians. Come to check up on little Lucia.'

'Oh,' said Maggie weakly. 'Ahm . . . come in.'

'I'll take your . . . milk, shall I?' said Roxanne help-fully, and reached for Maggie's baby bottle. 'Here. I'll leave it on your bedside table for later.'

'Thanks,' said Maggie. Her mouth was tight; she was obviously trying not to laugh.

'Maybe we'd better go,' said Candice.

'OK,' whispered Maggie.

'See you soon, babe,' said Roxanne. She downed her Pina Colada in one and thrust the empty bottle back into her bag. 'Nothing like a nice healthy drink of milk,' she said to the paediatrician, who nodded in surprise.

'Lucia's gorgeous,' said Candice, and bent over the bed to kiss Maggie. 'And well see you soon.'

'At the Manhattan Bar,' put in Roxanne. 'First of the month. You think you'll be able to make it, Maggie?'

'Absolutely,' said Maggie, and grinned at her. 'I'll be there.'

Chapter Ten

As Candice arrived home that evening her cheeks were flushed with happiness, and she still felt giggles rising whenever she thought of the baby bottles full of Pina Colada. She also felt more emotional than she had been expecting to. The sight of Maggie and her baby – a new little person in the world – had stirred her deep inside; more than she had been aware at the time. Now she felt overflowing with affection for both her friends.

The only awkward moment between the three of them had been over Heather – and that, thought Candice, was because they didn't understand. After all, how could they? Maggie and Roxanne had never felt her secret, constant guilt – so they couldn't know what it was like to feel that guilt alleviated. They couldn't understand the lightness she had felt inside over the past few weeks; the sheer pleasure it gave her to see Heather's life falling into place.

Besides which, neither of them had really met Heather properly. They had no idea what a warm and generous person she was; how quickly the friendship between them had developed. Perhaps she had started out thinking of Heather primarily as victim; perhaps her initial generosity had been spurred by guilt rather than anything else. But now there was a genuine bond between them. Maggie and Roxanne behaved as though having Heather living in her flat were a huge disadvantage. In fact, the opposite was true. Now that she had a flat-mate, Candice couldn't imagine living again without one. How had she spent the evenings before Heather? Sipping cocoa on her own, instead of snuggled up with Heather on the sofa in pyjamas, reading out horoscopes in fits of laughter. Heather wasn't a disadvantage, thought Candice affectionately. She was a life-enhancer.

As she closed the front door behind her, she could hear Heather's voice in the kitchen. She sounded as though she might be on the phone, and Candice advanced cautiously down the corridor, not wanting to disturb Heather's privacy. A few feet before she reached the kitchen, she stopped in slight shock.

'Don't give me any of your grief, Hamish!' Heather was saying, in a low, tense voice so far from her usual bubbling tones that Candice barely recognized it. 'What the fuck is it to you?' There was a pause, then she said, 'Yeah, well maybe I don't care. Yeah well, maybe I will!' Her voice rose to a shout and there was the sound of the phone slamming down. Out in the hall, Candice froze in panic. Please don't come out, she thought. Please don't come out and see me.

A moment later, she heard Heather putting the kettle on, and the sound seemed to jolt her into action. Feeling absurdly guilty, she tiptoed a few feet back down the hall, opened the front door again, then banged it shut.

'Hi!' she called brightly. 'Anyone in?'

Heather appeared at the kitchen door and gazed at Candice appraisingly, without smiling.

'Hi,' she said at last. 'How was it?'

'Great!' said Candice enthusiastically. 'Lucia's gorgeous! And Maggie's fine . . .' She tailed off, and Heather leaned against the door frame.

'I was on the phone,' she said. 'I expect you heard.'

'No!' said Candice at once. 'I've only just got in.' She felt herself flushing and turned her head away, pretending to fiddle with the sleeve of her jacket.

'Men,' said Heather after a pause. 'Who needs them?' Candice looked up in surprise.

'Have you got a boyfriend?'

'Ex-boyfriend,' said Heather. 'Utter bastard. You really don't want to know.'

'Right,' said Candice awkwardly. 'Well – shall we have some tea?'

'Why not?' said Heather, and followed her back into the kitchen.

'By the way,' said Heather, as Candice reached for the tea-bags, 'I needed some stamps, so I got some from your dressing table. You don't mind, do you? I'll pay you back.'

'Don't be silly!' said Candice, turning round. 'And of course I don't mind. Help yourself.' She laughed. 'What's mine is yours.'

'OK,' said Heather casually. 'Thanks.'

Roxanne arrived back at her flat cold and hungry, to see a cardboard box waiting outside the front door. She stared at it, bewildered, then opened the door and gave it little shoves with her foot until it was inside. She shut the front door, flicked on the lights then crouched down and looked at the box more closely. The postmark was Cyprus, and the writing on the label was Nico's. The sweetheart. What had he sent her this time?

Smiling a little, Roxanne ripped open the box, to see row upon row of bright orange tangerines, still with their green leaves attached to the stalks. She picked one up, closed her eyes, and inhaled the sweet, tangy, unmistakable scent. Then she reached for the handwritten sheet lying on top of the tangerines.

My dearest Roxanne. A small reminder of what you

*are missing, here in Cyprus. Andreas and I are still
hoping you will reconsider our offer. Yours as ever,
Nico.*

For a moment, Roxanne was quite still. Then she
looked at the tangerine consideringly, threw it into the
air and caught it. Bright and sweet, sunny and appeal-
ing, she thought. Another world altogether; a world
she'd almost forgotten about.

But her world was here. Here in the soft London
rain, with Ralph.

After all the visitors had left the ward, the lights had
been turned down and Lucia had settled to sleep,
Maggie lay awake, staring up at the high, white, insti-
tutional ceiling, trying to quell her feelings of panic.

The paediatrician had been very complimentary
about Lucia's progress. The jaundice had completely
gone, she was putting on weight well, and all was as it
should be.

'You can go home tomorrow,' he'd said, making a
mark on his white form. 'I expect you're sick of this
place.'

'Absolutely,' Maggie had said, and had smiled
weakly at him. 'I can't wait to get home.'

Later, Giles had arrived to visit – and when she'd
told him the good news, had whooped with delight.

'At last! What a relief. You must be thrilled. Oh, darling, won't it be great, having you home again?' He'd
leaned forward and hugged her so tightly she could
hardly breathe, and her spirits had, for a moment,
lifted to something near euphoria.

But now, lying in the dark, she could feel nothing
but fear. In ten days, she had become used to the
rhythm of life in hospital. She had become used to
three meals a day; to the friendly chatter of the midwives; to the cups of tea which appeared on trolleys at
four o'clock. She had become used to the feeling of

security: the knowledge that, if disaster struck, there was always a button to press, a nurse to summon. She had become used to Joan wheeling Lucia off at two in the morning and returning at six.

To her shame, she had secretly almost been relieved when Lucia's jaundice had responded more slowly than expected to phototherapy. Every extra night in hospital was putting off the day when she would have to leave the safety, familiarity and camaraderie of the maternity ward for her empty, chilly house. She thought of The Pines – her home – and tried to summon up some feeling of affection for it. But the strongest emotion she had ever felt for the house was pride in its grandeur – and somehow that no longer appealed to her. What was the point of all that cold, open space? She was used to her warm, cosy floral cell, with everything within arm's reach.

Giles, of course, would never understand that. He adored the house in a way she feared she would never be able to.

'I've been so looking forward to having you home,' he'd said that afternoon, holding her hand. 'You and the baby, home at The Pines. It'll be . . . just as I always imagined it.' And a twinge of surprise had gone through her. Of envy, almost. Giles so obviously had a clear vision in his mind of what life at home with a baby would be like. Whereas she still could hardly believe it was actually happening.

Throughout her pregnancy, she had been unable to picture herself with a child. She had known in her logical mind that there would be a baby; had occasionally tried to imagine herself pushing the smart Mamas and Papas pram or rocking the Moses basket. She had looked at the piles of new white sleeping suits and had told herself that a living, breathing child would soon be inhabiting them. But despite everything she'd said to herself, none of it had felt quite real.

And now, the thought of herself alone at home with Lucia seemed just as unreal. She exhaled sharply, then switched on her night light, glanced at Lucia's sleeping face, and poured herself a glass of water.

'Can't sleep?' A young midwife poked her head round the curtain. 'I expect you're excited about going home.'

'Oh yes,' said Maggie again, forcing a smile onto her dry face. 'Can't wait.'

The midwife disappeared and she stared miserably into her glass of water. She couldn't tell anyone how she really felt. She couldn't tell anyone that she was scared of returning to her own home, with her own baby. They would think she was absolutely mad. Perhaps she was.

Late that night, Candice woke with a start, and stared into the darkness of her room. For a moment she couldn't think what had woken her. Then she realized that a sound was coming from the kitchen. Oh my God, she thought: a burglar. She lay quite still, heart thumping in panic – then slowly and silently she got out of bed, wrapped a dressing gown around herself and cautiously opened the door of her room.

The kitchen light was on. Did burglars usually put lights on? She hesitated, then quickly padded out into the corridor. As she reached the kitchen, she stopped and stared in shock. Heather was sitting at the table, cradling a cup of coffee, surrounded by page proofs of the *Londoner.* As Candice stared, she looked up, her face drawn and anxious.

'Hi,' she said, and immediately looked back at the sheets of paper.

'Hi,' said Candice, staring at her. 'What are you doing? You're not working, surely?'

'I forgot all about it,' said Heather, staring down at the page proofs. 'I completely forgot.' She rubbed her red eyes, and Candice gazed at her in alarm. 'I brought these pages home to work on over the weekend, and I forgot to do them. How can I be so *stupid*?'

'Well . . . don't worry!' said Candice. 'It's not the end of the world!'

'I've got to redo five pages by tomorrow!' said Heather, a note of desperation in her voice. 'And then I've got to put all the corrections onto the computer by the time Alicia arrives! I promised they'd be ready!'

'I don't understand,' said Candice, sinking onto a chair. 'Why have you got so much work?'

'I got behind,' said Heather. She took a sip of coffee and winced. 'Alicia gave me a load of stuff to do, and I . . . I don't know, maybe I'm not as quick as everyone else. Maybe everyone else is cleverer than me.'

'Rubbish!' said Candice at once. 'I'll have a word with Alicia.' She had always liked Alicia, the earnest chief sub-editor; at one time they had even considered sharing a flat.

'No, don't,' said Heather at once. 'She'll just say—' She stopped abruptly and there was silence in the little kitchen, broken only by the ticking of the electric clock.

'What?' said Candice. 'What will she say?'

'She'll say I should never have got the job in the first place,' said Heather miserably.

'What?' Candice laughed. 'Alicia wouldn't say that!'

'She already has,' said Heather. 'She's said it several times.'

'Are you serious?' Candice stared at her in disbelief. Heather gazed back at her, as though debating whether to carry on, then sighed.

'Apparently a friend of hers applied for the job, too. Some girl with two years' experience on another magazine. And I got it over her. Alicia was a bit annoyed.'

'Oh.' Candice rubbed her nose, discomfited. 'I had no idea.'

'So I can't let her know I'm slipping behind. I've just got to somehow . . . manage.' Heather pushed her hair back off her shadowed face and took another sip of coffee. 'Go back to bed, Candice. Honestly.'

'I can't just leave you!' said Candice. She picked up a page proof covered in coloured corrections, then put it down again. 'I feel terrible about this. I had no idea you were being worked so hard.'

'It's fine, really. Just as long as I get it all done by tomorrow morning . . .' Heather's voice shook slightly. 'I'll be all right.'

'No,' said Candice, with a sudden decisiveness. 'Come on, this is silly! I'll do some of this work. It won't take me nearly as long.'

'Really? Would you?' Heather looked up at her entreatingly. 'Oh, Candice . . .'

'I'll go in early and do the work straight onto the computer. How's that?'

'But . . .' Heather swallowed. 'Won't Alicia know you've been helping me?'

'I'll send the pages over to your terminal when I've finished them. And you can print them out.' Candice grinned at her. 'Easy.'

'Candice, you're a star,' said Heather, sinking back into her chair. 'And it'll just be this once, I promise.'

'No problem,' said Candice, and grinned at her. 'What are friends for?'

The next day she went into work early and sat, patiently working through the pages Heather had been given to correct. It took her rather longer than she had expected, and it was eleven o'clock before she had perfected the final proof. She glanced over at Heather, gave her the thumbs-up, and pressed the button that would send the page electronically to Heather's computer terminal. Behind her she could hear Alicia saying, 'This page is fine, too. Well done, Heather!'

Candice grinned, and reached for her cup of coffee. She felt rather like a schoolchild, outwitting the teachers.

'Candice?' She looked up at Justin's voice and saw him standing at the door of his office, looking as polished as ever. His brows were knitted together in a thoughtful frown – which he'd probably been practising in the bathroom mirror, she thought with an inward grin. After having lived with Justin and seen his little vanities close at hand, she couldn't take his studied facial expressions seriously any more. Indeed, she could barely take him seriously as an editor at all. He could be as pompous as he liked and throw as many long words as he liked around at meetings, but he would never be half the editor Maggie was. He might have a large vocabulary and he might know the name of the maître d' at Boodles, but he didn't have the first idea about people.

Once again she felt a flicker of astonishment that, for a while, she had fallen for Justin's gloss; that she had actually believed that she might love him. It just showed, she thought, what an insidious influence good looks could have on one's judgement. If he'd been less attractive physically, she might have paid attention to his character from the start and realized sooner what a selfish person he was, underneath all the eloquent, superficial charm.

'What is it?' she said, reluctantly getting out of her seat and going towards his office. That was another thing which, in her opinion, made Justin inferior to Maggie. If Maggie had to say something, she came and said it. But Justin seemed to enjoy holding court in his little office, watching the staff of the magazine run in and out like faithful lackeys. Roll on Maggie's return, she thought wistfully.

'Candice, I'm still waiting for the profile list you promised me,' said Justin as she sat down. He had

144

retreated behind his desk and was gazing moodily out of the window as though being photographed for a fashion shoot.

'Oh yes,' she said, and felt herself flush with annoyance. Trust Justin to catch her out. She'd meant to type up the list that morning, but Heather's pages had taken priority. 'I'm onto it,' she said.

'Hmm.' He swivelled round so he was facing her. 'This isn't the first piece of work you've been late with, is it?'

'Yes it is!' said Candice indignantly. 'And it's only a list. It's not exactly front-page editorial.'

'Hmm.' Justin looked at her thoughtfully and Candice felt herself stiffen with irritation.

'So, how are you enjoying being acting editor?' she said, to change the subject.

'Very much,' said Justin, nodding gravely. 'Very much indeed.' He put his elbows on the desk and carefully placed his fingertips together. 'I see myself rather as—'

'Daniel Barenboim,' said Candice before she could stop herself, and stifled a giggle. 'Sorry,' she whispered.

'As a troubleshooter,' said Justin, shooting her a look of annoyance. 'I intend to institute a series of spot checks in order to locate problems with the system.'

'What problems?' said Candice. '*Are* there problems with the system?'

'I've been analysing the running of this magazine since I took power—'

Power! thought Candice scornfully. Next he'd be calling himself the Emperor.

' – and I've noticed several glitches which, frankly, Maggie just didn't pick up on.'

'Oh, really?' Candice folded her arms and gave him the least impressed look she could muster. 'So, you think, after a few weeks, you're a better editor than Maggie.'

145

'That's not what I said.' Justin paused. 'Maggie has, as we all know, many wonderful talents and qualities—'

'Yes, well, Ralph obviously thinks so,' put in Candice loyally. 'He sent her a magnum of champagne.'

'I'm sure he did,' said Justin, and leaned comfortably back in his chair. 'You know he's retiring in a couple of weeks' time?'

'What?'

'I just heard it this morning. Wants to spend more time with his family, apparently,' said Justin. 'So it looks like we're all going to have a new boss. It seems one of his sons is going to take over. He's coming in to meet us all next week.'

'Gosh,' said Candice, taken aback. 'I had no idea that was on the cards.' She frowned. 'Does Maggie know about this?'

'I doubt it,' said Justin, carelessly. 'Why should she? She's got other things to think about.' He took a sip of coffee, then glanced over her shoulder through the window at the editorial office. 'That friend of yours is doing well, by the way.'

'Who, Heather?' said Candice, with a glow of pride. 'Yes, she is good, isn't she? I told you she would be.' She turned to follow Justin's gaze, met Heather's eye and smiled.

'She came to me with an excellent idea for a feature the other day,' said Justin. 'I was impressed.'

'Oh yes?' said Candice, turning back interestedly. 'What's the idea?'

'Late-night shopping,' said Justin. 'Do a whole piece on it.'

'What?' Candice stared at him.

'We'll run it in the lifestyle section. Take a photographer down to a shopping mall, interview some customers . . .' Justin frowned at her flabbergasted expression. 'What's wrong? Don't you think it's a good idea?'

'Of course I do!' exclaimed Candice, feeling herself grow hot. 'But . . .' She broke off feebly. What could she say without looking as though she wanted to get Heather into trouble?

'What?'

'Nothing,' said Candice slowly. She turned round again and glanced out of the window, but Heather had vanished. 'It's . . . it's a great idea.'

Heather stood by the coffee machine with Kelly, the editorial secretary. Kelly was a sixteen-year-old girl with long bony legs and a thin, bright-eyed face, always eager for the latest gossip.

'You were working hard this morning,' she said, pressing the button for hot chocolate. 'I saw you, typing hard!' Heather smiled, and leaned against the coffee machine. 'And sending lots of things to Candice, weren't you?' added Kelly.

Heather's head jerked up.

'Yes,' she said carefully. 'How could you tell that?'

'I heard your e-mail pinging away!' said Kelly. 'The two of you, pinging away all morning!' She laughed merrily, and picked up her polystyrene cup full of hot chocolate.

'That's right,' said Heather after a pause. 'How observant of you.' She pressed the button for white coffee. 'You know what all that e-mail was?' she said in a lower voice.

'What?' said Kelly interestedly.

'Candice makes me send all my work to her to be checked,' whispered Heather. 'Every single word I write.'

'You're joking!' said Kelly. 'Why does she do that?'

'I don't know,' said Heather. 'I suppose she thinks I'm not up to scratch, or something . . .'

'Bloody nerve!' said Kelly. 'I wouldn't stand for it.' She blew on her hot chocolate. 'I've never liked that Candice very much.'

'Really?' said Heather and moved casually nearer. 'Kelly – what are you doing at lunchtime?'

Roxanne sat opposite Ralph at her little dining table and looked accusingly at him across her mound of beef stroganoff.

'You've got to stop cooking me such nice food!' she said. 'I'm going to be fat now.'

'Rubbish,' said Ralph, taking a sip of wine and running a hand down Roxanne's thigh. 'Look at that. You're perfect.'

'That's easy for you to say,' said Roxanne. 'You haven't seen me in a bikini.'

'I've seen you in a lot less than a bikini.' Ralph grinned at her.

'On the beach, I mean!' said Roxanne impatiently. 'Next to all the fifteen-year-olds. There were scores of them in Cyprus. Horrible skinny things with long legs and huge brown eyes.'

'Can't stand brown eyes,' said Ralph obligingly.

'You've got brown eyes,' pointed out Roxanne.

'I know. Can't stand them.'

Roxanne laughed and leaned back in her chair, lifting up her feet so that they nestled in Ralph's lap. As he reached down and began to massage them, she felt again the light tripping sensation in her heart; the lift of hope, of excitement. Ralph had arranged this meeting as an unexpected extra treat; a few days ago he had surprised her with a bouquet of flowers. It wasn't her imagination – he was definitely behaving differently. Ever since she'd got back from Cyprus he'd been different. A sudden fizz of hope rose through Roxanne like sherbet in a glass of lemonade and she felt a smile spread across her face.

'How did the trip go, by the way?' he added, stroking her toes. 'I never asked. Same old thing?'

'More or less,' said Roxanne. She reached for her wine and took a deep sip. 'Oh, except you'll never guess what. Nico Georgiou offered me a job.'

'A job?' Ralph stared at her. 'In Cyprus?'

'At the new resort he's building. Marketing manager or something.' Roxanne shook back her hair and looked provocatively at Ralph. 'He's offering a very good deal. What do you think? Shall I take it?'

Over the years, she had often teased him like this. She would mention job opportunities in Scotland, in Spain, in America – some genuine, some fabricated. The teasing was partly in fun – and partly from a genuine need to make him realize that she was choosing to be with him; that she was not staying with him simply by default. If she was utterly honest with herself, it had also, in the past, been from a need to see him hurt. To see his face fall; to see him experience, just for a second, the feeling of loss that she felt every time he left her.

But today, it was almost a test. A challenge. A way of getting him to talk about the future again.

'He even sent me a box of tangerines,' she added, gesturing to the fruit bowl, where the tangerines were piled up in a shiny orange pyramid. 'So he must be serious. What do you think?'

What she expected was for him to grin, and say, 'Well, he can sod off' as he usually did. What she wanted was for him to take her hands and kiss them and ask again what she wanted to be doing in a year's time. But Ralph did neither. He stared at her as though she were a stranger – then, eventually, cleared his throat and said, 'Do you want to take it?'

'For God's sake, Ralph!' said Roxanne, disappointment sharpening her voice. 'I'm only joking! Of course I don't want to take it.'

'Why not?' He was leaning forward, looking at her with an odd expression on his face. 'Wouldn't it be a good job?'

'I don't know!' exclaimed Roxanne. 'Since you ask, I expect it would be a marvellous job.' She reached for her cigarettes. 'And naturally they're *desperate* to have me. You know they'd even provide me with a house?' She lit her cigarette and looked at him through the smoke. 'I haven't noticed anyone at Allsopp Publications offering me any real estate.'

'So – what did you say to them?' said Ralph, meshing his hands together as though in prayer. 'How did you leave it?'

'Oh, the usual,' said Roxanne. 'Thanks but no thanks.'

'So you turned it down.'

'Of course I did!' said Roxanne, giving a little laugh. 'Why? Do you think I should have said yes?'

There was silence, and Roxanne looked up. At Ralph's tense expression she felt a sudden coldness inside her.

'You're joking,' she said, and tried to smile. 'You think I should have said yes?'

'Maybe it's time for you to move on. Take one of these opportunities up.' Ralph reached for his glass of wine with a trembling hand and took a sip. 'I've held you back far too long. I've got in your way.'

'Ralph, don't be stupid!'

'Is it too late to change your mind?' Ralph looked up. 'Could you still go to them and say you're interested?'

Roxanne stared at him in shock, feeling as though she'd been slapped.

'Yes,' she said eventually. 'I suppose I could, in theory . . .' She swallowed, and pushed her hair back off her face, scarcely able to believe they were having this conversation. 'Are you going to tell me I should?

Do you . . . do you *want* me to take this job?' Her voice grew more brittle. 'Ralph?'

There was silence, then Ralph looked up.

'Yes,' he said. 'I do. I think you should take it.'

There was silence in the room. This is a bad dream, thought Roxanne. This is a fucking bad dream.

'I . . . I don't understand,' she said at last, trying to stay calm. 'Ralph, what's going on? You were talking about the future. You were talking about Caribbean beaches!'

'I wasn't, you were.'

'You *asked* me!' said Roxanne furiously. 'Jesus!'

'I know I did. But that was . . . dreaming. Idle fantasies. This is real life. And I think if you have an opportunity in Cyprus, then you should take it.'

'Fuck the opportunity!' She felt close to tears, and swallowed hard. 'What about you and me? What about that opportunity?'

'There's something I need to tell you,' said Ralph abruptly. 'There's something which will . . . make a difference to you and me.' He stood up, walked to the window, then, after a long pause, turned round. 'I'm planning to retire, Roxanne,' he said without smiling. 'To the country. I want to spend more time with my family.'

Roxanne stared at his straight brown eyes. At first she didn't comprehend what he was saying. Then, as his meaning hit her, she felt a stabbing pain in her chest.

'You mean it's over,' she whispered, her mouth suddenly dry. 'You mean you've had your fun. And now you're off to . . . to play happy families.'

There was silence.

'If you want to put it that way,' said Ralph eventually, 'then yes.' He met her eye, then looked away quickly.

'No,' said Roxanne, feeling her whole body starting to shake. 'No. I won't let you. You can't.' She flashed a

151

desperate smile at him. 'It can't be over. Not just like that.'

'You'll go to Cyprus,' said Ralph, a slight tremor in his voice. 'You'll go to Cyprus and you'll make a wonderful new life for yourself. Away from all . . . all this.' He lifted a hand to his brow and rubbed it. 'It's for the best, Roxanne.'

'You don't want me to go to Cyprus. You don't mean it. Tell me you don't mean it.' She felt out of control, almost dizzy. In a minute she would start grovelling on the floor. 'You're joking.' She swallowed. 'Are you joking?'

'No, Roxanne. I'm not joking.'

'But you love me!' Her smile grew even wider; tears began to drip down her cheeks. 'You love me, Ralph.'

'Yes,' said Ralph in a suddenly choked voice. 'I do. I love you, Roxanne. Remember that.'

He stepped forward, took her hands and squeezed them hard against his lips. Then, without saying anything he turned, picked up his coat from the sofa and left.

Through a sea of pain, Roxanne watched him go; heard the front door shut. For a second she was silent, white-faced, quivering slightly, as though waiting to vomit. Then with a trembling hand she reached for a cushion, held it up to her face with both hands and screamed silently into it.

Chapter Eleven

Maggie leaned against a fence and closed her eyes, breathing in the clean country air. It was mid-morning, the sky was bright blue and there was a feel of summer about the air. In her previous life, she thought, she would have felt uplifted by the weather. She would have felt energized. But today, standing in her own fields, with her baby asleep in the pram beside her, all she could feel was exhausted.

She felt pale and drained through lack of sleep; edgy and constantly on the verge of tears. Lucia was waking every two hours, demanding to be fed. She could not breastfeed her in bed, because Giles, with his demanding job, needed to sleep. And so she seemed to be spending the whole night sitting in the rocking chair in the nursery, falling into a doze as Lucia fed, then waking with a start as the baby began to wail again. As the greyness of morning approached, she would rouse herself, pad blearily into the bedroom, holding Lucia in her arms.

'Good morning!' Giles would say, beaming sleepily from the big double bed. 'How are my girls?'

'Fine,' Maggie said every morning, without elaborating. For what was the point? It wasn't as if Giles could feed Lucia; it wasn't as if he could make her sleep. And she felt a certain dogged triumph at her own refusal to complain; at her ability to smile and tell Giles that everything was going wonderfully, and see him believe her. She had heard him on the phone, telling his friends, in tones of pride, that Maggie had taken to motherhood like a duck to water. Then he would come and kiss her warmly and say that everyone was amazed at how competent she was; at how everything had fallen into place so quickly. 'Mother of the Year!' he said one evening. 'I told you so!' His delight in her was transparent. She couldn't spoil it all now.

So she would simply hand Lucia to him and sink into the warm comfort of the bed, almost wanting to cry in relief. Those half-hours every morning were her salvation. She would watch Giles playing with Lucia and meet his eyes over the little downy head, and feel a warm glow creep over her; a love so strong, it was almost painful.

Then Giles would get dressed and kiss them both, and go off to work, and the rest of the day would be hers. Hours and hours, with nothing to do but look after one small baby. It sounded laughably easy.

So why was she so tired? Why did every simple task seem so mountainous? She felt as if she would never shift the fog of exhaustion that had descended on her. She would never regain her former energy, nor her sense of humour. Things that would have seemed mildly irritating before the birth now reduced her to tears; minor hitches that would once have made her laugh now made her panic.

The day before, she had taken all morning to get herself and Lucia dressed and off in the car to the supermarket. She had stopped halfway to feed Lucia in the Ladies', then had resumed and joined the queue – at which point Lucia had begun to wail. Maggie had flushed red as faces had begun to turn, and tried to soothe Lucia as discreetly as she could. But Lucia's cries had grown louder and louder until it seemed the whole shop was looking at her. Finally the woman in front had turned round and said knowledgeably, 'He's hungry, poor little pet.'

To her own horror, Maggie had heard herself snapping, 'It's a she! And she's not! I've just fed her!' Almost in tears, she had grabbed Lucia from the trolley and run out of the shop, leaving a trail of astonished glances behind her.

Now, remembering the incident, she felt cold with misery. How competent a mother could she be if she couldn't even manage a simple shopping trip? She saw other mothers coolly walking along the streets, chatting unconcernedly to their friends; sitting in cafés with their babies quietly sleeping beside them. How could they be so relaxed? She herself would never dare enter a café for fear that Lucia would start screaming: for fear of those irritated, judgmental glances from those trying to enjoy a quiet coffee. The sorts of glances she had always given mothers with squalling babies.

A memory of her old life rose in her mind – so tantalizing it made her want to sink down on the ground and weep. And immediately, as if on cue, Lucia began to cry; a small, plaintive cry, almost lost in the wind. Maggie opened her eyes and felt the familiar weariness steal over her. That piercing little cry dogged her every hour: she heard it in her dreams, heard it in the whine of the electric kettle, heard it in the running of the taps when she attempted to take a bath. She could not escape it.

'OK, my precious,' she said aloud, smiling down into the pram. 'Let's get you back inside.'

It was Giles who had suggested that she take Lucia outside for a walk that morning, and, seeing the cloudless blue sky outside, she had thought it a good idea. But now, pushing the pram back through resistant layers of thick mud, the countryside seemed nothing but a battleground. What was so superior about manure-scented air, anyway? she thought, shoving at the pram as it got stuck in a patch of brambles. Inside, Lucia began to wail even more piteously at the unaccustomed jolting movement.

'Sorry!' said Maggie breathlessly. She gave one final push, freeing the wheel, and began to march more quickly towards the house. By the time she arrived at the back door, her face was drenched in sweat.

'Right,' she said, taking Lucia out of the pram. 'Let's get you changed, and feed you.'

Did talking to a four-week-old baby count as talking to oneself? she wondered as she sped upstairs. Was she going mad? Lucia was wailing more and more lustily, and she found herself running along the corridor to the nursery. She placed Lucia on the changing table, unbuttoned her snow suit and winced. Lucia's little sleeping suit was sodden.

'OK,' she crooned. 'Just going to change you . . .' She pulled at the snowsuit and quickly unbuttoned the sleeping suit, cursing her fumbling fingers. Lucia's wails were becoming louder and louder, faster and faster, with a little catch of breath in between. Tears appeared at the tiny creases of her eyes, and Maggie felt her own face flush scarlet with distress.

'I've just got to change you, Lucia,' she said, trying to stay calm. She quickly pulled apart Lucia's wet nappy, threw it on the floor and reached for another one. But the shelf was empty. A jolt of panic went through her. Where were the nappies? Suddenly she remembered taking the last one off the shelf before setting off for her walk; promising herself to open the box and restock the shelf. But of course, she hadn't.

'OK,' she said, pushing her hair back off her face. 'OK, keep calm.' She lifted Lucia off the changing table and placed her on the safety of the floor. Lucia's screams became incomparably loud. The noise seemed to drive through Maggie's head like a drill.

'Lucia, please!' she said, feeling her voice rise dangerously. 'I'm just getting you a new nappy, OK? I'll be as quick as I can!'

She ran down the corridor to the bedroom, where she had dumped the new box of nappies, and began to rip hastily at the cardboard. At last she managed to get the box open – to find the nappies snugly encased in plastic cocoons.

'Oh God!' she said aloud, and began to claw frenziedly at the plastic, feeling like a contestant on some hideous Japanese game of endurance. Eventually her fingers closed over a nappy and she pulled it out, panting slightly. She ran back down the corridor to find Lucia in wailing paroxysms.

'OK, I'm coming,' said Maggie breathlessly. 'Just let me put your nappy on.' She bent down over Lucia and fastened the nappy around her as quickly as she could – then, with the baby in one arm, scrambled to the rocking chair in the corner. Every second seemed to count, with the noise of Lucia growing louder and louder in her ears. She reached with one hand under her jumper to unfasten her bra, but the catch was stuck. With a tiny scream of frustration, she placed Lucia on her lap and reached with the other hand inside her jumper as well, trying to free the catch; trying to stay calm. Lucia's screams were getting higher and higher, faster and faster, as though the frequency on the record had been turned up.

'I'm coming!' cried Maggie, jiggling hopelessly at the catch. 'I'm coming as quick as I can, OK!' Her voice rose to a shout. 'Lucia, be quiet! Please be quiet! I'm coming!'

'There's no need to scream at her, dear,' came a voice from the door.

Maggie's head jerked up in fright – and as she saw who it was, she felt her face drain of colour. There, watching her, lips tight with disapproval, was Paddy Drakeford.

*   *   *

Candice stood, holding a cup of coffee, peering at her computer screen over the shoulder of the computer engineer and trying to look intelligent.

'Hmm,' said the engineer eventually, and looked up. 'Have you ever had any virus screening programs installed?'

'Ahm . . . I'm not sure,' said Candice, and flushed at his glance. 'Do you think that's what it is, a virus?'

'Hard to tell,' said the engineer, and punched a few keys. Candice surreptitiously looked at her watch. It was already eleven-thirty. She had called out a computer engineer believing he would fix her machine in a matter of minutes, but he had arrived an hour ago, started tapping and now looked like he was settled in for the day. She had already called Justin, telling him she would be late, and he had 'Hmm'd' with disapproval.

'By the way, Heather says, can you bring in her blue folder,' he'd added. 'Do you want to have a word with her? She's right here.'

'No, I've . . . I've got to go,' Candice had said hastily. She had put down the phone, exhaled with relief, and sat down, her heart thudding slightly. This was getting ridiculous. She had to sort her own mind out; to rid herself of the tendrils of doubt that were growing inside her over Heather.

Outwardly, she and Heather were as friendly as ever. But inside, Candice had started to wonder. Were the others right? Was Heather using her? She had still paid no rent, neither had she offered to. She had barely thanked Candice for doing that large amount of work for her. And she had – Candice swallowed – she had blatantly stolen Candice's late-night shopping feature idea and presented it as her own.

A familiar twinge went through Candice's stomach and she closed her eyes. She knew that she should

158

confront Heather on the matter. She should bring the subject up, pleasantly and firmly, and listen to what Heather had to say. Perhaps, reasoned a part of her brain, it had all been a misunderstanding. Perhaps Heather simply hadn't realized that it wasn't done to take credit for someone else's idea. It was no big deal – all she had to do was mention it to Heather and see what the response was.

But she couldn't quite bring herself to. The thought of appearing to accuse Heather – of perhaps descending into an argument over it – filled her with horror. Things had been going so well between them – was it really worth risking a scene just over one little idea?

And so for more than a week she had said nothing, and had tried to forget about it. But there was a bad feeling inside her stomach which would not go away.

'Do you ever download from the Internet?' said the computer engineer.

'No,' said Candice, opening her eyes. Then she thought for a second. 'Actually, yes. I tried to once, but it didn't really work. Does that matter?'

The engineer sighed, and she bit her lip, feeling foolish. Suddenly the door bell rang, and she breathed out in relief.

'Excuse me,' she said. 'I'll be back in a minute.'

Standing in the hall was Ed, wearing an old T-shirt, shorts and espadrilles.

'So,' he said with no preamble. 'Tell me about your flat-mate.'

'There's nothing to tell,' said Candice, flushing defensively in spite of herself. 'She's just . . . living with me. Like flat-mates do.'

'I know that. But where's she from? What's she like?' Ed sniffed past Candice. 'Is that coffee?'

'Yes.'

'Your flat always smells so nice,' said Ed. 'Like a

coffee shop. Mine smells like a shit-heap.'

'Do you ever clean it?'

'Some woman does.' He leaned further into the flat and sniffed longingly. 'Come on, Candice. Give me some coffee.'

'Oh, all right,' said Candice. 'Come in.' At least it would be an excuse not to return to the computer engineer.

'I saw your friend leaving this morning without you,' said Ed, following her into the kitchen, 'and I thought – aha. Coffee time.'

'Don't you have any plans today?' said Candice. 'Properties to visit? Daytime TV to watch?'

'Don't rub it in!' said Ed. He reached for the salt cellar and tapped it on his palm. 'This bloody gardening leave is driving me nuts.'

'What's wrong?' said Candice unsympathetically.

'I'm bored!' He turned the salt cellar upside down and wrote 'Ed' in salt on the table. 'Bored, bored, bored.'

'You obviously don't have any inner resources,' said Candice, taking the salt cellar from his fingers.

'No,' said Ed. 'Not a one. I went to a museum yesterday. A *museum*. Can you believe it?'

'Which one?' said Candice.

'I dunno,' said Ed. 'One with squashy chairs.' Candice gazed at him for a moment, then rolled her eyes and turned away to fill the kettle. Ed grinned, and began to mooch about the kitchen.

'So, who's this kid?' he said, looking at a photograph tacked up on the pinboard.

'That's the Cambodian child I sponsor,' said Candice, reaching for the coffee.

'What's his name?'

'Pin Fu. Ju,' she corrected herself. 'Pin Ju.'

'Do you send him Christmas presents?'

'No. It's not considered helpful.' Candice shook

160

coffee into the cafetière. 'Anyway, he doesn't want some Western tat.'

'I bet he does,' said Ed. 'He's probably dying for a Darth Vader. Have you ever met him?'

'No.'

'Have you ever spoken to him on the phone?'

'No. Don't be stupid.'

'So how you do you know he exists?'

'What?' Candice looked up. 'Of course he exists! There he is.' She pointed at the photograph and Ed grinned wickedly at her.

'You're very trusting, aren't you? How do you know they aren't sending all you saps the same picture? Call him a different name each time; hive off the money for themselves. Does Pin Ju send you a personal receipt?'

Candice rolled her eyes dismissively. Sometimes Ed wasn't even worth responding to. She poured hot water into the cafetière and a delicious smell filled the kitchen.

'So, you haven't told me about Heather,' said Ed, sitting down. At the name, Candice felt a spasm inside her stomach, and looked away.

'What about her?'

'How do you know her?'

'She's . . . an old friend,' said Candice.

'Oh yeah? Well, if she's such an old friend, how come I never saw her before she moved in?' Ed leaned forward with an inquisitive gaze. 'How come you never even mentioned her?'

'Because . . . we lost touch, all right?' said Candice, feeling rattled. 'Why are so you interested, anyway?'

'I don't know,' said Ed. 'There's something about her that intrigues me.'

'Well, if she intrigues you so much, why don't you ask her out?' said Candice curtly.

'Maybe I will,' said Ed, grinning.

There was a sharp silence in the kitchen. Candice

handed Ed his cup of coffee and he took a sip. 'You wouldn't mind, would you, Candice?' he added, eyes gleaming slightly.

'Of course not!' said Candice at once, and shook her hair back. 'Why should I mind?'

'Ahem.' The voice of the computer engineer interrupted them, and they both looked up.

'Hi,' said Candice. 'Have you found out what's wrong?'

'A virus,' said the engineer, pulling a face. 'It's got into everything, I'm afraid.'

'Oh,' said Candice in dismay. 'Well – can you catch it?'

'Oh, it's already long gone,' said the engineer. 'These viruses are very slick. In and out before you know it. All I can do now is try to repair the damage it's left behind.' He shook his head reprovingly. 'And in future, Miss Brewin, I suggest you try to protect yourself a little better.'

Maggie sat at her kitchen table, stiff with humiliation. At the Aga, Paddy lifted the kettle and poured scalding water into the teapot, then turned round and glanced at the Moses basket by the window.

'She seems to be sleeping nicely now. I expect all that screaming wore her out.'

The implied criticism was obvious, and Maggie flushed. She couldn't bear to look Paddy in the eye; couldn't bear to see that disapproving look again. You try! she wanted to scream. You try keeping calm after nights and nights of no sleep. But instead she stared silently down at the table, tracing the pattern of the wood round and round with her finger. Just keep going, she told herself, and clenched her other hand in her lap. Keep going till she's gone.

After arriving on the scene in the nursery, Paddy had left her alone to breastfeed and she had sat in misery, feeling like a punished child. She arrived downstairs, holding Lucia, to find that Paddy had tidied the kitchen, stacked the dishwasher and even mopped the floor. She knew she should have felt grateful – but instead she felt reproved. A good mother would never have let her kitchen descend into such a sordid state. A good mother would never have gone out without wiping down the kitchen surfaces.

'Here you are,' said Paddy, bringing a cup of tea over to the table. 'Would you like some sugar in it?'

'No thanks,' said Maggie, still staring downwards. 'I'm trying to keep tabs on my weight.'

'Really?' Paddy paused, teapot in hand. 'I found I needed to eat twice as much when I breastfed, otherwise the boys would have gone hungry.' She gave a short little laugh and Maggie felt a spasm of irrational hatred for her. What was she saying now? That she wasn't feeding Lucia properly? That there was something inferior about her breast milk? A hot lump suddenly appeared in her throat and she swallowed hard.

'And how are the nights going?' said Paddy.

'Fine,' said Maggie shortly, and took a sip of tea.

'Is Lucia settling into a routine?'

'Not particularly,' said Maggie. 'But actually, these days they don't recommend bullying babies into routines.' She looked up and met Paddy's gaze square-on. 'They recommend feeding by demand and letting the baby settle into its own pattern.'

'I see,' said Paddy, and gave another short laugh. 'It's all changed since my day.'

Maggie took another gulp of tea and stared fixedly out of the window.

'It's a shame your parents couldn't visit for a little longer,' said Paddy. A spasm of pain went through Maggie and she blinked hard. Did the woman have to twist *every* knife? Her parents had visited for two days

163

while Maggie was in hospital – then, reluctantly, had had to leave. Both still worked, after all – and the drive from Derbyshire to Hampshire was a long one. Maggie had smiled brightly as they'd left, had promised she would be all right and would visit soon. But in truth their parting had hit her harder than she'd expected. The thought of her mother's kindly face could still sometimes reduce her to tears. And here was Paddy, reminding her of the fact.

'Yes, well,' she said, without moving her head, 'they're busy people.'

'I expect they are.' Paddy took a sip of tea and reached into the tin for a biscuit. 'Maggie—'

'What?' Reluctantly, Maggie turned her head.

'Have you thought about having any help with the baby? A nanny, for example.'

Maggie stared at her, feeling as though she'd been hit in the face. So Paddy really did think she was an unfit mother; that she couldn't care for her own child without paid help.

'No,' she said, giving a laugh that was nearer tears. 'Why, do you think I should?'

'It's up to you,' said Paddy, 'of course—'

'I'd rather look after my child myself,' said Maggie in a trembling voice. 'I may not do it perfectly, but . . .'

'Maggie!' said Paddy. 'Of course I didn't mean—' She broke off, and Maggie looked stiffly away. There was silence in the kitchen, broken only by Lucia's sleeping snuffles.

'Perhaps I should go,' said Paddy eventually. 'I don't want to get in your way.'

'OK,' said Maggie, giving a tiny shrug.

She watched as Paddy gathered her things together, shooting Maggie the odd anxious glance.

'You know where I am,' she said. 'Bye bye, dear.'

'Bye,' said Maggie, with careless indifference.

She waited as Paddy walked out of the kitchen and

164

let herself out of the front door; waited as the car engine started and the gravel crackled under the wheels. And then, when the car had disappeared completely and she could hear nothing more, she burst into sobs.

Chapter Twelve

Roxanne sat on a wooden bench, her shoulders
hunched and her face muffled in a scarf, staring across
the road at Ralph Allsopp's London home. It was a
narrow house in a quiet Kensington square with black
railings and a blue front door. A house that she'd seen
the outside of too many times to count; a house that
she'd cursed and wept at and stared at for hours – and
never once stepped inside.

At the beginning, years ago, she had secretly used to
come and sit outside the house for hours. She would
station herself in the square garden with a book and
stare at the façade behind which Ralph and his family
lived, as though trying to memorize each brick; each
stone in the path, wondering if today she would catch
a glimpse of her, or of him, or of any of them.

For at that time, Cynthia had still spent most of her
time in London – and Roxanne had quite often seen
her coming up or down the steps with Sebastian, both
dressed in exemplary navy blue overcoats. (From
Harrods, probably, judging by the number of times
Harrods delivery vans arrived at the front door.) The
front door would open, and Roxanne would stiffen,
and put down her book. Then Cynthia would appear.
Cynthia Allsopp, with her elegant, oblivious face. And
her little son Sebastian, with his innocent Christopher

Robin haircut. Roxanne would sit and stare at them as they came down the steps and got into the car or walked off briskly down the road. She would take in every new addition to Cynthia's wardrobe, every new hairstyle, every overheard word, every possible detail. The sight never failed to appal her; to fascinate her – and, ultimately, to depress her. Because Cynthia was his wife. That elegant, soulless woman was his wife. And she, Roxanne, was his mistress. His tawdry, tacky mistress. That initial excitement of seeing them – the feeling of power, almost – had always given way to a kind of emptiness; a black, destructive devastation.

And yet she'd been unable to stop coming back – unable to resist the draw of that blue front door – until the heart-stopping day when Ralph had come down the steps, holding a box full of books, glanced towards the garden square, and had seen her. She'd immediately hunched down, heart pounding, praying that he wouldn't give her away; that he would remain cool. To his credit, he had done. But he had not been cool on the phone that evening. He had been angry – more angry than she'd ever known him. She'd pleaded with him, reasoned with him; promised never to set foot in the square again. And she'd kept that promise.

But now she was breaking it. Now she didn't give a fuck who saw her. Now she *wanted* to be seen. She reached into her pocket for her cigarettes and took out her lighter. The irony was, of course, that now, years later, it didn't matter. The windows were dim; the house was empty. Cynthia didn't even live in the bloody house now. She'd decamped to the country manor, and only came up for the Harrods sale. And Sebastian rode his little ponies, and everyone was happy. And that was the life Ralph was choosing over her.

Roxanne inhaled deeply on her cigarette and exhaled with a shudder. She wasn't going to cry any more. She'd ruined enough fucking make-up already. For the past two weeks, she'd sat at home, drinking vodka and wearing the same pair of leggings every day, and staring out of her window, sometimes crying, sometimes shaking, sometimes silent. She'd left the answer machine on and listened to messages mount up like dead flies – irrelevant, stupid messages from people she couldn't be interested in. One, from Justin, had been to invite her to Ralph's retirement drinks party – and she'd felt a pain shoot through her like an electric shock. He was really doing it, she'd thought, tears welling up yet again. He was really fucking doing it.

Candice had left countless messages, and so had Maggie – and she had almost been tempted to phone back. Of all people, those were the ones she'd wanted to talk to. She'd even picked up the receiver once and begun to dial Candice's number. And then she had stopped, shaking in terror, unable to think of what she would say; how she would even start. How she would halt the flow once she'd begun. It was too big a secret. Easier – so much easier – to say nothing. She'd had six years' practice, after all.

They, of course, had assumed she was abroad. 'Or perhaps you're with Mr Married,' Maggie had said on one of her messages, and Roxanne had actually found herself half laughing, half crying. Dear Maggie. If she only knew. 'But we'll see you on the first,' Maggie had continued anxiously. 'You will be there, won't you?'

Roxanne looked at her watch. It was the first of the month. It was six o'clock. In half an hour's time they would be there. The two faces – at this moment – dearest to her in the world. She stubbed out her cigarette, stood up and faced Ralph Allsopp's house square-on.

'Fuck you,' she said out loud. 'Fuck you!' Then she turned and strode away, her heels clicking loudly on the wet pavement.

Ralph Allsopp lifted his head from the chair he was sitting in and looked towards the window. Outside, the sky was beginning to darken, and the street lights of the square were beginning to come on. He reached for a lamp and switched it on, and immediately the dim room brightened.

'Is there a problem?' said Neil Cooper, glancing up from his papers.

'No,' said Ralph. 'I just thought I heard something. Probably nothing.' He smiled. 'Carry on.'

'Yes,' said Neil Cooper. He was a young man, with a severe haircut and a rather nervous manner. 'Well, as I was explaining, I think your easiest option, in this instance, is to add a short codicil to the will.'

'I see,' said Ralph. He stared at the panes of the window, wet with London rain. Wills, he thought, were like family life itself. They started off small and simple – then expanded over the years with marriage and children; grew even more complex with infidelity; with accumulated wealth; with divided loyalties. His own will was now the size of a small book. A conventional family saga.

But his life had not been a mere conventional family saga.

'A romance,' he said aloud.

'I'm sorry?' said Neil Cooper.

'Nothing,' said Ralph, shaking his head as though to clear it. 'A codicil. Yes. And can I draw that up now?'

'Absolutely,' said the lawyer, and clicked his pen expectantly. 'If you give me, first of all, the name of the beneficiary?'

There was silence. Ralph closed his eyes, then opened them and exhaled sharply.

'The beneficiary's name is Roxanne,' he said, and his hand tightened slightly around the arm of his chair. 'Miss Roxanne Miller.'

Maggie sat at a plastic table in a Waterloo café and took another sip of tea. Her train had arrived in London an hour ago, and originally she had thought she might take the opportunity to go shopping. But, having made her way off the train, the very thought of shops and crowds had exhausted her. Instead, she had come in here and ordered a pot of tea and had sat, immobile, ever since. She felt shell-shocked by the effort it had taken to get herself here; could scarcely believe she had once made that long journey every single day.

She picked up the glossy magazine she'd bought at a kiosk, then put it down, unable to focus. She felt light-headed; almost high with fatigue. Lucia had been awake for most of the night before, with what she could only suppose was colic. She had paced up and down the bedroom furthest from Giles, trying to soothe the baby's cries, eyes half shut, almost sleeping on her feet. Then Giles had left for work, and instead of crawling back into bed, she had spent the entire remainder of the day preparing for her evening out. An occasion which, once upon a time, would have required no thought whatsoever.

She had decided to wash her hair, hoping the blast of the shower would wake her up. Lucia had woken up as she had started to dry it and she had been forced to carry on whilst simultaneously rocking Lucia's bouncy chair with her foot. For once, the situation had struck her as comical, and she had made up her mind to tell the other two about it that evening. Then she had opened her wardrobe, wondering what to wear – and her spirits had immediately sunk. She still fitted into none of her pre-pregnancy clothes. A whole wardrobe of designer clothes was hanging in front of her – and they might as well not have existed.

It had been her own decision not to buy any new

clothes in her larger size, as Giles had suggested. For one thing, it would be admitting defeat – and for another, she had seriously believed that within a month or so she would be slim again. Her handbook had assured her that she would lose weight from breastfeeding, and she had taken this to mean that within a few weeks she would be back to normal.

Seven weeks after the birth, however, she was still nowhere near. Her stomach was flabby, her hips were huge, and her breasts, full of milk, were even vaster than they had been during pregnancy. As she'd stared at herself in the mirror – large, dumpy and pale-faced with fatigue – she'd suddenly felt like cancelling the whole thing. How could she walk into the Manhattan Bar looking like that? People would laugh at her. She sank down onto the bed and buried her head in her hands, feeling easy tears rising.

But after a while, she looked up, and wiped her face and told herself not to be silly. She wasn't going up to London to pose. She was going to be with her two best friends. They wouldn't care what she looked like. Taking a deep breath, she stood up and approached her wardrobe again. Averting her eyes from all her old clothes, she assembled a well-worn outfit in unadventurous black, and placed it on the bed, ready to put on at the last moment. She didn't want to risk any spillages from Lucia.

At two o'clock, Paddy rang the doorbell and Maggie let her in with a polite greeting. Ever since that day when Paddy had interrupted her, there had been a certain distance between them. They were courteous to one another but nothing more. Paddy had offered to babysit for Maggie's evening out, and Maggie had politely accepted – but no warmth of feeling had flowered between them.

As Paddy came into the house she scanned Maggie's face with a frown, then said, 'My dear, you look very tired. Are you sure you want to go all the way up to London, just for a few cocktails?'

Count to ten, Maggie told herself. Count to ten. Don't snap.

'Yes,' she said eventually, and forced herself to smile. 'It's . . . it's quite important to me. Old friends.'

'Well, you look to me as if you'd do better with an early night,' said Paddy, and yet again gave that short little laugh. Immediately, Maggie had felt herself tense up all over.

'It's very kind of you to babysit,' she'd said, staring fixedly at the banisters. 'I do appreciate it.'

'Oh, it's no trouble!' Paddy had said at once. 'Anything I can do to help.'

'Right.' Maggie had taken a deep breath, trying to stay calm; to be pleasant. 'Well, let me just explain. The expressed milk is in bottles in the fridge. It needs to be warmed up in a saucepan. I've left it all in the kitchen for you. If she cries, she might need her colic drops. They're on the—'

'Maggie.' Paddy had lifted her hand with a little smile. 'Maggie, I've raised three children of my own. I'm sure I can manage little Lucia.'

Maggie had stared back, feeling snubbed; wanting to make some retort, but unable to.

'Fine,' she'd said at last, in a trembling voice. 'I'll just get ready.' And she'd run upstairs, suddenly not wanting to go to London at all. Wanting to tell Paddy to go away and to spend the evening alone, rocking her baby.

Of course she had done nothing of the sort. She had brushed her hair, put on her coat, imagining that she could already hear Lucia crying; telling herself not to be so foolish. But as she had come downstairs, the crying had got louder. She had run into the kitchen and felt her heart stop as she saw a wailing Lucia being comforted in Paddy's no-nonsense arms.

'What's wrong?' she'd heard herself say breathlessly as the doorbell rang.

'Nothing's wrong!' Paddy had said, laughing a little. 'That'll be your taxi. Now you go off and have a nice time. Lucia will calm down in a minute.'

Maggie had stood, stricken, staring at her daughter's red, crumpled face.

'Maybe I'll just take her for a moment—' she'd begun.

'Honestly, dear, she'll be fine! No point hanging about and confusing her. We'll go for a nice walk around the house in a moment, won't we, Lucia? Look, she's cheering up already!'

And sure enough, Lucia's cries had tailed off into silence. She gave a huge yawn and stared at Maggie with blue, teary eyes.

'Just go,' Paddy had said gently. 'While she's quiet.'

'OK,' Maggie had said numbly. 'OK, I'll go.'

Somehow she'd made herself walk out of the kitchen, through the hall to the front door. As she'd closed it behind her she'd thought she could hear Lucia sobbing again. But she hadn't gone back. She'd forced herself to keep going, to get in the taxi and ask for the station; she'd even managed to smile brightly at the ticket officer as she'd bought her ticket. It was only as the train to Waterloo pulled out of the station that tears had begun to fall down her cheeks, ruining her carefully applied make-up and falling on the pages of her glossy magazine.

Now she rested her head in her palms, listening to the railway Tannoy in the distance, and thought, with disbelief, how much things had changed in her life. There was no point even attempting to convey to Candice and Roxanne quite how much physical and emotional effort it had taken for her to be here this evening. No-one who was not herself a mother would comprehend; would believe what she had gone through. And so, in some way, that meant they would

173

never quite understand how highly she prized their friendship. How important their little threesome was to her.

Maggie sighed, and reached into her bag for a compact to check her reflection, wincing at the dark shadows under her eyes. Tonight, she decided, she would have as much fun as she possibly could. Tonight would make up for it all. Tonight she would talk and laugh with her dearest friends, and return – perhaps – to something like her former self.

Candice stood in front of the mirror in the Ladies', applying her make-up for the evening. Her hand shook slightly as she applied her mascara, and her face looked gaunt in the bright overhead light. She should have been looking forward to the evening out – a chance to see Maggie and Roxanne again; a chance to relax. But she felt unable to relax while she was still so confused about Heather. Another week had gone by, and still she had said nothing. She had not mentioned any of the matters troubling her, and neither had Heather. And so the unresolved situation remained and the niggling feeling remained in her stomach.

On the surface, of course, she and Heather were still the best of friends. She was sure that Heather suspected nothing was amiss – and certainly nobody else at the office had picked anything up. But Maggie and Roxanne were sharper than that. They would see the tension in her face; they would realize that something was wrong. They would quiz her until she admitted the truth – and then berate her for having ignored their advice. Half of her wanted to duck out of the meeting altogether.

The door opened, and she looked up to see Heather coming in, dressed smartly in a violet-coloured suit.

'Hi, Heather,' she said, and flashed an automatic little smile.

'Candice.' Heather's voice was full of distress. 'Candice, you must hate me. I feel so awful!'

'What about?' said Candice, half laughing. 'What are you talking about?'

'About your idea, of course!' said Heather, and looked at her with earnest grey eyes. 'Your late-night shopping feature!'

Candice stared at her and felt a thud of shock. She pushed back her hair and swallowed.

'Wh-what do you mean?' she said, playing for time.

'I've just seen the features list for July. Justin's put down that feature as though it was my idea.' Heather took hold of Candice's hands and grasped them tightly. 'Candice, I told him it was your idea in the first place. I don't know where he got the thought that it was mine.'

'Really?' Candice gazed at Heather, her heart thumping.

'I shouldn't even have said anything about it,' said Heather apologetically. 'But I just happened to mention it over a cup of coffee, and Justin got really enthusiastic. I told him it was your idea – but he can't have been listening.'

'I see,' said Candice. She felt hot with shame; with a drenching guilt. How could she have doubted Heather so readily? How could she have leapt to the wrong conclusion without even checking the facts. It was Maggie and Roxanne, she thought with a sudden flicker of resentment. They'd turned her against Heather

'You know, I could tell something was wrong,' said Heather, blinking a little. 'I could tell there was bad feeling between us. But I had no idea what it was. I thought maybe I'd done something in the flat to annoy you, or you were just getting tired of me . . . And then I saw the list and I realized.' Heather met Candice's eyes steadily. 'You thought I'd stolen your idea, didn't you?'

'No!' said Candice at once, then flushed. 'Well, maybe . . .' She bit her lip. 'I didn't know what to think.'

'You have to believe me, Candice. I would never do that to you. Never!' Heather leaned forward and hugged Candice. 'You've done everything for me. I owe you so much . . .' When she pulled away, her eyes were glistening slightly, and Candice felt her own eyes well up in sympathy.

'I feel so ashamed,' she whispered. 'I should never have suspected you. I might have known it was bloody Justin's fault!' She gave a shaky laugh and Heather grinned back.

'Let's go out tonight,' she said. 'Friends again.'

'Oh, that would be great,' said Candice. She wiped her eyes, and grinned ruefully at her smeared reflection. 'But I'm meeting the others at the Manhattan Bar.'

'Oh well,' said Heather lightly. 'Another time, perhaps . . .'

'No, listen,' said Candice, seized by a sudden fierce affection for Heather. 'Come with us. Come and join the gang.'

'Really?' said Heather cautiously. 'You don't think the others would mind?'

'Of course not! You're my friend – so you're their friend too.'

'I'm not sure about that,' said Heather. 'Roxanne—'

'Roxanne loves you! Honestly, Heather.' Candice met her gaze. 'Please come. It would mean a lot to me.' Heather pulled a doubtful face.

'Candice, are you sure about this?'

'Of course!' Candice gave Heather an impetuous hug. 'They'll love to see you.'

'OK.' Heather beamed. 'I'll see you downstairs, shall I? In about . . . fifteen minutes?'

'Fine,' smiled Candice. 'See you then.'

Heather stepped out of the Ladies' and looked around. Then she headed straight for Justin's office and knocked.

176

'Yes?' he said.

'I wondered if I could see you for a moment,' said Heather.

'Oh yes?' Justin smiled. 'Any more wonderful ideas for the magazine?'

'No, not this time.' Heather pushed back her hair and bit her lip. 'Actually . . . it's a bit of an awkward matter.'

'Oh,' said Justin in surprise, and gestured to a chair. 'Well, come on in.'

'I don't want to make a fuss,' said Heather apologetically, sitting down. 'In fact, I'm embarrassed even mentioning it. But I had to talk to somebody . . .' She rubbed her nose and gave a little sniff.

'My dear girl!' said Justin. 'What's wrong?' He got up from his chair, walked round behind Heather and shut the door. Then he walked back to his desk. Behind him, in the window, the reflected lights of the office shone back: a curved series of bright lozenges against the darkness.

'If you've got any kind of problem, I want to know,' said Justin, leaning back. 'Whatever it is.' He picked up a pencil and held it between his two hands, as though measuring something. 'That's what I'm here for.'

There was silence in the little office.

'Can this remain completely confidential?' said Heather at last.

'Of course!' said Justin. 'Whatever you say will remain between these four walls – ' he gestured ' – and our two selves.'

'Well . . . OK,' said Heather doubtfully. 'If you're absolutely sure . . .' She took a deep shuddering breath, pushed back her hair again and looked up beseechingly at Justin. 'It's about Candice.'

Chapter Thirteen

The Manhattan Bar was holding a Hollywood Legends night, and the glass door was opened for Maggie by a beaming Marilyn Monroe lookalike. Maggie walked into the foyer a few paces, staring at the vibrant scene before her, then closed her eyes and let the atmosphere just pour over her for a second. The buzz of people chatting, the jazzy music in the background, the scent of sizzling swordfish steaks, of cigarette smoke and designer fragrances wafting past. Snatches of over-heard conversation, a sudden shriek of laughter – and filtering through her closed eyelids, the brightness, the glitter, the colour. Metropolitan people enjoying themselves. As she opened her eyes, a happiness that was almost tearful began to well up inside her. She had not realized quite how much she'd missed it all. After the silence and mud of the fields, after the constant weary-ing wailing of Lucia, this warm noisy bar was like coming home.

She surrendered her coat to the coat check, took her silver button and turned towards the throng. At first she thought she must be the first to arrive. But then, suddenly, she spotted Roxanne. She was sitting alone at a table in the corner, a drink already in front of her. As she turned her head, unaware she was being watched, Maggie's stomach gave a small lurch.

Roxanne looked terrible. Her face was shadowed, her eyes looked bloodshot, and there was a weary downward crease to her mouth. A hangover, Maggie would have thought, or jetlag – had it not been for the expression in Roxanne's eyes. Those bright snappy eyes, usually so full of wit and verve, were tonight dull and unseeing, as though nothing around her interested her. As Maggie watched, Roxanne picked up her glass and took a deep gulp. Whatever was in it was obviously strong, thought Maggie, and she felt a slight pang of alarm.

'Roxanne!' she called, and began to make her way to the table, threading through the crowds of people. 'Roxanne!'

'Maggie!' Roxanne's face lit up and she stood up, holding her arms out. The two women embraced for slightly longer than usual; as Maggie pulled away, she saw that Roxanne's eyes were glistening with tears.

'Roxanne, are you OK?' she said cautiously.

'I'm fine!' said Roxanne at once. She flashed a bright smile and reached into her bag for her cigarettes. 'How are *you*? How's the babe?'

'We're all fine,' said Maggie slowly. She sat down, staring at Roxanne's trembling hands as she scrabbled for her lighter.

'And Giles? How's he enjoying being a father?'

'Oh, he loves it,' said Maggie drily. 'All ten minutes a day of it.'

'Not exactly a New Man, then, our Giles?' said Roxanne, lighting up.

'You could say that,' said Maggie. 'Roxanne—'

'Yes?'

'Are you OK? Seriously.'

Roxanne looked at her through a cloud of smoke. Her blue eyes were full of pain; she seemed to be struggling to keep control.

179

'I've been better,' she said eventually. 'Thanks for all your messages, by the way. They really kept me going.'

'Kept you going?' Maggie stared at her, aghast. 'Roxanne, what's going on? Where have you been?'

'I haven't been anywhere.' Roxanne gave a wobbly smile and dragged on her cigarette. 'I've been at home, drinking lots of vodka.'

'Roxanne, what the hell's happened?' Maggie's eyes sharpened. 'Is it Mr Married?'

Roxanne looked for a moment at the still-burning end of her cigarette, then stubbed it out with a suddenly vicious movement.

'You know I said watch this space? Well, you needn't have bothered.' She looked up. 'Mr Married is out of the picture. His choice.'

'Oh my God,' whispered Maggie. She reached for Roxanne's hands across the table. 'God, you poor thing. The bastard!'

'Hello there!' A cheery voice interrupted them and they both looked up. Scarlett O'Hara was smiling at them, notebook in hand. 'May I take your order?'

'Not yet,' said Maggie. 'Give us a few minutes.'

'No, wait,' said Roxanne. She drained her glass and gave it to Scarlett. 'I'd like another double vodka and lime.' She smiled at Maggie. 'Vodka is my new best friend.'

'Roxanne—'

'Don't worry! I'm not an alcoholic. I'm an alcohol-lover. There's a difference.'

Scarlett disappeared, and the two friends looked at each other.

'I don't know what to say,' said Maggie, and her hands clenched the table. 'I feel like going over to wherever he lives, and—'

'Don't,' cut in Roxanne. 'It's . . . it's fine, really.' Then, after a pause, she looked up with a glint in her eye. 'What, out of interest?'

'Scraping his car,' said Maggie fiercely. 'That's where it hurts them.' Roxanne threw back her head and roared with laughter.

'God, I've missed you, Maggie.'

'You too,' said Maggie. 'Both of you.' She sighed, and looked around the humming bar. 'I've been looking forward to this evening like a little kid. Counting off the days!'

'I would have thought there was no room in your grand country life for us any more,' said Roxanne, grinning slyly at her. 'Aren't you too busy going to hunt balls and shooting things?' Maggie gave her a wan smile, and Roxanne frowned. 'Seriously, Maggie. Is it all OK? You look pretty beat-up.'

'Thanks a lot.'

'You're welcome.'

'Here you are!' The voice of Scarlett O'Hara interrupted them. 'One double vodka with lime.' She put the glass down and smiled at Maggie. 'And can I get you anything?'

'Oh, I don't know,' said Maggie, picking up the cocktail menu and putting it down again. 'I was going to wait until we were all here.'

'Where is Candice, anyway?' said Roxanne, lighting another cigarette. 'She is definitely coming?'

'I suppose so,' said Maggie. 'Oh, come on, I can't wait any longer.' She looked up at the waitress. 'I'll have a Jamaican Rumba, please.'

'And a Margarita for me,' said Roxanne. 'Can't have you starting on the cocktails without me,' she added, at Maggie's look. As the waitress retreated, she leaned back in her chair and looked appraisingly at Maggie. 'So, come on. What's it like, being Mummy Drakeford of The Pines?'

'Oh, I don't know,' said Maggie, after a pause. She picked up a silver coaster and stared at it, twisting it round and round in her fingers. Part of her yearned to

181

confide in someone. To share her feelings of weariness and loneliness; to describe her deteriorating relationship with Giles's mother; to try and paint a picture of the monotonous drudgery that her life seemed, overnight, to have become. But another part of her couldn't bring herself to admit such defeat, even to such a close friend as Roxanne. She was used to being Maggie Phillips: editor of the *Londoner*, clever and organized and always on top of things. Not Maggie Drakeford, a pale, fatigued, disillusioned mother who couldn't even bring herself to go shopping.

And how could she begin to explain how these feelings of weariness and depression were bound up inextricably with a love; a joy so intense it could leave her feeling faint? How could she describe the wonderment every time she saw the flash of recognition in Lucia's eyes; every time those tiny wrinkled features broke into a smile? How could she convey the fact that during some of her happiest moments she was, nevertheless, in tears of exhaustion?

'It's different,' she said eventually. 'Not quite how I imagined it.'

'But you're enjoying it.' Roxanne's eyes narrowed. 'Aren't you?'

There was silence. Maggie put the coaster down on the table and began to trace circles on it with her finger.

'I'm enjoying it, of course I am,' she began after a while. 'Lucia's wonderful, and . . . and I love her. But at the same time . . .' She broke off and sighed. 'Nobody can have any idea what it's—'

'Look, there's Candice,' interrupted Roxanne. 'Sorry, Maggie. Candice!' She stood up and peered through the throng. 'What's she doing?'

Maggie turned in her seat and followed Roxanne's gaze.

'She's talking to someone,' she said, wrinkling her

brow. 'I can't quite see who . . .' She broke off in dismay. 'Oh no.'

'I don't believe it,' said Roxanne slowly. 'I don't believe it! She's brought that bloody girl.'

As Candice picked her way through the crowd of people to the table where Maggie and Roxanne were sitting, she felt Heather tugging at her sleeve, and turned back.

'What's wrong?' she said, looking at Heather's anxious expression in surprise.

'Look, Candice, I'm not sure about this,' said Heather. 'I'm not sure I'm going to be welcome. Maybe I'd better just go.'

'You can't go!' said Candice. 'Honestly, they'll be delighted to see you. And it'll be nice for you to meet them properly.'

'Well . . . OK,' said Heather after a pause.

'Come on!' Candice smiled at Heather and took her hand, pulling her forward. She felt buoyant tonight; overflowing with good spirits and affection. Towards Heather, towards Maggie and Roxanne; even towards the waitress dressed as Doris Day who crossed their path, forcing them to stop. 'Isn't this fun?' she said, turning to Heather. 'Just think, a few weeks ago it would have been you, dressing up.'

'Until you rescued me from my sad waitressing life,' said Heather, squeezing Candice's hand. 'My own Princess Charming.' Candice laughed, and pushed on through the crowds.

'Hi!' she said, arriving at the table. 'Isn't it busy tonight!'

'Yes,' said Roxanne, looking at Heather. 'Overpopulated, one might say.'

'You remember Heather, don't you?' said Candice cheerfully, looking from Roxanne to Maggie. 'I thought I'd ask her along.'

'Evidently,' muttered Roxanne.

'Of course!' said Maggie brightly. 'Hello, Heather. Nice to see you again.' She hesitated, then moved her chair round to make space at the little table.

'Here's another chair,' said Candice. 'Plenty of room!' She sat down and smiled at her two friends. 'So, how are you both? How's life, Roxanne?'

'Life's just fine,' said Roxanne, after a pause, and took a gulp of her vodka.

'And you, Maggie? And the baby?'

'Yes, fine,' said Maggie. 'Everything's fine.'

'Good!' said Candice.

There was an awkward silence. Maggie glanced at Roxanne, who was sipping her vodka, stony-faced. Candice smiled encouragingly at Heather, who grinned nervously back. Then, in the corner of the bar, the jazz band began to play 'Let's Face the Music' and suddenly a man in top hat and tails appeared, leading a woman in a white Ginger Rogers dress. As the crowd cleared a space for them, the two began to dance, and a round of applause broke out. The noise seemed to bring the group back to life.

'So, are you enjoying working for the *Londoner*, Heather?' said Maggie politely.

'Oh yes,' said Heather. 'It's a great place to work. And Justin's a wonderful editor.' Roxanne's head jerked up.

'That's what you think, is it?'

'Yes!' said Heather. 'I think he's fantastic!' Then she looked at Maggie. 'Sorry, I didn't mean—'

'No,' said Maggie, after a pause. 'Don't be silly. I'm sure he's doing marvellously.'

'Congratulations on the birth of your baby, by the way,' said Heather. 'I gather she's very sweet. How old is she?'

'Seven weeks,' said Maggie, smiling.

'Oh right,' said Heather. 'And you've left her at home, have you?'

184

'Yes. With my mother-in-law.'

'Is it OK to leave them that young?' Heather spread her hands apologetically. 'Not that I know anything about babies, but I once saw a documentary saying you shouldn't leave them for the first three months.'

'Oh, really?' Maggie's smile stiffened a little. 'Well, I'm sure she'll be fine.'

'Oh, I'm sure she will!' Heather blinked innocently. 'I don't know anything about it, really. Look, here comes a waiter. Shall we order?' She picked up her cocktail menu, looked at it for a second, then lifted her eyes to meet Roxanne's.

'And what about you, Roxanne?' she said sweetly. 'Do you think you'll ever have children?'

By the time the others were all ordering their second cocktails, Roxanne was on her fifth drink of the evening. She had eaten nothing since lunchtime, and the potent combination of vodka and Margaritas was beginning to make her head spin. But it was either keep drinking, and try somehow to alleviate the tension inside her, or scream. Every time she looked up and met Heather's wide-eyed gaze she felt acid rising in her stomach. How could Candice have fallen for her smooth talk? How could Candice – one of the most sensitive, observant people she knew – be so utterly blind in this case? It was crazy.

She glanced up, met Maggie's eye over her cocktail and rolled her eyes ruefully. Maggie looked about as cheerful as she felt. What a bloody disaster.

'I don't actually think much of this place,' Heather was saying dismissively. 'There's a really great bar in Covent Garden I used to go to. You should try it.'

'Yes, why not?' said Candice, looking around the table. 'We could probably do with a change.'

'Maybe,' said Maggie, and took a sip of her cocktail.

'That reminds me!' said Heather, suddenly bubbling

over with laughter. 'Do you remember that school trip to Covent Garden, Candice? Were you on it? Where we all got lost and Anna Staples got her shoulder tattooed.'

'No!' said Candice, her face lighting up. 'Did she really?'

'She had a tiny flower done,' said Heather. 'It was really cute. But she got in terrible trouble. Mrs Lacey called her in, and she'd put a plaster over it. So then Mrs Lacey said, "Is something wrong with your shoulder, Anna?"' Heather and Candice both dissolved into giggles, and Roxanne exchanged disbelieving looks with Maggie.

'Sorry,' said Candice, looking up with bright eyes. 'We're boring you.'

'Not at all,' said Roxanne. She took out a packet of cigarettes and offered it to Heather.

'No thanks,' said Heather. 'I always think smoking ages the skin.' She smiled apologetically. 'But that's just me.'

There was silence as Roxanne lit up, blew out a cloud of smoke and looked through it at Heather with dangerously glittering eyes.

'I think I'll go and check on Lucia,' said Maggie, and pushed her chair back. 'I won't be a minute.'

The quietest place to call from was the foyer. Maggie stood by the glass door looking out onto the street, watching as a group of people in black tie hurried past. She felt flushed, hyped up by the evening and yet exhausted. After all the preparation, all the effort, she was not enjoying herself as much as she had hoped. Partly it was that Candice had ruined the cosy familiar threesome by bringing along her awful friend. But partly it was because she herself felt frighteningly brain-dead; as though she could not keep up with the conversation. Several times she had found herself groping for the right word and having to give up. She,

186

who was supposed to be an intelligent, articulate person. As she leaned against the wall and took out her mobile phone, she caught a glimpse of herself in the mirror opposite, and felt a jolt of shock at how fat she looked; how grey her face looked, despite the make-up she had carefully put on. Her eyes looked miserably back at her, and suddenly she found herself wishing she were at home, away from Candice's hateful friend and her insensitive comments, away from the bright lights and the pressure to sparkle.

'Hello?'

'Hi! Paddy, it's Maggie.' A group of people entered the foyer and Maggie turned away slightly, covering her ear with one hand. 'I just thought I'd see how things were going.'

'All's well,' said Paddy briskly. Her voice sounded thin and tinny, as though she were miles away. Which of course she is, thought Maggie miserably. 'Lucia's been coughing a little, but I'm sure it's nothing to worry about.'

'Coughing?' said Maggie in alarm.

'I wouldn't worry,' said Paddy. 'Giles will be back soon, and if there's any problem, we can always send for the doctor.' A thin cry came from the background; a moment later, Maggie felt a telltale dampness inside her bra. Oh shit, she thought miserably. Shit shit.

'Do you think she's OK?' she asked, a perilous wobble in her voice.

'Really, dear, I wouldn't worry. You just enjoy yourself.'

'Yes,' said Maggie, on the verge of tears. 'Thanks. Well, I'll call later.' She clicked off the phone and leaned back against the wall, trying to breathe deeply; trying to gain some perspective. A cough was nothing to worry about. Lucia was fine with Paddy. This was her one night off; she was entitled to enjoy herself and forget about her responsibilities.

But suddenly it all seemed irrelevant. Suddenly the only person she wanted to be with was Lucia. A single tear ran down her face and she brushed it away roughly. She had to get a grip on herself. She had to go back in there and make an effort to be entertaining company.

Perhaps if it had just been the three of them, she thought miserably, she would have confided in the others. But she couldn't with Heather there. Heather with her smooth young skin and her innocent eyes and those constant snide little comments. She made Maggie feel slow-witted and middle-aged; the frump among the glamour girls.

'Hi!' A voice interrupted her and her head jerked up in shock. Heather was standing in front of her, an amused look on her face. 'Baby OK?'

'Yes,' muttered Maggie.

'Good.' Heather shot her a patronizing smile and disappeared into the Ladies'. God, I hate you, thought Maggie. I *hate* you, Heather Trelawney.

Oddly enough, the thought made her feel a little better.

As soon as Heather had disappeared to the Ladies', Roxanne turned to Candice and said, 'What the hell did you have to bring her for?'

'What do you mean?' said Candice in surprise. 'I just thought it would be fun for us all to get together.'

'Fun? You think it's fun listening to that bitch?'

'What?' Candice stared at her incredulously. 'Roxanne, are you drunk?'

'Maybe I am,' said Roxanne, stubbing out her cigarette. 'But to steal a phrase, she'll still be a bitch in the morning. Didn't you *hear* her? "I always think smoking ages the skin. But that's just me."' Roxanne's voice rose in savage mimicry. 'Stupid little cow.'

'She didn't mean anything by it!'

'Of course she did! Jesus, Candice, can't you see what she's like?'

Candice rubbed her face and took a few deep breaths, trying to stay calm. Then she looked up.

'You've had it in for Heather from day one, haven't you?'

'Not at all.'

'You have! You told me not to get involved with her, you gave her a nasty look at the office . . .'

'Oh, for God's sake,' said Roxanne impatiently.

'What's she ever done to you?' Candice's voice rose shakily above the chatter. 'You haven't even *bothered* to get to know her . . .'

'Candice?' Maggie arrived at the table and looked from face to face. 'What's wrong?'

'Heather,' said Roxanne.

'Oh,' said Maggie, and pulled a face. Candice stared at her.

'What, so you don't like her either?'

'I didn't say that,' said Maggie at once. 'And that's beside the point, anyway. I just think it would have been nice if the three of us could have . . .' She was interrupted by Roxanne coughing.

'Hi, Heather,' said Candice miserably.

'Hi,' said Heather pleasantly, and slid into her seat. 'Everything all right?'

'Yes,' said Candice, her cheeks aflame. 'I think I'll just . . . go to the loo. I won't be a minute.'

When she'd gone, there was silence around the table. In the corner, Marilyn Monroe had stepped up to the microphone and was singing a husky 'Happy Birthday' to a delighted-looking man with a sweating face and paunch. As she reached his name, the crowd around him cheered, and he punched the air in a victory salute.

'Well,' said Maggie awkwardly. 'Shall we all order another cocktail?'

'Yes,' said Roxanne. 'Unless you think cocktails age the skin, Heather?'

'I wouldn't know,' said Heather politely.

'Oh, really?' said Roxanne, her voice slightly slurred. 'That's funny. You seem to know about everything else.'

'Is that so?'

'Anyway,' said Maggie hastily. 'There's a full one here.' She picked up a highball, filled with crushed ice and an amber-coloured liquid and decorated with frosted grapes. 'Whose is this?'

'I think it was supposed to be mine,' said Heather. 'But I don't want it. Why don't you have it, Roxanne?'

'Have your lips touched the glass?' said Roxanne. 'If so, no thanks.'

Heather stared at her for a tense moment, then shook her head, almost laughing.

'You really don't like me, do you?'

'I don't like users,' said Roxanne pointedly.

'Oh, really?' said Heather, smiling sweetly. 'Well, I don't like sad old lushes, but I'm still polite to them.'

Maggie gasped and looked at Roxanne.

'What did you call me?' said Roxanne very slowly.

'A sad old lush,' said Heather, examining her nails. She looked up and smiled. 'A sad – old – lush.'

For a few seconds, Roxanne stared at her, shaking. Then, very slowly and deliberately, she picked up the highball full of amber liquid. She stood up and held the glass up to the glittering light for a moment.

'You wouldn't,' said Heather scathingly, but a flicker of doubt passed over her face.

'Oh yes she would,' said Maggie, and folded her arms. There was a moment of still tension as Heather stared disbelievingly up at Roxanne – then, with a sudden flick of the wrist, Roxanne up-ended the cocktail over Heather's head. The icy drink hit her straight in the face and she gasped, then spluttered

190

furiously, brushing crushed ice out of her eyes.

'Jesus Christ!' she spat, getting to her feet. 'You're a fucking . . . nutcase!' Maggie looked at Roxanne and broke into giggles. At the next table, people drinking cocktails put them down and began to nudge each other.

'Hope I haven't aged your skin,' drawled Roxanne, as Heather angrily pushed past. They both watched as Heather disappeared out of the door, then looked at each other and burst into laughter.

'Roxanne, you're wonderful,' said Maggie, wiping her eyes.

'Should have done it at the beginning of the evening,' said Roxanne. She surveyed the disarray on the table – empty glasses, puddles of liquid and crushed ice everywhere – then raised her head and met Maggie's eyes. 'Looks like the party's over. Let's get the bill.'

Candice was washing her hands when Heather burst into the Ladies'. Her hair and face were drenched, the shoulders of her jacket were stained, and she had a murderous expression on her face.

'Heather!' said Candice, looking up in alarm. 'What's happened?'

'Your bloody friend Roxanne, that's what!'

'What?' Candice, stared at her. 'What do you mean?'

'I mean,' said Heather, her jaw tight with anger, 'that Roxanne tipped a whole fucking cocktail over my head. She's crazy!' She headed towards the brightly lit mirror, reached for a tissue and began to blot her hair.

'She tipped a *cocktail* over your head?' said Candice disbelievingly. 'But why?'

'God knows!' said Heather. 'All I said was, I thought she'd had enough to drink. I mean, how many has she had tonight? I just thought maybe she should move onto the soft stuff. But the moment I suggested it, she went berserk!' Heather stopped blotting for a moment and met Candice's eye in the mirror. 'You know, I reckon she's an alcoholic.'

'I can't believe it!' said Candice in dismay. 'I don't know what she can have been thinking of. Heather, I feel awful about this! And your poor jacket . . .'

'I'll have to go home and change,' said Heather. 'I'm supposed to be meeting Ed in half an hour.'

'Oh,' said Candice, momentarily distracted. 'Really? For a . . .' She swallowed. 'For a date?'

'Yes,' said Heather, throwing a piece of sodden tissue into the bin. 'God, look at my face!' Heather stared at her dishevelled reflection, then sighed. 'Oh, I don't know, maybe I was tactless.' She turned round and met Candice's gaze. 'Maybe I should have kept my mouth shut.'

'No!' exclaimed Candice, feeling fresh indignation on Heather's behalf. 'God, don't blame yourself! You made every effort, Heather. Roxanne just—'

'She's taken against me all along,' said Heather, looking at Candice with distressed eyes. 'I've done my best to be friendly . . .'

'I know,' said Candice, her jaw firming. 'Well, I'm going to have a little word with Roxanne.'

'Don't argue!' said Heather, as Candice strode towards the door of the Ladies'. 'Please don't argue over me!' But her words were lost as the door closed behind Candice with a bang.

Out in the foyer, Candice saw Roxanne and Maggie at the table, standing up. They were leaving! she thought incredulously. Without apologizing, without making any effort whatsoever . . .

'So,' she said, striding towards them. 'I hear you've been making Heather feel welcome in my absence.'

'Candice, she had it coming,' said Maggie, looking up. 'She really is a little bitch.'

'Waste of a good drink, if you ask me,' said Roxanne.

She gestured to the green leather bill on the table. 'Our share's in there. I've paid for the three of us. Not for her.'

'I don't believe you, Roxanne!' said Candice furiously. 'Aren't you sorry? Aren't you going to apologize to her?'

'Is she going to apologize to me?'

'She doesn't have to! It was you who poured the drink over her! Bloody hell, Roxanne!'

'Look, just forget it,' said Roxanne. 'Obviously you can see nothing wrong in your new best friend—'

'Well, maybe if you'd made more of an effort with her, and hadn't just taken against her for no good reason—'

'No good reason?' exclaimed Roxanne in an outraged voice. 'You want to hear all the reasons, starting with number one?'

'Roxanne, don't,' said Maggie. 'There's no point.' She sighed, and picked up her bag. 'Candice, can't you understand? We came to see you. Not her.'

'What, so we're a little clique, are we? No-one else can enter.'

'No! That's not it. But—'

'You're just determined not to like her, aren't you?' Candice stared at them with a trembling face. 'I don't know why we bother to meet up, if you can't accept my friends.'

'Well, I don't know why we bother to meet up if you're going to sit chatting about school all night to someone we don't know!' said Maggie, with a sudden heat in her voice. 'I made huge sacrifices to be here, Candice, and I've hardly spoken a word to you all evening!'

'We can talk another time!' said Candice defensively. 'Honestly—'

'I can't!' cried Maggie. 'I don't *have* another time. This *was* my time!'

'Well, maybe I'd talk to you a bit more if you weren't

so bloody gloomy!' Candice heard herself snapping. 'I want to have fun when I go out, not just sit like a misery all night!'

There was an aghast silence.

'See you,' said Roxanne remotely. 'Come on, Maggie.' She took Maggie's arm and, without looking again at Candice, led her away.

Candice watched them walk through the noisy crush of people and felt a cold shame spread through her. Shit, she thought. How could she have said such an awful thing to Maggie? How could the three of them have ended up yelling so aggressively at each other?

Her legs suddenly felt shaky, and she sank down onto a chair, staring miserably at the wet table, the chaos of ice and cocktail glasses and – like a reprimand – the bill in its green folder.

'Hi there!' said a waitress dressed as Dorothy from *The Wizard of Oz*, stopping at the table. She briskly wiped the table and removed the debris of glasses, then smiled at Candice. 'Can I take your bill for you? Or haven't you finished?'

'No, I've finished, all right,' said Candice dully. 'Hang on.' She opened her bag, reached for her purse and counted off three notes. 'There you are,' she said, and handed the bill to the waitress. 'That should cover it.'

'Hi, Candice?' A voice interrupted her, and she looked up. It was Heather, looking clean and tidy, with her hair smoothed down and her make-up reapplied. 'Have the others gone?'

'Yes,' said Candice stiffly. 'They . . . they had to leave.' Heather looked at her closely.

'You had a falling-out, didn't you?'

'Kind of,' said Candice, and attempted a smile.

'I'm really sorry,' said Heather. 'Truly.' She squeezed Candice's shoulder, then looked at her watch. 'I've got to go, I'm afraid.'

'Of course,' said Candice. 'Have a good time. And say hello to Ed,' she added as Heather walked off, but Heather didn't seem to hear.

'Your bill,' said the waitress, returning the green folder.

'Thanks,' said Candice. She pocketed the slip of paper and got up from the table, feeling weary with disappointment. How could everything have gone so wrong? How could the evening have ended like this?

'Have a safe trip home and come back soon,' beamed the waitress.

'Yes,' said Candice dispiritedly. 'Maybe.'

Chapter Fourteen

The next morning, Candice woke with a cold feeling in her stomach. She stared up at the ceiling, trying to ignore it, then turned over, burying her head in the duvet. But the chill persisted; would not leave her. She had argued with Maggie and Roxanne, her brain relentlessly reminded her. Her two best friends had walked out on her. The thought sent a dripping coldness down her spine; made her want to hide under her duvet for ever.

As recollections of the evening began to run through her head, she squeezed her eyes tight shut and blocked her ears with her hands. But she could not avoid the images – the iciness in Roxanne's eyes; the shock in Maggie's face. How could she have behaved so badly? How could she have let them leave without sorting it out?

At the same time, as pieces of the evening resurfaced in her head, she felt a lingering resentment begin to lift itself off the lining of her mind. A slow self-justification began to pervade her body; a self-justification which grew warmer the more she remembered. After all, what crime had she really committed? She had brought along a friend, that was all. Perhaps Heather and Roxanne had not hit it off, perhaps Maggie had wanted to have a cosy tête-à-tête. But was she to blame for all that? If things had gone the other way – if they had all warmed to Heather and adopted her as a new chum – wouldn't they now be ringing Candice, and congratulating her on having such a nice friend? It wasn't her fault things hadn't worked out. She shouldn't have snapped at Maggie – but then, Maggie shouldn't have called Heather a bitch.

With a small surge of annoyance, Candice swung her legs out of the bed and sat up, wondering if Heather had already had her shower. And then it hit her. The flat was completely silent. Candice bit her lip and walked to the door of her little room. She pushed it open and waited, listening for any sounds. But there were none – and Heather's bedroom door was ajar. Candice walked towards the kitchen, and as she passed Heather's room, casually glanced in. It was empty, and the bed was neatly made. The bathroom was empty, too. The whole flat was empty.

Candice glanced at the clock on the kitchen wall. Seven-twenty. Heather could have got up extremely early, she told herself, putting on the kettle. She could have suffered from insomnia, or instituted a rigorous new regime.

Or she could have stayed out all night with Ed.

An indeterminate spasm went through Candice's stomach, and she shook her head crossly. It was none of her business what Ed and Heather did, she told herself firmly. If he wanted to ask her out, fine. And if Heather was desperate enough to want to spend the evening with a man who thought 'gourmet' meant three pizza toppings, fine again.

She walked briskly back into the bathroom, peeled off her nightshirt and stepped under the shower – noticing, in spite of herself, that it hadn't been used that morning. Quickly she lathered herself with a rose-scented gel marked 'Uplifting', then turned the shower on full hot blast to wash away the bubbles, the cold feeling in her stomach, her curiosity about Heather and Ed. She wanted to rinse it all away; to emerge refreshed and untroubled.

By the time she came back into the kitchen in her towelling robe, there was a pile of post on the mat and the kettle had boiled. Very calmly, she made herself a cup of camomile tea as recommended by the detox diet that had run in the *Londoner* the month before, and began to open her letters, deliberately keeping till last the mauve envelope at the bottom of the pile.

A credit card bill – higher than usual. Heather's arrival had meant more treats, more outings, more expenditure. A bank statement. Her bank balance also seemed rather higher than usual and she peered at it, puzzled, for a while, wondering where the extra money had come from. Then, shrugging, she stuffed it back into its envelope and moved on. A furniture catalogue in a plastic wrapper. A letter exhorting her to enter a prize draw. And then, at the bottom, the mauve envelope; the familiar loopy handwriting. She stared at it for a moment, then ripped it open, knowing already what she would find.

Dear Candice, wrote her mother. *Hope all is well with you. The weather is moderately fine here. Kenneth and I have been on a short trip to Cornwall. Kenneth's daughter is expecting another baby . . .*

Quietly, Candice read to the end of the letter, then put it back into the envelope. The same anodyne words as ever; the same neutral, distancing tone. The letter of a woman paralysed by fear of the past; too cowardly to reach out even to her own daughter.

A familiar flame of hurt burned briefly within Candice, then died. She had read too many such letters to let this one upset her. And this morning she felt clean and quiet; almost numb. *I don't care*, flashed through her head as she put the letters in a neat pile on the counter. *I don't care.* She took a sip of camomile tea, then another. She was about to take a third when the doorbell rang, startling her so much that her tea spilled all over the table.

She pulled her robe more tightly around her, cautiously walked to the front door and opened it.

'So,' said Ed, as though continuing a conversation begun three minutes ago, 'I hear one of your friends tipped a cocktail over Heather last night.' He shook his head admiringly. 'Candice, I never knew you ran with such a wild set.'

'What do you want?' said Candice.

'An introduction to this Roxanne character for a start,' said Ed. 'But a cup of coffee would do.'

'What's wrong with you?' said Candice. 'Why can't you make your own bloody coffee? And anyway, where's Heather?' Immediately the words were out of her mouth, she regretted them.

'Interesting question,' said Ed, leaning against the door frame. 'The implication being – what? That Heather should be making my coffee?'

'No!' snapped Candice. 'I just—' She shook her head. 'It doesn't matter.'

'You just wondered? Well . . .' Ed looked at his watch. 'To be honest, I have no idea. She's probably on her way to work by now, wouldn't you think?' He raised his eyes and grinned innocently.

Candice stared back at him, then turned on her heel and walked back into the kitchen. She flicked the kettle on, wiped down the tea-sodden table, then sat down and took another sip of camomile tea.

'I have to thank you, by the way,' said Ed, following her in. 'For giving me such sound advice.' He reached for the cafetière and began to spoon coffee into it. 'You want some?'

'No thank you,' said Candice coldly. 'I'm detoxing. And what did I give you advice about?'

'Heather, of course. You were the one who suggested I ask her out.'

'Yes,' said Candice. 'So I was.'

There was silence as Ed poured water into the cafetière and Candice stared into her cup of unappealing, lukewarm camomile tea. Don't ask, she told herself firmly. Don't ask. He's only come round to brag.

'So – how was it?' she heard herself saying.

'How was what?' said Ed, grinning. Candice felt a flush come to her cheeks.

'How was the evening?' she said in deliberate tones.

'Oh, the *evening*,' said Ed. 'The evening was lovely, thank you.'

'Good.' Candice gave an uninterested shrug.

'Heather's such an attractive girl,' continued Ed musingly. 'Nice hair, nice clothes, nice manner . . .'

'Glad to hear it.'

'Barking mad, of course.'

'What do you mean?' said Candice bad-temperedly. Typical bloody Ed. 'What do you mean, barking mad?'

'She's screwy,' said Ed. 'You must have noticed.'

'Don't be stupid.'

'Being her oldest friend and all,' said Ed, taking a sip of his coffee and looking at Candice quizzically over the rim of his mug. 'Or perhaps you hadn't noticed.'

'There's nothing to notice!' said Candice.

'If you say so,' said Ed, and Candice stared at him in frustration. 'And of course, you know her better than I do. But I have to say, in my opinion—'

'I'm not interested in your opinion!' cut in Candice. 'God, what do you know about people, anyway? All you care about is . . . is fast food and money.'

'Is that so?' said Ed, raising his eyebrows. 'The Candice Brewin Analysis. And in what order do I rate these two staples of life? Do I put money above fast food? Fast food above money? Even stevens?'

'Very funny,' said Candice sulkily. 'You know what I mean.'

'No,' said Ed after a pause. 'I'm not sure I do.'

'Oh, forget it,' said Candice.

'Yes,' said Ed, a curious look on his face. 'I think I will.' He put his coffee mug down and walked slowly towards the door, then stopped. 'Just let me tell you this, Candice. You know about as much about me as you do about your friend Heather.'

He strode out of the kitchen and down the hall, and, in slight dismay, Candice opened her mouth to say something; to call him back. But the front door banged closed, and she was too late.

As she arrived at work a couple of hours later, Candice paused at the door of the editorial office and looked at Heather's desk. It was empty and her chair was still tucked in. Heather had obviously not turned up yet.

'Morning, Candice,' said Justin, walking past towards his office.

'Hi,' said Candice absently, still staring at Heather's desk. Then she looked up. 'Justin, do you know where Heather is?'

'Heather?' said Justin, stopping. 'No. Why?'

'Oh, no reason,' said Candice at once. 'I was just wondering.' She smiled at Justin, expecting him to smile back or make some further conversational remark. Instead he frowned at her.

'You keep pretty close tabs on Heather, don't you, Candice?'

'What?' Candice wrinkled her brow. 'What's that supposed to mean?'

'You supervise a lot of her work, is that right?'

'Well,' said Candice, after a pause. 'I suppose I sometimes . . . check things for her.'

'Nothing more than that?'

Candice stared back at him and felt herself flush a guilty red. Had Justin realized that she'd been doing most of Heather's work for her? Perhaps he'd recognized her style of subbing; perhaps he'd seen her working on the articles Heather was supposed to have done; perhaps he'd noticed her constant e-mailing of documents to Heather.

'Maybe a bit more,' she said eventually. 'Just a helping hand occasionally. You know.'

'I see,' said Justin. He looked at her appraisingly, running his eyes across her face as though searching for typographical errors. 'Well, I think Heather can probably do without your little helping hand from now on. Would you agree?'

'I . . . I suppose so,' said Candice, taken aback by his harsh tone. 'I'll leave her to it.'

'I'm glad to hear it,' said Justin, and gave her a long look. 'I'll be watching you, Candice.'

'Fine!' said Candice, feeling rattled. 'Watch me all you like.'

A phone began to ring in Justin's office and, after a final glance at Candice, he strode off. Candice watched him go, feeling a secret dismay rising inside her. How had Justin worked out that she'd been helping Heather so much? And why was he so hostile about it? All she'd been trying to do, after all, was help. She frowned, and began to walk slowly towards her own desk. As she sat down and stared at her blank computer screen, a new, worrying thought came to her. Was her own performance suffering as a result of helping Heather? Was she genuinely spending too much time on Heather's work?

'People.' Justin's voice interrupted her thoughts and she swivelled round in her chair. He was standing at the door to his little office, looking round the editorial room with a strange expression on his face. 'I have some rather shocking news for you all.' He paused and waited for everyone in the office to turn away from what they were doing and face him. 'Ralph Allsopp is extremely ill,' he said. 'Cancer.'

There was silence, then someone breathed,

'Oh my God.'

'Yes,' said Justin. 'It's a bit of a shock for everyone. Apparently he's had it for a while, but no-one else knew. And now it's . . .' He rubbed his face. 'It's quite advanced. Quite bad, in fact.'

There was another silence.

'So . . . so that's why he retired,' Candice heard herself saying, in a faltering voice. 'He knew he was ill.' As she said the words, she suddenly remembered the message she'd once taken from Charing Cross Hospital, and a coldness began to drip down her spine.

'He's gone into hospital,' said Justin. 'But apparently it's spread everywhere. They're doing all they can, but . . .' He tailed off and looked around the stunned room. He appeared genuinely distressed by the news, and Candice felt a sudden flash of sympathy with him. 'I think a card would be nice,' he added, after a pause, 'signed by us all. Cheerful, of course . . .'

'How long do they think he's got?' asked Candice awkwardly. 'Is it . . .' She halted, and bit her lip.

'Not long, apparently,' said Justin. 'Once these things take hold, it's—'

'Months? Weeks?'

'I think . . .' He hesitated. 'I think from what Janet said, it'll be a matter of weeks. Or even . . .' He broke off.

'Jesus Christ!' said Alicia shakily. 'But he looked so . . .' She broke off and buried her head in her hands.

'I'll phone Maggie and let her know,' said Justin soberly. 'And if you can all think of anyone else who would like to be informed . . . Freelancers, for example. David Gettins will want to know, I'm sure.'

'Roxanne,' said somebody.

'Exactly,' said Justin. 'Maybe somebody should phone Roxanne.'

Roxanne flipped over on her sun lounger, stretched out her legs and felt the heat of the evening sun warm her face like a friendly smile. She had arrived at Nice airport at ten that morning and had immediately taken a taxi to the Paradin Hotel. Gerhard, the general manager, was an old friend and, after a quick call to the hotel group's publicity department, had managed to find her a spare room at a vastly reduced rate. She didn't want much, she had insisted. A bed, a shower, a place by the pool. A place to lie with her eyes closed, feeling the healing, warming sun on her body. A place to forget about everything.

She had lain all day on a sun-bed under the blistering sunshine, oiling herself sporadically and taking sips from a pitcher of water. At six-thirty she looked at her watch and felt a lurch of amazement that only twenty-four hours before, she'd been in the Manhattan Bar, about to descend into the evening from hell.

If she closed her eyes, Roxanne could still summon up the thrill she'd felt as she'd seen the first piece of crushed ice hit that little bitch in the face. But it was a faded thrill; an excitement that even at the time had been overshadowed by disappointment. She had not wanted to argue with Candice. She had not wanted to end up in the cold evening air, drunk and alone and miserable.

Maggie had abandoned her. After the two of them had walked out of the bar, both flushed and still buoyed up with adrenalin from the argument, Maggie had looked at her watch and said reluctantly, 'Roxanne . . .'

'Don't go,' Roxanne had said, the beginnings of panic in her voice. 'Come on, Maggie. This evening's been so shitty. We've got to redeem it somehow.'

'I've got to get back,' Maggie had said. 'It's already late—'

'It's not!'

'I have to get back to Hampshire.' Maggie had sounded genuinely upset. 'You know I do. And I have to feed Lucia, otherwise I'll burst.' She'd reached for Roxanne's hand. 'Roxanne, I'd stay if I could—'

'You could if you wanted to.' There had been a childish wobble in Roxanne's voice; she'd felt a sudden cold fear of being left alone. First Ralph, then Candice. Now Maggie. Turning to others in their lives. Their friends; their families. Preferring other people to her. She'd looked down at Maggie's warm hand clasping hers, adorned with its huge engagement sapphire and had felt a surge of jealousy. 'OK then, go,' she'd said savagely. 'Go back to hubby. I don't care.'

'Roxanne,' Maggie had said pleadingly. 'Roxanne, wait.' But Roxanne had wrenched her hand away and tottered down the street, muttering curses under her breath; knowing that Maggie would not run after her. Knowing in her heart of hearts that Maggie had no choice.

She had slept for a few hours, woken at dawn and made a snap decision to leave the country; to go anywhere as long as it had sunshine. She didn't have Ralph any longer. Perhaps she didn't even have her friends any longer. But she had freedom and contacts and a good figure for a bikini. She would stay here as long as she felt like it, she thought, then move on. Perhaps even further afield than Europe. Forget Britain, forget it all. She wouldn't pick up her messages, she wouldn't even file her monthly copy. Let Justin sweat a little. Let them all sweat a little.

Roxanne sat up on her sun lounger, lifted her hand and watched in pleasure as a white-jacketed waiter came walking over. That was service for you, she thought with pleasure. Sometimes she thought she would like to spend her whole life in a five-star hotel.

'Hello,' she said, beaming up at him. 'I'd like a club sandwich, please. And a freshly squeezed orange juice.' The waiter scribbled on his pad, then moved off again, and she sank comfortably back onto her sun lounger.

Roxanne stayed at the Paradin for two weeks. The sun shone every day, and the pool glistened, and her club sandwich arrived fat and crisp and delicious. She did not vary her routine, did not talk to her fellow guests and did not venture beyond the hotel portals more than once. The days passed by like beads on a string. She felt dispassionate; remote from everything but the sensation of sun and sand and the sharp tang of the first Margarita of the evening. Somewhere in England, all the people she knew and loved were going about their daily lives, but they seemed shadowy in her mind, almost like people from the past.

Only occasionally would flashes of pain descend upon her, so great that she could do nothing but close her eyes and wait for them to pass. One night, as she sat at her corner table in the bar, the band struck up a song that she used to listen to with Ralph – and with no warning she felt a stabbing in her chest that brought tears to her eyes. But she sat quietly, allowing the tears to dry on her cheeks rather than rub them away. And then the song ended, and another began, and her Margarita arrived. And by the time she'd finished it, she was thinking of something else completely.

After two weeks she woke up and strode to her window and felt the first stirrings of ennui. She felt energetic and restless; suddenly the confines of the hotel seemed narrow and limited. They had provided security, but now they were prison-like. She had to get away, she thought suddenly. Much further away. Without pausing to reconsider, she reached for her suitcase and began to pack. She didn't want to allow herself to sit still and think about her options.

206

Thinking brought pain. Travelling brought hope and excitement.

By the time she kissed Gerhard farewell in the hotel foyer, she had booked herself a seat on a flight to Nairobi and called her friends at the Hilton. A week at half-rate and concessions on a two-week safari. She would write the whole thing up for the *Londoner* and as many others as she could. She would take photographs of elephants and watch the sun rise over the horizon. She would sink her eyes into the vastness of the African plains and lose herself completely.

The flight was only half full, and after some discussion with the girl at the check-in desk, Roxanne managed to get herself an upgrade. She strode onto the plane with a satisfied smirk on her face and settled comfortably into her wide seat. As the flight attendants demonstrated the safety procedures, she reached for a complimentary copy of the *Daily Telegraph* and began to read the front-page stories, letting the familiar names and references fall onto her parched mind like rain. It seemed like a lifetime since she'd been in England. She flicked over a few pages and stopped at a feature about holiday fashions.

They were on the runway now, and moving more quickly; the roar of the engines was getting louder, almost deafening. The plane picked up speed until it seemed that it couldn't go any faster – and then, with a tiny jolt, lifted into the air. At that moment Roxanne turned the page again, and felt a mild surprise. Ralph was staring back at her, in stark black and white. Automatically, her mind skimmed over any acquisitions he'd been planning; over any newsworthy event he might have been involved with.

Then, as she realized what page she was on, her face grew rigid with disbelief.

Ralph Allsopp, read the obituary title. *Publisher who brought life to defunct magazine the 'Londoner'.*

'No,' said Roxanne in a voice that didn't sound like hers. 'No.' Her hands were shaking so much, she could barely read the text.

Ralph Allsopp, who died on Monday . . .

'No,' she whispered, searching the page desperately for a different answer, a punchline.

He left a wife, Cynthia, and three children.

Pain hit Roxanne like a hammer. She stared at his picture and felt herself start to shudder, to retch. With useless hands, she began to tug at her safety strap. 'No,' she heard herself saying. 'I've got to go.'

'Madam, is everything all right?' A stewardess appeared in front of her, smiling frostily.

'Stop the plane,' said Roxanne to the stewardess. 'Please. I've got to go. I have to go back.'

'Madam—'

'No! You don't understand. I have to go back. It's an emergency.' She swallowed hard, trying to keep outwardly calm. But something was bubbling up uncontrollably inside her, taking hold of her body.

'I'm afraid—'

'Please. Just turn the plane round!'

'We can't do that, I'm afraid,' said the stewardess, smiling slightly.

'Don't you fucking laugh at me!' Roxanne's voice rose to a roar; suddenly she couldn't keep control of herself any more. 'Don't laugh at me!' Tears began to course down her face in hot streams.

'I'm not laughing!' said the stewardess in surprise. She glanced at the crumpled page in Roxanne's hand and her face changed. 'I'm not laughing,' she said gently. She crouched down and put her arms around Roxanne. 'You can fly back from Nairobi,' she said quietly into Roxanne's hair. 'We'll sort it out for you.' And as the plane soared higher and higher into the clouds, she knelt on the floor, ignoring the other passengers, stroking Roxanne's thin, sobbing back.

Chapter Fifteen

The funeral was nine days later, at St Bride's, Fleet Street. Candice arrived early, to find groups of people clustering outside, exchanging the same numb, disbelieving looks they'd been exchanging all week. The whole building had been silenced by the news that Ralph had died only two weeks after being admitted into hospital. People had sat blankly at their computers, unable to believe it. Many had wept. One nervous girl, on hearing the news, had laughed – then burst into mortified tears. Then, while they were all still shell-shocked, the phones had started ringing and the flowers had started to arrive. And so they had been forced to put on brave faces and start dealing with the messages pouring in; the expressions of sympathy; the curious enquiries about the future of the company, veiled in layers of concern.

Ralph's son Charles had been glimpsed a few times, pacing the corridors with a stern look on his face. He had been at the company for such a short time, no-one knew what he was like, beneath the good looks and the expensive suit. His face was familiar, from the rows of photographs on Ralph's wall, but he was still a stranger. As he had toured the offices directly after his father's death, there had been a chorus of murmured sympathy; shy comments about what a wonderful man

Ralph had been. But no-one dared approach Charles Allsopp one-to-one; no-one dared to ask him what his plans for the company were. Certainly not until after the funeral. And so business had carried on as usual, with heads down and voices low and a feeling of slight unreality.

Candice shoved her hands in her pockets and went to sit alone on a bench. The news of Ralph's death had brought back her own father's death with a painful vividness. She could still remember the disbelief she'd felt; the shock, the grief. The hope every waking morning that it had all been a bad dream. The sudden realization she'd had, looking at her mother one morning, that their family unit was now down to two – that instead of expanding, it was prematurely closing in on itself. She could remember feeling suddenly alone and very vulnerable. What if her mother died, too, she'd thought? What if she was left all alone in the world?

And then, just as she'd felt she was levelling out and beginning to cope, the descent into nightmare had begun. The discoveries; the humiliation. The realization that the beloved husband and father had been a swindler, a conman. Roughly, Candice brushed a tear from her eye and stared at the ground, blinking hard. There was no-one she could share these memories and emotions with. Her mother would change the subject immediately. And Roxanne and Maggie – the only other two who knew the story – were out of the picture. Nobody had heard from Roxanne for weeks. And Maggie . . . Candice winced. She had tried to call Maggie, the day after the announcement of Ralph's death. She had wanted to apologize; to make friends again; to share the shock and grief. But as she'd said, falteringly, 'Hi, Maggie, it's Candice', Maggie had snapped back, 'Oh, I'm interesting now, am I? I'm worth talking to, am I?'

'I didn't mean . . .' Candice had begun helplessly. 'Maggie, please . . .'

'Tell you what,' Maggie had said. 'You wait until Lucia's eighteen, and call me then. OK?' And the phone had been slammed down.

Candice flinched again at the memory, then forced herself to look up. It was time to forget her own problems; to concentrate on Ralph. She glanced about the milling crowd for familiar faces. Alicia was standing alone, looking glum; Heather was in a corner comforting a weeping Kelly. There were lots of people she half recognized and even a few mildly famous ones. Ralph Allsopp had made many friends over the years, and had lost few.

Candice stood up, brushed down her coat and prepared to walk over to Heather. Then, as her gaze passed over the gates, she stopped. Coming in, looking more suntanned than ever, her bronzy-blond hair cascading down over a black coat, was Roxanne. She was wearing dark glasses and walking slowly, almost as though she were ill. At the sight of her, Candice's heart contracted, and tears suddenly stung her eyes. If Maggie wouldn't make up, Roxanne would.

'Roxanne,' she said, hurrying forward, almost tripping over herself. She reached her and looked up breathlessly. 'Roxanne, I'm so sorry about the other night. Can we just forget it ever happened?'

She waited for Roxanne to agree; for the two of them to hug and shed a few sentimental tears. But Roxanne was silent, then in a husky voice – as though with a huge effort – said, 'What are you talking about, Candice?'

'At the Manhattan Bar,' said Candice. 'We all said things we didn't mean—'

'Candice, I don't give a shit about the Manhattan Bar,' said Roxanne roughly. 'You think that's important now?'

'Well – no,' said Candice, taken aback. 'I suppose not. But I thought . . .' She broke off. 'Where've you been?'

'I went away,' said Roxanne. 'Next question?' Her face was inscrutable, unfriendly almost, behind her shades. Candice stared at her, discomfited.

'How . . . how did you hear the news?'

'I saw the obituary,' said Roxanne. 'On the plane.' With a quick, jerky gesture, she opened her bag and reached for her cigarettes. 'On the fucking plane.'

'God, that must have been a shock!' said Candice.

Roxanne looked at her for a long while, then simply said, 'Yes. It was.' With shaking hands, she tried to light her cigarette, flicking and flicking as the flame refused to catch light. 'Stupid thing,' she said, her breaths coming more quickly. 'Fucking bloody . . .'

'Roxanne, let me,' said Candice, taking the cigarette from her. She felt taken aback by Roxanne's obvious lack of composure – Roxanne, who normally took all of life's downs with a grin and a sparky comment. On this occasion, she seemed almost worse affected than anyone. Had she been very close to Ralph? She had known him for a while – but then, so had everybody. Candice looked puzzled as she lit the cigarette and handed it back to Roxanne.

'Here you are,' she said, then stopped. Roxanne was gazing transfixed at a middle-aged woman with a neat blond bob and a dark coat who had just got out of a black mourner's car. A boy of around ten got out and joined her on the pavement, then a young woman and, after a moment, Charles Allsopp.

'Oh,' said Candice curiously. 'That must be his wife. Yes, of course it is. I recognize her.'

'Cynthia,' said Roxanne. 'And Charles. And Fiona. And little Sebastian.' She put her cigarette to her lips and took a deep puff. On the pavement, Cynthia briskly brushed down Sebastian's coat and inspected his face.

'How old is he?' said Candice, gazing at them. 'The little one?'

'I don't know,' replied Roxanne, and gave an odd little laugh. 'I've . . . I've stopped counting.'

'Poor little thing,' said Candice, biting her lip. 'Imagine losing your father at that age. It was bad enough . . .' She broke off, and took a deep breath.

The Allsopps turned, and, led by Cynthia and Charles, began to head towards the church. As they passed Roxanne, Cynthia's gaze flickered towards her, and Roxanne stuck her chin out firmly.

'Do you know her?' said Candice curiously, when they'd gone by.

'I've never spoken to her in my life,' said Roxanne.

'Oh,' said Candice, and lapsed into a puzzled silence. Around them, people were beginning to file into the church. 'Well . . . shall we go in?' said Candice eventually. She looked up. 'Roxanne?'

'I can't,' said Roxanne. 'I can't go in there.'

'What do you mean?'

'I can't do it.' Roxanne's voice was a whisper and her chin was shaking. 'I can't sit there. With all of them. With . . . her.'

'With who?' said Candice. 'Heather?'

'Candice,' said Roxanne in a trembling voice, and pulled off her sunglasses. 'Will you get it through your bloody head that I don't care one way or the other about your stupid little friend?'

Candice stared back at her in pounding shock. Roxanne's eyes were bloodshot and there were dark grey shadows beneath them, unsuccessfully concealed by a layer of bronze make-up.

'Roxanne, what is it?' she said desperately. 'Who are you talking about?' She followed Roxanne's stare and saw Cynthia Allsopp disappearing into the church. 'Are you talking about *her*?' she said, wrinkling her brow in incomprehension. 'You don't want to sit with Ralph's wife? But I thought you said – you said . . .' Candice tailed off, and looked slowly at Roxanne's haggard face. 'You're not . . .' She stopped. 'No.'

She took a step backwards and rubbed her face, trying to steady her breath, to calm her thoughts; to stop herself leaping to ridiculous conclusions.

'You can't mean . . .' She raised her eyes to meet Roxanne's and, as she saw the expression in them, felt her stomach flip over. 'Oh my God.' She swallowed. 'Ralph.'

'Yes,' said Roxanne, without moving. 'Ralph.'

Maggie sat on the sofa in her sitting room, watching the health visitor scribbling in Lucia's little book. The others would all be at the funeral now. Ralph's funeral. She couldn't quite believe it. This had to be one of the worst periods in her life, she thought dispassionately, watching as the health visitor carefully recorded Lucia's weight on a graph. Ralph was dead. And she had fallen out with both her best friends.

She could hardly bear to remember that evening at the Manhattan Bar. So many hopes had been pinned on it – and it had ended so terribly. She still felt raw whenever she remembered Candice's cruel remarks. After all the effort she'd made, after all the sacrifice and all the guilt – to be told she wasn't interesting enough to bother with. To be – effectively – dismissed. She had travelled back to Hampshire that evening drained with exhaustion and in tears. When she'd arrived home it had been to find Giles holding a fretful Lucia, clearly at his wits' end, and Lucia frantic for a feed. She felt as though she'd failed them both; failed everybody.

'So, how was it?' Giles had said as Lucia started

ravenously feeding. 'Mum said you sounded as though you were having a good time.' And Maggie had stared at him numbly, unable to bring herself to tell the truth; to admit that the evening she'd been pinning all her hopes on had been a disaster. So she'd smiled, and said, 'Great!' and had sunk back in her chair, grateful to be home again.

Since then, she had been out only infrequently. She was getting used to her own company; was starting to watch a great deal of soothing daytime television. On the day she'd heard the news about Ralph she'd sat and wept in the kitchen for a while, then reached for the phone and dialled Roxanne's number. But there was no reply. The next day, Candice had rung, and she'd found herself lashing out angrily; not wanting to, but unable to stop herself retaliating with some of the hurt she still felt. Humiliation still burned in her cheeks when she remembered Candice's comments. Obviously Candice thought she was a miserable, boring frump. Obviously Candice preferred Heather's exciting, vibrant company to hers. She had slammed down the receiver on Candice and felt a moment of powerful adrenalin. Then, a moment later, the tears had begun to fall. Poor Lucia, thought Maggie. She lives in a constant shower of salt water.

'Solids at four months,' the health visitor was saying. 'Baby rice is widely available. Organic if you prefer. Then move on to apple, pear, anything simple. Cooked well and puréed.'

'Yes,' said Maggie. She felt like an automaton, sitting and nodding and smiling at regular intervals.

'And what about you?' said the health visitor. She put down her notebook and looked directly at Maggie. 'Are you feeling well in yourself?' Maggie stared at the woman, and felt her cheeks flame scarlet. She had not expected any questions about herself.

'Yes,' she said eventually. 'Yes, I'm fine.'

215

'Is husband nice and supportive?'

'He does his best,' said Maggie. 'He's . . . he's very busy at work, but he does what he can.'

'Good,' said the health visitor. 'And you – are you getting out much?'

'A . . . a fair bit,' said Maggie defensively. 'It's difficult, with the baby . . .'

'Yes,' said the health visitor. She smiled sympathetically, and took a sip of the tea Maggie had made her. 'What about friends?'

The word hit Maggie like a bolt. To her horror, she felt tears starting at her eyes.

'Maggie?' said the health visitor, leaning forward in concern. 'Are you all right?'

'Yes,' said Maggie, and felt the tears yet again begin to course down her face. 'No.'

A pale spring sun shone as Roxanne and Candice sat in the courtyard of St Bride's, listening to the distant strains of 'Hills of the North, Rejoice'. Roxanne gazed ahead, unseeingly, and Candice stared up at the gusting clouds, trying to work out whether she and Maggie had been incredibly blind, or Roxanne and Ralph had been incredibly discreet. Six years. It was unbelievable. Six years of complete and utter secrecy.

What had shocked Candice the most, as Roxanne had told her story, was how much the two had obviously loved each other. How deep their relationship had been, beneath all Roxanne's jokes, all her flippancy, her apparent callousness. 'But what about all your toyboys?' Candice had faltered at one point – to be rewarded with a searing blue gaze. 'Candice,' Roxanne had said, almost wearily, 'there *weren't* any toyboys.'

Now, in the stillness, she inhaled deeply on her cigarette and blew a cloud of smoke into the air.

'I thought he didn't want me any more,' she said,

without moving her head. 'He told me to go to Cyprus. To have a new life. I was utterly . . . devastated. All that bullshit about retiring.' She stubbed out her cigarette. 'He must have thought he was doing me a favour. He must have known he was dying.'

'Oh, he knew,' said Candice without thinking.

'What?' Roxanne turned and stared at her. 'What do you mean?'

'Nothing,' said Candice, wishing she'd kept her mouth shut. Roxanne stared at her.

'Candice, what do you mean? Do you mean . . .' She paused, as though trying to keep control of herself. 'Do you mean you knew Ralph was ill?'

'No,' said Candice, not quite quickly enough. 'I . . . I took a message once, from Charing Cross Hospital. It was meaningless. It could have been anything.'

'When was this?' asked Roxanne in a trembling voice, as, inside the church, the hymn came to a final chord. 'Candice, when was this?'

'I don't know,' said Candice, feeling herself flush. 'A while ago. A couple of months.' She looked up at Roxanne and flinched under her gaze.

'And you said nothing,' said Roxanne disbelievingly. 'You didn't even mention it to me. Or Maggie.'

'I didn't know what it meant!'

'Didn't you guess?' Roxanne's voice harshened. 'Didn't you *wonder*?'

'I . . . I don't know. Maybe I wondered a bit—'

Candice broke off and ran a hand through her hair. From inside the church came a rumble of voices in prayer.

'You knew Ralph was dying and I didn't.' Roxanne shook her head distractedly as though trying to sort out a welter of confusing facts.

'I didn't know!' said Candice in distress. 'Roxanne—'

'You knew!' cried Roxanne. 'And his wife knew. And the whole world knew. And where was I when he died? In the fucking south of France. By the fucking pool.'

Roxanne gave a little sob and her shoulders began to shake. Candice gazed at her in horrified silence.

'I should have known,' said Roxanne, her voice thick with tears. 'I could see something was wrong with him. He was thin, and he was losing weight, and he . . .' She broke off, and wiped her eyes roughly. 'But you know what I thought? I thought he was stressed out because he was planning to leave his wife. I thought he was planning to set up house with me. And all the time he was dying. And . . .' She paused disbelievingly. 'And you knew.'

In dismay, Candice tried to put her arm around her, but Roxanne shrugged it off.

'I can't stand it!' she said desperately. 'I can't stand that everyone knew but me. You should have told me, Candice.' Her voice rose like a child's wail. 'You should have told me he was ill!'

'But I didn't know about you and Ralph!' Candice felt tears pricking her own eyes. 'How could I have known to tell you?' She tried to reach for Roxanne's hand, but Roxanne was standing up, moving away.

'I can't stay,' she whispered. 'I can't look at you. I can't take it – that you knew, and I didn't.'

'Roxanne, it's not my fault,' cried Candice, tears running down her face. 'It's not my fault!'

'I know,' said Roxanne huskily. 'I know it's not. But I still can't bear it.' And without looking Candice in the eyes, she walked quickly off.

Maggie wiped her eyes and took a sip of hot, fresh tea.

'There you are,' said the health visitor kindly. 'Now don't worry, a lot of new mothers feel depressed to begin with. It's perfectly natural.'

'But I've got nothing to be depressed about,' said Maggie, giving a little shudder. 'I've got a loving

218

husband and a great big house, and I don't have to work. I'm really lucky.'

She looked around her large, impressive sitting room: at the grand piano covered in photographs, the fireplace stacked with logs; the french windows leading out onto the lawn. The health visitor followed her gaze.

'You're quite isolated out here, aren't you?' she said thoughtfully. 'Any family nearby?'

'My parents live in Derbyshire,' said Maggie, closing her eyes and feeling the hot steam of the tea against her face. 'But my mother-in-law lives a few miles away.'

'And is that helpful?'

Maggie opened her mouth, intending to say Yes.

'Not really,' she heard herself say instead.

'I see,' said the health visitor tactfully. 'You don't get on particularly well?'

'We do . . . but she just makes me feel like such a failure,' said Maggie, and as the words left her mouth she felt a sudden painful relief. 'She does everything so well, and I do everything so . . .' Tears began to stream down her face again. 'So badly,' she whispered.

'I'm sure that's not true.'

'It is! I can't do anything right!' Maggie gave a little shudder. 'I didn't even know I was in labour. Paddy had to *tell* me I was in labour. I felt so . . . so stupid. And I don't keep the house tidy, and I don't make scones – and I got rattled changing Lucia's nappy, and Paddy came in and saw me shouting at her . . .' Maggie wiped her eyes and gave a huge sniff. 'She thinks I'm a terrible mother.'

'I'm sure she doesn't—'

'She does! I can see it in her eyes every time she looks at me. She thinks I'm useless!'

'I don't think you're useless!' Maggie and the health visitor both started, and looked round. Paddy was standing at the door of the sitting room, her face flushed. 'Maggie, where did you get such a dreadful idea?'

Paddy had arrived at the house meaning to ask Maggie if she wanted anything from the shops, and had found the door on the latch. As she'd walked through the hall, she'd heard Maggie's voice, raised in emotion and, with a sudden jolt of shock, had heard her own name. She had told herself to walk away – but instead had drawn nearer the sitting room, unable to believe what she was hearing.

'Maggie, my darling girl, you're a wonderful mother!' she said now, in a trembling voice. 'Of course you are.'

'I'm sure it's all just a misunderstanding,' said the health visitor soothingly.

'No-one understands!' said Maggie, wiping her blotchy face. 'Everyone thinks I'm bloody super-woman. Lucia never sleeps . . .'

'I thought you said she was sleeping well,' said the health visitor with a frown, consulting her notes.

'I know!' cried Maggie in sudden anguish. 'I said that because everyone seems to think that's what she should be doing. But she's not sleeping. And I'm not sleeping either. Giles has no idea . . . no-one has any idea.'

'I've tried to help!' said Paddy, and glanced defensively at the health visitor. 'I've offered to babysit, I've tidied the kitchen . . .'

'I know,' said Maggie. 'And every time you tidy it you make me feel worse. Every single time you come round . . .' She looked at Paddy. 'Every time, I'm doing something else wrong. When I went up to London you told me I should have an early night instead.' Tears began to pour down her face again. 'My one night off.'

'I was worried about you!' said Paddy, her face

reddening in distress. 'I could tell you were exhausted; I didn't want you to make yourself ill!'

'Well, that's not what you said.' Maggie looked up miserably. 'You made me feel like a criminal.' Paddy stared at her for a few silent moments, then sank heavily down onto a chair.

'Perhaps you're right,' she said slowly. 'I didn't think.'

'I'm grateful for everything you've done,' muttered Maggie. 'I am, really. But . . .'

'It sounds like you could do with more emotional support,' said the health visitor, looking from Paddy to Maggie. 'You say your husband's got a very demanding job?'

'He's very busy,' said Maggie, and blew her nose. 'It's not fair to expect him . . .'

'Nonsense!' cut in Paddy crisply. 'Giles is this baby's father, isn't he? Then he can share the burden.' She gave Maggie a beady look. 'Anyway, I thought all you women were into New Men these days.' Maggie gave a shaky laugh.

'I am, in principle. It's just that he works so hard—'

'And so do you! Maggie, you must stop expecting miracles of yourself.'

Maggie flushed. 'Other women manage,' she said, staring at the floor. 'I just feel so inadequate . . .'

'Other women manage *with help*,' said Paddy. 'Their mothers come to stay. Their husbands take time off. Their friends rally round.' She met the health visitor's eye. 'I don't think any husband ever died from losing a night's sleep, did he?'

'Not to my knowledge,' said the health visitor, grinning.

'You don't have to do it all,' said Paddy to Maggie. 'You're doing marvellously as it is. Much better than I ever did.'

'Really?' said Maggie, and raised a shaky smile. 'Even though I don't make scones?'

221

Paddy was silent. She looked down at little Lucia, sleeping in her basket, then raised her eyes to meet Maggie's.

'I make scones because I'm a bored old woman,' she said. 'But you've got a lot more in your life than that. Haven't you?'

As people began to pour out of the church, Candice looked up. Her limbs felt stiff; her face felt dry and salty from tears; she felt internally bruised from Roxanne's powerful anger. She didn't want to see anyone, she thought, and quickly got up to leave. But as she was walking away, Justin suddenly appeared from nowhere and tapped her on the shoulder.

'Candice,' he said coldly. 'A word, please.'

'Oh,' said Candice, and rubbed her face. 'Can't it wait?'

'I'd like you to come and see me tomorrow. Nine-thirty.'

'OK,' said Candice. 'What's it about?'

Justin gave her a long look, then said, 'Let's just speak tomorrow, shall we?'

'All right,' said Candice, puzzled. Justin nodded curtly, then walked on into the crowds.

Candice stared after him, wondering what on earth he was talking about. The next moment, Heather appeared at her side.

'What did Justin want?' she said casually.

'I've no idea. He wants to see me tomorrow. Very serious about something or other.' Candice rolled her eyes. 'He was very cloak and dagger about it. Probably his latest genius idea about something.'

'Probably,' said Heather. She looked at Candice consideringly for a moment, then grinned and squeezed her waist. 'Tell you what, let's go out tonight,' she said. 'Have some supper somewhere nice. We could do with some fun after all this misery. Don't you think?'

'Absolutely,' said Candice in relief. 'I feel pretty wrung out, to tell you the truth.'

'Really?' said Heather thoughtfully. 'I saw you and Roxanne, earlier. Another row?'

'Kind of,' said Candice. An image of Roxanne's haggard face passed through her mind and she winced. 'But it . . . it doesn't matter.' She looked at Heather's wide, friendly smile and suddenly felt uplifted; warmed and encouraged. 'It really doesn't matter.'

Chapter Sixteen

The next morning, as Candice got ready for work, there was no sign of Heather. She smiled to herself as she made a cup of coffee in the kitchen. They had sat in a restaurant until late the night before, eating pasta and drinking mellow red wine and talking. There was an ease between the two of them; a natural, understated affection, which Candice treasured. They seemed to see life in exactly the same way; to hold the same values; to share the same sense of humour.

Heather had drunk more than Candice and, as their bill had arrived, had almost tearfully thanked Candice once again for everything she'd done for her. Then she'd rolled her eyes and laughed at herself. 'Look at me, completely out of it as usual. Candice, if I don't wake up in the morning, just leave me. I'll need the day off to recover!' She'd taken a sip of coffee and looked at Candice over her cup, then added, 'And good luck with your meeting with Justin. Let's hope it's something nice!'

It had been a healing evening, thought Candice. After the grief and drama of Ralph's funeral, it had been an evening to absorb the events of the day, to take stock and move on. She still felt raw from her parting with Roxanne; still felt a disbelieving shock whenever she thought about her and Ralph. But this morning she felt a new strength; an ability to look ahead and focus on other things in her life. Her friendship with Heather; her love of her job.

Candice finished her coffee, tiptoed to Heather's room and listened. There was no sound. She grinned, picked up her bag and left the flat. It was a crisp morning, with the feel of summer in the air, and she walked along briskly, wondering what Justin wanted to see her about.

As she arrived at work she saw that his office was empty. She went to her desk and immediately switched on her computer – then, validated, turned round to chat with whoever was about. But Kelly was the only one in the office, and she was sitting at her desk, furiously typing, not looking up for a second.

'I saw you at the funeral,' said Candice in friendly tones. 'It seemed very moving.' Kelly looked up and gave Candice a strange look.

'Yeah,' she said, and carried on typing.

'I didn't make it to the actual service,' continued Candice. 'But I saw you going in with Heather.'

To her surprise, a pink tinge spread over Kelly's face.

'Yeah,' she said again. She typed for a bit longer, then abruptly stood up. 'I've just got to . . .' she said, bit her lip and walked out of the room. Candice watched her go in puzzlement, then turned back to her computer. She tapped idly, then turned round again. There wasn't any point beginning work if she was seeing Justin at nine-thirty.

Again, she wondered what he wanted to see her about. Once upon a time she might have thought he was going to ask her advice on something, or at least her opinion. But since he'd taken over the running of the magazine, Justin had become more and more his own master, and behaved as though Candice – along with all the rest of the staff – was no longer his equal.

225

She would have resented it, had she not found it so ridiculous.

At nine twenty-five, Justin appeared at the door of the editorial office, still in conversation with someone in the corridor.

'OK, Charles,' he was saying. 'Thanks for that. Much appreciated. Yes, I'll keep you posted.' He lifted his hand in farewell, then came into the room and met Candice's eye.

'Right,' he said. 'In you come.'

He ushered Candice to a chair, then closed the door behind her and snapped the window blind shut. Slowly he walked round his desk, sat down and looked at her.

'So, Candice,' he said eventually, stopped, and gave a sigh. 'Tell me, how long have you been working for the *Londoner*?'

'You know how long!' said Candice. 'Five years.'

'That's right,' said Justin. 'Five years. And you've been happy here? You've been well treated?'

'Yes!' said Candice. 'Of course I have. Justin—'

'So you'd think, wouldn't you, that in all that time, a degree of . . . trust would have built up. You'd think that a satisfied employee would have no need to resort to . . . dishonesty.' Justin shook his head solemnly and Candice stared at him, half wanting to laugh at his gravitas, trying to work out what he was getting at. Had someone broken into the office? Or been pick-pocketing?

'Justin,' she said calmly. 'What are you talking about?'

'God, Candice, you're making this bloody difficult for me.'

'What?' said Candice impatiently. 'What are you talking about?' Justin stared at her as though in disbelief, then sighed.

'I'm talking about expenses, Candice. I'm talking about claiming false expenses.'

'Really?' said Candice. 'Who's been doing that?'

'You have!'

The words seemed to hit Candice in the face like a slap.

'What?' she said, and heard herself give an incongruous giggle. 'Me?'

'You think it's funny?'

'No! Of course not. It's just . . . ridiculous! Are you serious? You're not serious.'

'Oh, come on!' said Justin. 'Stop this act. You've been caught, Candice.'

'But I haven't done anything!' said Candice, her voice coming out more shrilly than she had intended. 'I don't know what you're talking about!'

'So you don't know about these?' Justin reached into his desk drawer and produced a pile of expense claim forms with receipts attached. He flicked through it and, with a slight lurch, Candice caught a glimpse of her name. 'Haircut at Michaeljohn,' he read from the top form. 'Are you telling me that's a legitimate editorial expense?'

'What?' said Candice, flabbergasted. 'I didn't submit that! I would never submit that!' Justin was turning to the next page. 'A beauty morning at Manor Graves Hotel.' He turned again. 'Lunch for three at the Ritz.'

'That was Sir Derek Cranley and his publicist,' said Candice at once. 'I had to give them lunch to get an interview. They refused to go anywhere else.'

'And Manor Graves Hotel?'

'I've never even been to Manor Graves Hotel!' said Candice, almost laughing. 'And I wouldn't claim something like that! This is a mistake!'

'So you didn't sign this hotel receipt and fill in this claim form.'

'Of course not!' said Candice incredulously. 'Let me see.'

She grabbed the piece of paper, looked at it and felt her stomach flip over. Her own signature stared up at her from a receipt she knew she'd never signed. An expenses claim form was neatly filled in – in what looked exactly like her handwriting. Her hands began to tremble.

'A total of one hundred and ninety-six pounds,' said Justin. 'Not bad, in a month.'

Suddenly a cold feeling came over Candice. Suddenly she remembered her bank statement; the extra money which had seemed to come out of nowhere. The extra money – which she hadn't bothered to question. She looked quickly at the date on the hotel receipt – a Saturday, six weeks ago – and again at the signature. It looked like hers, but it wasn't. It wasn't her signature.

'Perhaps it doesn't seem like a big deal to you,' said Justin. Candice looked up to see him standing by the window, facing her. The light from the window silhouetted his face so she couldn't see his expression, but his voice was grave. 'Fiddling expenses.' He made a careless gesture. 'One of those little crimes that doesn't matter. The truth is, Candice, it does matter.'

'I know it matters!' spat Candice in frustration. 'Don't bloody patronize me! I know it matters. But I didn't do it, OK?'

She took a deep breath, trying to keep calm – but her mind felt like a fish on the deck, thrashing back and forth in panic, trying to work it out.

'So what are these?' Justin pointed to the expense forms.

'Someone else must have filled them in. Forged my signature.'

'And why would they do that?'

'I . . . I don't know. But look, Justin! It isn't my handwriting. It just looks like it!' She flipped quickly through the pages. 'Look at this form compared to . . . this one!' She thrust the pages at Justin but he shook his head.

'You're saying somebody – for a reason we have yet to ascertain – forged your signature.'

'Yes!'

'And you knew nothing about it.'

'No!' said Candice. 'Of course not!'

'Right,' said Justin. He sighed as though disappointed by her reply. 'So when the expenses came through a week ago – expenses you say you knew nothing about – and you found a load of unexplained money in your account, you naturally pointed out the mistake and returned it straight away.'

He looked at her evenly and Candice stared back dumbly, feeling her cheeks flame bright red. Why hadn't she queried the extra money? Why hadn't she been honest? How could she have been so . . . so stupid?

'For God's sake, Candice, you might as well admit it,' said Justin wearily. 'You tried to fleece the company and you got caught.'

'I didn't!' said Candice, feeling a sudden thickness in her throat. 'Justin, you *know* I wouldn't do something like that.'

'To be honest, Candice, I feel at the moment as though I don't know you very well at all,' said Justin.

'What's that supposed to mean?'

'Heather's told me all about your little power trips over her,' said Justin, a sudden hostile note in his voice. 'To be honest, I'm surprised she didn't make an official complaint.'

'What?' said Candice in astonishment. 'Justin, what the hell are you talking about?'

'All innocent again?' said Justin sarcastically. 'Come on, Candice. We even spoke about it the other day. You admit you've been insisting on supervising all

229

Heather's work. Using your power over her to intimidate her.'

'I've been *helping* her!' said Candice in outrage. 'My God! How can you—'

'It probably made you feel pretty big, didn't it, getting a job for Heather?' Justin folded his arms. 'Then she started to make progress, and you resented it.'

'No! Justin—'

'She told me how badly you treated her after she presented her feature idea to me.' Justin's voice harshened. 'You just can't stand the fact that she's got talent, is that it?'

'Of course not!' said Candice, flinching at his voice. 'Justin, you've got it all wrong! It's twisted! It's—'

Candice broke off, and gazed at Justin, trying to marshal her flying thoughts. Nothing was making sense. Nothing was making—

She stopped, as something hit her. The receipt for the Michaeljohn haircut. That was hers. Her own private receipt, from her own pile of papers on the dressing table in her bedroom. Her own bedroom, in her own flat. No-one else could have—

'Oh my God,' she said slowly.

She picked up one of the expense forms, gazed at it again and slowly felt herself grow cold. Now that she looked closely, she could see the hint of another handwriting beneath the veneer of her own. Like a mocking wave, Heather's handwriting was staring up at her. She looked up, feeling sick.

'Where's Heather?' she said in a trembling voice.

'On holiday,' said Justin. 'For two weeks. Didn't she tell you?'

'No,' said Candice. 'No, she didn't.' She took a deep breath, and pushed her hair back off her damp face. 'Justin, I think . . . I think Heather forged these claims.'

'Oh really?' Justin laughed. 'Well, there's a surprise.'

'No.' Candice swallowed. 'No, Justin, really. You have to listen to me—'

'Candice, forget it,' said Justin impatiently. 'You're suspended.'

'What?' Utter shock drained Candice's face of colour.

'The company will carry out an internal investigation, and a disciplinary hearing will be held in due course,' said Justin briskly, as though reading lines from a card. 'In the meantime, until the matter is resolved, you will remain at home on full pay.'

'You . . . you can't be serious.'

'As far as I'm concerned, you're lucky not to be fired on the spot! Candice, what you did is fraud,' said Justin, and raised his chin slightly. 'If I hadn't instituted random spot-checks of the expenses system, it might not even have been picked up. Charles and I had a little chat this morning, and we both feel that this kind of thing has to be cracked down on firmly. In fact, we're going to be using this as an opportunity to—'

'Charles Allsopp.' Candice stared at him in sudden comprehension. 'Oh my God,' she said softly. 'You're doing this to impress bloody Charles Allsopp, aren't you?'

'Don't be stupid,' said Justin angrily, and flushed a deep red. 'This is a company decision based on company policy.'

'You're really doing this to me.' Candice's eyes suddenly smarted with disbelieving, angry tears. 'You're treating me like a criminal, after . . . everything. I mean, we lived together for six months, didn't we? Doesn't that count for *anything*?'

At her words, Justin's head jerked up and he gave her an almost triumphant look.

He's been waiting for me to say that, thought Candice in horrified realization. He's been waiting for me to grovel.

'So you think I should make an exception for you

because you used to be my girlfriend,' said Justin. 'You think I might do you a special favour and turn a blind eye. Is that it?'

Candice stared at him, feeling sickened.

'No,' she said, as calmly as she could manage. 'Of course not.' She paused. 'But you could . . . trust me.'

There was silence as the two stared at each other and, for an instant, Candice thought she saw the old Justin looking at her – the Justin who would have believed her; possibly even defended her. Then, as though coming to, he turned and reached into his desk drawer.

'As far as I'm concerned,' he said coldly, 'you've forfeited my trust. And everybody else's. Here.' He looked up and held out a black plastic bin liner. 'Take what you want and go.'

Half an hour later, Candice stood on the pavement outside the glass doors, holding her bin liner and flinching at the curious gazes of passers-by. It was ten o'clock in the morning. For most people the day was just beginning. People were hurrying to their offices; everyone had somewhere to go. Candice swallowed and took another step forward, trying to look as though she was standing here on the pavement with a bin bag on purpose. But she could feel her calm face slipping; could feel raw emotion threatening to escape. She had never felt so vulnerable; so frighteningly alone.

As she'd come back into the editorial office, she'd managed to maintain a modicum of dignity. She'd managed to hold her head up high and – above all – had refused to look guilty. But it had been difficult. Everyone obviously knew what had happened. She could see heads looking up at her, then quickly looking away; faces agog with curiosity; with relief that it wasn't them. With a new member of the Allsopp family in charge of the company, the future was uncertain for everybody. At one point she'd caught Alicia's eye and saw a genuine flash of sympathy before Alicia, too, looked away. Candice didn't blame her. No-one could afford to take any chances.

She'd shaken the bin bag open with trembling fingers, sickened by its slithery touch. She had never felt so sordid; so humiliated. Around the room, every-one was working silently at their computers, which meant they were all listening. Almost unable to believe she was doing it, Candice had opened her top desk drawer and looked at its familiar contents. Notebooks, pens, old disks, a box of raspberry tea-bags.

'Don't take any disks,' Justin had said, passing by. 'And don't touch the computer. We don't want any company information walking out with you.'

'Just leave me alone!' Candice had snapped savagely, tears coming to her eyes. 'I'm not going to *steal* any-thing.'

Now, standing outside on the hard pavement, a hot-ness rose to her eyes again. They all believed she was a thief. And why shouldn't they? The evidence was convincing enough. Candice closed her eyes. She still felt dizzy at the idea that Heather had fabricated evidence about her. That Heather had, all the time, been plotting behind her back. Her mind scurried backwards and forwards, trying to think logically; try-ing to work it all out. But she could not think straight while she was fighting tears; while her face was flushed and her throat blocked by something hard.

'All right, love?' said a man in a denim jacket, and Candice's head jerked up.

'Yes thanks,' she muttered, and felt a small tear escape onto her cheek. Before he could say anything else she began walking along the pavement, not know-ing where she was going, her mind skittering wildly about. The bin liner banged against her legs, the plas-tic was slippery in her grasp; she imagined that everyone she passed looked at it with a knowing glance. In a shop window she glanced at her reflection and was shocked at the sight. Her face was white, and busy with suppressed tears. Her suit was already crumpled; her hair had escaped from its smooth fastening. She had to get home, she thought frantically. She would take off her suit, take a bath, hide away mindlessly like a small animal in a hole until she was feeling able to emerge.

At the corner she reached a telephone box. She pulled open the heavy door and slipped inside. The interior was cool and quiet; a temporary haven. Maggie, she thought frantically, picking up the receiver. Or Roxanne. They would help her. One of them would help her. Roxanne or Maggie. She reached to dial, then stopped.

Not Roxanne. Not after the way they'd parted at Ralph's funeral. And not Maggie. Not after the things she'd said to her; not after that awful phone call.

A cold feeling ran down Candice's spine and she leaned against the cool glass of the kiosk. She couldn't call either of them. She'd lost them both. Somehow she'd lost her two closest friends in the world.

Suddenly a banging on the glass of the telephone box jolted her, and she opened her eyes in shock.

'Are you making a call?' shouted a woman holding a toddler by the hand.

'No,' said Candice dazedly. 'No, I'm not.'

She stepped out of the telephone box onto the street, shifted her bin liner to the other hand and looked around confusedly, as though resurfacing from a tunnel. Then she began to walk again in a haze of misery, barely aware of where she was going.

As Roxanne came up the stairs, holding a loaf of bread and a newspaper, she heard the telephone ringing inside her flat. Let it ring, she thought. Let it ring.

There was no-one she wanted to hear from. Slowly she reached for her key, inserted it into the lock of the front door and opened it. She closed the door behind her, put down the loaf of bread and the newspaper, and stared balefully at the phone, still ringing.

'You don't bloody give up, do you?' she said, and reached for the receiver. 'Yes?'

'Am I speaking to Miss Roxanne Miller?' said a strange male voice.

'Yes,' said Roxanne. 'Yes, you are.'

'Good,' said the voice. 'Let me introduce myself. My name is Neil Cooper and I represent the firm of Strawson and Co.'

'I don't have a car,' said Roxanne. 'I don't need car insurance. And I don't have any windows.'

Neil Cooper gave a nervous laugh. 'Miss Miller, I should explain. I am a lawyer. I'm telephoning you in connection with the estate of Ralph Allsopp.'

'Oh,' said Roxanne. She stared at the wall and blinked furiously. Hearing his name unexpectedly on other people's lips still took her by surprise; still sent shock-waves through her body.

'Perhaps I could ask you to come into the office?' the man was saying, and Roxanne's mind snapped into focus. Ralph Allsopp. The estate of Ralph Allsopp.

'Oh God,' she said, and tears began to run freely down her face. 'He's gone and left something to me, hasn't he? The stupid, sentimental bastard. And you're going to give it to me.'

'If we could just arrange a meeting . . .'

'Is it his watch? Or that crappy ancient typewriter.' Roxanne gave a half-laugh in spite of herself. 'That stupid bloody Remington.'

'Shall we say half-past four on Thursday?' the lawyer said, and Roxanne exhaled sharply.

'Look,' she said. 'I don't know if you're aware, but Ralph and I weren't exactly . . .' She paused. 'I'd rather stay out of the picture. Can't you just send whatever it is to me? I'll pay the postage.'

There was silence down the line, then the lawyer said, more firmly, 'Half-past four. I'll expect you.'

Candice became aware that her steps were, unconsciously, taking her towards home. As she turned into her street she stopped at the sight of a chugging taxi outside her house. She stood still, staring at it, her mind ticking over – then stiffened as Heather appeared, coming out of the front door. She was wearing jeans and a coat and carrying a suitcase. Her blond hair was just as bouncy as ever, her eyes just as wide and innocent – and as Candice stared at her she felt herself falter in confusion.

Was she really accusing Heather – this cheery, warmhearted friend – of deliberately setting her up? Logically, the facts drew her to that conclusion. But as she gazed at Heather talking pleasantly to the taxi driver, everything in her resisted it. Could there not be some other plausible explanation? she thought frantically. Some other factor she knew nothing about?

As she stood transfixed, Heather turned as though aware of Candice's gaze, and gave a slight start of surprise. For a few moments the two girls stared at each other silently. Heather's gaze ran over Candice, taking in the bin bag; her flustered face, her bloodshot eyes.

'Heather.' Candice's voice sounded hoarse to her own ears. 'Heather, I need to talk to you.'

'Oh yes?' said Heather calmly.

'I've just been . . .' She paused, barely able to say the words aloud. 'I've just been suspended from work.'

'Really?' said Heather. 'Shame.' She smiled at Candice, then turned and got into the taxi.

Candice stared at her and felt her heart begin to pound.

'No,' she said. 'No.' She began to run along the pavement, her breath coming quickly, her bin bag bouncing along awkwardly behind her. 'Heather, I . . . I don't understand.' She reached the taxi door just as Heather was reaching to close it, and grabbed hold of it.

'Let go!' snapped Heather.

'I don't understand,' said Candice breathlessly. 'I thought we were friends.'

'Did you?' said Heather. 'That's funny. My father thought your dad was his friend, too.'

Candice's heart stopped. She stared at Heather and felt her face suffuse with colour. Her grip on the door weakened and she licked her lips.

'When . . . when did you find out?' Her voice was strangled; something like cotton wool seemed to be blocking her airway.

'I didn't have to find out,' said Heather scathingly. 'I knew who you were all along. As soon as I saw you in that bar.' Her voice harshened. 'My whole family knows who you are, Candice Brewin.'

Candice stared at Heather speechlessly. Her legs were trembling; she felt almost dizzy with shock.

'And now you know how I felt,' said Heather. 'Now you know what it was like for me. Having everything taken away, with no warning.' She gave a tiny, satisfied smile and her gaze ran again over Candice's dishevelled appearance. 'So – are you enjoying it? Do you think it's fun, losing everything overnight?'

'I trusted you,' said Candice numbly. 'You were my friend.'

'And I was fourteen years old!' spat Heather with a sudden viciousness. 'We lost everything. Jesus, Candice! Did you really think we could be friends, after what your father did to my family?'

'But I tried to make amends!' said Candice. 'I tried to make it up to you!' Heather shook her head, and wrenched the taxi door out of Candice's grasp. 'Heather, listen!' said Candice in panic. 'Don't you understand?' She leaned forward, almost eagerly. 'I was trying to make it up to you! I was trying to help you!'

'Yes, well,' said Heather coldly. 'Maybe you didn't try hard enough.'

She gave Candice one final look, then slammed the door.

'Heather!' said Candice through the open window, her heart thumping. 'Heather, wait! Please. I need my job back.' Her voice rose in desperation. 'You have to help me! Please, Heather!'

But Heather didn't even turn round. A moment later the taxi zoomed away up the street.

Candice watched it go in disbelief, then sank shakily down onto the pavement, the bin bag still clutched in her hand. A couple passing by with their dog looked at her curiously, but she didn't react. She was oblivious of the outside world, oblivious of everything except her own thudding shock.

Chapter Seventeen

There was a sound behind her and Candice looked up. Ed was standing at the door of the house, gazing at her, for once without any glint of amusement in his eye. He looked serious, almost stern.

'I saw her getting all her stuff together,' he said. 'I tried to call you at work, but they wouldn't put me through.' He took a couple of steps towards her, and looked at the bin liner lying in a crumpled heap on the ground. 'Does that mean what I think it does?'

'I've been . . . suspended,' said Candice, barely able to manage the words. 'They think I'm a thief.'

'So – what went wrong?'

'I don't know,' said Candice, rubbing her face wearily. 'I don't know what went wrong. You tell me. I just . . . All I wanted, all along, was to do the right thing. You know?' She looked up at him. 'I just wanted to . . . do a good deed. And what happens?' Her voice began to thicken dangerously. 'I lose my job, I lose my friends . . . I've lost everything, Ed. Everything.'

Two tears spilled onto her cheeks, and she wiped them away with the sleeve of her jacket. Ed looked at her consideringly for a moment.

'It's not so bad,' he said. 'You haven't lost your looks. If that's of any interest to you.' Candice stared at him, then gave a shaky giggle. 'And you haven't lost—' He broke off.

'What?'

'You haven't lost me,' said Ed, looking straight at her. 'Again — if that's of any interest to you.'

There was a taut silence.

'I . . .' Candice swallowed. 'Thanks.'

'Come on.' Ed held out his hand. 'Let's get you inside.'

'Thanks,' whispered Candice, and took his hand gratefully. 'Thanks, Ed.'

They trudged up the stairs in silence. As she arrived at the front door of her flat Candice hesitated, then pushed it open. Immediately she had a feeling of emptiness. Heather's coat was gone from the stand in the hall; her message pad had disappeared from the little phone table; her bedroom door was ajar and the wardrobe visibly empty.

'Is everything still there?' said Ed behind her. 'If she's stolen anything we can call the police.'

Candice walked a few steps into the sitting room and looked around.

'I think everything's still here,' she said. 'Everything of mine, anyway.'

'Well, that's something,' said Ed. 'Isn't it?'

Candice didn't reply. She walked over to the mantelpiece and looked silently at the photograph of herself, her mother and her father. Smiling into the sun, innocently happy, before any of it happened. Her breath began to come more quickly; something hot seemed to rise through her, burning her throat, her face, her eyes.

'I feel so . . . stupid,' she said. 'I feel so completely stupid.' Tears of humiliation began to run down her cheeks and she buried her face in her hands. 'I believed every bloody thing she said. But she was lying. Everything she said was . . . lies.'

Ed leaned against the door frame, frowning.

240

'So – what – she had it in for you?'

'She had it in for me all along.' Candice looked up and wiped her eyes. 'It's a . . . it's a long story.'

'And you had no idea.'

'I thought she liked me. I thought we were best friends. She told me what I wanted to hear, and I . . .' A fresh wave of humiliation passed through Candice. 'And I fell for it.'

'Come on, Candice,' said Ed. 'You can't just blame yourself. She fooled everyone. Face it, she was good.'

'You weren't fooled by her though, were you?' retorted Candice, looking up with a tearstained face. 'You told me you thought she was mad.'

'I thought she was a bit weird,' said Ed, shrugging. 'I didn't realize she was a fucking psycho.'

There was silence. Candice turned away from the mantelpiece and took a few steps towards the sofa. But as she reached it she stopped, without sitting down. The sofa no longer seemed welcoming. It no longer seemed hers. Everything in the flat suddenly seemed tainted.

'She must have been plotting all along,' she said, and began to pick distractedly at the fabric of the sofa. 'From the moment she walked in the door with all those flowers. Pretending to be so grateful.' Candice closed her eyes, feeling a sharp pain run up her body. 'Always so sweet and grateful. Always so . . .' She swallowed hard. 'In the evenings, we used to sit on this sofa together watching the telly. Doing each other's nails. I'd be thinking what a great friend she was. I'd be thinking I'd found a soulmate. And what was Heather thinking?' Candice opened her eyes and looked bleakly at Ed. 'What was she really thinking?'

'Candice—'

'She was sitting there, hating me, wasn't she? Wondering what she could do to hurt me.' Fresh tears began to fall down Candice's face. 'How could I have

241

been so *stupid*? I did all her bloody work for her, she never paid me a penny rent . . . and I kept thinking I still owed her! I kept feeling guilty about her. Guilty!' Candice wiped her streaming nose. 'You know what she told them at work? She said I was bullying her.'

'And they believed her?' said Ed incredulously.

'Justin believed her.'

'Well,' said Ed. 'That figures.'

'I tried to tell him,' said Candice, her voice rising in distress. 'I tried to explain. But he wouldn't believe me. He just looked at me as though I was a . . . criminal.'

She broke off into a shuddering silence. Outside in the distance, a siren gave a long wail, as though in imitation of her voice, then broke into whoops and faded away.

'You need a stiff drink,' said Ed finally. 'Have you got any drink in the house?'

'Some white wine,' said Candice after a pause. 'In the fridge.'

'White wine? What is it with women and white wine?' Ed shook his head. 'Stay here. I'm going to get you a proper drink.'

Roxanne took a sip of cappuccino and stared blankly out of the café window at a group of lost tourists on the street. She had told herself that today she would spring back into action. She'd had, in all, nearly a month off. Now it was time to get back on the phone, start working again; start leading her former life.

But instead, here she was, sitting in a Covent Garden café, sipping her fourth cappuccino, letting the morning slip past. She felt unable to concentrate on anything constructive; unable to pretend to herself that life was anything like back to normal. Grief was like a grey fog that permeated every move, every thought;

that made everything seem pointless. Why write any more articles? Why make the effort? She felt as if everything she had ever done over the last few years had been in relation to Ralph. Her articles had been written to entertain him, her trips abroad had been to provide anecdotes that would make him laugh; her clothes had been bought because he would like them. She had not realized it at the time, of course. She'd always thought herself completely, ferociously independent. But now he was gone – and the point seemed to have gone out of her life.

She reached in her bag for her cigarettes and, as she did so, her fingers came across the scrap of paper bearing the name of Neil Cooper and an address. Roxanne looked at the paper for a few steady seconds, then thrust it away from her, feeling sick. She had been thrown by the lawyer's call; still felt shaky when she remembered it. In her memory, his voice seemed to have had a patronizing note. A smooth, oh-so-discreet knowingness. A firm like his probably dealt with dead clients' mistresses every day. There was probably a whole bloody department dedicated to them.

Tears stung Roxanne's eyes and she flicked her lighter savagely. Why had Ralph had to tell a fucking *lawyer* about the two of them? Why had he had to tell anyone? She felt exposed; vulnerable at the idea that an entire plushy office was laughing at her. She would walk in and they would smile behind their hands; eye her outfit and hairstyle; suppress a giggle as they asked her to sit down. Or, even worse, stare at her with blatant disapproval.

For they were on Cynthia's side, weren't they? These lawyers were all part of that secure, established life Ralph had enjoyed with his wife. A union that had been legitimized by a marriage certificate, by children, by solid shared property; that had been buttressed by family friends, by distant cousins, by accountants and lawyers. An entire support system, dedicated to propping up and validating the joint entity of Ralph and Cynthia.

And what had she and Ralph had in comparison? Roxanne drew on her cigarette, feeling the acrid smoke burning her lungs. What had she and Ralph had? Mere ephemera. Fleeting experiences, memories, stories. A few days here, a few days there. Furtive embraces; secretly whispered endearments. Nothing public, nothing solid. Six whole years of wishes and whimsy.

A tree falls in the forest, thought Roxanne, staring bleakly out of the window. A man tells a woman he loves her. But if no-one is present to hear it – does he really make a sound? Did it really happen?

She sighed, and stubbed out her cigarette. Forget Neil Cooper, she thought, draining her cappuccino. Forget the meeting on Thursday. Forget. That was all she wanted to do.

Candice sat silently on the sofa, head buried in her hands, her eyes closed and her mind a whirl of images and memories. Heather's innocent smile and gushing words. Heather leaning forward in the candlelight and asking her what meant most to her in the world. Heather squeezing her waist affectionately. And her own pride and delight in her new friend; her idealistic belief that she was atoning for her father's crimes.

The memories made her wince in pain; in mortification. How could she ever have believed that life was that easy; that people were that accepting? How could she have seen things so simplistically? Her attempt to make amends now suddenly seemed laughable; her trust in Heather almost criminally naive.

'I was a fool,' she muttered aloud. 'A gullible, stupid—'

'Stop talking to yourself,' came Ed's voice from above her, and her head jerked up. 'And get that inside you,' he added, holding out a glass of transparent liquid.

'What is it?' she said suspiciously, taking it.

'Grappa. Wonderful stuff. Go on.' He nodded at the glass and she took a gulp, then gasped as the fiery liquid hit her mouth.

'Bloody hell!' she managed, her mouth tingling with pain.

'Like I said.' Ed grinned. 'Wonderful stuff. Go on, have some more.'

Candice braced herself, and took another gulp. As the alcohol descended inside her, a warm glow began to spread through her body, and she found herself smiling up at Ed.

'There's plenty more,' said Ed, replenishing her glass from the bottle in his hand. 'And now,' he added, reaching for the phone, 'before you get too comfortable, you've got a call to make.' He plonked the phone in her lap and grinned at her.

'What?' said Candice, confused.

'Phone Justin. Tell him what Heather said to you – and that she's scarpered. Prove she's a nutcase.' Candice gazed up at him and, gradually, realization descended on her.

'Oh my God,' she said slowly. 'You're right! That changes everything, doesn't it? He'll have to believe me!' She took another gulp of grappa, then picked up the receiver. 'OK. Let's do it.' Briskly she dialled the number and, as she heard the ringing tone, felt a surge of excitement.

'Hello,' she said, as soon as she got through, 'I'd like to speak to Justin Vellis, please.'

'I'll just check for you,' said the receptionist. 'May I say who's calling?'

'Yes,' said Candice. 'It's . . . it's Candice Brewin.'

'Oh yes,' said the receptionist, in tones which might have been scorn or merely indifference. 'I'll just try the line for you.'

As she heard Justin's phone ringing, Candice felt a pang of apprehension. She glanced at Ed, leaning against the arm of the sofa, and he gave her the thumbs-up.

'Justin Vellis.'

'Hi, Justin,' said Candice, winding the telephone cord tightly around her fingers. 'It's Candice.'

'Yes,' said Justin. 'What do you want?'

'Listen, Justin.' Candice tried to speak quickly but calmly. 'I can prove that what I said in your office was true. Heather's admitted she set me up. She's got a vendetta against me. She yelled at me in the street!'

'Oh, really?' said Justin.

'Yes! And now she's cleared out of the flat with all her stuff. She's just . . . disappeared!'

'So what?'

'So, isn't that a bit suspicious?' said Candice. 'Come on, think about it!'

There was a pause, then Justin sighed. 'As I recall, Candice, Heather's gone on holiday. Hardly suspicious.'

'She hasn't gone on holiday!' cried Candice in frustration. 'She's gone for good! And she admitted she'd got me into trouble on purpose.'

'She actually said that she'd forged your hand-writing?'

'No,' said Candice after a pause. 'Not exactly in those words. But she said—'

'Candice, I'm afraid I don't have time for this,' interrupted Justin coolly. 'You'll have an opportunity to state your case at the hearing. But please don't telephone me again. I'll be telling reception not to put through your calls.'

'Justin, how can you be so bloody obtuse?' yelled Candice. 'How can you—'

'Goodbye, Candice.' The phone went dead and Candice stared at it in disbelief.

246

'Let me guess,' said Ed, taking a gulp of grappa. 'He apologized and offered you a pay rise.'

'He doesn't believe me,' said Candice. 'He doesn't bloody well believe me!' Her voice rose in outrage. 'How can he believe her over me? How *can* he?'

She rose to her feet, letting the phone fall to the ground with a crash, and strode to the window. She was shaking with anger, unable to keep still.

'Who the hell does he think he is, anyway?' she said. 'He gets a bit of temporary power, and suddenly he thinks he's running the whole bloody company. He spoke to me as if I was some bloody . . . shopfloor worker, and he was the president of some huge corporation. It's pathetic!'

'Tiny dick, obviously,' said Ed.

'Not tiny,' said Candice, still staring out of the window. 'But fairly meagre.' She turned round, met Ed's eyes, and gave a bursting gasp of laughter. 'God, I can't believe how furious I am.'

'Neither can I,' said Ed in impressed tones. 'Angry Candice. I like it.'

'I feel as though—' She shook her head mutely, smiling tightly as though suppressing more laughter. Then a tear ran quickly down her face.

'So what do I do now?' she said more quietly. She wiped the tear away and exhaled. 'The hearing won't be for another two weeks, apparently. At least. So what do I do in the meantime?' She pushed a hand through her dishevelled hair. 'I can't even get back into the building. They took my security card away.'

There was silence for a few seconds, then Ed put down his glass of grappa and stood up.

'Come on,' he said. 'Let's get out of here. Go to my aunt's house.'

'What?' Candice looked at him uncertainly. 'The house you inherited?'

'Change of scene. You can't stick in this flat all day.'

247

'But . . . it's miles away, isn't it? Wiltshire or some-where.'

'So what?' said Ed. 'Plenty of time.' He looked at his watch. 'It's only eleven.'

'I don't know.' Candice rubbed her face. 'I'm not sure it's such a great idea.'

'Well, what else are you going to do all day? Sit around and go crazy? Sod that.'

There was a long pause.

'You're right,' said Candice eventually. 'I mean, what else am I going to do?' She looked up at Ed and felt a smile licking across her face; a sudden euphoria at the thought of escaping. 'You're right. Let's go.'

Chapter Eighteen

At midday, Giles knocked on the bedroom door and waited until Maggie sleepily lifted her head.

'Someone to see you,' he said softly. Maggie rubbed her eyes and yawned as he advanced into the room, holding Lucia in his arms. The room was bright with sunshine and she could smell coffee in the air. And she didn't feel tired. She grinned, and stretched her arms high above her head, enjoying the sensation of the cotton sheets against her well-rested limbs. What a wonderful place bed was, she thought happily.

'Oh, I feel good!' she said, and sat up, leaning against a mound of pillows. She gave a huge yawn, and smiled at Giles. 'I feel fantastic. Except I'm bursting with milk . . .'

'I'm not surprised,' said Giles, handing Lucia to her and watching as Maggie unbuttoned her nightshirt. 'That's fourteen hours you've been asleep.'

'Fourteen hours,' said Maggie wonderingly, as Lucia began to feed. 'Fourteen hours! I can't remember the last time I slept for more than . . .' She shook her head. 'And I can't believe I didn't wake up!'

'You've been a noise-free zone,' said Giles. 'I turned all the phones off and took Lucia out for a walk. We only got back a few minutes ago.'

'Did you?' Maggie looked down at Lucia's little face

and smiled, with a sudden tenderness. 'Isn't she pretty?'

'She's gorgeous,' said Giles. 'Like her mother.'

He came and sat down on the bed, and watched them both in silence. After a while, Maggie looked up at him.

'And how was she during the night? Did you get much sleep?'

'Not much,' said Giles ruefully. 'She doesn't seem to like that cot much, does she?' His gaze met Maggie's. 'Is that what it's been like, every night?'

'Pretty much,' said Maggie after a pause.

'I don't understand why you never told me.' Giles pushed a hand back through his rumpled hair. 'We could have got help, we could have—'

'I know.' Maggie bit her lip and looked out of the window at the blue sky. 'I just . . . I don't know. I couldn't face admitting how awful it was.' She hesitated. 'You thought I was doing so well, and you thought Lucia was so perfect, and you were so proud of me . . . If I'd told you it was a nightmare . . .'

'I would have said sod the baby, let's send it back,' said Giles promptly and Maggie giggled.

'Thanks for taking her last night,' she said.

'Maggie, don't *thank* me!' said Giles, almost impatiently. 'She's my child too, isn't she? I've got just as much right to curse her at three o'clock in the morning as you have.'

'Bloody baby,' said Maggie, smiling down at her.

'Bloody baby,' echoed Giles. 'Bloody silly Mummy.' He shook his head in mock-disapproval. 'Lying to the health visitor. I don't know. You could get put in prison for that.'

'It wasn't lying,' said Maggie, transferring Lucia to the other breast. 'It was . . .' She thought for a moment. 'It was spin.'

'Good PR, you mean.'

'Exactly,' said Maggie, giving a self-mocking smile. '"Life with my new baby is utter bliss," commented Ms Phillips. "Yes, she is an angel, and no, I have encountered no problems. For I am Supermum."' She stared at Lucia's tiny, sucking face, then looked up seriously at Giles. 'I thought I had to be like your mother. But I'm nothing like your mother.'

'You're not as bossy as my mother,' said Giles, pulling a face. 'She gave me a real earful about my responsibilities. I felt as if I was about ten years old again. She can be pretty fearsome when she wants to, my mum.'

'Good,' said Maggie, grinning.

'Which reminds me,' said Giles. 'Would Madam like breakfast in bed?'

'Madam would *adore* breakfast in bed.'

'And what about Mademoiselle? Shall I take her with me or leave her?'

'You can leave Mademoiselle,' said Maggie, stroking Lucia's head. 'I'm not sure she's quite finished her own breakfast.'

When Giles had gone she lay back comfortably against the pillows, staring out of the window at the fields beyond the garden. From that distance, no mud was visible; no brambles could be seen. A bright sun was beating down and wind was ruffling the long green grass; a small bird fluttered out of one of the hedges. The countryside at its most idyllic. The kind of backdrop she'd imagined for her fantasy rustic picnics.

'What do you think?' she said, looking down at Lucia. 'You like rustic? You like cows and sheep? Or you like cars and shops? Cows and sheep or cars and shops. You choose.'

Lucia looked at her intently for a moment, then screwed up her tiny face in a yawn.

'Exactly,' said Maggie. 'You don't really give a toss, do you?'

'Voilà!' Giles appeared at the door holding a tray on which reposed a glass of orange juice, a cafetière full of steaming coffee, a plate of warm croissants and a pot of Bonne Maman Apricot Conserve. He looked at Maggie silently for a second, then put the tray down on a table.

'You look beautiful,' he said.

'Yeah, right,' said Maggie, flushing slightly.

'You do.' He came towards the bed, plucked Lucia from Maggie's arms and placed her carefully on the floor. He sat down on the bed and stroked Maggie's hair, her shoulder; then, very gently, her breast. 'Any room in that bed for me, do you think?'

Maggie stared back at him and felt her well-rested body respond to his touch. Remembered sensations began to prickle at her skin; her breath began to come slightly more quickly.

'Could be,' she said, and smiled self-consciously.

Slowly Giles leaned forward and kissed her. Maggie closed her eyes in delight and wrapped her arms around his body, losing herself in delicious sensation. Giles's lips found her earlobe, and she gave a little moan of pleasure.

'We could make number two,' came Giles's voice in her ear. 'Wouldn't that be lovely?'

'What?' Maggie stiffened in horror. 'Giles . . .'

'Joke,' said Giles. She pulled away, to see him laughing at her. 'Joke.'

'No!' said Maggie, her heart still thudding. 'That's not a joke! That's not even . . . not even half-funny. It's . . . It's . . .' Suddenly she found herself giggling. 'You're evil.'

'I know,' said Giles, and nuzzled her neck. 'Aren't you glad you married me?'

Ed's car was a navy blue convertible. As he bleeped it open, Candice stared at it in disbelief.

'I didn't know you had a . . . what is this?'

'BMW,' said Ed.

'Wow,' said Candice. 'So how come I've never seen you in it?'

Ed shrugged. 'I don't drive a lot.'

Candice wrinkled her brow.

'So then – why have you got a flash car like this if you never drive?'

'Come on, Candice.' He grinned disarmingly. 'I'm a boy.'

Candice laughed in spite of herself, and got into the car. Immediately she felt ridiculously glamorous. As they drove off, her hair began to blow about her face. The sun glinted on the windscreen and the shiny chrome of the wing mirrors. They stopped at a traffic light and Candice watched a girl of about her own age cross the road. She was dressed smartly and obviously hurrying back to the office. Back towards a secure job; a trusting environment; a secure future.

At the beginning of the day she'd been just like that girl, thought Candice. Oblivious and trusting, completely unaware of what was about to happen. And in a matter of hours it had all changed.

'I'll never be the same again,' she said, without quite meaning to. Ed swivelled in his seat and looked at her.

'What do you mean?'

'I'll never be so . . . trusting. I was a stupid, gullible fool.' She rested her elbow on the door, supporting her head with her hand. 'What a bloody disaster. What a bloody . . .'

'Candice, don't get like that,' said Ed. Candice turned her head to look at him.

'What?' she said sarcastically. 'Don't blame myself?'

Ed shrugged. 'Don't tear yourself to bits. What you did, helping Heather – it was a . . . a generous, positive thing to do. If Heather'd been a different person, maybe it would have worked out fine.'

'I suppose so,' muttered Candice after a pause.

'It wasn't your fault she was a nutter, was it? She didn't arrive with a sign round her neck.'

'But I was so bloody . . . idealistic about the whole thing.'

'Of course you were,' said Ed. 'That's what makes you . . . you.'

There was a sudden stillness between them. Candice gazed back into Ed's dark, intelligent eyes and felt a faint tinge in her cheeks. Then, behind them, a horn sounded. Without speaking, Ed put the car into gear and drove off, and Candice sat back in her seat and closed her eyes, her heart thumping.

When she opened her eyes again, they were on the motorway. The sky had clouded over a little and the wind had become too strong to allow talking. Candice struggled up to a sitting position and looked about. There were fields, and sheep, and a familiar country smell. Her legs felt stiff and her face dry from the wind, and she wondered how much further away it was.

As though reading her mind, Ed signalled left and turned off the motorway.

'Are we nearly there?' shouted Candice. He nodded, but said nothing more. They passed through a village and she peered with interest at the cottages and houses, wondering what Ed's house might be like. He had said nothing about it; she didn't know if it was large or small, old or new. Suddenly the car was swinging off the main road up a narrow track. They bumped along for two miles or so, then Ed turned in at a gate. The car crackled down a sloping drive, and Candice gazed ahead of her in disbelief.

They were approaching a low, thatched cottage, turned slightly away from them as though too shy to show its face. The walls were painted a soft apricot; the window frames were turquoise; from inside a window she caught a splash of lilac. Around the corner she could see several brightly painted pots clustering outside the wooden front door.

'I've never seen anything like it,' Candice said in astonishment. 'It's like a fairytale.'

'What?' said Ed. He switched the engine off and looked around with a suppressed gleam. 'Oh yes. Didn't I say? She was a painter, my aunt. Liked a bit of colour.' He opened the car door. 'Come on. Come and see inside.'

The front door opened onto a low hall; a bunch of dried flowers hung from a low beam.

'That's to warn tall bastards,' said Ed. He glanced at Candice, who was peering into the flagstoned kitchen. 'What do you think? You like it?'

'I love it,' said Candice. She took a few steps into the warm red kitchen and ran her hand over the wooden table. 'When you said a house, I imagined . . . I had no idea.'

'I stayed here quite a bit,' said Ed. 'When my parents were splitting up. I used to sit in front of that window, playing with my trains. Sad little git, really.'

'How old were you?' said Candice.

'Ten,' said Ed. 'The next year, I went away to school.'

He turned away, staring out of the window. Somewhere in the house, a clock was still ticking; outside was a still, country silence. Over Ed's shoulder, through the glass, Candice could see a bird pecking anxiously in a pink-painted flowerpot.

'So,' said Ed, turning to face her. 'What do you reckon I'd get for it?'

'You're not going to sell it!' said Candice in horror.

'No,' said Ed, 'I'm going to become a bloody farmer and live in it.'

'You wouldn't have to live in it all the time. You could keep it for—'

'Weekends?' said Ed. 'Drive down every Friday rush

255

hour to sit and freeze? Give me a break, Candice.'

'Oh well,' said Candice. 'It's your house.' She looked at a framed sampler on the wall. *Absence makes the heart grow fonder.* Next to it was a charcoal drawing of a shell, and below that a child's painting of three fat geese in a field. Looking more closely, Candice saw the name 'Edward Armitage' written in a teacher's hand in the bottom left-hand corner.

'You never told me it was like this,' she said, turning round. 'You never told me it was so . . .' She spread her hands helplessly.

'No,' said Ed. 'Well, you never asked.'

'So what happened to my breakfast,' murmured Maggie, lying in the crook of Giles's arm. Lazily he shifted, and opened one eye.

'You want breakfast, *too*?'

'You bet I do. You don't get off that lightly.' Maggie sat up to allow Giles to move, then flopped back on the pillows and watched as he sat up and reached for his T-shirt. Halfway through putting it on, he stopped.

'I don't believe it!' he whispered. 'Look at this!' Maggie sat up and followed his gaze. Lucia was fast asleep on the carpet, her little hands curled into fists.

'Well, we obviously didn't disturb her,' she said with a giggle.

'How much did that cot cost?' said Giles ruefully. He tiptoed past Lucia, lifted the tray of breakfast off the table and presented it to Maggie.

'Madam.'

'Fresh coffee, please,' she said at once. 'This is luke-warm.'

'The management is devastated,' said Giles. 'Please accept this complimentary glass of orange juice and array of fine croissants with our humblest apologies.'

'Hmmm,' said Maggie, taking a doubtful sip. 'Plus a meal for two at the restaurant of my choice?'

'Absolutely,' agreed Giles. 'It's the least the management can do.'

He took the cafetière and headed out of the room. Maggie sat up, pulled open a croissant and spread it thickly with the amber-coloured conserve. She took a huge bite and then another, savouring the buttery taste, the sweetness of the jam. Simple food had never tasted so delicious. She felt as though her taste buds, along with everything else, had been temporarily dulled and then sprung back to life.

'This is more like it,' said Giles, coming back into the room with fresh coffee. He sat down on the bed, and smiled at Maggie. 'Isn't it?'

'Yes,' said Maggie, and took a gulp of tangy orange juice. Sunlight glinted off the glass as she put it back down on the tray and took another bite of apricot croissant. Warm colours, sweet and light, like heaven in her mouth. She looked out of the window again at the green fields, shining in the sunshine like an English paradise, and felt a momentary pull towards them.

Brambles and weeds, she reminded herself. Mud and manure. Cows and sheep. Or cars and shops and taxis. Bright lights. People.

'I think,' she said casually, 'I might go back to work.' She took a sip of grainy, delicious coffee and looked up at Giles.

'Right,' he said cautiously. 'To your old job? Or . . .'

'My old job,' said Maggie. 'Editor of the *Londoner*. I was good at it, and I miss it.' She took another sip of coffee, feeling pleasurably in command of the situation. 'I can still take a few months more maternity leave, and then we can hire a nanny, and I can go back.'

Giles was silent for a few minutes. Cheerfully, Maggie finished her first croissant and began to spread jam on the second.

'Maggie . . .' he said eventually.

'Yes?' She smiled at him.

'Are you sure about this? It would be hard work.'

'I know. And so is being a full-time mother.'

'And you think we could find a nanny . . . just like that?'

'Thousands of families do,' said Maggie. 'I don't see why we should be any different.'

Giles frowned. 'It would be a very long day. Up on the train, all day at work, back again . . .'

'I know. It would if we carried on living here.' Maggie looked at Giles and her smile broadened. 'And that's why we're going to have to move back to London.'

'What?' Giles stared at her. 'Maggie, you're not serious.'

'Oh yes I am. Lucia agrees, too, don't you, sweetheart? She wants to be a city girl, like me.' Maggie glanced fondly over at Lucia, still fast asleep on the floor.

'Maggie . . .' Giles swallowed. 'Darling, aren't you over-reacting just a tad? All our plans have always been—'

'Your plans,' put in Maggie mildly.

'But with my mother so close, and everything, it seems absolutely crazy to—'

'Your mother agrees with me.' Maggie smiled. 'Your mother, in case you didn't know, is a star.'

There was silence as Giles gazed at her in astonishment. Then, suddenly, he threw his head back and laughed.

'You women! You've been bloody plotting behind my back, haven't you?'

'Maybe.' Maggie smiled wickedly.

'You'll be telling me next you've sent for house details in London.'

'Maybe,' said Maggie after a pause, and Giles guffawed.

'You're unbelievable. And have you spoken to them at work?'

'Not yet,' said Maggie. 'But I'll phone the new chap today. I want to catch up with what's been going on, anyway.'

'And do I have any function in any of this?' said Giles. 'Any role whatsoever?'

'Hmmm.' Maggie looked at him consideringly. 'You could make some more coffee, if you like.'

Candice and Ed sat outside in the sunshine, side by side on the front doorstep, drinking instant coffee out of oddly shaped pottery mugs. Beside them was a plate of elderly digestive biscuits, found in a tin and abandoned after the first bite.

'You know the really stupid thing?' said Candice, watching a squirrel dart across the top of the barn roof. 'I still feel guilty. I still feel guilty towards her.'

'Heather?' said Ed in amazement. 'You're joking. After everything she did?'

'Almost *because* of everything she did. If she could hate me that much . . .' Candice shook her head. 'What does that mean about what my father did to her family? He must have utterly ruined their lives.' She looked soberly at Ed. 'Every time I think about it I feel cold all over.'

There was silence. In the distance a peewit called shrilly and flapped out of a tree.

'Well, I don't know a lot about guilt,' said Ed at last. 'Being a lawyer.' He took a sip of coffee. 'But one thing I do know is that you have nothing to feel bad about. You didn't rip off Heather's family. Your father did.'

'I know. But . . .'

'So. You can feel sorry about it – like you feel sorry about an earthquake. But you can't feel guilty about it. You can't blame yourself.' He looked directly at her. 'It wasn't you, Candice. It wasn't you.'

259

'I know,' said Candice after a pause. 'You're right. In my head, I know you're right. But . . .' She took a sip of coffee and sighed miserably. 'I've got everything wrong, haven't I? It's as if I've been seeing everything upside down.' Carefully she put down her coffee cup and leaned back against the painted door frame. 'I mean, these last few weeks, I was so happy. I really thought Heather and I were . . .'

'In love with each other?'

'Almost that.' Candice gave a shamefaced laugh. 'We just got on so well . . . And it was silly things. Like . . .' She gave a little shrug. 'I don't know. One time she gave me a pen.'

'A pen?' said Ed, grinning.

'Yes,' said Candice defensively. 'A pen.'

'Is that all it takes to win your heart? A pen?' Ed put down his coffee and reached into his pocket.

'No! Don't be—' Candice stopped as Ed produced a scruffy old biro.

'Here you are,' he said, presenting it to her. 'Now do you like me?'

'Don't laugh at me!' said Candice, feeling a flush come to her cheeks.

'I'm not.'

'You are! You think I'm a fool, don't you?' she said, and felt an embarrassed flush suffuse her face. 'You think I'm just a stupid . . .'

'I don't think you're stupid.'

'You despise me.'

'You think I despise you.' Ed looked at her without the glimmer of a smile. 'You really think I despise you, Candice.'

Candice raised her head and looked up into his dark eyes. And as she saw his expression, she felt a sliding sensation, as though the ground had fallen away from beneath her; as though the world had swung into a different focus. She stared silently at Ed, unable to speak;

scarcely able to breathe. A leaf blew into her hair, but she was barely aware of it.

For an endless, unbearable time, neither of them moved. Then, very slowly, Ed leaned towards her, his eyes still pinned on hers. He raised one finger and ran it down her cheek. He touched her chin and then, very gently, the corner of her mouth. Candice gazed back, transfixed by a longing so desperate it was almost fear.

Slowly he leaned closer, touched her earlobe, softly kissed her bare shoulder. His lips met the side of her neck and Candice shuddered, unable to control herself, unable to stop herself wanting more. And then, finally, he bent his head and kissed her, his mouth first gentle, then urgent. They paused, and looked at each other, not speaking; not smiling. As he pulled her, determinedly, to her feet and led her into the house, up the stairs, her legs were as staggery as those of a newborn calf.

She had never made love so slowly; so intensely. The world seemed to have dwindled to Ed's two dark eyes, staring into hers, mirroring her own hunger; her own gradual, unbelieving ecstasy. As she'd come to orgasm, she'd cried out in tears, at the relief of what seemed like a lifetime's tension. Now, sated, she lay in his arms, gazing up at the ceiling, in a room whose details she was only now beginning to notice. Plain white walls; simple blue and white curtains; an old oak bed. A surprising haven of tranquillity after the riot of colour downstairs. Her gaze shifted to the window. In the distance she could see a flock of sheep hurrying down a hill, jostling each other as though afraid of being late.

'Are you asleep?' said Ed after a while. His hand caressed her stomach and she felt a fresh, undeserved delight run through her body.

'No.'

'I've wanted you ever since I've known you.'

There was a pause, then Candice said, 'I know.' Ed's hand moved slowly up to her breast and she felt a renewed *frisson* of self-consciousness; of strangeness at being so close to him.

'Did you . . . want me?' he said.

'I want you now,' said Candice, turning towards him. 'Is that enough?'

'It'll do,' said Ed, and pulled her down to kiss him.

Much later, as the evening sun crested the hills, they wandered downstairs.

'There should be some wine somewhere,' said Ed, going into the kitchen. 'See if you can find some glasses on the dresser.'

Yawning slightly, Candice went into the little adjoining parlour. A pine dresser in the corner was covered with colourful crockery, postcards of paintings and thick, bubbled glasses. As she went towards it, she passed a writing desk, and glanced down as she did so. A handwritten letter was poking out of the tiny drawer, beginning, 'Dear Edward'.

Edward, she thought hazily. Ed. Dear Ed.

Curiosity overwhelmed her. She struggled with herself for a few moments – then glanced back at the door and pulled the letter out a little further.

Dear Edward, she read quickly. *Your aunt was so pleased to see you last week; your visits do her the power of good. The last cheque was much appreciated and so generous. I can hardly believe—*

'Found them?' Ed's voice interrupted Candice, and she hastily stuffed the letter away.

'Yes!' she said, grabbing two glasses off the dresser. 'Here we are.' As Ed entered the room she looked at him anew.

'You must miss your aunt,' she said. 'Did you . . . visit her much?'

'A fair bit.' He shrugged. 'She was a bit gaga by the end. Had a nurse living in, and everything.'

'Oh, right,' said Candice casually. 'That must have been pretty expensive.'

A faint colour came to Ed's cheeks.

'The family paid,' he said, and turned away. 'Come on. I've found some wine.'

They sat outside, sipping wine, watching as the sun grew lower and a breeze began to blow. As it got chillier, Candice moved closer to Ed on the wooden bench, and he put an arm round her. The silence was complete, thought Candice. Unlike anything in London. Her mind floated absently for a while, landed on Heather and quickly bounced away again, before the flash of pain could catch light from her thoughts. No point thinking about it, she told herself. No point reliving it all.

'I don't want to go back,' she heard herself saying.

'Then let's not. Let's stay the night,' said Ed.

'Really?'

'It's my house,' said Ed, and his arm tightened around Candice's shoulders. 'We can stay as long as we like.'

Chapter Nineteen

It was three days later that Maggie got round to ringing Charles Allsopp about coming back to work. She waited until Paddy arrived for morning coffee, then handed Lucia to her, together with a load of house details.

'I want to sound businesslike,' she explained. 'No wailing babies in the background.'

'Good idea,' said Paddy cheerfully. 'Are these more London houses?'

'Arrived this morning. I've put red crosses on the ones I think are possibles.'

Maggie waited until Paddy had carried Lucia carefully off to the sitting room, then dialled the number of Allsopp Publications.

'Hello, yes,' she said, as soon as the phone was answered. 'Charles Allsopp, please. It's Maggie Phillips.' Then she beamed in pleasure. 'Yes, I'm fine, thanks, Doreen. Yes, she's fine, too. An absolute poppet.'

Paddy, from inside the sitting room, caught Maggie's eye and gave her an encouraging smile. This, she thought, as she dangled a pink furry octopus in front of Lucia's waving hands, this is what the real Maggie was like. Confident and cheerful and in command. Thriving on a challenge.

'I'll miss you,' she murmured to Lucia, letting the

baby grasp her finger and tug at it. 'I'll miss you. But I think you'll be happier. Don't you?' Paddy reached for one of the estate agents' house details and began to read the description, trying to conceal her shock at the pitiful size of the garden and the enormous figure printed in bold black and white at the top of the page. For that money around here . . . she found herself thinking – then smiled at herself. For that money around here you could buy The Pines. And look what a success that had been.

'Yes, I look forward to it, too, Charles,' she could hear Maggie saying in the kitchen. 'And I'll be in contact with Justin. Oh, could you? Well, thank you. And I look forward to our meeting. Yes. Bye.' She looked up, caught Paddy's eye and gave the thumbs-up. 'He seems really nice!' she hissed. 'He even suggested I have a computer set up at home, so I can . . . Oh, hello, Justin,' she said in a louder voice. 'Just wondering how it's all going?'

'Shall we get you a computer?' said Paddy, smiling down at Lucia. 'Would you like that?' She tickled Lucia's little tummy and watched in pleasure as the baby began to chortle. 'Are you going to be clever like your mummy? Are you going to be—'

'What?' Maggie's voice came ripping out of the kitchen, and both Paddy and Lucia jumped. 'You did *what*?'

'Goodness,' said Paddy. 'I wonder . . .'

'And she didn't have any explanation?' Maggie stood up and began to pace furiously about the kitchen. 'Oh, she did. And you followed that up, did you?' Maggie's voice grew colder. 'I see. And nobody thought to consult me?' There was a pause. 'No, I'm not angry, Justin. I'm livid.' There was another pause. 'Justin, I don't give a fuck about your spot-checks!'

'Goodness!' said Paddy again, and glanced nervously at Lucia.

'Yes, I am challenging your authority!' shouted Maggie. 'To be frank, you don't deserve any!' She thrust the phone down and said angrily, 'Wanker!' Then she picked up the phone again and jabbed in a number.

'Oh dear,' said Paddy faintly. 'I wonder what—'

'Come on,' said Maggie in the kitchen, drumming her nails on the wooden table. 'Come on, answer the phone. Candice, where the hell are you?'

Candice was lying in the garden of the cottage, staring up at the leaves above her. The early summer sun was warm on her face and she could smell the sweet scent of lavender on the breeze. But she was cold inside as thoughts she had tried to put from her mind during the last few days came crowding in.

She had been suspended from work. She had been publicly branded dishonest. And she had ruined the two friendships that meant most to her in the world. A sharp wave of pain went through Candice and she closed her eyes. How long ago was it that the three of them had been sitting in the Manhattan Bar, innocently ordering their cocktails, unaware that the girl in the green waistcoat standing at their table was about to enter their lives and ruin everything? If only she could rewind and play the scene again, thought Candice miserably. If only Heather hadn't been serving that night. If only they'd gone to a different bar. If only . . . A sickening self-reproach went through Candice and she sat up, trying to escape her thoughts, wondering what Ed was doing. He had disappeared mysteriously off that morning, muttering something about a surprise. As long as it wasn't more hideous local cider, she thought, and raised her face, enjoying the warm breeze on her cheeks.

They had been down at the cottage for four days now, but it felt as though it could have been weeks.

They had done little but sleep and eat and make love, and lie on the grass in the early summer sun. Their only forays into the local village had been to buy essentials: food, soap and toothbrushes. Neither had brought any spare clothes – but in the spare room, Ed had found a pile of colourful extra-large T-shirts advertising a screen-printing exhibition, and, for Candice, a wide-brimmed straw hat decorated with a bunch of cherries. They had not spoken to a soul, had not even read a paper. It had been a haven; a place for sanctuary and healing.

But although her body was well rested, thought Candice, her mind was not. She could push the thoughts from her brain, but they only came rushing back in when she wasn't expecting it. Emotions would suddenly hit her, causing pain to spread through her body and tears to start to her eyes. She felt bruised, humiliated; full of shame. And her mind constantly circled around Heather.

Heather Trelawney. Blond hair, grey eyes, snub nose. Warm hands which had held Candice's affectionately; bubbling infectious laughter. Thinking back, Candice felt sickened, almost violated. Had every single moment of their friendship been an act? She could hardly believe it.

'Candice!' Ed's voice interrupted her thoughts and she stood up, shaking out her stiff legs. He was coming towards her, a strange look in his eye. 'Candice,' he said, 'don't get angry – but I've got someone to see you.'

'What?' Candice stared at him. 'What do you mean, someone to see me?' Her gaze shifted over his shoulder but she could see no-one.

'He's in the house,' said Ed. 'Come on.'

'Who is?' said Candice, her voice truculent. Ed turned and looked at her steadily. 'Someone I think you need to speak to,' he said.

267

'Who?' She followed him with hasty legs, stumbling with nerves. 'Who is it? Oh God, I know who it is,' she said at the door, her heart pounding. 'It's Justin, isn't it?'

'No,' said Ed, and pushed the door open.

Candice peered into the gloom and saw a young man of about twenty standing by the dresser in the kitchen. He looked up apprehensively and pushed a hand back through his long fair hair. Candice stared at him in puzzlement. She had never seen him before in her life.

'Candice,' said Ed, 'this is Hamish.'

'Hamish,' said Candice wrinkling her brow. 'You're . . .' She stopped as a memory surfaced in her mind like a bubble. 'Oh my God. You're Heather's ex-boyfriend, aren't you?'

'No, I'm not,' said Hamish, and looked at her with steady grey eyes. 'I'm her brother.'

Roxanne sat in the office of Strawson and Co., sipping tea out of a bone china cup and wishing that her hand wouldn't shake every time she put it down. There was a smooth, thickly carpeted silence about the place; an air of solid opulence and respectability which made her feel flimsy and cheap, even though she was wearing one of the most expensive, sober outfits she possessed. The room she was sitting in was small but grand – full of heavy oak bookcases and a muted atmosphere, as though the very walls themselves were aware of the confidential nature of their contents.

'I'm so glad you decided to come,' said Neil Cooper.

'Yes, well,' said Roxanne shortly. 'Curiosity won in the end.'

'It often does,' said Neil Cooper, and picked up his own cup to take a sip.

He was much younger than Roxanne had expected, and had an earnest, guarded expression on his face, as though he didn't want to disappoint her. As though he didn't want to let down the hopes of the gold-digging mistress. A flash of humiliation passed through Roxanne and she put down her cup.

'Look,' she said, more aggressively than she'd intended. 'Let's just get this over with, shall we? I wasn't expecting anything, so whatever it is, I'll just sign for it and leave.'

'Yes,' said Neil Cooper carefully. 'Well, it's not quite as simple as that. If I can just read to you a codicil which the late Mr Allsopp added to his will shortly before dying . . .'

He reached for a black leather folder, opened it and shuffled some papers together, and Roxanne stared at his calm, professional face in sudden realization.

'Oh God,' she said, in a voice which shook slightly. 'He really has left something to me, hasn't he? Something serious. What is it? Not money.'

'No,' said Neil Cooper, and looked up at her with a tiny smile. 'Not money.'

'We're fine for money,' said Hamish, taking a sip of tea from the mug Ed had made. 'In fact, we're pretty loaded. After my parents split up, my mum remarried this guy Derek. He's . . . well, he's stinking. He gave me my car . . .' He gestured out of the window, to where a new Alfa Romeo was sitting smartly on the gravel next to Ed's BMW. 'He's been really good to us. Both of us.'

'Oh,' said Candice. She rubbed her face, trying to marshal her thoughts; trying to let yet another astonishing fact sink in. She was sitting across the table from Hamish, and every time she looked up at him she could see Heather in his face. Heather's little brother. She hadn't even known Heather had a brother. 'So . . . so why was Heather working as a cocktail waitress?'

'It's the kind of thing she does,' said Hamish. 'She starts something like an art course or a writing course and then she drops out and takes some crummy job so we all feel bad.'

.'Oh,' said Candice again. She felt slow and very stupid, as though her brain had overloaded on information.

'I knew she'd gone to live with you,' said Hamish. 'And I thought she might do something stupid. I told her the two of you should just talk about it. You know – work it out. But she wouldn't listen.' He paused, and looked at Candice. 'I really didn't think she'd go as far as . . .' He broke off, and took another sip of tea.

'So . . . she really hated me,' said Candice, managing to keep her voice low and calm.

'Oh God,' said Hamish, exhaling sharply. 'This is . . .' He was silent for a few moments, then looked up. 'Not you,' he said. 'Not you as a person. But . . .'

'But what I represented.'

'You have to understand. What your dad did – it split up our family. My dad was wrecked. He went a bit crazy. And my mum couldn't cope with it, so . . .' Hamish broke off for a few moments. 'And it was easy to blame your dad for everything. But now I look back – I think maybe it would have happened anyway. It wasn't like my parents had such a great marriage.'

'But Heather didn't agree?' said Candice tentatively.

'Heather never saw the whole picture. She was away at school, so she didn't see my parents rowing the whole time. She thought they had the perfect set-up. You know, big house, perfect marriage . . . Then we lost all our money and they split up. And Heather couldn't deal with it. She went a bit . . . screwy.'

'So when she saw me in the Manhattan Bar . . .' Candice rested her head in her hands.

'Candice, let me get this straight,' said Ed, leaning forward. 'Both of you knew about what your dad had done – but neither of you ever mentioned it?'

'Heather behaved as if she had no idea!' said Candice defensively. 'And I didn't say anything to her because I didn't want her to think I was helping her out

270

of pity. I wanted to . . .' She flushed slightly. 'I really wanted to be her friend.'

'I know,' said Hamish. He met Candice's eyes. 'For what it's worth, I think you were probably the best friend she ever had. But of course she wouldn't have seen that.'

There was silence in the kitchen, then Candice said apprehensively, 'Do you know where she is now?'

'No idea,' said Hamish. 'She disappears for weeks. Months. But she'll turn up eventually.'

Candice swallowed. 'Would you . . . would you do me a favour?'

'What?'

'Come and tell Justin, my boss, what Heather's really like? Tell him that she set me up?'

There was a long pause.

'No,' said Hamish at last. 'No, I won't. I love my sister, even if she is a bit—' He broke off. 'I'm not going to go into some office and tell them she's a conniving, crazy bitch. I'm sorry.' He looked at Candice, then pushed his chair back with a scraping sound. 'I have to get going.'

'Yes,' said Candice. 'Well . . . thanks for coming.'

'I hope everything works out,' said Hamish, shrugging slightly.

Ed followed him out, then after a few minutes came back into the kitchen as the Alfa Romeo disappeared up the track. Candice stared at him, then said incredulously, 'How did you find him?'

'Heather told me her family lived in Wiltshire. I looked them up and paid them a visit.' Ed gave a rueful grin. 'To be honest, I was half hoping to find her there, too. Catch her out.'

Candice shook her head. 'Not Heather.'

Ed sat down beside Candice and took her hand.

'But anyway. Now you know.'

'Now I know. Now I know I was harbouring a

psychopath.' Candice smiled at him, then buried her head in her hands. Tears began to ooze out of the corners of her eyes.

'What?' said Ed in alarm. 'Oh, Jesus. I'm sorry. I should have warned you. I shouldn't have just—'

'It's not that.' Candice looked up and wiped her eyes. 'It's what Hamish said about me being a good friend.' She stared straight ahead, her face trembling slightly. 'Roxanne and Maggie were the best friends I ever had. They tried to warn me about Heather. And what did I do?' She took a deep, shuddering breath. 'I got angry with them. I argued with them. I was so . . . *besotted* with Heather, I would rather lose them than hear the truth.'

'You haven't lost them!' said Ed. 'I'm sure you haven't.'

'I said some unforgivable things, Ed. I behaved like a . . .'

'So call them.'

'I tried,' said Candice miserably. 'Maggie put the phone down on me. And Roxanne is furious with me. She thinks I was keeping Ralph's illness a secret from her, or something . . .'

'Well, it's their loss,' said Ed. 'It's their bloody loss.'

'It's not, though, is it?' said Candice, as tears began to roll down her face again. 'It's mine.'

Roxanne stared at Neil Cooper, feeling a whooshing in her head, a pounding in her ears. The walls of the office seemed to be closing in on her; for the first time in her life, she thought she might faint.

'I . . . that can't be right,' she managed. 'It can't be right. There must be . . .'

'To Miss Roxanne Miller,' repeated Neil Cooper deliberately, 'I leave my London house. 15 Abernathy Square, Kensington.' He looked up from his leather folder. 'It's yours. To live in, sell – whatever you prefer.

We can provide you with advice on the matter if you like. But obviously there's no hurry to decide. In any case, it will all take a while to go through.'

Roxanne stared back at him, unable to speak; unable to move. Ralph had left her his house. He'd sent a message to her – and to the world – that she had meant something. That she hadn't been a nothing. He'd almost . . . legitimized her.

Something hot and powerful began to rise up inside her body; she felt as though she was going to be sick.

'Would you like another cup of tea?' said Neil Cooper.

'I . . .' Roxanne stopped, and swallowed hard against the lump in her throat. 'I'm sorry,' she gulped, as tears suddenly began to stream down her face. 'Oh God. It's just I never expected . . .'

Sobs were overtaking her; she was powerless to stop them. Furiously she scrabbled for a tissue, trying to control herself, aware of Neil Cooper's politely sympathetic gaze.

'It's just . . .' she managed eventually '. . . a bit of a shock.'

'Of course it is,' said Neil Cooper diplomatically, and hesitated. 'Do you . . . know the property?'

'Only the outside,' said Roxanne, wiping her eyes. 'I know every blasted brick of the outside. But I've never been inside.'

'Well. If you would like to visit it, that can be arranged.'

'I . . . No. I don't think so. Not yet.' Roxanne blew her nose, and watched as Neil Cooper made a note on the pad in front of him.

'What about . . .' she began, then stopped, almost unable to say the words. 'The . . . the family. Do they know?'

'Yes,' said Neil Cooper. 'Yes, they do.'

'Are they . . .' Roxanne broke off, and took a deep breath. 'Do they hate me?'

'Miss Miller,' said Neil Cooper earnestly, 'there's no need for you to concern yourselves with the other members of the Allsopp family. Let me just reassure you that Mr Allsopp's will was very generous to all parties concerned.' He paused, and met her gaze. 'But his bequest to you is between you and him.'

There was a pause, then Roxanne nodded.

'OK,' she said quietly. 'Thanks.'

'If you have any further questions . . .'

'No,' said Roxanne. 'No thanks. I think I'd just like to go and . . . digest it all.' She stood up and met the young man's eyes. 'You've been very kind.'

As they walked to the panelled door, she caught a glimpse of herself in a wall mirror and winced at her bloodshot eyes. It was obvious she'd been crying – but then, that was probably pretty standard for a family law firm, she thought with a half-grin.

Neil Cooper adroitly opened the door for her and stood aside, and Roxanne walked into the hall to see a man in a navy blue overcoat standing at the reception desk.

'I'm sorry,' he was saying. 'I am rather early . . .'

Roxanne stopped in her tracks. Beside her, she was aware of Neil Cooper giving a small start of shock. At the desk, Charles Allsopp looked up, saw Roxanne and froze.

There was an instant of silence, as they stared at each other – then Roxanne turned quickly away, trying to keep calm.

'Well, thank you very much,' she said to Neil Cooper in a voice which trembled with nerves. 'I'll . . . I'll be in touch. Thanks very much.' And without looking him in the eye she began to walk towards the exit.

'Wait.' Charles Allsopp's voice halted her in her tracks. 'Please.'

Roxanne stopped and very slowly turned round, aware that her cheeks were flushed; that her mouth was lipstickless and reddened; that her legs were still shaking. But she didn't care. And suddenly, as she met his gaze, she wasn't nervous. Let him say what he liked. He couldn't touch her.

'Are you Roxanne Miller?'

'I really think,' said Neil Cooper, hurrying forward protectively, 'that for all parties concerned . . .'

'Wait,' said Charles Allsopp, and lifted a hand. 'All I wanted was to introduce myself. That's all.' He hesitated – then slowly held out his hand. 'How do you do. My name's Charles Allsopp.'

'Hello,' said Roxanne after a pause, and cleared her throat. 'I'm Roxanne.'

Charles nodded gravely and Roxanne found herself wondering how much he knew about her; whether Ralph had said anything to his eldest son before he died.

'I hope they're looking after you,' said Charles, glancing towards Neil.

'Oh,' said Roxanne, taken aback. 'Yes. Yes, they are.'

'Good,' said Charles Allsopp, and looked up at an elderly lawyer descending the stairs into the hall. 'Well, I must go,' he said. 'Goodbye.'

'Goodbye,' said Roxanne awkwardly, watching as he walked towards the stairs. 'And . . . and thanks.'

Outside, on the pavement, she leaned against a wall and took a few deep breaths. She felt confused; euphoric; shattered with emotion. Ralph had left her his house: the house she'd spent obsessive hours staring at. It was hers. A house worth a million pounds was hers. The thought made her feel tearful, almost sick.

She hadn't expected Ralph to leave her anything. She hadn't expected Charles Allsopp to behave so politely to her. The world was suddenly being nice to her, and she didn't know how to react.

Roxanne reached inside her bag for her cigarettes, and as she did so, felt again the vibrating motion of her mobile phone. She'd noticed it several times during the meeting; someone was trying to contact her. She hesitated, then took the phone out and half reluctantly put it to her ear.

'Hello?'

'Roxanne! Thank God.' Maggie's voice crackled urgently down the line. 'Listen, have you spoken to Candice recently?'

'No,' said Roxanne. 'Is something wrong?'

'That little twerp Justin has suspended her from work. Some nonsense about expenses.'

'*What?*' exclaimed Roxanne, her mind snapping back into focus.

'And she's disappeared off the face of the earth. No-one knows where she is. She isn't answering her phone . . . she could be dead in a ditch somewhere.'

'Oh my God,' said Roxanne, her heart beginning to thump. 'I had no idea.'

'Hasn't she called you, either? When did you last speak to her?'

'At the funeral,' said Roxanne. She paused. 'To be honest, we didn't part very well.'

'The last time I spoke to her was when she phoned up to apologize,' said Maggie miserably. 'I snapped at her and put the phone down.'

There was a subdued silence.

'Anyway,' said Maggie. 'I'm coming up to London tomorrow. Breakfast?'

'Breakfast,' agreed Roxanne. 'And let me know if you hear anything.' She switched off her phone and began to walk on, her face clouded with sudden worry.

Chapter Twenty

At eleven o'clock the next morning, Maggie and Roxanne stood outside Candice's front door, fruitlessly ringing the bell. After a while, Maggie bent down and peered through the letterbox into the communal hall.

'There's a load of letters piled up on the table,' she reported.

'Addressed to Candice?'

'I can't see. Possibly.' Maggie dropped the letterbox flap, stood up and looked at Roxanne. 'God, I feel shitty.'

'I feel awful,' agreed Roxanne. She sank down onto the front step, and Maggie sat down beside her. 'I gave her such a hard time at Ralph's funeral. I was just . . . oh, I don't know. Beside myself.'

'Of course you were,' said Maggie at once. 'It must have been a terrible time.'

Her voice was sympathetic, but again she felt a *frisson* of shock at the idea of Roxanne and Ralph as lovers. Roxanne had, haltingly, told her everything on the journey from Waterloo to Candice's flat, and for at least five minutes Maggie had been utterly unable to speak. How could two people be friends for such a long time and one of them have a secret as big as that? How could Roxanne have talked about Ralph so normally, without once giving their relationship away?

How could she have let Maggie moan on to her so many times about Ralph's annoying little ways without somehow warning her that they were talking about her lover? Of course it was understandable, of course she hadn't had any choice – but even so, Maggie felt hurt; as though she would never look at Roxanne in quite the same way.

'It was as if I'd finally found someone to blame,' said Roxanne, staring bleakly ahead. 'So I took it all out on her.'

'It's a natural reaction,' said Maggie after a pause. 'You feel grief, you need a scapegoat.'

'Perhaps it is,' said Roxanne. 'But Candice, of all people . . .' She closed her eyes briefly. 'Candice. How could I have blamed Candice?'

'I know,' said Maggie shamefacedly. 'I feel the same. I can't believe I slammed the phone down on her. But I just felt so hurt. Everything seemed so awful . . .' She looked at Roxanne. 'I can't tell you what these last few weeks have been like. I honestly think I lost it for a bit.'

There was a short silence. A car drove by and its occupants looked curiously out of the window at the pair of them.

'I had no idea,' said Roxanne eventually. 'You always looked so . . . in control. It all seemed so perfect.'

'I know,' said Maggie, staring at the pavement. 'I was stupid. I couldn't bear to admit how terrible I felt to anyone. Not to Giles, not to anyone.' She paused in sudden recollection. 'Actually that's not true. I was going to tell you about it once. That night at the Manhattan Bar. But we got interrupted. And then . . .' She gave a rueful smile. 'You know, that night has to be one of the worst in my life. I felt fat, I was exhausted, I was guilty at leaving Lucia . . . Then we all end up arguing with each other. It was . . .' She gave a short laugh. 'It was one to forget.'

'God, I feel terrible.' Roxanne looked miserably at Maggie. 'I should have realized you were depressed. I should have called. Visited.' She bit her lip. 'Some friend I've been. To both of you.'

'Come on,' said Maggie. 'You've had it worse than either of us. Much worse.'

She put an arm round Roxanne's shoulders and squeezed them. For a while they were both silent. A postman arrived, looked at them oddly, then reached past them to post a bundle of letters through the letter-box.

'So, what do we do now?' said Roxanne finally.

'We go and put Justin on the spot,' said Maggie. 'He's not going to get away with this.' She stood up and brushed down her skirt. 'Let's find a taxi.'

'That's a nice suit, by the way,' said Roxanne, look-ing up at her. Then she frowned. 'In fact, now I come to think of it, you're looking very good all over.' She surveyed Maggie's silk, aubergine-coloured suit; her simple white T-shirt; her gleaming nut-brown hair. 'Have you just had your hair cut?'

'Yes,' said Maggie, a half-smile coming to her face. 'This is a whole new me. New hair, new clothes, new lipstick. I went shopping yesterday afternoon. Spent a bloody fortune, I might add.'

'Good for you,' said Roxanne approvingly. 'That's a fantastic colour on you.'

'I just have to avoid hearing any crying babies,' said Maggie, pulling Roxanne to her feet. 'Or I'll leak milk all over the jacket.'

'Oooh.' Roxanne pulled a face. 'You didn't have to tell me that.'

'The joys of motherhood,' said Maggie cheerfully, and began to stride ahead to the corner. If someone had told her a few weeks ago, she thought, that she'd be *laughing* about breastfeeding, she just wouldn't have believed them. But then, neither would she have believed that she'd be wearing a suit two sizes bigger than normal and feeling good in it.

As they got out of a chugging taxi outside the Allsopp Publications building, Maggie tilted her head back and stared at it. The building where she'd spent most of her working life looked as familiar as ever – and yet different. In just a few weeks it seemed, almost imperceptibly, to have changed.

'This is so strange,' she murmured as Roxanne swiped her security card and pushed open the glass doors to reception. 'I feel as if I've been away for years.'

'Ditto,' muttered Roxanne. 'In fact, I'm surprised my card still works.' She looked at Maggie. 'Ready?'

'Absolutely,' said Maggie. The two grinned at each other, then, side by side, walked into the foyer.

'Maggie!' exclaimed Doreen at the reception desk. 'What a surprise! Don't you look well? But where's the baby?'

'At home,' said Maggie, smiling. 'With my mother-in-law.'

'Oh! What a shame! You should have brought her in! Little pet.' Doreen nudged the girl sitting next to her at the desk – a shy-looking redhead whom Maggie didn't recognize. 'This is Maggie who I was telling you about,' she said to the girl. 'Maggie, this is Julie. Just started on reception yesterday.'

'Hello, Julie,' said Maggie politely. 'Doreen—'

'And is she a good little baby? I bet she's as good as gold.'

'She's . . . she's great,' said Maggie. 'Actually, Doreen, I'm here to see Justin. Could you give him a quick call?'

'I don't think he's in,' said Doreen in surprise. 'He and Mr Allsopp have gone off somewhere together. I'll just check.' She pressed a button and said, 'Hello, Alicia? Doreen here.'

'Damn!' said Maggie, and looked at Roxanne. 'It didn't even occur to me he wouldn't be in.'

'Back in about an hour, apparently,' said Doreen, looking up. 'They've gone to a design presentation.' Maggie stared at her.

'What for? What design presentation?'

'Don't ask me, dear.'

Maggie's jaw tightened and she glanced at Roxanne.

'Nice of them to keep me informed,' she said. 'They're probably redesigning the whole bloody magazine without telling me.'

'So what do we do?' said Roxanne.

'We wait,' said Maggie firmly.

An hour later, Justin was still not back. Maggie and Roxanne sat on leather chairs in the foyer, leafing through old copies of the *Londoner* and looking up every time the door opened. Some of those entering were visitors who gave them polite, interested looks; others were members of staff who came over to greet Maggie warmly and ask where the baby was.

'The next time someone asks me that,' Maggie muttered to Roxanne, as a group of marketing executives walked off to the lifts, 'I'm going to say it's in my briefcase.'

Roxanne didn't answer. She was transfixed by a photograph of Candice she had just come across in an old issue of the *Londoner. Staff writer Candice Brewin investigates the plight of the elderly in London's hospitals,* read the caption. And next to it, Candice's round face stared out, eyebrows slightly raised, as though surprised. Roxanne gazed down at the familiar picture as though for the first time, and felt a pain in her chest at the innocence of Candice's expression. She didn't look like a hard-hitting reporter. She looked like a child.

'Roxanne?' said Maggie curiously. 'Are you OK?'

'We should have seen it coming,' said Roxanne in a trembling voice. She put the magazine down and looked at Maggie. 'We knew that little bitch was up to no good. We should have . . . I don't know.' She rubbed her face. 'Warned Candice, or something.'

'We tried, remember?' said Maggie. 'Candice kept defending her.'

'But we could have done *something*. Tried to protect her, instead of standing back and letting her walk right into it . . .'

'What could we have done?' said Maggie reasonably. 'We didn't know anything. I mean, let's face it, it was nothing more than instinct. We just didn't like the girl.'

There was silence. A couple of businessmen came into the foyer, glanced at Maggie and Roxanne, then headed for the reception desk.

'Where do you think she is?' said Roxanne, and looked up at Maggie with a sober face. 'It's been days. People don't just disappear for days.'

'I . . . I don't know,' said Maggie. 'I'm sure she's fine. She's probably . . . having a holiday or something,' she added unconvincingly.

'We should have been there for her,' said Roxanne in a low, fierce voice. 'I'll never forgive myself for shutting her out. Or you, for that matter.' She looked up at Maggie. 'I should have been there for you when you were feeling down.'

'You weren't to know,' said Maggie awkwardly. 'How could you have known?'

'But that's my point!' said Roxanne urgently. 'We shouldn't keep secrets . . . or . . . or put on acts for each other. None of us should ever feel we have to struggle through on our own.' She gazed at Maggie with blue eyes suddenly glittering with tears. 'Maggie, ring me next time. If it's the middle of the night, or . . . whenever it is, if you're feeling low, ring me. I'll come straight over and take the baby for a walk. Or Giles. Whichever one you want off your hands.' She grinned, and Maggie gave a giggle. 'Please,' said Roxanne

282

seriously. 'Ring me, Maggie. Don't pretend everything's fine when it isn't.'

'I won't,' said Maggie, blinking away her own tears. 'I'll . . . I'll ring you, I promise. Maybe even when things *aren't* bad.' She smiled briefly, then hesitated. 'And next time you have a six-year-long affair with the boss – you tell me too, all right?'

'It's a deal.' Impulsively, Roxanne leaned forward and hugged Maggie tightly. 'I've missed you,' she murmured. 'Come back to London soon.'

'I've missed you too,' said Maggie, her throat blocked with emotion. 'God, I've missed you all. I feel as though—'

'Shit,' said Roxanne, staring over her shoulder. 'Shit. Here they come.'

'What?' Maggie swivelled round and saw Justin walking along the pavement towards the glass doors of the building. He was dressed in a dark green suit, talking enthusiastically and gesturing to Charles Allsopp at his side. 'Oh God!' she said in dismay and turned back to Roxanne. She gave a huge sniff and lifted her hands to her eyes. 'Quickly. Do I look all right? Has my make-up run?'

'A bit,' said Roxanne, leaning forward and quickly wiping away a smudge of eye-liner. 'How about mine?'

'It looks fine,' said Maggie, peering intently at her face. 'All intact.'

'That's waterproof mascara for you,' said Roxanne lightly. 'Copes with sea, sand, strong emotions . . .' She broke off as the glass doors swung open. 'Oh fuck,' she murmured. 'Here they are. What are we going to say?'

'Don't worry,' said Maggie. 'I'll do the talking.' She stood up, smoothing her skirt down, and took a deep breath. 'Right,' she said, glancing nervously at Roxanne. 'Here goes. Justin!' she exclaimed, raising her voice and taking a step forward. 'How are you?'

Justin turned at the sound of Maggie's voice as

though he'd been scalded. As he saw her, his face fell spectacularly – then, just as spectacularly, repositioned itself in an expression of delight.

'Maggie!' he said, opening his arms wide as though to hug her. 'What a charming surprise.'

'I thought I'd just pop in and see how things were going,' said Maggie, smiling back and making no effort to mirror his gesture.

'Great!' said Justin with a forced enthusiasm. 'What a . . . marvellous idea!'

'So this is the famous Maggie Phillips,' said Charles Allsopp, giving her a friendly smile and extending his hand towards her. 'Maggie, I'm Charles Allsopp. Congratulations on the birth of your baby. It must be a very exciting time for you.'

'Thank you,' said Maggie pleasantly. 'And, yes it is.'

'I have to say though, not a day goes by without my being asked when you're coming back to the *Londoner.*'

'Really?' said Maggie, allowing herself a tiny, satisfied glance at Justin's crestfallen face. 'Well, I'm very glad to hear it. And let me tell you, I'm intending to return to work in a matter of weeks.'

'Good!' said Charles Allsopp. 'Glad to hear it.'

'Charles, this is Roxanne Miller,' said Justin in a loud, attention-seeking voice. 'One of our regular freelancers.'

'Miss Miller and I have already met,' said Charles after a tiny pause, and gave Roxanne a friendly little smile. 'Now, may I offer the two of you a cup of tea? A drink?'

'Very kind,' said Maggie in a businesslike manner. 'But I'm afraid this visit isn't social. I'm actually here on an unfortunate matter. The suspension of Candice Brewin. I was a little perturbed to hear about it.'

'Ah,' said Charles Allsopp, and glanced at Justin. 'Justin?'

'It was completely justified,' said Justin defensively. 'The fact is, Candice has been found to be defrauding the company. If you don't think that's a serious offence, Maggie—'

'Of course I do,' said Maggie calmly. 'But I can't believe Candice is capable of doing such a thing.'

'I've got the evidence in my office,' said Justin. 'You can see it with your own eyes if you like!'

'Fine,' said Maggie, and gestured towards the lifts. 'Let's see it.'

As Maggie strode through the door of the editorial office, she felt suddenly proprietorial. Here was her magazine; here was her team. It was almost as though she were coming home.

'Hi, Maggie,' said Alicia casually as she walked past, then double-took. 'Maggie! How are you! Where the hell's that bump gone?'

'Damn,' said Maggie in mock-alarm. 'I knew I was missing something.' There was a giggle round the office. Bright-eyed faces looked up from desks, glanced at Justin and back to Maggie.

'I'm just popping in briefly,' said Maggie, looking around the room. 'Just a quick hello.'

'Well, good to see you,' said Alicia. 'Bring the baby next time!'

'Will do,' said Maggie cheerily, then turned and walked into Justin's office where he, Charles and Roxanne were waiting. She pulled the door shut behind her and for a few moments there was silence.

'I have to say,' said Charles eventually to Maggie, 'I'm a little unclear as to why you're here. The evidence against Candice seems, I'm afraid, fairly strong. And she will, of course, be given a chance at the hearing . . .'

'Hearing!' said Maggie impatiently. 'You don't need a hearing to sort this out!'

285

'Here we are,' said Justin, producing from a drawer a pile of photocopied forms, each headed with Candice's name. His voice sharpened slightly with triumph. 'What do you make of these?'

Maggie ignored him. 'Did you hear her explanation?' she asked Charles.

'Some story about being set up by one of her colleagues?' He wrinkled his brow. 'It seems a little fanciful.'

'Well, frankly, the idea that Candice Brewin is capable of fraud is even more fanciful!' exclaimed Roxanne.

'You're her friend,' said Justin scathingly. 'You would defend her.'

'Correct me if I'm wrong,' retorted Roxanne, 'but you're her ex-boyfriend. You *would* get rid of her.'

'Really?' said Charles in surprise. He frowned, and looked at Justin. 'You didn't tell me that.'

'It's irrelevant!' said Justin, flushing. 'I behaved in a completely fair and impartial way.'

'On the contrary,' said Maggie in her calm, competent voice. 'If you ask me, you behaved in a completely high-handed and irresponsible way. You took the word of Heather Trelawney – a girl who has been at the company for a matter of weeks – over that of Candice, who's worked here for, what, five years? You fell for this ridiculous story of office bullying – did you ever actually see it going on with your own eyes? You took at face value these expenses claims –' Maggie picked one up and dropped it dismissively on the desk. 'But I'm a hundred per cent sure that if they were analysed, they would be shown to be an imitation of Candice's handwriting, not the real thing.' She paused, letting her words sink in. 'I would say, Justin, that not only have you shown a partisan and improper haste to get rid of a talented employee, but that your lack of judgement has cost the company substantially in terms

286

of lost time, disruption and damaged morale.'

There was silence. Roxanne glanced at Charles Allsopp and gave an inward grin. He was staring at Maggie open-mouthed.

'There were witnesses to the bullying,' said Justin, leafing through his papers. 'There was definitely a . . . Yes.' He pulled out a sheet of paper. 'Kelly Jones.' He stood up, stalked to the door and called, 'Kelly? Could you step in here a moment please? Our secretary,' he added, in a lower voice to Charles. 'Heather said she had witnessed some instances of Candice's unpleasant behaviour.'

'Unpleasant behaviour?' said Roxanne. 'Oh, for God's sake, Justin. Can't you wake up and smell the bullshit?'

'Let's just hear what Kelly has to say, shall we?' said Justin coolly.

As the sixteen-year-old girl came into the office, a hot pink blush spread over her face. She stood by the door, her legs wound awkwardly around each other, her gaze steadily fixed on the floor.

'Kelly,' said Justin, adopting a smooth, patronizing tone. 'I'd like to ask you about Candice Brewin – who, as you know, has been suspended from the company – and Heather Trelawney.'

'Yes,' whispered Kelly.

'Did you ever see any unpleasantness between them?'

'Yes,' said Kelly after a pause. 'I did.'

Justin shot a pleased glance around the room.

'Could you tell us a little more?' he said.

'I feel really bad about it now,' added Kelly miserably, twisting her hands together. 'I was going to come and say something before. But I didn't want to . . . you know. Cause trouble.'

'Never mind that,' said Justin kindly. 'What were you going to say?'

'Well, just that . . .' Kelly hesitated. 'Just that Heather hated Candice. Really . . . hated her. And she knew Candice was going to get in trouble, even before it happened. It was expenses, wasn't it?' Kelly looked up nervously. 'I think maybe Heather had something to do with it.'

Roxanne looked at Justin's face, gave a snort of laughter and clamped her hand to her mouth.

'I see,' said Charles Allsopp heavily and looked at Justin. 'I would say, at the very least, this matter could have done with a little further investigation before action. What do you think, Justin?'

There was a short, still silence.

'I . . . I . . . I utterly agree,' said Justin finally, in a furious, stammering voice. 'Obviously there has been some . . . some gross misrepresentation of the facts . . .' He shot an angry look at Kelly. 'Perhaps if Kelly had come to me sooner . . .'

'Don't blame *her*!' said Roxanne. 'It's you who got rid of Candice!'

'I think what we need in this case is a . . . a full and thorough investigation,' said Justin, ignoring her. 'Clearly some errors have been made . . .' he swallowed, 'and clearly some . . . some clarification of the situation is needed. So what I suggest, Charles, is that as soon as Heather gets back—'

'She isn't coming back,' said Kelly.

'What?' said Justin, impatient at the interruption.

'Heather's not coming back.' Kelly twisted her hands even harder. 'She's gone to Australia.'

Everyone stared at her.

'For good?' said Justin, his voice rising in disbelief.

'I don't know,' said Kelly, flushing. 'But she's not coming back here. She . . . she gave me a goodbye present.'

'The sweetheart,' said Roxanne.

Charles Allsopp shook his head disbelievingly.

'This is ludicrous,' he said. 'Utterly—' He stopped himself and nodded at the blushing girl. 'Thank you, Kelly. You can go now.'

As the door closed behind her, he looked at Maggie.

'What we must do, straight away, is contact Candice and arrange a meeting. Could you do that, Maggie? Ask her to come in as soon as possible. Tomorrow, perhaps.'

'I would do,' said Maggie. 'But we don't know where she is.'

'What?' Charles stared at her.

'She's disappeared,' said Maggie soberly. 'She isn't answering the phone, her letters are all piled up in her hallway . . . We're actually rather alarmed.'

'Christ!' said Charles in dismay. 'This is all we need. Has anyone called the police?'

'Not yet,' said Maggie. 'But I think perhaps we should.'

'Jesus God,' said Charles, lifting a hand to his brow. 'What a bloody fiasco.' For a moment or two he was silent. Then he turned to Justin, his face stern. 'Justin, I think the two of us need to have a little talk.'

'Ab-absolutely,' said Justin. 'Good idea.' He reached for his desk planner with a trembling hand. 'Ahm . . . when were you thinking of?'

'I was thinking of now,' said Charles curtly. 'Right now, upstairs in my office.' He turned to the others. 'If you'll excuse me . . .'

'Absolutely,' said Maggie.

'Go right ahead,' said Roxanne, and grinned maliciously at Justin.

When the two of them had left, Roxanne and Maggie sank heavily onto chairs and looked at each other.

'I feel absolutely . . . shattered,' said Maggie. She lifted her hands to her head and began to rub her temples.

'I'm not surprised!' said Roxanne. 'You were fantastic. I've never seen anything like it.'

'Well, I think I made my point,' said Maggie, giving a satisfied smile.

'Made your point? I tell you, after your performance, Charles will be welcoming Candice back with the whole red carpet treatment.' Roxanne stretched out her legs in front of her and kicked off her shoes. 'He'll probably give her a pay rise on the spot. Flowers on her desk every day. E-mails to the whole company, extolling her virtues.' Maggie began to giggle, then stopped.

'If we find her,' she said.

'If we find her,' echoed Roxanne, and looked soberly at Maggie. 'Were you serious about calling the police?'

'I don't know.' Maggie sighed. 'To be honest, I'm not sure the police can actually do anything. They'll probably tell us to mind our own business.'

'So what can we do?' said Roxanne.

'God knows,' said Maggie, and rubbed her face. 'Call her mother?'

'She won't have gone there,' said Roxanne, shaking her head. 'She can't stand her mother.'

'She hasn't got anyone, has she?' said Maggie, sudden tears starting to her eyes. 'Oh shit, I can't bear to think about it. She must have felt so completely alone.' She looked miserably at Roxanne. 'Think about it, Roxanne. She's been let down by us, by Heather . . .'

There was a sound at the door, and she stopped midstream. Outside the glass panel of the door, the new receptionist Julie was peering in anxiously. As Maggie beckoned, she cautiously opened the door.

'Sorry to bother you,' she said, looking from face to face.

'That's OK,' said Maggie, dabbing at her eyes. 'What is it?'

'There's somebody downstairs to see Justin,' said

Julie nervously. 'Doreen wasn't sure if he was in a meeting or not.'

'He is, I'm afraid,' said Maggie.

'And he may be some time,' added Roxanne. 'At least, we hope he will.'

'Right.' Julie paused doubtfully. 'So what should I say to the person?'

'What do you think?' said Maggie, glancing at Roxanne. 'Shall I see them myself?'

'I don't see why you should,' said Roxanne, stretching her arms above her head. 'You're not here to work. You're on maternity leave, damn it.'

'I know,' said Maggie. 'But even so . . . it might be important.'

'You're too conscientious,' said Roxanne. 'Nothing's that important.'

'Maybe you're right,' said Maggie after a pause, then pulled a face. 'Oh, I don't know.' She looked at Julie. 'Do you happen to know what the name was?'

There was a pause as Julie consulted her little piece of paper.

'She's called . . . Candice Brewin.' Julie looked up. 'Apparently she used to work here or something?'

Candice stood by the reception desk, trying desperately to fight the impulse to run out of the door and never return. Her legs were trembling in their brand new tights, her lips were dry, and every time she thought of having to face Justin she felt as if she might vomit. But at the same time, there was a determination inside her like a thin steel rod; a determination which kept her trembling legs pinned to the floor. I have to do this, she told herself yet again. If I want my job back, my integrity back – I have to do this.

That morning at the cottage, she had awoken feeling a strange lightness inside her. A sense of release, almost. For a while she had stared silently up at the ceiling, trying to place this new sensation; trying to work out what had happened.

And then it had hit her. She didn't feel guilty any more.

She didn't feel guilty any more. It was as though she'd been absolved; as though she had been cured. As though a burden that she'd unconsciously been carrying for years had been lifted – and suddenly she was able to stretch her shoulders; to enjoy the sensation of freedom; to move in any way she liked. The guilt she'd been carrying for her father's crimes was gone.

Deliberately she had tested herself by bringing Heather to the forefront of her mind; waiting – amid all the anger and humiliation – for the flash of guilt. That spark of shame that she always felt; the twinge in her stomach as she remembered her father's misdemeanours. It was such an automatic reaction, she had got used to it over the years. But this morning there had been nothing. A new absence inside her. A numbness.

She had lain still and silent, marvelling at her transformation. Now she was able to view Heather with uncluttered eyes; to view the whole relationship between them in a different way. She had owed Heather nothing. Nothing. As Ed shifted beside her in bed, Candice had felt clear-headed and cool.

'Morning,' he'd murmured sleepily and leaned over to kiss her.

'I want my job back,' she'd replied, staring straight at the ceiling. 'I'm not waiting for any hearing. I want my job back, Ed.'

'Good,' he'd said, and kissed her ear. 'Well, go and get it.'

They'd eaten breakfast and packed up the cottage almost silently, as though to chat would be to destroy the mood; the focus. As they'd driven back to London, Candice had sat tensely, her hand gripping the top of the door, staring straight ahead. Ed had taken her home, waited while she changed into the smartest outfit she possessed, then had driven her here. Somehow she'd managed to stride confidently into the foyer and ask for Justin. Somehow she'd got that far.

But now, standing on the marble floor, flinching under Doreen's curious gaze, her confidence was evaporating. What exactly was she going to say to Justin? How was she going to change his mind? She felt suddenly vulnerable beneath her veneer, as though the slightest confrontation would blow away her poise completely. The clear-headedness she'd felt that morning was now clouded; her chest was beginning to heave with a renewed humiliation.

What if Justin wouldn't listen? What if he simply had her ejected from the building? What if he called her a thief again? She had rehearsed her story, had planned exactly what she would say – but now it seemed unconvincing in her own mind. Justin would simply dismiss her explanation and order her to leave. Candice felt her cheeks burn in mortification and she swallowed hard.

'Yes,' said Doreen, looking up. 'It's as I thought. Justin is in a meeting at the moment.'

'Oh,' said Candice in a trembling voice. 'I see.'

'But you've been asked to wait here,' said Doreen coldly. 'Someone will be down presently.'

'What – what for?' said Candice, but Doreen merely raised her eyebrows.

Candice felt her heart pound with fright. Perhaps they were going to charge her. Perhaps they were going to bring the police in. What had Justin said to them? Her face began to burn harder than ever; her breaths were shallow and nervous. She should never have come back, she thought frantically. She should never have come.

At the back of the foyer, there was a ping as the lift

arrived at the ground floor. Candice felt her stomach
lurch in panic. She took a deep breath, steeling herself
for the worst. Then the lift doors opened, and her face
went numb with shock. It couldn't be. She blinked
several times, feeling giddy; wondering if she was hal-
lucinating. There, in front of her, was Maggie, coming
out of the lift, her hazel eyes looking ahead anxiously.
And, behind her, Roxanne, her face taut, almost stern
with worry.

They stopped as they saw Candice and there was a
tense silence as the three gazed at each other.

'It's you,' whispered Candice at last.

'It's us,' said Roxanne, nodding. 'Isn't it, Maggie?'

Candice stared at her friends' unsmiling faces
through a haze of fear. They hadn't forgiven her. They
were never going to forgive her.

'I . . . Oh God. I'm so sorry.' Tears began to stream
down her face. 'I'm so sorry. I should have listened to
you. I was wrong and you were right. Heather was . . .'
She swallowed desperately. 'She was a . . .'

'It's OK,' said Maggie. 'It's OK, Candice. Heather's
gone.'

'And we're back,' said Roxanne, and started to walk
towards Candice with glittering eyes. 'We're back.'

Chapter Twenty-One

The grave was plain and white; almost anonymous-looking amongst the rows in the suburban, functional cemetery. Perhaps it was a little untidier than most – overgrown with grass, its gravel scattered around the plot. But it was the plainly engraved name which differentiated it; which turned it from a meaningless slab of stone into a memorial of a life. She stared at it, chiselled into the stone in capital letters. The name she'd been ashamed of for all her adult life. The name she'd come, over the years, to dread hearing.

Candice clutched her bunch of flowers more tightly, and walked towards her father's grave. She hadn't been to visit it for years. Neither, judging by its state, had her mother. Both of them too consumed by anger, by shame, by denial. Both wanting to look ahead; to forget the past.

But now, staring at the overgrown stone, Candice felt a sense of release. She felt as though, in the last few weeks, she had handed all the blame, all the guilt, back to her father. It was his again, every last drop of it; her shoulders were light again. And in return she was beginning to be able to forgive him. After years of feeling nothing for him but shame and hatred, she was beginning to recall her father in a different light; to remember all those good qualities which she'd almost forgotten. His wit, his warmth. His ability to put people at their ease; to singlehandedly entertain a whole table full of dullards. His generosity; his impulsiveness. His sheer enjoyment of the good things in life.

Gordon Brewin had caused a lot of misery in his life. A lot of pain and a lot of suffering. But he had also given a lot of people a great deal of pleasure. He had brought light and laughter; treats and excitement. And he had given her a magical childhood. For nineteen unsullied years, right up until his death, she had felt loved, secure and happy. Nineteen years of happiness. That was worth something, wasn't it?

With shaky legs, Candice took a step nearer the grave. He hadn't been an evil man, she thought. Only a man with flaws. A happy, dishonest, generous man with too many flaws to count. As she stared at his name, etched in the stone, hot tears came to her eyes and she felt again a childish, unquestioning love for him. She bent down, placed the flowers on his grave and brushed some of the spilled gravel back onto the plot, tidying the edges of the grave. She stood up and stared at it silently for a few moments. Then she turned abruptly and walked away, back to the gates where Ed was waiting for her.

'Where's the other godmother?' said Paddy, bustling up to Maggie in a rustle of blue flowery crêpe. 'She's not going to be late, is she?'

'On her way, I'm sure,' said Maggie calmly. She fastened a final button on Lucia's christening robe and held her up to be admired. 'What do you think?'

'Oh, Maggie!' said Paddy. 'She looks an angel.'

'She does look rather fine, doesn't she?' said Maggie, surveying the frothing trail of silk and lace. 'Roxanne, come in here! See your god-daughter!'

'Let's have a look,' said Roxanne, and sauntered into the room. She was wearing a tightly fitted black and white suit, and a stiff, wide-brimmed hat with a curling ostrich feather. 'Very nice,' she said. 'Very nice indeed. Although I'm not sure about that bonnet affair. Too many ribbons.' Maggie gave a little cough.

'Actually,' she said, 'Paddy very kindly made this bonnet, especially to match the christening robe. And I . . . I rather like the ribbons.'

'All my boys wore that robe when they were christened,' put in Paddy proudly.

'Hmm,' said Roxanne, looking the robe up and down. 'Well, that explains a lot.' She met Maggie's eye and, without meaning to, Maggie gave a snort of laughter.

'Paddy,' she said, 'do you think the caterers have brought napkins, or should we have provided them?'

'Oh dear,' said Paddy, looking up. 'Do you know, I'm not sure. I'll just pop down and check, shall I?'

When she'd left the bedroom, there was silence for a while. Maggie popped Lucia under her baby gym on the floor and sat down at the dressing table to do her make-up.

'Budge up,' said Roxanne presently, and sat down next to her on the wide stool. She watched as Maggie hastily brushed shadow onto her eyelids and stroked mascara onto her lashes, checking her appearance peremptorily after each stage.

'Glad to see you still take your time with your maquillage,' she said.

'Oh absolutely,' said Maggie, reaching for her blusher. 'We mothers enjoy nothing more than spending an hour in front of the mirror.'

'Slow down,' said Roxanne, and reached for a lip pencil. 'I'll do your lips. Properly.' She swivelled Maggie's face towards her and carefully began to outline her mouth in a warm shade of plum. She finished the outline, studied her work, then reached for a lipstick and a lip brush.

297

'Listen here, Lucia,' she said as she brushed the colour on. 'Your mother needs time to put on her lipstick, OK? So you just give her time. You'll realize why it's important when you're a bit bigger.' She finished, and handed Maggie a tissue. 'Blot.'

Maggie pressed her lips slowly on the tissue, then drew it away from her mouth and looked at it.

'God, I'm going to miss you,' she said. 'I'm really going to . . .' She exhaled sharply and shook her head. 'Cyprus. I mean, *Cyprus*. Couldn't it have been . . . the Isle of Wight?'

Roxanne laughed. 'Can you see me living on the Isle of Wight?'

'Well, I can't see you living in Cyprus!' retorted Maggie. There was a long pause, then she said reluctantly, 'Well – perhaps I can. If I try hard.'

'I'll be back at least every month,' said Roxanne. 'You won't know I'm gone.' Her blue gaze met Maggie's in the mirror. 'And I meant what I said, Maggie. I still stand by it. If you ever feel down, if you're ever depressed – ring me. Whatever time it is.'

'And you'll fly back,' said Maggie, laughing.

'I'll fly back,' said Roxanne. 'That's what you do for family.'

As Ed turned into the drive of The Pines, he gave an impressed whistle.

'So this is the house she's *selling*? What the hell's wrong with it?'

'She wants to live in London again,' said Candice. 'They're going to live in Ralph's house. Roxanne's house. Whatever.' She looked anxiously in the mirror. 'Do I look all right?'

'You look bloody fantastic,' said Ed without turning his head.

'Should I have worn a hat?' She stared at herself. 'I hate hats. They make my head look stupid.'

'No-one wears hats to christenings,' said Ed.

'Yes they do!' As they approached the house, Candice gave a wail. 'Look, there's Roxanne. And she's wearing a hat. I knew I should have worn one.'

'You look like a cherub.' Ed leaned over and kissed her. 'Babyface.'

'I'm not supposed to be the baby! I'm supposed to be the godmother.'

'You look like a godmother, too.' Ed opened his door. 'Come on. I want to meet your friends.'

As they crunched over the gravel, Roxanne turned and beamed at Candice. Then her gaze shifted to Ed and her eyes narrowed appraisingly.

'Jesus Christ,' muttered Ed to Candice. 'She's checking me out with her bloody X-ray vision.'

'Don't be silly! She loves you already.' Candice strode breathlessly towards Roxanne and hugged her. 'You look fantastic!'

'And so do you,' said Roxanne, standing back and holding Candice by the shoulders. 'You look happier than you have for a long time.'

'Well . . . I feel happy,' said Candice, and glanced shyly at Ed. 'Roxanne, this is—'

'This is the famous Ed, I take it.' Roxanne's gaze swivelled and her eyes gleamed dangerously. 'Hello, Ed.'

'Roxanne,' replied Ed. 'Delighted to meet your hat. And you, of course.' Roxanne inclined her head pleasantly and surveyed Ed's face.

'I have to say, I thought you'd be better looking,' she said eventually.

'Yup. Easy mistake to make,' said Ed, unperturbed. 'A lot of people make it.' He nodded confidentially at Roxanne. 'Don't let it worry you.'

There was a short silence, then Roxanne grinned.

'You'll do,' she said. 'You'll do nicely.'

'Hey, godmothers!' came Maggie's voice from the

front door. 'In here! I need to give you this sheet on what your duties are.'

'We have duties?' said Roxanne to Candice, as they walked together across the gravel. 'I thought we just had to be able to pick out silver.'

'And remember birthdays,' said Candice.

'And wave our magic wands,' said Roxanne. 'Lucia Drakeford, you *shall* go to the ball. And here's a pair of Prada shoes to go in.'

The church was thick-walled and freezing, despite the heat of the day outside, and Lucia wailed lustily as the unheated water hit her skin. When the ceremony was over, Candice, Roxanne and Lucia's godfather – an old university friend of Giles – posed together for photographs in the church porch, taking turns to hold her.

'I find this very stressful,' muttered Roxanne to Candice through her smile. 'What if one of us drops her?'

'You won't drop her!' said Candice. 'Anyway, babies bounce.'

'That's what they say,' said Roxanne ominously. 'But what if they forgot to put the indiarubber in this one?' She looked down at Lucia's face and gently touched her cheek. 'Don't forget me,' she whispered, so quietly that not even Candice could hear. 'Don't forget me, little one.'

'OK, that's enough pictures,' called Maggie eventually, and looked around the crowd of milling guests. 'Everybody, there's champagne and food at the house.'

'Well, come on then!' said Roxanne. 'What are we waiting for?'

Back at The Pines, a long trestle table had been laid out on the lawn and covered with food. A pair of ladies from the village were serving champagne and offering canapés, and a Mozart overture was playing from two speakers lodged in trees. Roxanne and Candice collected their drinks, then wandered off, a little way from the main crowd.

'Delicious!' said Candice, taking a sip of icy cold champagne. She closed her eyes and let the warm summer sun beat down on her face, feeling herself expand in happiness. 'Isn't this lovely? Isn't it just . . . perfect?'

'Nearly perfect,' said Roxanne, and gave a mysterious grin. 'There's just one more thing we have to do.' She raised her voice. 'Maggie! Bring your daughter over here!'

As Candice watched in puzzlement, she reached into her chic little bag, produced a miniature of brandy and emptied it into her champagne glass. Then she produced a sugar lump and popped that in, too.

'Champagne cocktail,' she said, and took a sip. 'Perfect.'

'What is it?' Maggie joined them, holding Lucia, her eyes bright and her cheeks flushed with pleasure. 'Didn't it all go well? Wasn't Lucia good?'

'It was beautiful,' said Candice, squeezing her shoulder. 'And Lucia was an angel.'

'But it's not quite over,' said Roxanne. 'There's one more vital ceremony that needs to be performed.' Her voice softened slightly. 'Come here, Lucia.'

As the others looked on in astonishment, Roxanne dipped her finger into the champagne cocktail and wetted Lucia's brow.

'Welcome to the cocktail club,' she said.

For a few moments there was silence. Maggie stared down at her daughter's tiny face, then looked up at the others. She blinked hard a few times, then nodded. Then, without speaking, the three turned and slowly walked back across the grass to the party.

THE END